WHAT THE DUKE DESIRES

"A totally engaging, adventurous love story . . . with a strong plot, steamy desire, and an oh-so-wonderful ending."

—*RT Book Reviews*

"This unusual tale of interlocking mysteries is full of all the intriguing characters, brisk plotting, and witty dialogue that Jeffries's readers have come to expect."

—*Publishers Weekly*, starred review

"Another sparkling series" (*Library Journal*) from Sabrina Jeffries—read all of the "exceptionally entertaining" (*Booklist*) novels of the HELLIONS OF HALSTEAD HALL

A LADY NEVER SURRENDERS

"Jeffries pulls out all the stops. . . . Not to be missed."
—*RT Book Reviews* (4½ stars, Top Pick)

"Sizzling, emotionally satisfying. . . . Another must-read."

—*Library Journal* (starred review)

"Superbly shaded characters, simmering sensuality, and a splendidly wicked wit . . . *A Lady Never Surrenders* wraps up the series nothing short of brilliantly."

—*Booklist*

TO WED A WILD LORD

"Wonderfully witty, deliciously seductive, graced with humor and charm."

—*Library Journal* (starred review)

"A beguiling blend of captivating characters, clever plotting, and sizzling sensuality."

—*Booklist*

HOW TO WOO A RELUCTANT LADY

"A delightful addition. . . . Charmingly original."

—*Publishers Weekly* (starred review)

"Steamy passion, dangerous intrigue, and just the right amount of tart wit."

—*Booklist*

A HELLION IN HER BED

"Jeffries's sense of humor and delightfully delicious sensuality spice things up!"

—*RT Book Reviews* (4½ stars)

THE TRUTH ABOUT LORD STONEVILLE

"Jeffries combines her hallmark humor, poignancy, and sensuality to perfection."

—*RT Book Reviews* (4½ stars, Top Pick)

"Delectably witty dialogue . . . and scorching sexual chemistry."

—*Booklist*

Sabrina Jeffries

If the Viscount Falls

POCKET BOOKS

New York London Toronto Sydney New Delhi

Pocket Books
A Division of Simon & Schuster, Inc.
1230 Avenue of the Americas
New York, NY 10020

First Pocket Books paperback edition February 2015

POCKET and colophon are registered trademarks of Simon & Schuster, Inc.

For information about special discounts for bulk purchases, please contact Simon & Schuster Special Sales at 1-866-506-1949 or business@simonandschuster.com.

The Simon & Schuster Speakers Bureau can bring authors to your live event. For more information or to book an event contact the Simon & Schuster Speakers Bureau at 1-866-248-3049 or visit our website at www.simonspeakers.com.

Front cover art by Alan Ayers
Cover typography by Iskra Design

Manufactured in the United States of America

10 9 8 7 6 5 4 3 2 1

ISBN 978-1-4767-8604-9
ISBN 978-1-4767-8613-1 (ebook)

*For my husband, Rene, whose support for
my writing has stayed steady throughout
our thirty years of marriage.
And for my sweet son, Nicholas, whose autism
prevents him from reading this
but who is always in my heart.
I love you both so much!*

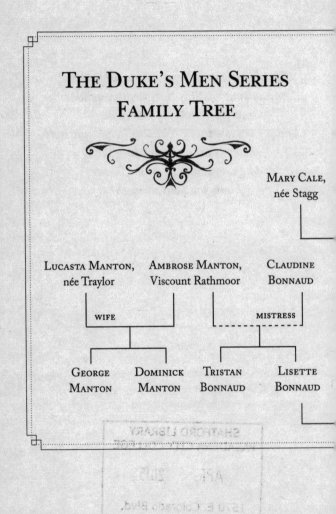

The Duke's Men Series
Family Tree

MARY CALE,
née Stagg

LUCASTA MANTON,
née Traylor

AMBROSE MANTON,
Viscount Rathmoor

CLAUDINE
BONNAUD

WIFE

MISTRESS

GEORGE
MANTON

DOMINICK
MANTON

TRISTAN
BONNAUD

LISETTE
BONNAUD

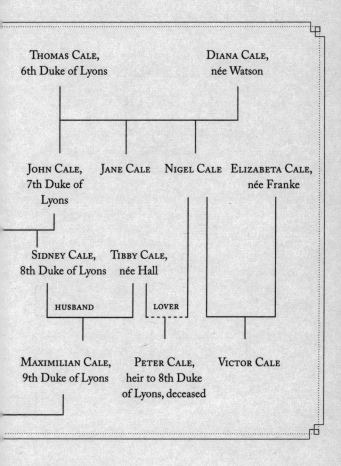

PROLOGUE

London
February 1817

DOMINICK MANTON HAD never expected to spend his twentieth birthday peering covertly through open terrace doors into the Earl of Blakeborough's ballroom. But he had to find Jane Vernon, his fiancée, before some footman ousted him.

She pirouetted into his line of sight, and his breath settled like a lead weight in his chest. In her pearly gown, she shone so brightly under the candles that she fairly blinded him. Her pert freckled nose, her full red mouth, her wild auburn curls were all so essentially Jane. And now completely out of his reach.

Blast it, he couldn't even dance with her. Instead, she was partnered with Edwin Barlow, heir to the earl and a good friend of her family's. The man was as remote as ever, and Jane was trying to soften his melancholy by being animated and vibrant and . . .

Young. So very young. Only seventeen. She'd be eighteen soon, but the two years between her and Dom felt like ten, now that he'd lost everything.

His vision of Jane was suddenly blocked by a blond, curvier version of her: Miss Nancy Sadler, Jane's cousin on her mother's side.

"Mr. Manton?" she whispered as she peeked through the French doors onto the terrace. "Is that really you? Why aren't you inside?"

He backed up to allow Nancy to join him. "I wasn't invited."

"Whyever not?"

He eyed the wealthy merchant's daughter askance. "Because society can't abide the sight of disinherited, disgraced second sons with no respectable future."

She winced. "Oh. Right. So how did you get in?"

"Scaled the back fence." He gazed inside to where Jane and Edwin had finished the dance and were joining Samuel Barlow, Edwin's younger brother. "I need to speak to Jane alone. She keeps refusing to meet with me."

"What do you expect? At your last meeting you tried to convince her to jilt you. She's afraid that at your next one you'll end the engagement yourself."

"Nonsense. *She* has to end it. If I cry off, it will look bad for her."

One peculiarity of good society was that a woman could end a betrothal without suffering too badly. But not the reverse. People would always assume the woman had done something awful to cause the rift. He didn't want Jane's reputation besmirched.

"Can you get her to talk to me privately?" Dom asked. "This terrace connects to the library. I could meet her there."

If anyone could coax Jane to do anything, it was Nancy. Her father was Jane's uncle and had been Jane's guardian since Jane was orphaned, so the two girls had grown up together. And Mr. Sadler wanted to see the engagement broken as much as Dom, though neither could convince Jane of it.

A secret part of Dom exulted in that. But the part of him that knew what lay before him in the coming years despaired.

Nancy gave a girlish shake of her head. "I could probably trick her into going into the library, but you won't get her to throw you over. Jane loves you."

As much as a girl her age could, anyway. Except for the accidental drowning of her parents when Jane was eight, she'd led a sheltered life. The Sadlers gave her whatever she wanted, and she loved them deeply. Unlike Dom's parents, the couple had a true love match, so Jane saw marriage as an idyll.

Meanwhile, he was heading into hell—a long stretch of uncertainty and hard work and poverty. How could her love for him survive that?

Nancy shot him a petulant look. "I *thought* you loved Jane, too."

He stiffened. Of course he loved her, had loved her from the moment they'd met in a bookshop. While unconsciously humming the first few bars of Haydn's *Surprise* Symphony, he'd been jarred from his book by someone on the other side of the bookcase humming the next few bars.

It had proved to be Jane, taking respite from the endless rounds of parties and balls that constituted her debut. Until that moment, he'd never encountered anyone with his memory for music. Or his avid interest in symphonies. Or his penchant for humming while reading. He'd never come across a soul who liked both books *and* people. At once, she fascinated him.

From there, he'd courted the baron's daughter through a succession of musicales, operas, and even the occasional ball. Though the foolish woman preferred Beethoven to Mozart, he easily forgave that because she overlooked so many of his own flaws. She didn't seem to care that his dancing was more precise than heartfelt, that his exacting memory for music and conversation was downright freakish, or even that his prospects were limited.

Clearly, the woman was as daft as she was lovely. Which, of course, meant he'd wanted to marry her. Still did.

"It doesn't matter what I feel for Jane," he said dully. "Or even what she feels for me. She deserves someone like Blakeborough's heir, who can give her a decent future."

"Don't be ridiculous. She's never once thought of Edwin romantically. He's much too gruff for Jane's taste. And unlike me, Jane would prefer a barrister to a—" Nancy broke off with a groan. "I'm sorry. I forgot."

"That I no longer have a future as a barrister?" he

said bitterly. "Jane may not crave an earl's son, but she sure as blazes doesn't want a Bow Street runner for a husband."

With a peevish look, Nancy said, "I don't understand why you had to go off and take a position doing something so low. Why not live on credit until your brother relents and gives you back your allowance?"

Dom stifled an oath. As usual, Nancy saw the world through rainbows. "George will never relent."

"Perhaps he would if you reasoned with him." She gestured across the ballroom, and Dom spotted his elder brother standing among his cronies. "It's him you should talk to privately. I don't know exactly what happened between you, but—"

"No, you don't," he clipped out. "Jane does, and that's enough." Well, most of it, anyway. There were certain aspects he dared not tell even her.

"She says that George behaved badly," Nancy persisted. "So if you would just explain to people what he did, perhaps everyone wouldn't be suggesting all these awful things *you* did to cause your falling-out."

His fingers curled into fists. "Like what?"

She colored. "I don't know—that you were too friendly with your late father's . . . mistress and by-blows. That George didn't approve, so your father refused to give you an inheritance."

That was bad, but not as damaging as the truth. Father had added a codicil to his will on his deathbed in the presence of George and their half brother, Tristan Bonnaud. George had been so angry over it, he'd burned the thing the moment Father perished. And Tristan had been so angry over *that* that he'd stolen the horse left to him in the codicil.

Then Dom had found himself in the unenviable position of having to protect Tristan from George's attempt to have him hanged. George had made Dom choose: Give Tristan over or lose everything.

It had been no choice at all. Dom would do it again, except that in losing everything he had essentially lost Jane, too. And not even revealing the truth publicly would change that.

Because while Dom couldn't prove the burning of the codicil, George could damned well prove the horse theft. The arse had kept quiet about it so far, but if Dom broke his silence, George would surely retaliate by hinting that Dom was somehow involved. Then Dom's benefactor, Jackson Pinter, would have no choice but to dismiss Dom from the post as Bow Street runner that the man had generously offered. And Dom would not only lack money, he'd lack a means of earning any.

So he was stuck with the gossip, stuck with his lowered station, stuck with no future. And there wasn't a damned thing he could do about it. Except make sure that Jane wasn't equally stuck.

He'd already suffered much because Father and George had neglected to do what was right. He refused to be like them. "It's precisely because of the gossip that Jane must break with me. She'll be seen as sensible. And I won't be any worse off than I already am."

"Perhaps if you just gave yourself time to get on your

feet. You couldn't marry Jane right now even if you wanted to," Nancy reminded him. "Papa already said you had to wait until she comes of age. And by then—"

"By then, I will *still* be nobody, damn it!"

Nancy blinked.

Good God, his new life was already changing him; a gentleman never cursed in front of a lady.

"Forgive me," he went on, "but clearly you don't understand what my future holds. In four months as a runner, I've earned a mere twenty pounds."

She gasped. Twenty pounds was probably two weeks' pin money for her.

"Sixty pounds a year will barely support *me*," he went on, "much less a wife and a family."

"But with Jane's dowry—"

"By the terms of her father's will, if she marries anyone other than a gentleman of means before she turns thirty-five, the money goes to some cousin of hers. Only after thirty-five can she access her fortune without restriction."

"*You're* a gentlem—" Nancy caught herself. "Well, you *were* born and bred a gentleman of means, anyway. Besides, Jane's father set up that will to protect her from fortune hunters."

"In society's eyes, *I* am a fortune hunter. I have nothing to offer an heiress and everything to gain from one."

A troubled look crossed Nancy's face. "Papa knows better."

"It doesn't matter. He already made it clear that his hands are tied by the terms of the will. So if I marry her now, she loses her fortune. My measly income will scarcely enable us to survive. And that's assuming I succeed in my new profession, which is by no means certain. Even if I do, I'll never be able to afford servants or a carriage or any of the comforts she's accustomed to."

His voice turned grim. "There will be no opera performances for her to attend, no concerts, no pianoforte for her to play." Oddly enough, that was what he missed most about his former life—the ease with which he could hear excellent music. Now he was reduced to drinking up the strains of whatever spilled out into the street from the drawing rooms of Mayfair.

Nancy chewed on her lower lip. "Jane does enjoy her sonatas."

"And her waltzes and reels. If she marries me, there will be no dancing. She won't be able to attend balls. She'll have to leave society entirely."

"How dreadful!" Nancy cast a worried glance through the open doors into the ballroom. "But she could come to parties at our house."

"To be shunned by her friends? Do you really think your parents would invite a runner's wife and risk the gossip? Would you happily chat with Jane in front of your suitors, knowing that being seen with her would damage your own marriage prospects?"

Given how she blanched, that hadn't occurred to her. "Well, I-I . . . don't know . . ."

"That's assuming she'd have time to visit you," he said coldly, pressing his case. If he could persuade Nancy, she might persuade Jane. "With no servants,

Jane would have to keep house for us, something she's never done a day in her life."

"Dear me, that's true. Although she has—"

"I'll be gone for days on end doing investigations, while she is banished from good society and left alone in my one-room lodgings in Spitalfields." The thought of his fair Jane forced to live in that slum chilled his heart. "And what if I'm killed in the pursuit of some criminal?"

"Heavens, is your work really so very dangerous?"

"More than you think." More than he'd expected, too. "And if I died, she'd be left alone, impoverished and exiled, with no one to turn to."

"She would hate that." Nancy looked downcast. "All the same, I would never abandon Jane."

"Wouldn't you? What if your future husband didn't wish you to take in your poor relation? What if your father was dead? We can't predict what might happen."

"Stop it! You're making it all sound so awful!"

"Because it *is*." He fixed her with a sharp stare. "Nothing lies before me but years of clawing my way up into a position where I can afford a wife."

"Oh, Dom," she moaned.

"If she waits until I'm financially secure enough to marry her, she'll be waiting a long time. And if I fail to succeed, she'll have sacrificed her youth for naught."

He gazed past her to where Edwin Barlow was saying something that made Jane smile. Dom fought the irrational urge to march over and punch Blakeborough's heir in the nose. "But if she jilts me, the whole world is before her. Her dowry is enough to tempt any gentleman, and her amiable character and her sweetness and her—"

God, how could he stand the thought of losing her to another?

He gritted his teeth. Better that than to watch her become beaten down through years of hard living and worry for him. Or worse, watching her grow to hate him for tearing her away from everything she held dear. Watching their hard life snuff the light from her eyes, drain the animation from her face . . .

No, he must give her up while he still could, while she was young enough to find someone new. It was the only way.

"Don't you see? She should marry someone like Blakeborough's heir, a man with a future. Or even his brother. Barlow is a midshipman in the navy, isn't he?"

"Yes." Nancy's gaze flicked admiringly over Samuel Barlow's uniform. "But she won't marry him, either. She won't give you up, and not just because she loves you. She already told me she would find it dishonorable to abandon you simply because you've fallen on hard times. It would go against her principles."

He was quite familiar with Jane's principles, which mirrored his own. But hers hadn't been forged in the cruel fires of experience. His had. "There must be a way to convince her."

"You'd have to show yourself to be a man of awful character—a thief or a murderer . . . or an adulterer, which is silly, since you're not married."

An ugly thought wormed its way into his consciousness. "I don't need to be married to betray Jane's trust. If she thought I was intimately involved with another woman—"

"Dominick Manton! Don't even suggest such a dreadful thing!"

"But it would work, wouldn't it?"

"I suppose." An anxious expression crossed her brow. "Do you mean you would take up with some soiled dove?"

"Of course not," he said impatiently. "Unless Jane actually witnessed me entering a brothel, which would be impossible to arrange, she would never believe any rumors of such a dalliance. She knows my character too well for that."

Nancy sniffed. "I doubt she would believe rumors of your dallying with a respectable woman, either."

"If she witnessed it herself, she'd have to." He slanted a glance at Nancy. "If Jane actually caught me pressing my attentions on some rich heiress, she might be persuaded to think me desperate enough to go after a woman with money."

"But how could she see you with an heiress when you don't even go out into society anymore?"

He stared hard at her. "It would have to be an heiress who was in on the plan. Who understood what I was trying to do and knew the importance of it."

Nancy caught his stare and froze. "Me?" At his terse nod, she said, "Oh no, Dom, I could never . . . Jane would never forgive me!"

"She would if she thought I was forcing a kiss on you. If you were protesting. We could make it seem as if I'd cornered you and was trying to seduce you."

"No!" Nancy stared off into the ballroom, her lower lip trembling. "No, it would destroy her."

An ache rose in his chest. Ruthlessly he ignored it. "For a time, she would be . . . hurt. But she'd get over it. She'd rail against me, and you'd support her outrage with your own, and eventually she'd come to see herself as better off without me."

"Good Lord, Dom. Is there no other way?"

"I can see none. We must use Jane's fixed principles against her. It's for her own good."

"I doubt she would see it that way," Nancy mumbled.

"But surely *you* do."

She sighed. "Yes. Still, it shan't be easy. I'll need someone to help me. Jane will get suspicious if I tell her to meet me in the library, and then you're there kissing me."

"True. But whomever you find must not drag anyone else into it. We don't want to inadvertently spawn rumors that would ruin *you*. Whomever you choose must keep the truth of it secret once the deed is done, or it will all be for naught."

She paced the terrace. "Samuel Barlow will do. He fancies me—or so he says, not that I believe a word of it." She gave a dismissive wave belied by her coquettish smile. "He's a shameless flirt."

So was she, from all accounts. Dom searched her face. "Are you hoping he'll marry you?"

"Good heavens, no!" Her laugh rang false. "Samuel

is only eighteen; he certainly isn't ready to set up house. Besides, can you imagine me married to a sailor I only got to see once every great while? I think not. I want a husband who will make me the toast of London, not the toast of some dirty wardroom."

"Very sensible."

And typically shallow, though not surprising. Nancy's father had pots of money, all of which had been settled on her. She could easily catch a high-ranking husband. She needn't marry a mere midshipman.

"Do you think Barlow would help us?" Dom asked.

"Of course. I can get him to do whatever I want." She sobered. "If you're sure about this, that is."

Dom scanned the ballroom for Jane. She stood alone now, drumming her fingers on a table in a decidedly un-ladylike fashion. He could practically hear the rhythm, feel it beat in his blood the way *she* beat in his blood.

A soft, absent smile crossed her face, the one she always got when listening to a new piece of music, and the familiarity of it stabbed deep into his heart. Could he really do this? Make her hate him? Make her cut him out of her life forever?

"Dom?" Nancy prodded. "Is this really what you want?"

He numbed himself to the pain. "No." It would never be what he wanted. "But it has to be done."

✦ ✦ ✦

AN HOUR LATER, Jane Vernon was surprised when Samuel Barlow asked her to waltz. While his siblings

Edwin and Yvette were grand friends of Jane's, Samuel rarely paid her any attention, saving his flirtations for Nancy.

Jane didn't mind that. She was used to being eclipsed by her older cousin, whose golden curls, fine bosom, and flawless skin captivated every fellow who entered her orbit.

Not that Jane remained entirely unnoticed. She'd had an admirer or two, despite her deplorable plethora of freckles and unmanageable red hair. But around Nancy, Jane had felt like a clay pot beside a Wedgwood vase.

Until Dom.

Jane's pulse leapt at the thought of her handsome fiancé. *He* saw her as Wedgwood. He might be quiet and enigmatic, but his eyes lit up whenever he spotted her. A woman could always trust a man's eyes. Although lately . . .

Lately, *everything* was a problem. After being disinherited, Dom had retreated into himself. He kept talking about how she was too good for him now, how she would lose everything if they married.

Curse Papa and his stupid will. And curse Uncle Horace for enforcing it. Her whole life was dictated by rules! She didn't care if Dom had to work. She didn't care if *she* had to work. She'd already learned a great deal about running a household from her aunt, and whenever Auntie was ill, Jane was the one who took over her duties. So surely she and Dom could manage, even in a garret, as long as they were together.

It would be better, of course, if Dom could continue his studies and become a barrister, but she would endure *anything* to be with him. Now if only she could get the stubborn man to believe it. He was such a worrier!

That was the only reason he'd tried to convince her to jilt him. The only one. She was sure of it.

Forcing any gnawing doubt from her mind, she focused on her dancing partner. "Is this the Dettingen Waltz?"

"How should I know?" Samuel frowned. "All these dances sound the same."

Poor Samuel had no soul. Come to think of it, even Edwin's soul had a big hole in it. Only Dom had a soul that was pure perfection.

"You're surly tonight," she said. "Are you taking after Edwin? Or are you and Nancy at odds again?"

"When have Nancy and I ever been at evens?" Samuel caught her eyeing him with curiosity and smoothed his features. "This has nothing to do with her. I'm merely upset by something that occurred in the hall a short while ago. And I can't decide whether to tell you of it."

"Why shouldn't you?" She smiled brightly. "I daresay I'm the most discreet person of your acquaintance."

"It's not your discretion that worries me." As they whirled through the dance, he lowered his voice. "Did you know that your fiancé is here?"

"What? Where?" She scanned the room for Dom but didn't see him. And he would certainly stand out, tall as he was.

"He's not in the ballroom," Samuel said. "That's the tricky part. I ran across him sneaking into the library."

Why on earth would he be sneaking— Oh, right. He hadn't been invited. Still, she could think of only one reason he would make the effort to enter where he wasn't wanted.

Her heart sank. "I suppose he asked you to arrange a meeting with me." She kept hoping that if she put Dom off long enough, the foolish fellow would give up trying to get her to end their engagement. But putting him off was killing her. She hadn't seen him in weeks, and she ached for at least a glimpse of him.

"Actually, no," Samuel said blandly. "He wasn't happy to see me. Indeed, he asked me not to tell you he was here."

How odd. Dom was never secretive. A cold finger of premonition stroked down her spine. What could he be up to? And why wouldn't he wish her to know of it?

"Did he say why?" she asked.

"I gathered he was meeting someone, though he denied it."

She glanced around the ballroom. Who was missing? It had to be a friend or relation of hers, someone he was trying to convince to talk to her, perhaps her uncle or aunt or—

Nancy! There was no sign of Nancy.

Her blood rose. Now he meant to enlist her *cousin* in his scheme to end their betrothal? That tore it. Enough of this nonsense. She would make it clear to the silly man that she loved him no matter what his prospects were.

Leaving the floor mid-dance, she headed for the library.

Samuel hastened after her. "Now see here, just forget I said anything." Yet he made only a halfhearted attempt to stop her.

"The devil I will!" She skirted a group of gentlemen to reach the hall and caught sight of Dom's brother George Manton, the new Viscount Rathmoor.

That scoundrel. This was all George's fault. Given that he'd never spoken publicly of what had occurred, she suspected he was ashamed of his behavior. Unfortunately, a proud man like him would never admit his error.

Perhaps he needed a push. He needed to see just what a pass he'd brought his brother to. Then he might change his mind and return to giving Dom his allowance and paying for his education as a barrister. That would do more to solve their problems than anything.

It was worth a try, wasn't it? And this might be her only chance to get the two men in the same room.

She halted in front of the viscount. His friends stopped talking to nudge each other as his lordship turned to see her standing there.

"Miss Vernon," he said with a cool nod.

Samuel moved up next to her to hiss, "What are you doing?"

She ignored him to address Dom's brother. "I should very much like a word with you in private, sir. Would you join me in the library?"

The other gentlemen murmured among themselves,

and she heard chuckles, but she didn't care. If she could just get Dom and his estranged brother together, she could make his lordship see sense and mend the rift.

George skimmed her with an interested glance, then flashed that toothsome smile that had most girls her age quivering in their dancing slippers. "I would be delighted," he said, and offered her his arm.

She took his cordiality as a good sign, so when Samuel murmured, "Jane, I need to speak to you *this moment*," she seized George's arm and said, "Thank you, Mr. Barlow, but I will talk to you later."

As soon as they were alone in the hall, George said, "I think I can guess what this is about, Miss Vernon."

"Please, sir, I would prefer some privacy for our discussion."

He cast her a sharp glance. "Would you, now?" Stopping at the library door, he said, "Well, then, here we are."

George opened it and she sailed through, expecting to find Dom and Nancy in deep discussion. Instead, she spotted them at the other end of the room, silhouetted by the firelight and locked in an intimate embrace.

She stopped so quickly that the viscount bumped into her. No, it couldn't be them. That was absurd! Surely Dom would never . . . *Nancy* would never—

One figure separated itself from the other to hiss, "Stop that, Dom! You don't know what you're doing!"

Nancy. Oh, Lord.

Jane's stomach began to churn. No. This couldn't be happening! She must have misunderstood.

But she couldn't misunderstand the grab Dom made

for Nancy's waist as he attempted to pull her back into his embrace. "I know exactly what I'm doing."

Hearing Dom's voice made it all real. Too real. Jane's head swam. She was going to faint.

"You're only interested in my money," Nancy protested. "I know it's Jane you really want."

"That's not true. You and I get along very well, don't you think?" Dom lowered his head to Nancy. "Let me show you just how well—"

The crack of a hand against his cheek sounded, and Nancy shoved free. As Jane's vision narrowed and the room began to spin, Nancy headed for the door, but halted when she saw Jane there. "Oh. Um . . . this . . . it isn't how it looks."

"Isn't it?" drawled George. "Because it looks to me like my brother is throwing his fiancée over for a wealthier heiress."

Shocked speechless, Jane glanced at Dom. If she could just see his eyes, she would know what he felt.

But he avoided her gaze to glare at George. "This has naught to do with you, brother. And I swear, if you attempt to harm Miss Sadler's reputation by breathing a word of this—"

"I've no intention of talking about this to anyone." George bowed to Nancy. "The lovely Miss Sadler's secret is safe with me."

Nancy's secret? *Nancy's* reputation? That was all Dom and his brother cared about? Dom wasn't even attempting to protest his innocence. He just stood there wooden, still avoiding her gaze, a sure sign of his guilt.

Jane swallowed the bile rising in her throat. "What the devil is this, Dom? We're engaged!"

His stance was ramrod rigid. "I suppose that loose-lipped Barlow told you about seeing me arrive." His voice held a remote chill that struck her to the heart. It reminded her of how Papa used to talk to Mama.

Too late she remembered Samuel trying to stop her, worrying over telling her about Dom's presence.

Heat rose up her neck to her cheeks. "So you really did come here to court Nancy?" Jane fought the urge to throw up. "You are not the man I thought you were."

Oh, God, she couldn't even summon up a clever set-down! She was about to be sick right here in front of them all. That would be the worst humiliation imaginable.

Mustn't cast up my accounts, mustn't cast up my accounts. The chant ran in her head as she whirled to push past George and out into the hall.

"Wait, Jane!" her cousin called after her, but Jane just shook her head and kept running.

As she fled, she heard Dom say, in a clipped voice, "Let her go."

It was the final insult in a line of them. Her stomach roiled, and she clapped her hand over her mouth. Praying no one saw her before she made it to the retiring room, she lurched down the hall to the stairs.

Dom. Oh, Lord, Dom! He wasn't hers. He'd never really been hers, had he? Clearly she'd read too much into their animated talks. Had she invented the Dom she'd fallen in love with? She must have, building her image upon their heavily chaperoned conversations and a handful of dances.

All this time she thought he'd been trying to get her to break off their engagement out of some noble concern for her, when really it had been so he could court a rich heiress whose money *wasn't* restricted by a stupid will. Not to mention someone prettier than her.

Tears rolled down her cheeks as she stumbled into the retiring room. She'd believed in him. Even when Uncle Horace had warned that he wouldn't give his blessing to the union, she'd ignored him, putting her faith in Dom's goodness, his virtue, his loyalty. And for what? To be made a fool of.

Never again would she trust some two-faced man who spouted a string of lies and told her he loved her madly. Never again would she claim that fortune and consequence didn't matter in the wake of true love.

Because clearly true love was the greatest lie of all.

1

Winborough Estate in Yorkshire
May 1829

FOUR DAYS AFTER his arrival at Winborough's
Whitsuntide house party, Dom rummaged through the
drawers of the desk in his half brother's study. Where
in blazes did Tristan keep his sealing wax? So far, Dom
had found a penknife, some string, seventeen quills, a
lint-clad lemon drop, a stack of foolscap, and a lacy garter, but no sign of wax.

He didn't even want to think about why the garter
was in there. The thought of Tristan and Dom's new
sister-in-law, Zoe, doing . . . whatever upon the desk
made him feel like a Peeping Tom.

Just as Dom slammed the top drawer shut, he spotted the sealing wax, set neatly beside an inkpot atop the
desk. Right there before his eyes, blast it all. Clearly he
was losing his mind.

Dom dropped into the chair. It was all Jane's fault.

Set to inherit the Rathmoor title now that George was dead, he ought to be concentrating on his return to Rathmoor Park today and his attempts to get it out of arrears. Instead, Jane consumed his thoughts.

It was ludicrous. They were nothing to each other now. Certainly, he was nothing to *her*. After more than twelve years unmarried, she'd finally gone and got herself engaged to Edwin Barlow, the newly minted Earl of Blakeborough.

She would soon be out of Dom's reach for good, and he couldn't change that. He didn't *want* to change it. That time of his life was gone forever, as well it should be. He was quite a bit older and wiser, not to mention rougher, and she was still an heiress. They had nothing in common. They were different people.

And perhaps if he said it enough, he would finally believe it. He had to believe it. He had to excise her from his mind somehow.

"Zoe wants to know if you intend to join us for services at their church in town."

He jerked his head up so quickly that he nearly knocked over the Argand lamp. "Blast it, Lisette, don't sneak up on me like that!"

With a toss of her black curls, his half sister approached the desk. "Don't blame me if your mind is in the clouds. I've been standing here waiting for you to notice me for a good five minutes while you muttered and cursed and scowled."

"Sorry. I'm a bit . . . distracted, is all."

She sniffed. "Is that what you call it? And here I thought you were merely rude."

"Now, Lisette—"

"You were such a grump at the celebration yesterday! I don't even know why you bothered to drive the two hours over from the coast for the house party. Even Tristan noticed your foul mood, which takes some doing, since he only has eyes for Zoe."

Dom snorted. He would never have expected his half brother, of all people, to fall in love. Especially so spectacularly. "I'm surprised he and Zoe even remember we exist, given their billing and cooling." He narrowed his gaze on her. "Although you and Max are just as bad."

"Lord, I hope not. We're parents now; we have to show *some* decorum." She tucked a stray tendril of hair behind her ear. "Though it's difficult since Max likes me a little . . . indecorous."

"Good God, I don't even want to think about that," he said irritably. "Stop talking about all the ways Max likes you."

"Why? Because it makes you feel lonely?"

"Because you're my *sister*."

"It's your own fault you're lonely, you know," she said, ignoring his answer. "You've got Jane right under your nose at Rathmoor Park while she's staying with Nancy, and instead of taking advantage of that to court her, you're hiding over here at our brother's estate."

"I am *not* hiding," he said coolly, though perhaps he

was. "Besides, why would I court Jane? She's engaged to another man. And if you'll recall, *she* was the one to jilt me, not the other way around."

"So you say."

That brought him up short. "You think I'm lying?"

"I think that the woman I met at your betrothal party years ago was so in love with you she wouldn't have jilted you over any loss in station or fortune. Which means you must have done something to run her off."

Damn. Lisette was fishing for information, as usual. And hitting uncomfortably close to the mark.

By the night of that blasted ball where he'd maneuvered Jane into breaking with him, Lisette and Tristan had already fled to France to avoid George's wrath. So all his sister knew of what had happened was what she'd pieced together from gossip.

Dom wasn't fool enough to tell her and Tristan the truth. They would never let him hear the end of it. They already brought Jane up more often than he could stand. "None of that changes the fact that Jane is engaged to someone else."

Lisette released an exasperated breath. Clearly she'd been hoping for an explanation. She ought to know better by now.

"So even if I wanted to 'court' Jane," Dom continued, "I could not."

"Still, she seems in no hurry to marry her fiancé," Lisette pressed on, undaunted by the facts. "She came running up to Yorkshire almost the minute George died."

"To be with George's *widow*. I would think less of her if she did *not* try to comfort her cousin."

"Don't be obtuse, Dom. It doesn't suit you. She came because she's desperate to see you before she marries a man she has to know is wrong for her."

"Desperate? Hardly. She's been staying with Nancy at the dowager house a mile away from the manor, and I haven't come across her once during her entire visit."

"No doubt you went to great lengths to make sure of that." When he didn't rise to her bait, Lisette turned pensive. "How is Nancy doing, anyway?"

"How the blazes should I know? I just told you— I don't see them."

"I hope you realize how rude that is. You should at least pay them a visit from time to time. To show there are no hard feelings."

"Hard feelings? Are you mad?" He eyed her askance. "Nancy doesn't care about my feelings toward her. She undoubtedly hates me and Tristan both. Because of us, George is dead."

"He was going to murder you two!"

"A minor detail that she will undoubtedly overlook in the face of George's death," he said dryly.

"I always found it odd that they married in the first place. I mean, if he'd been trying to get back at you over your helping Tristan, why didn't he just go after Jane?"

Because George had believed what he'd seen that night at the ball—that Dom wanted Nancy for her money. So, resentful of Dom as ever, George had set out to gain the woman for himself. That was undoubtedly what Nancy had intended when she'd somehow arranged for Jane to stumble upon them with George in tow.

Though that probably hadn't turned out as well as Nancy had planned. George couldn't possibly have been much of a husband, even for someone as shallow and undiscriminating as Jane's cousin.

Leaning back in his chair, he clasped his hands over his stomach. "George didn't go after Jane precisely because he knew Jane would never have married him after how he'd cut me off. Besides, Nancy was more his sort of woman—pretty, but vapid and malleable."

"Nonetheless, even she deserved better. And now she's a widow beholden to the very man her husband hated. Thank heaven she's got Jane to help her deal with that."

"Yes, thank heaven," he echoed absentmindedly.

And thank heaven Jane had apparently held Nancy blameless for that scene in the library years ago. At least his subterfuge hadn't torn her from the woman most like a sister to her.

Though sometimes it irked him that Jane had believed the lie so easily. That she'd instantly accepted the picture of him as an unscrupulous fortune hunter. That's what he'd wanted, of course, but it rankled.

Because he was an arse who wanted to have his cake and eat it, too.

"So," Lisette said, "*are* you joining us for services this morning?"

Thank God the inquisition about Jane was over. "Afraid not. As soon as I put the seal on this document that you and Max are carrying back to Victor, transferring the running of Manton's Investigations to him, I'm returning to Rathmoor Park."

He sat up and bent over the papers laid out on the desk. "I'm still dealing with those tenants George mistreated. We must reach some sort of agreement about how to compensate them fairly without bankrupting the estate, so I'm meeting with them tomorrow morning."

"And does this urgent meeting involve Nancy? Might you see Jane?"

Good God, Lisette was like a trickle of water that wore away at the stone until it cracked.

He concentrated on melting the sealing wax onto the parchment. "Actually, Jane is gone. She left from Hull the day before yesterday by packet boat to return to London." To her fiancé, the man Dom wanted to throttle simply because Blakeborough got to have Jane for the rest of his days.

So much for excising Jane from his mind.

"Aha! *That's* why you've been so cross." Lisette huffed out a breath. "I swear, you're impossible. You'll let the only woman you ever cared about marry some other fellow, even though you now possess everything you need to support a wife. For a man who's faced down thieves and murderers unflinchingly, you can be quite the coward, Dom."

Grimly, he pressed his signet ring into the wax. Lisette would never understand. Jane might have been his once, but she despised him now and that was that. Even if he told her the truth about that night, they'd spent so many years apart that whatever she'd felt for him had clearly withered.

Otherwise, she wouldn't be marrying Blakeborough. Dom, of all people, knew that Jane wouldn't get engaged to a man she didn't love.

When he didn't respond to his sister's barbs, her gaze grew calculating. "You know, you ought to carry that document to London in person. I'm sure Victor has hundreds of questions about the running of the agency. Besides, you still haven't met little Eugene. I know he'd be delighted to see his Uncle Dom."

He chuckled at her blatant attempt to manipulate him. "I doubt little Eugene delights in anything but being nursed and having his swaddling changed. He's what, two months old? Has he even learned how to sit up yet?"

She glared at him. "Sometimes you can be so . . . so . . ."

"Practical?"

"Unsentimental. He's your very first nephew. Don't you *want* to see him?"

So he could be reminded of all he'd lost because of George? No. Though he supposed he must, eventually. "I will happily come to visit little Eugene once he's old enough to recognize me. But I do have a meeting tomorrow, so I can't run off to London." He patted the document on the desk. "Would you make sure Max gets this before you leave?"

With a murderous glance, she whirled on her heels and headed for the door.

"Don't I at least get a goodbye kiss?" he called after her. "I probably won't see you for some weeks."

"Foolish gentlemen who don't know what's good for them don't get goodbye kisses," she said as she kept going.

Her peevish tone made him grin. "I suppose I should be glad you're not stabbing me toward Jane with your embroidery needles."

She halted to cast him an arch glance. "Would that work?"

Good God, she might actually do it. "It would not. And don't be angry. I'm fine as I am, really."

"Liar. Anyone can see you're not the least bit fine."

It frightened him sometimes, how well she knew him. "I'm content, at least. I inherited the estate I never expected to own. What more can I ask for?"

"A wife. Children. Happiness."

"Those three don't always go hand in hand, dear girl."

"Especially if you make no attempt to acquire the first one."

"Lisette, give it over," he said softly. "Being angry at me won't change the past."

An oath escaped her. "I'm frustrated by your obstinacy, stymied by your reserve, and perplexed by your acceptance of this ridiculous state of affairs between you and Jane." She apparently noticed the tightening of his jaw, for her expression softened. "But not angry. I could never be angry at you."

She marched back to plant a kiss on his cheek.

"There. That should prove it." With a fond smile, she said, "Do take care not to work too hard, will you?"

"Certainly," he lied.

He waited until she left before wandering over to the window to watch the family leave. She didn't understand that he welcomed the work. It kept his mind off the "ridiculous state of affairs" between him and Jane.

An image of his former fiancée as she'd looked in London a few months ago sprang into his mind. He'd been shocked to encounter her at the soiree thrown by Zoe's father. It had only been the second time he'd seen her in their years apart, and the first had been so fleeting he'd scarcely had time to register that she was there before she was gone.

Not so at the soiree.

He'd been unable to look away from the glory that was Jane in a blue evening gown. In the time they'd been apart, she'd filled out just enough to have lusher curves. Wrapped in expensive satin, those curves had been quite enticing.

It had been all he could do to keep his gaze on her face. Especially since her brown eyes had sparked fire at him. It was as if no time at all had passed since that horrible night at Blakeborough's.

He had expected her to lose her anger over time, but her eyes had been hot, her words cool, and her tone a mix of condescension and implied meanings he couldn't decipher. He'd only endured the encounter by taking on his investigator persona—aloof, unruffled, and always certain of his position.

But her enigmatic comment about tiring of waiting for her life to begin had rattled him. It still did. What the blazes had she meant? Surely she hadn't been waiting for *him*, not after what had happened.

Her remark had plagued him for months. Because if she really *had* been waiting all these years . . .

God, the very notion was idiotic. She hadn't. And if she had, it didn't matter. He couldn't have renewed his attentions toward her, even if she would have accepted them.

He'd spent his first two years at Bow Street proving himself. His next few, during the years of political unrest, had been an endless series of missions for Jackson Pinter and occasionally even Lord Ravenswood, undersecretary to the Home Office—secret, *dangerous* missions.

He stroked the scar carved into his right cheek. More dangerous than he'd ever imagined.

Those years were a blur. But they'd earned him the respect of the other runners and better chances at more lucrative cases. He'd saved enough to open Manton's Investigations. And then he'd had new challenges to contend with, new missions to absorb him, all of which kept him from starting up again with Jane.

You can be quite the coward, Dom.

He clenched his jaw. It wasn't cowardice—not a bit. He'd been busy, damn it. And too aware of how deeply he had hurt Jane to want to risk it again.

Now she was betrothed, and that was that. So he would put her behind him—put that part of his life behind him—and learn to be happy with what he had. It was more than he'd expected, after all.

With that settled, he returned to the desk. He penned a quick note to Max and set it atop the document for Victor, weighing them both down with a paperweight. Then he tidied up his mess and headed out the door. He'd called for his equipage earlier, so his bag should already be stowed. He merely had to—

"If I give you my name," said a painfully familiar voice from the foyer, "will you promise to make Lord Rathmoor come out here to talk to me? And not put me off with some nonsense about how he's not here? I *know* he's here. I saw his phaeton out front. And it's imperative that I speak with him."

Dom's stomach knotted. How could it be? Why would *she* be here?

"I understand, madam," the butler was saying as Dom hurried toward them, "but if the matter is so urgent, why will you not tell me what name to announce—"

"It's all right," Dom said as he approached. "I know Miss Vernon."

Jane started, her pretty eyes widening as she caught sight of him. Today she wore a riding habit of purple wool that nipped in at the waist, ballooned at the hips, and accentuated every curve to good effect. Looking agitated and windblown and heartbreakingly beautiful, she sucked the air quite out of his lungs.

God save him.

"I need to speak with you at once." With a furtive glance at the butler, she added, "Privately."

He nodded and gestured for her to precede him toward an open door down the hall. The second they entered, he wished he'd chosen another room. Jane looked so lovely against the backdrop of gold and red silk that his blood ran hot.

"What the blazes are you doing here?"

She lifted an eyebrow. "How delightful to see *you*, too."

Damn, he hadn't meant to sound annoyed. "Forgive me. I'm merely surprised to find you still in Yorkshire. I assumed you'd be well on your way to London by now. Weren't you supposed to leave by packet boat the day before yesterday?"

"The spring rains washed out the bridge on the road to Hull, so I had to return to Rathmoor Park." Something indecipherable glinted in her eyes. "I was unaware you were paying such close attention to my schedule."

Blast. He hadn't meant to give that away. "I pay attention to everything regarding my estate and those in my charge," he said smoothly. "Which includes any visitors to the dowager house."

Was that disappointment in her face? No, surely not.

"I see," she said in a colder tone. "Then it's a pity you haven't been around the past two days. Because while you've been gone, one of those 'in your charge' has gone missing."

"Who?"

"Nancy. According to the servants, she headed off alone on the mail coach to York to visit her great-aunt, Mrs. Patch, directly after I left for Hull. Nancy told them she was going only for the day, but she hasn't returned."

He let out a breath. Was that all? "York is only half a day's journey from Rathmoor Park. Nancy probably decided to remain in town a day or two with her aunt, and since she assumed you were on your way to London, she didn't bother to inform anyone at the estate."

"Well, she *did*, actually. Indeed, it's what is in her letter to the housekeeper, which arrived late in the evening on the day she left, that alarms me."

She held out the missive and he moved close enough to take it from her, which, unfortunately, was also close enough to smell her lavender scent. God, why must she still be wearing lavender after all these years? It conjured up memories of their far-too-brief kisses under the arbor behind her uncle's house, the ones he'd refused to think of in their years apart.

Determinedly he retreated out of smelling distance and forced his attention to the letter. Obviously Jane thought she had cause for concern, though he couldn't imagine why. She probably wouldn't even have known Nancy was gone, if not for having missed the packet boat to London.

With one look at the letter, he had memorized it, part of his peculiar talent for remembering words and images at a glance. He gave it back to her. "This only proves that she's not missing at all. She writes that she's decided to travel with her great-aunt to Bath."

"Yes, but that's not true!"

This got more perplexing by the moment. "How do you know?"

"Because I sent an express to Mrs. Patch to ask if Nancy wanted her maid to join them, and *this* is what I received in reply early this morning."

Jane jerked another letter from the pocket of her riding habit and thrust it at him. It was written with a formality that Nancy's had lacked:

> *Dear Miss Vernon,*
> *I believe there has been some misunderstanding. I have not had the pleasure of my dear Nancy's company since before her husband's demise. She is certainly not here, nor had we made any plans to travel anywhere. Have you perhaps confused me with another relation of hers?*
> *If I can be of any further assistance in this matter, do let me know. I would be very happy to see you when next you are in York.*
> *Very Sincerely Yours,*
> *Mrs. Lesley Patch*

A twinge of unease slid down his spine. "Blast it all."

"Exactly. And you read Nancy's letter. She was clearly referring to her great-aunt in York."

"One of them must be lying."

"Yes," she said in a tone of pure exasperation, "but what reason would Mrs. Patch have for doing so? From what I understand, Nancy has been visiting her for years. They are very close."

"And what do they do when she visits?" he asked, falling easily into his role as investigator, though it had been months since he'd had anything to investigate other than what crops worked best in Yorkshire soil.

"I don't know." Jane tapped her foot impatiently. Obviously investigative techniques were rather lost on her. "Gossip. Discuss their dogs—between them, they have seven. I think one of the footmen said they used to go shopping together. According to him, George encouraged Nancy's trips when he was alive. He even let her use the carriage, which is why it's so odd that she took the mail coach this time."

"She didn't have a choice," he pointed out. "I've got the phaeton, and I assume you took the family carriage to Hull the day she left."

"I did, but why didn't she just wait to set off for York until you were back or the family carriage had returned? For that matter, why not just get off at the village here while on her way, so she could get the phaeton from you? Nancy doesn't like being crowded, so why go all the way to York in the mail coach? She had no reason to rush if this was just some little shopping venture."

"Perhaps it was more than that. You said she went without her maid. Is that usual?"

"I don't think so, but Nancy's regular maid, Meredith, left service for a while to help her ill papa in London, and the present maid hasn't been with her long enough to go on one of her jaunts. I don't have any first-hand knowledge about the York trips, because Nancy has never taken one, with or without me, while I was at Rathmoor Park."

How peculiar. "Why not?"

"How the devil should I know?"

Why were his perfectly logical questions annoying Jane? She eyed him as if he were a half-wit.

"But don't you see?" she went on. "This visit is clearly different. Her going off on the mail coach, and without her maid. Her letter to the servants about her supposed trip to Bath, which didn't mention any requests for clothes. Or, for that matter, her dogs."

"You expected her to take her *dogs*?"

"Absolutely. She never leaves them at home for days at a time. They go everywhere with her—to London, to Brighton, anywhere she travels. At the very least, she would have mentioned them in her letter. The fact that she didn't is worrisome."

He eyed her closely. "So, what are you saying, Jane?"

"Something dreadful must have happened to my cousin. She obviously had a mishap between here and York."

"And then wrote a letter to lie about being off on a jaunt to Bath?"

She huffed out a frustrated breath. "The letter has to be forged, don't you see? Nancy wouldn't create such a tale out of whole cloth. She isn't capable of perpetrating such a falsehood."

He bit his tongue to keep from admitting that Nancy had been more than capable of perpetrating falsehoods twelve years ago. But Jane didn't know about that, and now wasn't the time to tell her. First he must soothe her concerns.

"Do you have any reason for thinking that the letter is forged?" he asked. "Is there anything in the handwriting that you find suspect?"

"Not to the naked eye, but—"

"So you assume that a master forger has learned to copy Nancy's hand well enough to fool her own cousin."

A look of desperation flickered in her eyes. "It's possible, isn't it?"

"Possible? Yes. Probable? No."

"Why not? I read about kidnappers in the paper all the time!"

"Yes, and they have reasons for their actions." He fell back on what usually worked with sensible people whose panic kept them from thinking straight: simple logic. "What would be a kidnapper's purpose in sending a forged letter?"

She crossed her arms over her chest. "To put off anyone who might grow alarmed when she didn't return. He had to throw possible pursuers off his trail."

Dom flashed her a tight smile. "This mysterious kidnapper already had a day's head start. By the time the servants grew alarmed enough to head to York after her, he could be in another county. So why trump up some tale about her traveling to Bath?"

"I don't know!" Her cheeks bloomed a fetching shade of pink. "Sadly, my education didn't include how to think like a kidnapper."

"Ah, but mine did. Some of those cases you read about in the papers were ones I solved." When that made her frown, he softened his tone. "This isn't how kidnappers operate. If a man carries off a woman, it's usually for one of three reasons: to elope with her, to force himself on her, or to ransom her off."

Her lips began to thin ominously, but he pressed on, ticking each reason off on his fingers. "In the first case, Nancy can marry whom she pleases, so there's no need for evasive letters. In the second, he'd simply force her; again, no reason for evasive letters. In the final and most rare case, which you seem to be considering, the only letter he'd send would be a ransom request. Have you received any?"

"Not yet," she said sullenly.

Clearly, she wasn't fond of simple logic. "Kidnappers don't generally send evasive forged letters in the victim's hand and then notes of ransom. They want to strike fear, not confusion, into the hearts of the family."

She thrust out her chin. "I'm beginning to remember how sanctimonious you can be."

He regarded her coldly. "I'm being logical. You simply don't like my logic."

"Because you keep dwelling on what *couldn't* have happened. I need to know what *could*."

"Fine. Instead of conjuring up criminal assaults, you should consider the possibility that Nancy merely wanted to get away. She did just lose her husband, after all."

"That makes it sound as if she misplaced him somehow, instead of his being killed by your half brother." When Dom tensed, she let out an exasperated oath. "I realize that Tristan was merely defending himself. If anyone is aware of how vicious George could be, it's me. I'm simply . . ."

"Angry at me because I'm telling you what you don't want to hear."

She advanced on him with a dark light in her eyes. "And what exactly is that? Your theory that Nancy merely wanted to get away? Why should that bother me? Unless you're implying that it was *me* she wanted to escape."

"Certainly not. She thought you were gone off to London and unlikely to return anytime soon."

"Well then, according to your logic, *whom* might Nancy have been trying to escape?" She started ticking possibilities off on her fingers, mimicking him. "The servants? The villagers? The tenants? *You*, perhaps?"

Her rapid-fire questions unnerved Dom. He wasn't used to this new Jane, who threw his logic back in his face and didn't simply accept his opinions. She was maddening.

She was magnificent.

Damn her. "Don't be absurd—you know perfectly well that I never see Nancy. She would have no reason to escape me. But that's not the point."

"Oh? Then what *is* the point, Lord Rathmoor?"

Her use of his title added to his irritation. Officially he wasn't even viscount yet, although everyone behaved as if he were, since George had sired no sons. "I never said she was trying to get away *from* anyone. It's more likely she was trying to get away *to* someone."

That stole the color from Jane's face. "*To*. What do you mean?"

"Come now, you aren't a girl anymore. After several years of marriage, Nancy has, well, certain needs. Her husband is dead, and she's alone. Since either you or I have been at Rathmoor Park from the day George died, this would have been her first chance to get away to be with someone."

Jane just kept gaping at him as if he were some foreigner newly alighted on English shores.

"It would explain her mysterious jaunts to York," he went on. "And why Nancy concocted her ruse of a trip to Bath and left her maid behind. She wants to preserve her reputation before her staff, which is perfectly understandable."

Thunderclouds wrought her brow. "Are you saying that my cousin would be so unprincipled, so shameless, so *deceptive*, as to run away to consort with a . . . a . . ."

"Paramour. Yes. It's the only thing that makes sense. Nancy has obviously been having an affair."

2

JANE WANTED TO throttle him. How dared he? She didn't remember his being so cynical. So ungentlemanly.

So handsome.

Curse it, she didn't find Dom at all attractive anymore, for one perfectly good reason. He'd thrown their future away, and she could never forgive him for that.

But it would be so much easier to stand firm against him if he'd grown a paunch and his hair had thinned in the past twelve years. Instead, he'd gained a rakish scar and a broader chest than she remembered.

And he wasn't even a tiny bit gray! His hair was still as black as his iron heart, which seemed unaffected by their past together. Meanwhile, just being this close to him had revived her own cold, dead heart.

She'd have to make sure he couldn't tell. He used to be wickedly good at reading her emotions, and she would *die* before she let him see how vulnerable she was to him after all these years.

"So without having any facts to support your theory you've decided that Nancy ran off to meet a paramour," she told him. "Aren't investigators supposed to consider all the evidence before they jump to conclusions?"

A muscle flexed in his jaw. "I'm not jumping to anything. It's the explanation that makes the most sense."

"To you, perhaps. But if Nancy had a lover, I would know, I assure you. The woman is incapable of that level of deception."

"Is she?" His eyes were cold and brittle as green glass in the morning light. "Perhaps you don't know your cousin as well as you think."

A pox on him! Was he alluding to the subterfuge he and Nancy had pulled off that horrible night at the Blakeborough ball? Because if so, he ought to come out and say it.

Then again, he was unaware that she knew the truth. He still thought she'd *believed* their nonsense. And at first she had. She'd assumed Dom was a villain, that somehow she'd missed a serious flaw in his character.

But as the years had passed and he hadn't married any heiresses or become the subject of gossip about fortune hunters or even attempted to push his way into other society functions, she'd grown suspicious. By then, Nancy had been wed to George for a few years and the bloom of her marriage had withered. She'd been lonely enough to want to share confidences with Jane again.

It hadn't taken much to get the truth out of her—that Dom had set up the entire thing. That the arrogant wretch had deliberately made Jane think he was a fortune hunter just to force her to jilt him.

He hadn't even given her a choice! He'd placed her in a position where her pride demanded that she break with him, because he'd known exactly how she would react to seeing him make advances to her cousin. Because he'd known exactly where to insert the knife.

He'd gotten away with it, too. It still infuriated her every time she thought about it. Of all the pompous, unfeeling—

Jane gritted her teeth to silence the hot retorts she wanted to throw at him. After their encounter last year at George's town house, she'd decided that if Dom hadn't loved her enough to fight for her back then—or come back to fight for her later, when he was more financially secure—then he wasn't worth the years she'd wasted on him.

The only thing she wanted now was for him to confess what he'd done and why. For him to admit that it had been a mistake. That he'd ended up alone without her because of his foolish pride and his assumptions about her character. The dratted man owed her that, at least.

Unfortunately, she wasn't likely to get any such admission. Dom the Almighty had clearly grown even more arrogant now that he'd gained his inheritance and become Lord Rathmoor. Like Papa with Mama, he thought his opinion was the only important one, which was clear from his dratted elucidation of all the reasons Nancy was some sort of devious harlot.

Well, Dom could sling as much mud at Nancy as he pleased—Jane knew the truth. Simply because he'd once manipulated Nancy into a deception didn't mean she was capable of adultery. If he intended to argue that, he'd have to provide evidence, not just vague insinuations.

"Actually," Jane said, forcing sweetness into her tone, "I know my cousin *quite* well. I can't imagine why you would think otherwise. Do you have any particular instance of deceptiveness you're alluding to?"

When his eyes darkened at her aggressive pursuit of the matter, she added, "Because if you're hinting at how I found the two of you together at the Blakeborough ball, I happen to know that Nancy didn't want you to kiss her that night. It was perfectly clear from what I overheard."

Wriggle out of that, *Dominick Manton!*

A shuttered look crossed his face. "I'm merely falling back on my years of experience as an investigator, which tell me that something other than a kidnapping is at work here."

His voice was cool, remote—a far cry from the warm one she remembered from her youth, whispering sweet compliments in her ear.

It saddened her. When had he become so unfeeling and controlling? She remembered him as an amiable gentleman, who loved books and music and dogs and spoke to her with perfect candor. Now he was autocratic and dictatorial.

Had something happened to him during his career

as a Bow Street runner to turn him into this rigid fellow without a heart? Or had he always been that way and she just hadn't seen it, blinded by love?

"Very well," she said. "You have your theory of what happened to Nancy, and I have mine. But either way, you have to go look for her."

Stubborn to a fault, he crossed his arms over his chest. "Why?"

"Because I can't go looking for her alone, of course. You know perfectly well it would be improper for me to wander the streets of York asking questions. Besides, even if it weren't frowned upon, investigation is *your* particular skill, not mine. So you have to help me search for her."

Irritation furrowed his brow. "What I meant was, why must *anyone* look for her? She's a grown woman. If she wishes to run off, that's her affair."

"But you aren't sure that's what happened!"

He pointed to the letter from Nancy, which Jane clutched in her hand. "I'd swear that her missive isn't forged. So she made her own choice to leave and to hide her reasons for it. We should respect that." He searched her face. "Unless there's something you're not telling me."

Drat the man. How was it he could always read her so well? She'd better take care or she'd wind up spilling the secret Nancy had made her swear to keep some days ago. After all, Nancy wasn't certain of anything yet. No point in stirring things up until she was.

But that didn't mean Jane would give up on looking for her cousin.

"I'm merely anxious about her, and you should be, too. You're her brother-in-law; she's your responsibility now. Even if you're right and she ran off with a paramour, that doesn't mean she's safe." Mama hadn't even been safe with her own husband, for pity's sake.

She shoved thoughts of her long-dead parents from her mind. "Men do take advantage of widows with dower portions, as you well know. So don't you think you should at least attempt to protect her, if only from herself?"

He muttered an oath under his breath. Oh, Dom the Almighty didn't like having his sense of chivalry used against him, did he? He prided himself on his character, and a responsible gentleman didn't allow a female relation to be misused.

She pressed her advantage. "If you won't help me, you'll force me to go alone. Either way, I'm not letting Nancy stumble into an awful situation where some deceptive fellow—"

"Fine," he cut in. "I'll travel to York and make inquiries of this Mrs. Patch."

"Right away?"

He raised his eyes heavenward. "If I must. But I have to return to the coast in time for my tenants' meeting tomorrow."

"And you'll take me with you to York, right?"

"There's no need." A flush darkened his angular features, making the scar he'd acquired in their years apart stand in high relief. "And anyway, you can't go riding the roads with me unchaperoned."

"I'm nearly thirty, Dom—it's not as if I'm some schoolgirl. If we travel in your open phaeton, no one will suspect us of anything scandalous. I realize that York is a couple of hours away, but with the days lengthening, we can be there and back before dark. And you did say you must go on from here to Rathmoor Park for your meeting."

He advanced on her with a fierceness that took her aback. "You're betrothed, or have you forgotten? What will your fiancé say when he hears you're running about the countryside alone with me?"

When he stopped just short of her, forcing her to look way up to meet his gaze, she glared at him. "He'll say that he trusts me. That he believes in me, no matter what. That he knows I'll always do what's right, regardless of the situation."

And that's more than you ever did, she nearly added. Because that was what stuck in her craw about how Dom had behaved in their youth. Without ever giving her a chance to prove herself, he'd simply assumed she couldn't handle the massive changes in his circumstances.

Dom stared at her, then slowly lowered his gaze to her lips. "That's what Blakeborough would say, is it? Somehow I doubt that."

"Because I'm not trustworthy?"

"Because he's a man." Something hard and hungry glittered in his eyes, putting her on her guard. "He knows we were once engaged, so he'll assume I'm still tempted by you."

That took her by surprise. Lord help her, the covetous look he was giving her would stir the very marrow in a woman's bones. "And are you?" she managed to eke out. "Still tempted by me, I mean?"

Time halted as they stood there, with eyes locked and breaths mingling, so close that a mere lowering of his head would bring their mouths together, too.

Then he tore his gaze from hers and stepped away. "That's of no consequence. Blakeborough will think I am, which is all that matters. And I know you don't wish to spoil things with him."

Vexed that he wouldn't reveal what he felt for her, she snapped, "Odd, how you always seem to 'know' what I'm thinking or wishing." When her sarcasm made him shoot her a veiled glance, she added, "In any case, no acquaintance of Edwin's is likely to see you and me in York, so there's little chance that news of our jaunt will get back to him. I, for one, am willing to risk it."

"I, for one, am not."

"You don't have a choice. You've never met Mrs. Patch, which makes it highly unlikely that she'd talk to you, especially with your being Nancy's estranged brother-in-law and the man partly responsible for George's death."

A muscle worked in his jaw. "Have *you* met her?"

"Well, no, but you notice that she invited me to consult with her further if it became necessary. And I'm sure Nancy has spoken of me frequently enough for her to feel comfortable talking to me."

For a long moment, Dom simply scowled at her, as if somehow that would frighten her into compliance.

It had been a long time since she'd seen that cutting frown. He'd only used it on her once—that day in her uncle's study when he'd tried to convince her to jilt him. She'd withstood it then well enough, so why he expected her to behave any differently now was beyond her.

"You refuse to leave this to me," he finally said.

"If it was Lisette in trouble, would you leave it to one of your men? Or would you insist on handling it yourself?"

He hesitated. Then to her shock, he flashed her a rueful smile. "You know the answer to that."

Of course she did. She could read *him*, too, after all. "Then I suggest that we leave at once. No point in letting the trail grow any colder."

◆ ◆ ◆

THE ROAD TO York was quiet—not surprising, since it came from the coast and encompassed only a few sleepy towns and estates along the route. Normally Dom would have enjoyed having just the steady clop-clop of the horses as an accompaniment to his reverie.

But normally Dom didn't have Jane bumping up against him on the seat. He didn't have her scent filling his senses, mingling with the smell of the spring grasses and wildflowers. He didn't have her arm within touching distance. Her very presence put him on edge, which made the silence between them unbearable.

How odd. Dom had never been a chatty sort, and in their youth he'd been happy to let Jane do most of the talking. He hadn't always even heard what she was saying, too enthralled by the animation on her face to pay attention.

She used to have this way of imbuing every word with emotion. Judging from their argument earlier, she still did, even if the emotion was panic and concern. And accusation.

He scowled. The blasted woman had manipulated him into this trip quite well. It had been a masterful performance, but a performance nonetheless. Not for nothing had he spent the past years uncovering deceptions. Jane was hiding something. She wouldn't be this alarmed unless there was more at stake than she was saying.

He'd better find out what it was before this went any further. "So tell me, how was Nancy's mood when last you saw her?"

Instantly she stiffened, heightening his suspicions. "Why?"

"I merely wondered if there was anything to indicate why she would leave Rathmoor Park. Did she seem melancholy? Relieved by George's death? Angry?"

"Nancy is never angry," Jane said.

"Unlike you. Who seem to be quite angry right now." *At me, anyway.*

"I'm worried, not angry." Jane leaned away from him, putting the lie to her words. "Nancy doesn't do things like this."

"You did say she's made these jaunts to York before."

"Yes, but never for more than a day, and never

without telling anyone in the family. It's not like her." She breathed deeply. "But to answer your question, she *has* seemed rather melancholy of late. That's not how someone who is racing off to meet a lover reacts, is it?"

"It depends. Perhaps she hadn't heard from him. Perhaps she thought he'd given her up, now that she was free. Perhaps—"

"Faith, are you always so cynical?" She twisted a little to stare at him. "You believe the worst of everyone. In your eyes, Nancy is an adulteress and Lord Blakeborough a jealous and distrustful suitor. You seem to see the entire world through dark glasses."

He kept his gaze fixed on the road ahead. "Until a few months ago, I dealt regularly with the worst specimens of humanity, so I lost the habit of trusting people unequivocally. You would have, too, if you'd ever witnessed—" Blast it, he shouldn't even have said that much.

"Witnessed what?"

"Nothing." He'd engineered the end of their engagement precisely to keep her out of the nightmarish world he'd entered, so he sure as blazes wasn't going to drag her into it now. "It wouldn't interest you."

"And once again, you decide what would or would not interest me." She sniffed. "It must be nice to be able to read minds."

He shot her a sidelong glance. "It does have its uses," he said blandly.

She narrowed her gaze on him. "I'm not entirely

unaware of what you've been doing all this time, you know. I've followed your career in the papers."

Oh, God. Was that good or bad? "I didn't realize I'd been mentioned all that often in the press," he said, hoping she'd elaborate.

"Often enough." A mischievous smile tugged at her lips. "Like that case where you and several armed men stormed a barn full of criminal chickens in the dead of night."

Wonderful. She really *had* kept up with him. "Ah, yes, the chickens. Now, *that* was an attack I'll never forget." He cast her a mock frown. "It didn't help that the weather was fowl."

She blinked, then burst into laughter. "I can't believe I forgot your love of wordplay." Her eyes gleamed at him. "And did the chickens resist your attempts to arrest them?"

"I've never seen fugitives so cocksure. But in the end they were too birdbrained to fly the coop, which is how we managed to capture them."

"And did you wring their necks?"

"No, we left that to the farmer. We figured a bird in his hand was better than two in our gaol."

She chuckled. "Why *did* you attack a barn full of chickens, anyway?"

He sobered. "We'd been given what we thought was sound information that the place held guns intended for use at a demonstration in Chelsea. After the Spa Fields Riots, we could take no chances."

"I assume that you got there and found no guns?"

"It turned out that our information was . . . er . . ."

"Fowl?"

He stifled a smile. "Unreliable."

"I shouldn't tease you about it, I suppose. Most of your cases were quite impressive." She said it almost grudgingly. "I read how you brought that murderer from Spitalfields to justice. And recovered part of the funds stolen from the Bank of England. Oh, and the most spectacular case, when you single-handedly captured the Cato Street conspirators. That one got you lots of attention in the press."

"I didn't do it single-handedly, and we were lucky that day. It could have ended much worse." Much, *much* worse.

He felt her gaze on him, probing him.

"Is that where you got the scar on your cheek?" she asked.

God, now she was the one reading minds. "No." He swiftly changed the subject. "Do you have any theories about why Nancy might have been melancholy?"

Jane frowned, and he thought she might persist in her questions about his past. Then, with a sigh, she gazed ahead at the road. "As you said, Nancy just lost her husband. That would depress any woman's spirits."

"Assuming she had a happy marriage. But did she?"

"It was . . . happy enough, I suppose."

"You *suppose?*"

A flustered expression crossed her face. "You grew up with George. Did he seem like a fellow who would treat his wife well?"

"No." And that bothered Dom. Because if not for George mistaking the situation that night in the library, Nancy might never have ended up with the arse.

One more sin to add to his conscience. But that didn't mean he was going to run off on some wild-goose chase to find her while Rathmoor Park, which desperately needed oversight just now, languished. "So it's not far-fetched that Nancy might have taken a lover."

"Under George's nose?" She snorted. "He would have killed her if he'd ever learned of such a thing."

A chill swept down Dom's spine. "But if he was willing to let her go off alone to York sometimes—"

"Not alone. She had servants with her." Her voice turned acid. "And you can be sure that they knew better than to keep anything from him."

"Then perhaps we should be questioning *them*."

"I already did. As I told you, the present maid is a temporary replacement, so she had no information. But the coachman revealed that he always left Nancy and her regular maid at Mrs. Patch's lodgings and picked them up there when it was time to return. He assumed they went shopping with her great-aunt."

Jane's tone turned defensive. "Mrs. Patch doesn't have horses to stable, so the coachman had to go to a local inn where he and the horses might be fed while he waited for Nancy and Meredith."

"That still means it's possible that Nancy went to York to meet with a man, and that Mrs. Patch and Meredith were complicit in the affair."

"Oh, for the love of— You seem determined to think

Nancy some hussy. Why is that? What is it about her that has your back up?"

He tensed. He could hardly say that he knew the woman to be capable of at least one deception. Then again, perhaps he should tell Jane the truth about that. Just clear the air between them.

But it wasn't as if it would change anything. She was finally betrothed and moving on with her life, which he'd expected her to do long before now. What would be the point of revealing what he'd done? If he learned nothing of use in York today and Jane persisted in this pointless pursuit then he would confess all. But for now, he'd rather not muck with her life any further.

Coward. You're afraid that you'll tell her and it will make no difference. That she'll thank you for setting her free. That you'll finally have the definitive answer to how she feels about you, and it will be the one you can't bear to hear. At least this way, you can go on believing she could still love you.

He grimaced. That wasn't it at all. Not a bit. "I do not have my back up about Nancy. I'm merely trying to prepare you for disappointment in case I'm right about her character. I want to protect you, that's all."

She muttered something under her breath about "idiot men," which hardly seemed an appropriate reaction to what he'd said.

It fairly stirred his temper, which, as always, set him on the offensive. "You still haven't given a sufficient explanation for why she might have run off." He couldn't help the sarcasm that crept into his voice. "Other than your theory that some stranger kidnapped her and forged her name to a note."

He cast Jane a sharp glance, and what he saw in her face only confirmed his suspicions that Jane knew something she wasn't telling him. Something important.

"I have no theories," Jane said smoothly. "Unlike you, I want to see the entirety of the evidence before I make a decision. So perhaps we should suspend this discussion until we have more of it."

Oh, yes, *definitely* something important. But it would do no good to continue to press her on it. Once she dug in her heels, she was damned hard to persuade. He'd learned that years ago.

Very well. He could be patient. Because in the end, he always uncovered the truth.

3

JANE LAUNCHED INTO a subject she hoped Dom would consider neutral—how he intended to handle his estate now that he'd inherited. But her heart hammered so hard that she could barely pay attention as he spoke of his plans for new crops and breeds of livestock and what all. Because she feared that he had somehow guessed she was hiding something.

After all, Dom had come by his reputation as a good investigator honestly. Which made it all the more imperative that she not reveal Nancy's secret until she was sure it had something to do with Nancy's disappearance. If it didn't, and Jane broke Nancy's confidence, Nancy would never forgive her—especially given how Dom was sure to react to the news.

After a while, listening to Dom lay out his plans for the estate began to depress her. It reminded her that no matter what happened, one day he would find a wife and have children of his own, and—

Lord, she hated to think of that, which in itself was

awful. He had a right to marry. She certainly intended to. She'd considered remaining a spinster and just claiming her fortune when she turned thirty-five, when it would revert to her.

Unfortunately, she wanted children and she needed a husband for that. She might not love Edwin, nor he her, but they were friends with a deep affection for each other that was far more practical than any passionate and romantic love.

They had an understanding. She was to give him an heir and help his difficult sister, Yvette, find a husband. In exchange, Jane would get babies and a household to manage in any way she saw fit.

Edwin would never try to control her future. He might be something of a curmudgeon, but he was never dictatorial. Unlike the hard-nosed individual at her side, Edwin would treat her as an equal partner in their marriage, consulting her on important matters before he made his decisions. Jane refused to tread the same dangerous path as Mama and Nancy, marrying a man who told her what to do, when to do it, and how to please him in the doing of it.

And because Jane had no intention of giving her heart to Edwin, he would never break it. That was the most important thing.

So why did the very idea of her tidy, arranged marriage dampen her spirits? Because she was a fool. Because despite all her efforts to stamp the dream of love out of her heart, the dratted weed always sprouted anew.

Not this time.

"You said Mrs. Patch has no stables," Dom remarked. "Do you know what inn the coachman used to frequent?"

Dragged from her woolgathering, she forced herself to concentrate on his question. "Is there one called the Elephant and Church?"

"The Elephant and Castle, you mean."

"If it's on Skeldergate, then yes."

"We can leave the phaeton there. And that will allow us to question the innkeeper, in case Nancy came through there. We'd kill two birds with one stone." As they reached a long, straight bit of road, he flicked the reins to urge the horses into a faster pace. "How much do you know about this Mrs. Patch?"

"She's a knight's daughter related to Nancy on her mother's side. Her maternal grandmother's sister, I believe."

"So, not a blood relation of yours."

"Exactly. That's why we've never met."

Uncle Horace was the brother of Jane's late mother. The siblings had been cits, the children of a wealthy cotton merchant. Uncle Horace had followed in their father's footsteps. Meanwhile, his sister had married a baron, lending her wealth to Papa's dwindling coffers. That was why Jane had quite a nice dowry. Not nearly as large as Nancy's, but certainly enough to make her sought after.

"One thing I should warn you about," Jane said. "I gather that Mrs. Patch is even more fanatical about her spaniels than Nancy. But given your fondness for dogs, you shouldn't have any trouble. You were always so good with Archer, though that wasn't difficult. I've never seen a sweeter foxhound."

Dom tightened his grip on the reins. "He was even-tempered, indeed."

The note of pain in his voice gave her pause. "I suppose he must be quite old by now."

"Assuming he's still alive."

"You don't know?"

He stared rigidly at the road. "I had to give him away. Haven't seen him in . . . some years."

"Oh, Dom, why? You adored that dog!"

"And where was I to keep him?" His eyes blazed over at her. "I was gone for days at a time, following cases wherever they led. Who was to look after him while I stalked criminals and invaded barns?"

She met his gaze steadily. "I would have. If you had let me."

Surprise showed in his features before he returned his attention to the road. "You mean, if I had not chosen Nancy over you."

Sweet Lord, the man was stubborn. "Of course," she said snidely, annoyed that he persisted in upholding that farce. "In any case, once your business got on its feet, you could have found another dog."

"I still traveled too much for that," he said in a dead tone. "It wouldn't have been fair to the animal."

Was that the real reason? She had to wonder. He'd deliberately cut both her and his dog out of his life out of some misguided sense of doing what was best for them. What else—*who* else—had he eliminated?

"Is there anything more you can tell me about Mrs. Patch?" he asked, clearly determined to avoid talking about Archer. "Other than the fact that she lives in Stonebow Lane?"

"How did you even know *that*?"

"Her address was on the letter."

"Oh. Right." One more thing she'd forgotten about him—his ability to memorize written and spoken words with ease.

"I wonder why a knight's daughter would live in such cramped lodgings in town, rather than out here in one of these manor houses."

She gazed about her and got a start. Faith, they were nearly to York, and she hadn't even noticed. The ancient Roman walls loomed up ahead as they drove toward Walmgate Bar. Within a mile or so, they'd be inside the old city. How had the time passed so quickly?

"I believe Nancy said that her aunt married beneath her." *Which you wouldn't let me do.*

He went rigid beside her. "Ah. That does happen."

Unless you're Dom the Almighty. "The marriage seems to have turned out well enough." Jane would goad him into revealing the truth of what he'd done, no matter what it took. "Nancy said Mrs. Patch misses her late husband dreadfully and refuses to decamp from York, though she could easily live with my uncle. Apparently, she doesn't miss her life as a knight's daughter."

"Oh? And exactly how far beneath herself *did* she marry?"

Jane colored as she dredged that little detail from her memory. "Her late husband was an architect, I believe."

"So, not a gentleman of leisure but still in a profession respectable enough that Nancy felt no compunction about visiting her." He smirked as he navigated the phaeton expertly through the narrow streets of York. "There are levels of marrying beneath one, after all."

Oh, she could just smack his face for that. After all these years, that he could still be so certain of the wisdom of the course he'd set them upon . . . "Yes, just as there are levels of being in love. Some people's love for each other transcends all obstacles. *Some* people's love does not."

His smug expression vanished. "And some people do not understand the meaning of the word."

"Really? I thought love was about enduring any sacrifice to be with the object of one's affection."

He drove through an archway and reined in the horses. "Here we are. The Elephant and Castle."

So he was avoiding the subject. Again.

As grooms scurried to seize the reins, Dom jumped out and came around to help her down. When he took her gloved hand, her breath caught in her throat. Because the yearning that flashed over his face as she stepped down was so raw and untamed that it made her want to leap into his arms.

Drat the man. That wouldn't do, not at all. She was engaged to another, for pity's sake! Never again would she put her heart in the care of Dominick Manton. He'd already proved he didn't want it badly enough to keep it.

She resisted the urge to snatch her hand free and thus betray her agitation. Instead she slid it nonchalantly from his grip. "Do we have time to eat something?" She flashed him an airy smile. "I'm positively famished."

He stared at her a long moment, his expression cooling to remoteness once more. "I'm not hungry myself, but you could eat while I question the innkeeper. Then we'll walk over to Mrs. Patch's."

"An excellent plan." And she would visit the retiring room as well. After a long ride from the coast to Winborough, and then on from there to here, she desperately needed to freshen up.

Half an hour later, they left the inn and headed toward Stonebow Lane. As they approached a puddle, he laid his hand against the small of her back to steer her around it, and her stomach flipped over.

Stupid, traitorous stomach, performing acrobatics for the likes of Dom Manton. Why couldn't it do that with Edwin? He, at least, *wanted* to marry her.

But sadly, Edwin didn't have smoldering eyes the exotic color of the finest jade. Or hair cropped unfashionably short, which only emphasized the carved masculine lines of his face. Or a body that looked so amazing in blue superfine it made a grown woman want to weep.

She would *not* weep over Dom's body, curse it! "What did you find out from the innkeeper?"

He dropped his hand from her back. "Not much. But I didn't expect to learn anything about this particular trip of Nancy's, anyway. If she took the mail coach, she would have stopped at Ringrose's Inn, not here. Still, I'd hoped he might at least reveal something about her prior visits."

"And did he?"

"Sadly, no. As the coachman told you, he dropped her off at her great-aunt's house and picked her up there, too. The innkeeper had never even met Nancy. Nor had he heard any local gossip about her."

Jane tipped up her chin. "Of course not. I told you she wasn't doing anything wrong."

"If you don't mind, I'll reserve judgment until I speak with Mrs. Patch and the ostlers at Ringrose's Inn. With any luck, one of them will know if Nancy is still in York, and where she went from here if she's not. The ostlers may even be able to tell me if anyone met her when she disembarked."

"Fine," she said, annoyed that he persisted in his conviction that Nancy had come here to run off with a man. "And what happens when you can find no evidence of her collusion with some mysterious lover? What then?"

"Then I'll institute a full investigation." He glanced at her. "I'm no more eager than you to see something awful happen to Nancy. One way or another, I'll make sure she's safe before I return to Rathmoor Park, I promise you."

"Thank you."

He had better keep his promise. Because if he didn't,

she would be forced to search the countryside on her own. And even her accommodating fiancé might take umbrage at that.

◆ ◆ ◆

DOM DIDN'T KNOW what he'd been expecting when they'd entered Mrs. Patch's, but this tiny, fearful female clutching three small spaniels to her bosom wasn't it. She wasn't as old as he would have thought—she couldn't be more than sixty-five—but she looked as if a stiff wind might blow her over.

It did explain why they'd had such a difficult time getting in to see the woman. Oh, the maidservant had been perfectly happy to admit Jane, but had insisted that Dom must stay outside. Only after Jane threatened to leave without telling Mrs. Patch anything about the missing Nancy did the maid agree to let Dom inside, too.

Now, standing in a brightly lit drawing room littered with an assortment of ragged leather balls and torn socks, he felt distinctly out of place. Especially when, as he stepped forward, Mrs. Patch squeaked loudly enough to send one of her dogs into loud barks. For God's sake, did the woman think he meant to murder her?

"Sh, sh, Rogue, I won't let anyone hurt you." She struggled to rise, no small feat when she had her arms full of spaniels.

Rogue? She named a dog Rogue, yet jumped when Dom cleared his throat? Good God.

Jane cast him a glance that said, *I told you so,* reminding him of why she'd insisted on joining him. Then she performed the necessary introductions.

Although Mrs. Patch said, sotto voce, that she was pleased to meet them both, she wouldn't look at him, preferring instead to smile timidly at Jane. "I'm so delighted to have you here at last, Miss Vernon. Nancy has told me what a wonderful lady you are."

"She's very fond of you as well, ma'am."

Jane's words were so gentle it made something twist in his gut. When was the last time she'd spoken gently to *him*? No, he wouldn't think of that. He refused to be like those writhing, whimpering dogs struggling to escape Mrs. Patch's grip—a slave to his instincts. He had spent years banishing Jane from his heart. If he let her inside even an inch, he would be lost.

Jane stepped toward Mrs. Patch. "I take it you've heard nothing more about Nancy?"

"Oh no, my dear, or I would have said at once." Mrs. Patch looked genuinely anxious. "You're certain she came *here*?"

He began to wonder how this nervous creature could perpetrate any sort of deception. Which meant that Nancy couldn't have met a lover here. Or while shopping with Mrs. Patch. Something wasn't right.

"Your niece spoke of you specifically in her letter," Dom interjected, determined to make the woman acknowledge him.

She acknowledged him, all right, shooting him a

frantic look, which so alarmed her dogs that Rogue broke free and jumped out of her arms.

With his tiny feet skittering wildly on the polished wooden floor, the spaniel dashed up to Dom and barked repeatedly.

"Rogue!" Mrs. Patch cried. "Come back here at once!"

"It's fine." Dom knelt to hold his hand out to the little rascal. "Good afternoon, Rogue. Pleased to make your acquaintance."

As Rogue sniffed him, Dom very carefully reached into his pocket with his free hand and pulled out a packet of ham. He'd bought it at the inn after Jane had warned him about Mrs. Patch's fanatical love for her dogs, and now he was thankful he had, for Rogue sat back on his haunches with a drooling doggy smile.

Dom suppressed a grin. Ah, if only people could be so easy to bribe. He glanced at Mrs. Patch. "Does the little scoundrel like ham?"

For the first time since he'd entered, she actually looked him in the eye, but she still didn't speak to him. Instead, she bobbed her head.

"Here you go, lad," he said and laid a small piece in front of the fellow.

The other dogs barked their displeasure at being left out, and Mrs. Patch released them. After they ran over to greet him with wagging tails and imploring looks, he gave them each a bit of ham, then ventured to pet the one who seemed most eager to make his acquaintance, a capering little lass with a winsome pair of eyes.

"What's her name?" he asked.

For a moment, he thought Mrs. Patch might not answer, but then she ventured, "That one's Nell. And the other female's name is Braganza."

He burst into laughter. When Jane looked bewildered, he explained, "They're King Charles spaniels, so named because Charles II had several. He called his favorite one Rogue."

Jane broke into a grin. "Oh, right! So the others are named after his mistress, Nell Gwyn, and his queen, Catherine of Braganza."

Slanting a glance at Mrs. Patch, Dom told Nell, "Your owner is a very droll woman, my dear. As was your namesake."

"She was also a shameless flirt," Mrs. Patch said in an arch tone. "Just like my Nell, who can clearly be bought for a bit of ham."

"Or who recognizes that she has naught to fear from me," Dom answered, meeting Mrs. Patch's gaze head-on. "Dogs know when someone means them harm. I mean none to anyone."

Mrs. Patch reddened. "And yet my Nancy has gone missing while in your care."

He frowned at her. The woman dared to *accuse* him?

"Mrs. Patch," Jane said hastily, "Nancy was with me until the day she left, an hour after I attempted to return to London. At that point, his lordship was visiting his family in Winborough. He didn't even know Nancy was gone until I informed him."

"And I assure you," Dom said tersely, "I would have

no reason to harm your great-niece. None whatso-
ever."

"Even if she—" The woman halted, then glanced at
Jane.

Something passed between the two women that he
was *not* meant to see. It only confirmed his impression
that Jane was keeping secrets from him, secrets that
Mrs. Patch was apparently privy to. And that infuriated him.

He rose to face the woman with a grim expression.
"Even if she what?"

Mrs. Patch's eyes went wide. "In truth, it's nothing.
Nothing, I assure you!"

"Forgive me, madam," he said, crossing his arms
over his chest, "but if you're hiding something about
my sister-in-law, I expect you to tell me at once."

"Hiding something? Oh, dear, oh, dear . . ." Mrs.
Patch's hands fluttered at her chest, and she collapsed
onto the settee, alarming him with her sudden quick
breathing. "Heavens . . . my cordial. I need my cordial!"

Her maid produced a bottle and poured some in a
glass for her. Dom suppressed a curse. He'd pushed the
woman too hard.

Sparing a dire glance for him, Jane took the glass
from the servant and hurried to sit beside the widow.
Mrs. Patch seized it gratefully and sipped it.

Jane patted the woman's hand. "It's all right, madam.
His lordship is just concerned and impatient to find out
what happened to Nancy, that's all. He didn't mean to
upset you."

"Indeed I did not." Dom deliberately loosened his stance and looked apologetic. He would get nothing out of Mrs. Patch if the woman jumped every time he asked a probing question. "Do forgive me, Mrs. Patch."

He was generally much better at questioning people, at reading what would upset them or make them reveal their secrets. But this situation had thrown him entirely off-kilter.

For one thing, even though he'd seen the like before, he'd somehow failed to grasp that Mrs. Patch was a particular kind of recluse. Once, during an investigation, he'd met a woman who panicked at every upset and was loath to leave the comforts of her home.

The other woman hadn't been so afraid of him, however. And clearly Mrs. Patch *was* afraid of him. No doubt she'd heard some of the gossip concerning his final confrontation with George.

Somehow he must put her at ease. Although Jane was already doing a decent job at it.

Jane. She's the other reason you're off-kilter.

He stiffened. No, he refused to accept that. Jane meant nothing to him anymore. Or at least she shouldn't, not with her fiancé waiting in the wings.

Mrs. Patch darted an anxious look from Jane to him and back. "Honestly, I don't know where Nancy is. But she certainly didn't come here. When she visits me, she always sends a note ahead. She knows I do not . . . like surprises of any kind."

"But this time she refrained from informing you?" Jane asked.

"Exactly!" Her high-pitched tone betrayed her alarm. "That's why I don't understand why she would claim to be traveling to Bath with *me*. She knows I don't leave my house."

"Not at all?" Dom asked. When she started, he added in a softer tone, "You never leave? Not even to go to the market?"

"Absolutely not," Mrs. Patch said. "It's a dangerous world for a lady. Criminals run rampant through the streets. And so many people crowd York these days, pushing up against one and making one nervous, taking all the air out of rooms . . ."

Just talking about it seemed to panic her, for she began to tremble and breathe heavily again. As Jane urged more cordial on her, Dom knelt to pet the eager Nell. As he'd hoped, just seeing him with her dogs and not looming over her helped to calm Mrs. Patch.

Only when he was sure the lady was no longer upset did he continue his questions. "So, if I am to understand you correctly, when Nancy came to visit you, the two of you did not go shopping."

She recoiled. "Oh no! Certainly not. It was one thing when my dear Mr. Patch was alive, but go out with just Nancy and our maids? Only think what could happen to us!"

He narrowed his gaze on her. "So Nancy just stayed here to keep you company? Or did she go shopping alone?"

"Not alone, no. I'd *never* stand for that. She came to take tea with me, and then she and Meredith would shop. I always tried to dissuade her, pointing out the sure dangers of pickpockets and ruffians, but she would only laugh." She wrung her hands. "My poor girl was too brave for her own good. And now look at her, gone missing! Whatever shall I tell her father?"

"You must leave that to us," Jane said. "But first let us attempt to find her. Perhaps you're right, and she did go visit another relation or a friend."

But her eyes were on him, and they mirrored his thoughts. If Nancy had come to York and spent a part of the day with just Meredith—who'd conveniently gone off to join her brother in London sometime after George's death—then Nancy *could* have been up to something. Mrs. Patch wouldn't have needed to be privy to it.

His legs were starting to cramp in his kneeling position, so he rose. "Tell me, Mrs. Patch. Do you know of any friends Nancy might have had in York? Did she ever mention any with whom we could speak?"

A tiny frown marred her brow. "No, I don't believe so. And I am the only one of her relations who lives here."

Jane avoided his gaze, clearly uncomfortable with the direction this discussion was going. But he *had* warned her.

"To your knowledge," he went on, "has she ever come to visit you by mail coach?"

"I should hope not!" Mrs. Patch said stoutly. "Only think of the foul air in such a close place. And all those dirty people and their dirty hands; why, it would not do! Not at all."

Yet, according to the servants at the estate, Nancy *had* left for York by mail coach. Perhaps it was time they moved on to Ringrose's Inn to ask their questions. Clearly, Mrs. Patch wasn't going to be much more help.

Unless . . .

"My dear lady," he said, "I have to go, but perhaps while I am asking questions about town, Miss Vernon might stay here with you? I hate to drag her about with me when there's no need."

Jane opened her mouth as if to protest, then shut it. He could see the exact moment when it dawned on her that she and Mrs. Patch could discuss their secret concerns if he weren't around.

And that was what he wanted. If they hashed it out together, he'd more easily be able to get the story out of Jane later. She would keep stubbornly silent as long as she wasn't sure of Mrs. Patch's part of the story.

"Oh, yes!" Mrs. Patch said with profound relief. "I'd be delighted to entertain Miss Vernon for the afternoon while your lordship is in town."

"We have to return before dark," he said, "so it won't be very long."

"Take all the time you need." Mrs. Patch patted Jane's hand. "I'm sure Miss Vernon and I have a great deal to talk about."

He was counting on it. One way or the other, he meant to get the truth out of Jane eventually. Because there was definitely more to this than met the eye.

4

THE MOMENT DOM was gone, Mrs. Patch sent her maid off for tea, then seized Jane's hand. "Is his lordship aware that Nancy is with child?"

Jane's heart sank. So Mrs. Patch knew. That meant it wasn't quite the secret Nancy had made it out to be. "Nancy told you for certain that she was breeding?"

"No, she merely said she was hopeful of it." Mrs. Patch looked first one way, then the other, as if watching for spies, before lowering her voice. "She said there were signs. That she hadn't had her . . . you know . . . in some time. Did she say as much to you?"

"All she said was that she *might* be with child."

In the three months since George's death, Nancy hadn't once had her menses, and she'd been feeling other effects—nausea, a violent urge to cry, a tenderness in her breasts.

Unfortunately, that didn't necessarily mean it would continue. "But she also said that given her past experiences, she dared not get her hopes up."

They sighed together. Nancy had already miscarried thrice; it was possible she would do so again.

"Still, this time the child *could* take root," Mrs. Patch said brightly.

"Yes." And if that happened, it was going to be quite a problem. For everyone.

"So his lordship has no idea that she is breeding?" Mrs. Patch asked.

"No. I certainly didn't tell him."

"Oh, thank heavens! That's one thing we needn't worry about then."

Jane stared at her. "What do you mean?"

"Well, if he doesn't know, he can't take steps to . . . prevent it."

"Like *what*?" Jane exploded. "I assure you that Lord Rathmoor wouldn't lay a finger on Nancy, no matter what the possible outcome of her pregnancy!"

Mrs. Patch flinched, clearly unnerved by Jane's vitriol. "I-I'm only saying that he would have good reason for alarm. If Nancy bears George's son in six months' time, Lord Rathmoor will no longer be the heir presumptive. He won't be able to inherit the title or the lands, and he'll go back to being plain Mr. Manton. So he *might* . . . I mean, I have to wonder, with Nancy missing and all . . ."

Jane drew herself up stiffly. "I beg your pardon, madam, but you clearly do not know his lordship if you think he would ever harm a woman. *Any* woman. And certainly he'd never do anything criminal to gain an inheritance!"

A flush spread over Mrs. Patch's cheeks. "But Nancy said that he and his bastard brother were the ones who murdered George."

"After George tried to kill *them*," Jane snapped. "They were defending themselves. Did she say that, too?"

"Well . . . yes, but I just thought—"

"You thought wrong," Jane said sharply.

Mrs. Patch dropped her gaze to her hands, which were now fluttering wildly. "Oh, dear, I've insulted you. I'm so sorry! It's just that I'm worried about Nancy. But I-I didn't mean to . . . I should not have . . ."

Her breathing sped up as before, and she clutched at her chest, which brought the dogs racing to her side. Rogue jumped into her lap and licked her face.

"My cordial . . ." she gasped. "Wh-where is my cordial?"

"I have it here." Stifling a sigh, Jane pressed the bottle into the woman's hand. "Don't be alarmed. I'm not insulted. We're both just very upset, that's all."

"Yes." Mrs. Patch uncorked the bottle and sipped some cordial. "Very upset . . . indeed."

"It will be all right." Jane rubbed Mrs. Patch's shoulder, relieved to notice the older woman's breathing was already evening out. "I brought his lordship here precisely because I trust his ability to find people. I wouldn't have asked for his help if I'd had any fears about his character, I promise."

Mrs. Patch nodded and drank a bit more cordial, but she seemed to be calming. "Rogue and Braganza did like him very well." She petted the dogs. "And Nell, the little flirt, would have climbed into his lap if she could have."

"You see? You needn't worry. If anyone can locate Nancy, it's his lordship."

Mrs. Patch lifted an anxious face to Jane. "But you won't . . . you shan't tell him about the coming baby, shall you?"

"Not until I have to. And I very well may." Jane glanced away. The thought of how that conversation would go made her nearly as nervous as Mrs. Patch. "But I'd prefer not to until we find Nancy or it becomes absolutely necessary."

"Good, good." Mrs. Patch clutched Rogue to her hard enough to make the dog squirm. "Because you know that the minute his lordship hears of it, he'll insist that my niece have those embarrassing doctor's examinations. And if she *has* managed to keep the baby, that could very well make her lose it."

"I know."

It was one reason Jane was so reluctant to mention the possibility to Dom. Before she raised that specter, she had to be sure it was likely. What if she said something and then they found Nancy tomorrow? Dom might indeed insist that she be examined for signs of a pregnancy.

A great deal was at stake, after all. Because if he didn't take such a dire measure and he chose to wait until it was clear she was carrying a child, he wouldn't be able to do anything with the estate. Everything would stop while there were endless discussions about the future, about what would happen if Nancy bore a son.

Jane wasn't privy to the terms of George's will. There was no telling whom George might have appointed to oversee his child's future, but it wasn't likely to be Dom. So Dom's hands would be tied until they learned whether the babe was a boy—and thus an heir—or a girl, in which case Dom would inherit. Meanwhile, the tension of living in such an atmosphere of uncertainty could easily make Nancy miscarry again.

Could that be why Nancy had run away—to find a quiet place while the child grew in her belly? To avoid the questions and examinations until she was further along in her pregnancy? That might explain Nancy's lack of need for clothes, if she thought she'd have to buy new ones to fit her advancing figure.

But then why not tell *someone* about her trip and where she was going, who could reach her if there was an emergency? For that matter, why not take her maid? Nancy wasn't the sort to fend for herself for months, especially if she was with child. So why leave in such a rush, and on the mail coach, no less?

It made no sense. And that was precisely why Jane couldn't tell Dom about the possible pregnancy until she gained more information.

For the next couple of hours, she fretted. She was forced to wait for Dom and listen while Mrs. Patch voiced her many worries: about the strange noises outside in the street at night, the noxious smells coming from the butcher's shop next door, her dogs' safety when they went for walks with the servants.

Incredibly, Mrs. Patch didn't take the spaniels out herself. Apparently she hadn't lied about the fact that she never left her house. In that, she was much like Nancy's mother, who'd grown more reclusive with age, to the point that she'd relied on Jane to do anything that required leaving their home.

Jane couldn't imagine being cooped up in one house all the time. Already, she was impatient to be gone from Mrs. Patch's. Much as she liked the woman's adorable spaniels, she was dying to know what Dom had discovered. Was it possible he'd actually found Nancy? Could that be why he was taking so long? Perhaps Nancy had simply stopped for a few nights at Ringrose's Inn, and he was even now coming back to give them the triumphant news.

But no, when he arrived, there was nothing in his grim expression to say that he'd met with success. He *had* discovered something, however. She could tell. And it was clearly something he didn't want to share with Mrs. Patch.

That made it all the harder for Jane to wait through the necessary goodbyes and repeated assurances that they would keep Mrs. Patch informed of what they learned.

By the time they were in the street, she was fit to be tied. "All right," she said without preamble, "what took you so long? What did you find out at the inn?"

He walked with such long strides toward the Elephant and Castle that she had to hurry to keep up with him. "I didn't go to the inn right away. I spent some time in this neighborhood first, asking about Nancy and Meredith. The neighbors said that after visiting Mrs. Patch the two women always headed off for the more fashionable area of shops."

"That means they were together," Jane mused aloud. "So it's highly unlikely that Nancy was doing anything but shopping."

A scowl knit his brow. "There's something else. Since finding out where they shopped and questioning shopkeepers would require more time than we have today, I went on to the inn. I learned that Nancy arrived there around noon on the day you left Rathmoor Park for Hull. And then she apparently vanished."

"What?" She seized his arm. "What do you mean, 'vanished'?"

He stared over at her. "No one saw her leave. Unfortunately, that doesn't tell us much, because not all of the ostlers from that day were working today." Frustration crept into his voice. "They said I'd have to return tonight to speak with everyone who would have been here then. But . . ."

When he hesitated, she shook his arm. "But *what*?"

"One of the ostlers said that when he asked if he could fetch a hackney coach for Nancy, she told him there was no need, because she was meeting a friend."

Jane's heart began to pound. "Mrs. Patch?"

"I doubt that." Eyes hard and brittle as emeralds glittered at her. "She would have said 'aunt.' Besides, 'meeting' implies that Nancy expected someone to come there for her. And you heard Mrs. Patch say she never ventures from her house."

This was getting worse by the moment. "Perhaps Nancy has a female friend in York."

"One you've never heard of? Never met? How likely is that?"

Oh, the man was so infuriating! "I take it you're determined to believe that Nancy was meeting with a lover."

"As I said—it's the most likely explanation." When she frowned at him, he said smoothly, "Certainly the ostler's words don't fit *your* pet theory—that she was kidnapped."

Jane was sorely tempted to tell him that Nancy wouldn't be indulging her "needs" with a lover while she had a babe growing in her belly, but that would only complicate matters.

Seething with worry and anger and frustration that he could be such a . . . a *man* about this, she dropped his arm and quickened her pace. "You are attributing a great deal to one remark by an ostler." She turned onto the street that led directly to the inn. "He might have misheard or misunderstood the fact that she really was heading to Mrs. Patch's."

He followed her. "Without telling the woman ahead of time? Didn't Mrs. Patch say that Nancy always sent a note before she came?"

"She also said that murderers run rampant in the streets of York, but I don't hear you quoting the woman on *that*."

"Admit it, Nancy did lie about the fact that she wasn't shopping *with* Mrs. Patch."

"No, she didn't. I told you, although the servants assumed as much, *Nancy* merely said she went to York to visit her aunt and do some shopping. Which is true."

"Yes, but Jane—" he began in that condescending, arrogant tone of his that pricked her harder than any embroidery needle.

"So that's it," she bit out. "You've got your mind made up. Nancy ran off with a lover, and you're washing your hands of the whole thing."

"Can you give me a good reason why I shouldn't?"

Something in his voice made her glance at him. He was regarding her as a naturalist regarded a beetle he intended to dissect.

That was when it dawned on her—Dom wanted to unearth her secrets. *Nancy's* secrets. Just as Jane had feared, he really had deduced that she hid some.

A shiver ran down her spine, and she jerked her gaze from him, fighting to hide her consternation. "Merely the same reason I gave you before. Nancy could be in trouble. And it's your duty as her brother-in-law to keep her safe."

"From what?" he demanded. "From whom? Is there more to this than you're saying?"

Ooh, the fact that he was so determined to unveil the truth about Nancy while hiding his former collusion with her scraped Jane raw. "I could ask the same of you," she said primly. "You're obviously holding something back. You have *some* reason for your determination to believe ill of Nancy. I wonder what that might be."

Two can play your game, Almighty Dom. Hah!

He was silent so long that she ventured a glance at him to find him looking rather discomfited. Good! It was about time.

"I am merely keeping an open mind about your cousin, which is more than I can say for you," Dom finally answered. "She isn't the woman you think she is."

"Because she wouldn't give in to your advances twelve years ago, you mean?" She would make him admit the truth about that night if it was the last thing she did! "Perhaps that's why you're determined to blacken her character. You're angry that she resisted you and married your brother instead."

"That's a lie!" When several people on the street turned to look in his direction, Dom lowered his voice. "It wasn't like that."

She stifled a smile of satisfaction. At last she was getting a reaction from him that was something other than levelheaded logic. "Wasn't it? If you'd convinced Nancy to marry you, you might not have had to go off to be a Bow Street runner. You could have had an easier life, a better life in high society than you could have had with me if you'd married me. Without being able to access my fortune, I could only have dragged you down."

"You don't really believe that I wanted to marry her for her money," he gritted out.

"It's either that or assume that you fell madly in love with her in the few weeks we were apart." They were nearly to the inn now, so she added a plaintive note to her voice. "Or perhaps it was her you wanted all along. You knew my uncle would never accept a second son as a husband for his rich heiress of a daughter, so you courted me to get close to her. Nancy was always so beautiful, so—"

"Enough!"

Without warning, he dragged her into one of the many alleyways that crisscrossed York. This one was deeply shadowed, the houses leaning into each other overhead, and as he pulled her around to face him, the brilliance of his eyes shone starkly in the dim light.

"I never cared one whit about Nancy."

She tamped down her triumph—he hadn't admitted the whole truth yet. "It certainly didn't look that way to me. It looked like you had already forgotten me, forgotten what we meant to each—"

"The hell I had." He shoved his face close to hers. "I never forgot you for one day, one hour, one moment. It was you—always you. Everything I did was for *you,* damn it. No one else."

The passionate profession threw her off course. Dom had never been the sort to say such sweet things. But the fervent look in his eyes roused memories of how he used to look at her. And his hands gripping her arms, his body angling in closer, were so painfully familiar . . .

"I don't . . . believe you," she lied, her blood running wild through her veins.

His gleaming gaze impaled her. "Then believe this." And suddenly his mouth was on hers.

This was *not* what she'd set out to get from him.

But oh, the joy of it. The *heat* of it. His mouth covered hers, seeking, coaxing. Without breaking the kiss, he pushed her back against the wall, and she grabbed for his shoulders, his surprisingly broad and muscular shoulders. As he sent her plummeting into unfamiliar territory, she held on for dear life.

Time rewound to when they were in her uncle's garden, sneaking a moment alone. But this time there was no hesitation, no fear of being caught.

Glorying in that, she slid her hands about his neck to bring him closer. He groaned, and his kiss turned intimate. He used lips and tongue, delving inside her mouth in a tender exploration that stunned her. Enchanted her. Confused her.

Something both sweet and alien pooled in her belly, a kind of yearning she'd never felt with Edwin. With *any* man but Dom.

As if he sensed it, he pulled back to look at her, his eyes searching hers, full of surprise. "My God, Jane," he said hoarsely, turning her name into a prayer.

Or a curse? She had no time to figure out which before he clasped her head to hold her still for another darkly ravishing kiss. Only this one was greedier, needier. His mouth consumed hers with all the boldness of Viking raiders of yore. His tongue drove repeatedly inside in a rhythm that made her feel all trembly and hot, and his thumbs caressed her throat, rousing the pulse there.

Thank heaven there was a wall to hold her up, or she

was quite sure she would dissolve into a puddle at his feet. Because after all these years apart, he was riding roughshod over her life again. And she was letting him.

How could she not? His scent of leather and bergamot engulfed her, made her dizzy with the pleasure of it. He roused urges she'd never known she had, sparked fires in places she'd thought were frozen. Then his hands swept down her possessively as if to memorize her body . . . or mark it as belonging to him.

Belonging to *him*. Oh, Lord!

She shoved him away. How could she have fallen for his kisses after what he'd done? How could she have let him slip that far under her guard?

Never again, curse him! Never!

For a moment, he looked as stunned by what had flared between them as she. Then he reached for her, and she slipped from between him and the wall, panic rising in her chest.

"You do not have the right to kiss me anymore," she hissed. "I'm engaged, for pity's sake!"

As soon as her words registered, his eyes went cold. "It certainly took you long enough to remember it."

She gaped at him. "You have the audacity to . . . to . . ." She stabbed his shoulder with one finger. "You have no business criticizing *me*! You threw me away years ago, and now you want to just . . . just take me up again, as if nothing ever happened between us?"

A shadow crossed his face. "I did not throw you away. *You* jilted *me*, remember?"

That was the last straw. "Right. I jilted you." Turning

on her heel, she stalked back toward the road. "Just keep telling yourself that, since you're obviously determined to believe your own fiction."

"Fiction?" He hurried after her. "What are you talking about?"

"Oh, why can't you just admit what you really did and be done with it?"

Grabbing her by the arm, he forced her to stop just short of the street. He stared into her face, and she could see when awareness dawned in his eyes. "Good God. You know the truth. You know what really happened in the library that night."

"That you manufactured that dalliance between you and Nancy to force me into jilting you?" She snatched her arm free. "Yes, I know."

Then she strode out of the alley, leaving him to stew in his own juices.

5

DOM STOOD DUMBFOUNDED as Jane disappeared into the street. Then he hurried to catch up to her, to get some answers.

She *knew.* How the blazes did she know?

The answer to that was obvious. "So, Nancy told you the truth, did she?" he snapped as he fell into step beside her.

Jane didn't reply, just kept marching toward the inn like a Hussar bent on battle.

"When?" he demanded. "How long have you known?"

"For nine years, you . . . you conniving . . . lying—"

"*Nine* years? You knew all this time, and you didn't say anything?"

"Say anything!" She halted just short of the innyard entrance to glare at him. "How the devil was I to do that? You disappeared into the streets of London as surely as if you were a footpad or a pickpocket."

She planted her hands on her hips. "Oh, I read about your heroic exploits from time to time, but other than that, I neither heard nor saw anything of you until last year, when you showed up at George's town house. It was only pure chance that I happened to be at dinner with Nancy that day. As you'll recall, you didn't stay long. Nor did you behave as if you would welcome any confidences."

Remembering the cool reception he'd given her, he glanced away, unable to bear the accusation in her eyes. "No, I suppose I didn't."

"Besides," she said, "it hardly mattered that I knew the truth. I assumed that if you ever changed your mind about making a life with me, you would seek me out. Since you never did, you were clearly determined to remain a bachelor."

His gaze shot back to her. "It was more complicated than that."

She snorted. "It always is with you. Which is precisely why I'm happy I'm engaged to *someone else*."

That sent jealousy roaring through him. "Yet you let me kiss you."

A pretty blush stained her cheeks. "You . . . you took me by surprise, that's all. But it was a mistake. It won't happen again."

The blazes it wouldn't. He intended to find out if the past was as firmly in the past as she claimed. But obviously he couldn't do it here in the street. He glanced up at the gloomy sky. Or right now.

She followed the direction of his gaze. "Yes," she said in a dull voice. "It looks like we'll have a rainy trip back." She headed into the innyard. "Perhaps if we hurry, we can reach Winborough before it starts. Besides, we've got only three hours until sunset, and it's not safe to ride in an open phaeton after dark."

She was right, but he didn't mean to drop this discussion. He needed answers, and once they were on the road, he meant to get them.

He strode into the innyard, his mind awhirl. He'd never been one for snap judgments, which was precisely what made him a good investigator. He liked to be sure he had all the facts before he sorted them by their implications and importance so he could come to some conclusions.

With Jane, though, getting all the facts was proving difficult. She was obviously too angry to tell him rationally what he needed to know. And he was too unsettled to make sense of what little she'd said.

Fortunately, calling for his phaeton, putting the top up, and getting on the road gave him time to settle his thoughts. Certain things seeped into his memory. Like how Jane had called him "Saint Dominick" three months ago, which he'd thought odd at the time for a woman who should have believed him a fortune hunter. Or how she'd spoken of being tired of "waiting" for her "life to begin."

Good God. She really *might* have been talking about him then. About waiting for *him* to come after her. All this time . . .

No, he couldn't believe that. She'd only been seventeen when they'd ended things, and women that age were still feeling their way in life. She couldn't possibly have been carrying a torch for him all these years.

Why not? You've been carrying one for her.

He stifled a curse. Nonsense. He'd cut her out of his heart.

God, he was such a liar.

They were now well out of the city. She sat quietly beside him, obviously uncomfortable after what had happened between them.

She couldn't be any more uncomfortable than he was. He could still taste her mouth, still feel the moment when she'd turned to putty in his arms. He was aware of every inch of her that touched him now. Her hand lay in her lap, so close he could reach over and take it.

Or perhaps not. The last thing he needed was her shoving him off the phaeton, which she was liable to do if she took a mind to it. She was damned angry.

Though he wasn't entirely sure why. She was engaged to a very rich, very well-connected earl, all because Dom had set her free. So why did she look as if she wanted to throttle him?

Nancy. The chit must have made everything sound worse than it was. "Tell me how much your cousin told you about our . . . supposed dalliance."

"Everything, as far as I know." Jane smoothed her skirts with a nonchalance he might have believed if he hadn't also noticed her trembling hands. "That you coaxed her into pretending you were making advances to her. That she then convinced Samuel Barlow to help get me into the library without my suspecting, so I could see your manufactured tableau."

Nancy really *had* told her everything. "She promised she would never say a word."

"I gave her no choice." Her voice lowered to an aching murmur. "I'm not the fool you take me for, you know."

"I have *never* taken you for a fool."

"No? You didn't think I'd notice when you made no further attempts to court Nancy? Or any other rich ladies? There was no gossip about you, no tales of fortune hunting. It wasn't long before I smelled a rat."

Blast it all. "So you went to Nancy and forced her to tell the truth."

She got very quiet. He glanced over to find her looking chagrined.

"Actually, I claimed that I had encountered you in Bond Street, and you'd revealed the truth then. I told her I just wanted to hear her side of things."

A groan escaped him. "In other words, you tricked her."

"Pretty much." She fiddled with her reticule. "It wasn't difficult. Nancy isn't, well . . ."

"The brightest star in the sky?"

Jane winced. "Exactly. She's fairly easy to manipulate. Indeed, that was all it took to have her blurting out everything. That you told her a bunch of nonsense about how I would be better off without you—"

"It wasn't nonsense," he interrupted. "You *were* better off without me."

"Was I? You don't know that."

"I do, actually." He clicked his tongue at the horses

to have them step up the pace. "Do you know where I lived for my first three years as a Bow Street runner?"

"It doesn't matter. I wouldn't have cared."

He uttered a harsh laugh. "Yes, I'm sure you would have been delighted to share a garret above a tavern in Spitalfields with me. To eat only bread and cheese four days a week in order to save money. To forgo coal in the dead of winter so we'd have enough money to pay the rent."

"That does sound dreadful." Her voice held an edge. "But that was three years of the twelve we were apart. What about later? After you started to have some success?"

"I didn't move out of the garret because of any great success. I moved out because I . . . was traveling too much to sustain lodgings in London. That's how I spent the rest of my time as a runner."

In Manchester and wherever else the Spenceans and their ilk were calling for reform, or, as the government saw it, fomenting rebellion. But he couldn't talk about that to her. She would never understand those difficult years, what he'd done, what he'd been expected to do. How could she? She was a lady encased in a castle of privileged living. She didn't know anything about the struggle between the poor and the rich. He wouldn't want her to.

"That was your choice, though, wasn't it?" she said softly. "Not all Bow Street runners travel."

He tensed. "No, but neither do they make much of a living. I was paid far more for . . . er . . . traveling than for catching criminals in London. I was able to save up enough to start my business concern precisely because of all those years when I was willing to go anywhere for my position."

To take any risk. To spy on his fellow countrymen. It still left a bad taste in his mouth.

"And what about after you started Manton's Investigations? That was four years ago, Dom. If you had wanted me, you could have approached me then."

"Of course," he said bitterly. "I could have marched up to your uncle's house and begged you to marry me. To forgo your fortune, leave your comfortable position, risk being cut off by all your friends and relations so you could marry a man whom I was sure you considered a fortune hunter."

"Yes. You could have."

"And you would have gladly accepted my suit. Even though you had your pick of the men. Even though you had an earl and a marquess sniffing at your skirts—"

"You knew about the marquess?"

He cursed his quick tongue. "The point is, you would have been a fool to choose me over one of them. And I was astute enough to realize it."

"No, the point is that you'll never *know* whether I would have accepted your suit or not. You didn't offer it. You never took the chance, and that is your loss."

The words stabbed a dagger through his chest. She spoke as if she'd given up on him. But of course she had, hadn't she? She'd accepted Blakeborough's marriage proposal. And given how hard she'd fought twelve years ago not to jilt Dom, she was certainly not going to jilt Blakeborough.

What if Dom *had* asked? What if he had blundered into her life again and wrenched her from everything she knew?

No, that couldn't have ended anything but badly.

It had begun to drizzle. Since the phaeton top only extended so far, he pulled out a blanket to put over their laps to keep some of the damp off. When he took the reins in one hand so he could reach over to tuck the blanket about her, she froze.

So did he, painfully aware of his hand lingering on her thigh. He had half a mind to stop the phaeton, drag her into his arms, and kiss her until she softened and remembered what they had been to each other.

But she did remember. She'd made that clear earlier. She just no longer cared.

He drew his hand back and the moment blew away on the breeze.

A stilted silence fell over them. Mile after mile of dreary gray seeped into his blood, weighing him down. He didn't know which was worse. Being without her entirely all these years, or being so close and not having her.

After a long while, she released a sigh. "Do you even regret what you did to end our engagement?"

"No," he said bluntly.

He could feel her gaze on him.

"After all this time," she said, "you still think you and Nancy did the right thing."

"Absolutely." It was the truth. Wasn't it?

Another uncomfortable silence stretched between them.

"Nancy regrets it," Jane said at last. "She says she regretted it from the moment she agreed to go along with it."

He was tempted to point out that Nancy had certainly hidden her regret well behind her triumphant marriage to George. But pointing that out would merely put Jane on the defensive again regarding her cousin. Jane seemed determined to believe Nancy some sort of saint, and until he had more facts, he couldn't dispute her view. Which was precisely why he had to investigate further.

"So, *are* you going to get to the bottom of Nancy's disappearance?" she asked.

Good God, did the woman read minds? "I think I must. You made a valid point earlier. If Nancy *has* been duped by some fortune-hunting scoundrel, it would be unwise to let the matter lie."

"You mean, because he might hurt her," she said, her tone anxious.

"Because he could hurt Rathmoor Park and Nancy's future along with it. Her dower portion comes out of the estate's income. Any husband she takes will want to look after her interests, and won't care what strain that puts on Rathmoor Park." Or how much trouble it caused Dom.

Shock emanated from her side of the phaeton. "You know, Dom, whether or not I was better off without you, it's clear that *you* were not better off without *me*."

"What's that supposed to mean?"

"You used to have a heart, to care about people." She uttered a ragged oath. "Or perhaps I just thought you did. Perhaps you were always this cold-blooded, and I merely missed it."

He bristled at the accusation. "And what is it that makes you think me cold-blooded? The fact that I questioned the need to rush off after Nancy?"

"The fact that you only seem to see the financial aspects of this. She's a woman alone. That should secure your concern."

"I lost my concern for Nancy the day she married George," he snapped.

"So that's what this is about. She married your enemy, and that made her your enemy as well."

He tightened his grip on the reins, not sure what to say. "I suppose you could see it that way."

"Well, she's still my cousin and my friend, so I hope you have enough . . . softness left in your heart toward *me* that you would search for her on my behalf, if not on hers."

"Don't worry, I'm not so 'cold-blooded' as all that," he said irritably. "Tristan and I will return to York tonight to speak with the ostlers at Ringrose's Inn who weren't there today. Then we'll comb the town, see what more we can learn." He shot her a hard glance. "You'll only get in our way, so you should stay with Lady Zoe at Winborough."

"That's probably best," she surprised him by saying.

Was she agreeing with him because she feared he

would attempt to kiss her again? Or because she'd learned what she wanted to know from him, and now only needed him to find Nancy?

Either possibility chafed him.

They traveled farther without speaking, but when he caught himself humming some doleful notes from Mozart's *Requiem Mass*, he winced. Damn it, there were things he wanted—he *needed*—to know from her. "Jane, have you been happy all these years?" *Was my sacrifice worth it?*

When she didn't speak, he looked over to find her regarding him with a stark gaze that chilled him. "You don't have the right to ask. You didn't attempt to find out or ensure that I was, so think whatever makes you sleep better at night."

And she called *him* cold-blooded?

She squared her shoulders. "But I do intend to be quite deliriously happy from now on. I intend to marry Edwin and have his children and live to a ripe old age surrounded by people I care about. I assume that sets your mind at ease."

It should. But it damned well didn't. Because for the first time, he saw his life laid out before him, devoid of Jane in a different way from before. And it made him want to howl and gnash his teeth. A fat lot of good that would do him.

The gray light grew dimmer by the moment, making him worry they would slip past nightfall before they reached their destination. Then he saw the signpost for the local village. Tristan and Zoe's estate was only a few miles beyond. They'd be there within the half hour, thank God.

"Before we reach Winborough," he said, "you should tell me how much you wish me to reveal to Tristan about the situation."

"If you're to gain his help, I imagine you'll have to reveal everything. Though I would prefer that you not mention your more . . . lurid suspicions about Nancy."

"There's no need for that. Yet."

"Have you considered the fact that if Nancy *had* been planning on going to York to meet a lover, she could have just delayed her trip for one day so she could have the coach, and then told her servants that she and her aunt were headed to Bath? She could have packed up clothes for the trip and everything."

He mused a moment. "Then she would have had to take her maid."

"Not necessarily. She could have said there was no room for one at the place they were staying, or that her aunt's maid would do for both of them. She could have lied in all manner of ways that wouldn't have roused their suspicions. But she didn't. That in itself should alarm you. It certainly does me."

He grudgingly admitted that her concerns made sense. Why *hadn't* Nancy set up a more elaborate ruse, one that wouldn't have left questions in anyone's mind? "You did say Nancy isn't terribly clever."

"Which is precisely why she would have operated in a more straightforward manner."

"Well, we'll know the truth soon enough, I expect."

Or would they? He still didn't know the secret Jane was hiding about Nancy. He'd been so caught up in the turmoil over their past together that he'd forgotten to get it out of her.

"By the way, did Mrs. Patch say anything of use after I left?" he asked. "Did she have any theories about why Nancy ran off?"

A shutter dropped over her features. "No. Why?"

"She seemed very agitated about the situation."

"Only because her home had been invaded by strangers. Nancy's mother was much like her before she died. By the time you and I met, she'd already given over to me the responsibility of dealing with the servants and tradesmen, because that particular duty made her very nervous."

He stared at her, stunned. "How is it I never knew that about you?"

"Why should you? It's not as if I could talk about it in front of her or my uncle when you came to visit. And the few times at balls and such that we weren't chaperoned so closely, I preferred to speak of less boring things. Like music."

"That *was* our favorite topic of conversation," he said, the memories washing over him.

As if she remembered them, too, she shivered. He stripped off his coat and laid it over her shoulders as best he could while holding on to the reins. Her eyes met his and a fleeting smile touched her lips. Then, as abruptly as it had come, it faded and she glanced away.

He felt the loss of that smile more keenly than the absence of fine music in his life.

They passed through the village in silence and soon reached the estate's drive. After only a few moments, he spotted the halos of candles and lamps through the gloom of the foggy dusk, so many that it appeared as if every window in the manor house was lit.

A groan escaped him. "I should warn you that not only are my brother and sister-in-law at Winborough, but so are her father, aunt, and cousin. Lisette and Max are there, too. It will be chaotic." He slanted a glance at her. "And they will all wonder about your presence."

They would all *comment* on her presence, too, especially his sister, who would spin it into romantic possibilities of mythical proportions.

"Let them wonder," Jane said primly. "I'm not afraid of them, Dom. And I can handle a bit of chaos."

"Don't be too sure of that. Trust me, Bedlam doesn't begin to compare to the insanity of my family when they're all together."

6

JANE INITIALLY ASSUMED that Dom had exaggerated, since their arrival began innocuously enough. Tristan and his wife welcomed them warmly, but before Jane could exchange more than a couple of pleasantries with Lady Zoe, whom she'd met at the Keane soiree in town, the woman's father and aunt descended to the entrance hall to join the conversation.

Then those two began to argue with Tristan and Lady Zoe about which bedchamber Jane should occupy, while Lisette rushed up to greet Jane with a flurry of questions. Jane had just fielded all of those when the duke entered with Mr. Jeremy Keane, Lady Zoe's artist cousin.

"How pleasant to see you again, Lady Jane," the man said with a gleam in his eye. "I'd begun to despair over the lack of eligible females at this party, and then you appear from out of the mist to save me."

"Not a mist," Dom growled. "A proper rain, which is why we are somewhat in a hurry to—"

"Nonsense," Jane said sweetly, relishing Dom's disgruntlement. "I always enjoy talking to a man as talented as Mr. Keane."

"And which of my particular talents are you enamored of, may I ask?" Mr. Keane smirked at her. "I have more than one, you know. I'd be happy to show your ladyship any of them whenever you like."

"I'm sure you would," Dom snapped and tried to take her arm.

She brushed him off to smile at Mr. Keane. "Oh, I'm afraid we don't have time for what I'm sure would be a long and . . . interesting encounter. But perhaps we could pursue it at a later date."

Dom looked fit to be tied, but before he could say a word, new queries erupted from the others about where he'd been all day and how long Jane was staying. Within moments, the din had grown to rival the shouts of "Encore!" in any London opera house. She was surprised that the cherubs on the ceiling didn't swoop down to add their angelic voices to the chorus.

"Quiet!" boomed Dom's voice over the clamor.

A startled silence fell on the crowd.

"Miss Vernon and I have had a very trying day," Dom continued, "and there are decisions to be made. So while I realize that order is anathema to you lot, could we for once attempt to go about this in an orderly fashion?"

If he had given that rather rude speech to Uncle Horace, Dom would have found himself thrown out of the house on his ear, but his family only burst into laughter.

"Good idea," Lord Olivier said, eyes twinkling. He nodded to Lady Zoe's aunt. "If you would be so good as to go tell Cook that there will be two more for dinner, his lordship and I will herd this 'lot' into the drawing room so we can have a glass of wine and a more civilized discussion."

"Of course," the woman said, though the bright speculation in her eyes showed that she was none too happy to miss any of the impending discussion.

As soon as she'd left, Dom said, "Actually, Miss Vernon and I need to consult Tristan and Lisette privately right away. So if you don't mind, sir, we'll join the rest of you after that."

"If you prefer," Lord Olivier said, though curiosity shone in his face now, too.

He gestured toward the drawing room, and the others headed in that direction while Dom led her and his siblings the opposite way, down the hall toward what proved to be a man's study.

As soon as the four of them entered, Tristan strolled over to lean against the desk. "What's going on, old chap?"

Briefly, Dom laid out the facts of Nancy's disappearance. To Jane's vast relief, he limited the discussion to the contents of the two pertinent letters, followed by a bald recitation of what they'd learned so far.

"I could use some help with pursuing the matter further in York," Dom told his brother. "I want to return there tonight, if possible, so we can speak to the ostlers at Ringrose's Inn. With any luck, they'll help us figure out where Nancy might have gone from there. If not, we'll have to investigate further."

"What about your meeting tomorrow morning?" Lisette asked.

"I'll send a note to the estate canceling it." He shot Jane a veiled glance. "I have no choice. I promised Miss Vernon I would find my sister-in-law, and I mean to do what I can in that regard." He turned his attention to Tristan. "Can you get away to help me?"

"I don't see why not," Tristan said. "I can certainly be gone for one night. Most everyone is leaving tomorrow, which will ease Zoe's burden."

"Speaking of that . . ." Dom turned to his sister. "Since you and Max are heading for London, would you mind taking Miss Vernon with you? She missed her packet boat the day before yesterday, and there's no telling when the next one leaves Hull. Nor can she stay at Rathmoor Park alone, with Nancy gone."

"Now see here," Jane said before Lisette could answer, "I am *not* returning to London while you're still searching for Nancy."

Dom pierced her with a dark look. "The hell you aren't. I've got the situation well in hand, so there's no point to your lingering here. Besides, your uncle is undoubtedly worried by now. Not to mention your fiancé."

"The day I discovered Nancy gone, I wrote to my uncle informing him of my plan to stay in Yorkshire a while longer and asking him to pass on the message to Edwin." Jane braced herself for battle. "Uncle Horace will be far more worried if I return to tell him that I have no idea where his daughter is than if I merely take a few days to find out where she's headed."

"That sounds perfectly logical," Lisette chimed in.

"I didn't ask for your opinion," Dom told his sister irritably. "And I've already explained that Miss Vernon cannot stay at Rathmoor Park."

"Then she can stay here," Tristan said. "Zoe and I won't mind."

"Or Max and I could delay our trip a day or so," Lisette put in.

"You two need to stay out of this," Dom warned.

Lisette didn't even bat an eyelash at his tone, merely turning to exchange a glance with Jane. "Has he been this cranky all day?"

"Worse. When things aren't going his way, he becomes downright rude," Jane said lightly. "Your brother has a bad habit of making assumptions based on his own peculiar logic, and then pursuing them in spite of the facts."

Tristan arched an eyebrow. "Really? That doesn't sound like Dom."

"That's because it isn't," Dom clipped out, "which Miss Vernon knows perfectly well. Meanwhile, she has a bad habit of taking everything personally."

"Only because you make everything personal," Jane said. "Otherwise, you wouldn't care at all if I stayed in Yorkshire while you searched."

"Oh, for God's sake—"

"Might I make a suggestion?" Lisette said.

"No!" Dom snarled at the same time that Jane said, "Absolutely."

When Dom muttered an oath under his breath, Jane suppressed a smile. It certainly was fun watching Dom's sister get under his skin.

Especially since Lisette simply ignored his protests. "While you and Tristan go investigate, I'll send back to Rathmoor Park for Jane's maid and her things. In the morning, Jane and Max and I will pack up and leave for London. We have to go through York anyway to get there."

Lisette looked at Tristan. "We'll meet the two of you there, at which time you can report on the results of your search. If you've found Nancy, then Jane can continue with us to London or remain with her cousin, whichever she chooses. If you haven't, we'll reassess the situation. Jane can always return here to stay with Tristan and Zoe if she likes. But there's no point in making a definitive decision when we're still not sure what's going on."

"Actually, that sounds sensible to me," Tristan drawled. "Dom?"

Dom's eyes were fixed on her. Idly he rubbed his scar. "Don't you trust me to find her, Jane?"

Why was it that every time he spoke her Christian name in that husky voice, shivers danced over her skin? It was most annoying.

"Of course I trust you," she said smoothly. "But you may need my help. *She* may need my help." She clasped her hands in front of her. "I'm not returning to London until she's found or we learn where she's headed. You will just have to put up with me until then, my lord."

Some unreadable emotion flickered in his eyes that roused an unwanted heat in her blood.

I never forgot you for one day, one hour, one moment. It was you—always you. Everything I did was for you, damn it.

Curse him and his heat-rousing looks and shiver-producing words. They meant nothing. He'd had plenty of chances to get her back, and he hadn't taken any of them. So she was *not* going to fall prey to some terribly inconvenient attraction to him. She absolutely would not!

As if he sensed her reaction, Dom swept her with a slow, heated look meant to arouse her. Or cow her. Perhaps both.

Then he nodded. "As you wish. But you three should leave as early in the morning as you can. If I learn something of use, I won't wait around for you before pursuing it."

Of course not. When had Dom ever waited around for *her*? She did all the waiting. "Fine. We'll meet you at Ringrose's Inn tomorrow for a late breakfast. Say, around ten A.M.?"

Tristan barked a laugh.

"What?" Jane asked. "Is that too late?"

Now Dom laughed, too, and Tristan laughed even harder.

"What's so funny?" Jane snapped.

"It's not about you," Lisette said dryly. "They're

laughing at *me*. My brothers think me incapable of rising early. Or getting off in a timely fashion."

"That's because, dear girl, we have yet to see you rise before eleven or leave by noon for a trip," Dom teased.

Tristan grinned at Jane. "Better schedule that meeting in York for a bit later, Freckles."

Freckles. Tristan had dubbed her with the nickname during Dom's courtship of her, and that reminder of her past with Dom and his family roused an ache in her chest.

She avoided Dom's gaze. "How about midafternoon then?"

"Nonsense." Lisette rolled her eyes. "I can rise early, no matter what my idiot brothers think. We'll be there midmorning for breakfast if I have to dunk my head in ice water to accomplish it. Max wanted to get an early start, anyway."

Dom chuckled. "Max always wants to get an early start. But he'd have to have a different wife in order to manage that."

The two men nudged each other with smug looks.

"Yes, he would," Lisette said in a voice of pure sweetness, "one he wasn't quite so enamored of. But since sampling my particular charms always takes him so very *long* in the morning, I admit that we do end up lying abed late more times than not."

Jane knew she ought to be shocked by such frankness, but she was having too much fun watching the men's mouths fall open, and a red flush creep up their faces.

Lisette flashed them a coy look. "But I shall endeavor to prevent my husband from enjoying his usual pleasures tomorrow morning. That should resolve the matter." She threaded her arm through Jane's. "Now come, my dear, let's join the others for dinner. I'd love a glass of wine, wouldn't you?"

The two women had barely made it out into the hall before they burst into laughter. "That'll teach . . . *them,*" Lisette gasped. "Did you see . . . Tristan's face?"

"And Dom's," Jane choked out. "Oh, Lord, you are so *wicked!*"

"Why, of *course.*" Lisette's eyes sparkled with mischief. "What's the point of being a duchess if you can't shock people from time to time?"

They both laughed again as they walked briskly toward the drawing room.

Then Lisette's amusement faded, and she made a face. "But it does mean I'm actually going to have to get up at dawn tomorrow. I refuse to let those two get the last word."

"I certainly understand that impulse." Darting a glance back down the hall, Jane lowered her voice. "Which is precisely why I need your help. You said you'd send for my maid and my things, but I'd rather go back to Rathmoor Park myself to fetch them. I want to make sure Nancy hasn't returned. And if she hasn't, I want to question her servants more thoroughly."

Jane had to ask the lady's maid for details concerning her mistress's possible pregnancy. Nancy had been quite vague about it. And the lady's maid might also know something that would put paid to Dom's belief that Nancy had taken a lover.

"You do realize it will take you half the night to do all that," Lisette said.

"It can't be helped. I need to have more information by the time we meet the gentlemen in the morning."

"Very well. Then Zoe and I will go with you."

"Absolutely not." Jane could ask questions more freely without them. "You need your sleep if you're leaving in the morning. So does Lady Zoe, who's undoubtedly had an exhausting few days with so many visitors in residence."

Lisette sighed. "Good point. And Lady Zoe is with child, so she particularly needs rest." The duchess stopped short of the drawing room to level Jane with a concerned glance. "But she's not the only one. You need sleep, too, my dear."

"Yes, and I'll get more of it in the carriage if I'm alone. If Lady Zoe will agree to send a footman with me for safety's sake, I'll welcome it, but I need no other company."

Lisette looked furtively down the hall. "Dom won't like your traveling at night with just a footman."

"Which is why I shan't tell him. As soon as the men leave to go their way, I shall go mine." When a frown creased Lisette's brow, Jane patted her hand. "Honestly, I'll be fine. I came here alone from the coast in the first place. It's only two hours there and two back, and it won't take me long at the estate. I'll return in plenty of time for us to leave in the morning."

With any luck, by then she'd be armed with enough new facts to put Dom's suspicions about Nancy to rest once and for all.

+ + +

IT WAS NEARLY ten o'clock the next morning by the time Jane and her companions arrived at Ringrose's Inn. The duke took a private dining room for them and ordered an elaborate breakfast, much more costly than she'd ever eaten herself while traveling.

But the man *was* a duke, after all. Obviously, he had pots of money to throw around. She assumed that was why Dom's investigative agency had been dubbed "the Duke's Men." His Grace had probably invested heavily in the struggling concern once they'd found his cousin for him. No doubt he'd played a large part in helping the agency reach its pinnacle of success.

The breakfast was soon brought, but despite its extravagance, Jane could barely eat. Indeed, she managed to swallow only a few mouthfuls of shirred eggs before she rose from the table.

"I miss Eugene," Lisette was saying. "I am never leaving him with a wet nurse again, I swear."

"You said it would be fine for only a few days," the duke remarked as he continued to eat.

"I was wrong. I do hope Nurse remembers to . . ."

Unable to pay attention to the conversation anymore, Jane began to pace. It was now well past ten o'clock. Where were Dom and Tristan?

"Come, Miss Vernon." The duke set down his fork.

"They will get here when they get here, and your agitation won't bring them a moment sooner."

"I know." She flashed him a sheepish glance. "I've never been good at waiting."

"Seems to me you've been excellent at waiting," Lisette mumbled as she buttered her toast.

Jane chose to ignore the reference to the many years she and Dom had spent apart. That was different. She'd thought she was waiting for the only man who'd ever loved her. But she'd been wrong about his feelings, or else he would have come for her when he had the chance.

What if he wants you as his wife now that he's gained the title?

That was all she'd been able to think about since their kisses yesterday, but the answer was always the same. Years ago, Dom had dictated the terms of their "friendship" without consulting her. He now wanted to dictate the terms of the search for Nancy. If Jane married him, she could only imagine what else he would dictate. He'd wrap her in cotton wool while trying to manage everything alone.

At seventeen, she might have put up with a husband who commanded her entire world and treated her like a wide-eyed innocent who must be led through life. But that was before she'd learned the truth about her parents' death.

Now, at nearly thirty, she would rather eat glass than be married to a man like Papa. She'd spent the years since Auntie's death running a household however she pleased, and very competently, too. So why should she have to put up with the dictates of Dom the Almighty?

He had even tried to prevent her from coming here to York with him yesterday. Lord only knew what ridiculous restrictions he would put on her as his wife.

"Despite all Dom's grousing about *my* inability to show up on time, he and Tristan are late," Lisette said. "Who knows when they'll be here? Perhaps, Jane, you should use the time to rest."

"I'm fine," Jane said. "I couldn't possibly sit still right now."

"Are you sure? Forgive me, my dear, but you look quite tired. Lady Zoe's butler said you didn't arrive from Rathmoor Park until nearly five A.M."

Jane nodded. "I had a few more matters to take care of than expected. With Nancy and me both gone, the household was at sixes and sevens, and I had to invent some reason for her sudden trip to Bath that wouldn't alarm the servants."

That had been no small feat, since she'd also had to question Nancy's maid. The nature of the questions had only put the poor woman into a more anxious state, but it couldn't be helped. Especially once Jane learned—

A knock at the door made her jump. She hurried to open it, relieved to find Dom and Tristan standing there. But the looks on their faces struck dread in her heart. Tristan wouldn't meet her eyes as he came inside. Dom, however, met her gaze with a look of banked anger that heightened her alarm.

"Is that sausages?" Tristan said, hurrying to the table. "Thank God. I'm half-starved."

"You live in a permanent state of starvation, I declare," Lisette said behind Jane. "Sit down and eat before it gets any colder." She paused. "Dom? Will you have some breakfast?"

"In a minute." His eyes never left Jane's. "First I need to speak to Miss Vernon. Alone."

That did *not* bode well.

The duke rose from the table. "We probably need to . . . er . . . check on the horses, eh, Tristan?"

Grimly, Tristan nodded. Pausing only to make himself a sandwich out of sausages and toast, he wrapped it in a napkin, shoved it into his coat pocket, and hurried for the door.

"I should probably go make sure our servants are being adequately fed downstairs," Lisette mumbled as she, too, rose and went out.

Jane's maid was with Lisette's maid and the duke's valet in the taproom. At the moment, Jane wished she were with them.

After everyone left, Dom closed the door, and her heart began to thunder in her chest. If he was bending the rules of propriety to closet them alone together in an inn room, he must have found out something awful indeed.

Still, he said nothing at first, removing his greatcoat and throwing it over a chair, then staring at her for a long, tension-fraught moment that rattled her nerves.

"What is it?" she rasped. "What did you learn?"

"A number of things," he said, his voice hard. "We were lucky to find an ostler here who'd seen Nancy leave with a gentleman about her age. Fortunately, he recognized the man—a local fellow. He was even able to give us directions to the chap's lodgings." He clasped his hands behind his back, looking very investigator-like. "Were you aware that Samuel Barlow now lives in York?"

A sour sickness churned in her stomach. Good heavens, not Samuel. Anyone but Samuel. "No, I did not . . . realize that." As Dom kept staring at her skepti-cally, she thrust out her chin. "Do you think I'm lying?"

"I don't know. Are you?"

"Certainly not!" Moving away from his disturbing gaze, she began to pace. "I only knew that Samuel no longer lived at the Blakeborough estate. He lost his commission in the navy a few years ago and then was disinherited by his father. Perhaps you heard about it."

"I haven't traveled in those circles in some time, re-member?" he said tersely.

She colored. "Well, no one outside of his family knows what caused the estrangement between him and the old earl. I asked Edwin once, but all he would say is that their father didn't approve of Samuel's way of living. Judging from gossip, Samuel had become quite the . . . er . . . rogue in recent years, but I never heard what happened to him after his family cut him off."

As something occurred to her, she faced Dom. "Still, he and Nancy were always good friends. Perhaps that was the impetus for their meeting . . . to share a meal or something. You went to his lodgings. Was he there? Was *she* there?"

"No." Dom approached her, his eyes like shards of ice. "Barlow was seen leaving his place the morning of her arrival. And he hasn't returned since."

"Oh no," she breathed.

"It took us half the night, but we checked with every coaching inn in York and finally found the one from which they left for London."

"London?" This got worse and worse. "They left *together*? You're sure?"

"Very sure. They went off in a post chaise. What's more, Samuel was quite specific about their needs when he hired it. He said he required the most comfortable one the inn had." Dom stared her down. "And do you know why he had such a specific request?"

Jane swallowed. She was afraid that she did.

When she didn't answer, he added, "Because, or so he told the innkeeper, his 'wife' was pregnant."

7

DOM COULD TELL from Jane's expression that she knew of Nancy's condition. Of course she knew. She'd probably known all along.

Betrayal sliced through him. "When were you going to tell me?" With leaden legs, he walked to the window to look out over the bustling innyard below. "When did you first find out?"

"Only a short while ago," Jane said hastily. "And Nancy was by no means certain. She said she *might* be pregnant. If I'd been sure I would have told you at once, but I didn't think it wise to stir it all up if it came to naught."

"No, much better to imply that this disappearance was some fey whim of hers. Much better to leave out the most important part of this entire affair." He could hardly speak for the pressure on his chest. Nancy could very well be bearing George's son. "Much better to let me go on thinking that I have a new life, when in reality it may be over before it even begins."

"Oh, Dom, I'm so sorry—" she began in a soft voice.

"Don't." He turned from the window to shoot her a baleful glance. "Don't you *dare* pity me."

She flinched. "I'm not, I swear. But I doubt that it will come to anything. Nancy has conceived three times already and has never carried the babe beyond the first few months. There's no reason to believe this time will be different."

"Isn't there? *This* time the child may not be borne of George's inadequate seed, which makes a great deal of difference. Because it could mean she has a better chance of carrying the child until birth."

That arrested Jane. "I-I don't understand."

"Of course you do." He paced the room, unable to keep still. "Nancy came running right here to Samuel Barlow the moment you left Rathmoor Park. She probably wanted to tell him in person that he was going to be a father."

Jane's mouth dropped open. "That's absurd! If she was having Samuel's baby, she would have tried to cover it up. She wouldn't have hurried off to meet him, rousing everyone's suspicions."

There was a certain logic in that, but he couldn't think past the idea of Nancy pregnant. Nancy having a son that could be passed off as George's.

Nancy's son inheriting Rathmoor Park while Dom, once more, lost everything.

The thought fueled his mounting rage. "If she was having *George's* baby, why wouldn't she share it with the world? Why keep it a big secret?"

"I told you why! She wasn't yet sure." Jane tipped up her chin. "And she didn't keep it *that* big a secret. I knew. Mrs. Patch knew. And Nancy's maid definitely knew."

"Yet none of you said anything to *me* about it."

As the bitterness in his voice registered with her, guilt flashed over her face. "We had our reasons."

"Oh? What might those be?" When Jane turned her face from his, a ball of ice settled in his belly. "Damn it, what possible reasons could you have for—"

"We were afraid of what you might do if you knew!"

"Do!" he cried, recoiling from the knife she'd just thrust in his gut. "Like *what*? Kidnap her? Murder her?"

"No, of course not!" Her vehemence only slightly dulled the blade of her betrayal. When he just stood staring at her, her cheeks reddened. "But I know that in cases like these, it's customary to . . . have the lady in question undergo a physical exam to make sure that she is indeed bearing a possible heir."

He stiffened. "It certainly is. So why would you wish to deprive me of that opportunity? It's my right."

"I know, but such an exam, as well as all the uproar that news of a possible heir would cause among the family and staff, might lead her to miscarry again." She steadied her gaze on him. "I was protecting my cousin, that's all."

"From *me*?" He could hardly breathe for the twist of pain in his belly. "You think me that much a monster? You think that once I knew the situation, I would still force a pregnant woman to undergo an exam that might cause her to lose her child."

"No! Well . . ." She rubbed her arms fitfully. "You might have thought you had no choice. I didn't want to put you in the position of having to decide, when there could be no reason. And I certainly didn't want to risk her losing the baby." She dropped her gaze. "I know you'll think it awful of me, but I wanted her to have it—even if it meant you had to go back to being plain Mr. Manton."

There, in the starkest of words, was the truth. Jane didn't care if he lost everything again, as long as her precious cousin got to bear a child. George's child.

Or perhaps not George's child.

Raw fury burned his throat. He ought to be more sympathetic toward his sister-in-law. But it was hard to be so when it could spell the end to all his hopes. Especially when it could also be part of a scheme dreamed up between Barlow and Nancy to rip the estate from him. The estate he deserved to have, damn it!

He dug his fingernails into his palms. "So, in your zeal to protect Nancy, you decided it was acceptable to overlook her many deceptions."

Jane cast him a mutinous glance. "What deceptions? I only spoke to the servants last night—"

"Last night?"

Briefly she got the look of a hare caught in a trap. Then she smoothed her features. "When I returned to Rathmoor Park to get my things, yes."

"You went to the estate in the middle of the night," he said incredulously. One more thing she hadn't informed him of. "Tell me you didn't go the two hours back alone on horseback, the way you came to Winborough."

"Of course not. That would be reckless." As Dom began to breathe a little easier, she added, "I went in Lady Zoe's coach and took a footman with me."

"And that wasn't reckless at all," he said sarcastically. The thought of her traveling for hours late at night on dark country roads with only a servant to protect her curdled his blood. "Are you mad? Anything could have happened to you, for God's sake!"

"Do not shout at me, Lord Rathmoor!" She planted her hands on her hips. "You don't have the right to command me. If I wish to take a ship to India to learn blowhunting from Bedouins, I can do so with or without your approval."

He lifted an eyebrow. "There are no Bedouins in India; they reside in Arabia. And it's not 'blowhunting.' I believe you're referring to blowguns, but—"

"I don't care! The point is that I don't need your permission to do anything." She cocked her head. "Besides, Lord Olivier's footman and coachman are former soldiers. I'm sure they would be just as useful to me in a fight as any fine gentleman."

He grimaced. She was probably right about that.

"And in any case," Jane went on, "your sister saw no problem with it."

"She wouldn't," he said dryly.

Lisette would do just about anything to keep Jane happy, as long as it meant reuniting Jane with him. Yesterday, he'd felt the same way. Their kisses, which had haunted him all night, had made him almost certain that Jane still had feelings for him.

Clearly he'd been wrong. If Jane could keep such a monumental secret from him, knowing what it could mean to his future . . .

"You ought to be glad I went," Jane continued. "I learned quite a bit. The servants confirmed what I suspected—that they had always just assumed that Mrs. Patch accompanied Nancy for her shopping, but they never knew it for a certainty. In fact, they didn't really know how Nancy spent her time in York."

"Which supports *my* theory as easily as yours. Nancy could have been spending that time with Barlow."

"She came back with packages," Jane said stoutly.

"Her maid was with her, right? Meredith could have shopped for her while Nancy joined Barlow."

Jane's lips thinned. "You're determined to believe Nancy a harlot."

"*You're* determined to believe her a saint." He clasped his hands behind his back to keep from shaking some sense into her. "And what about Meredith, anyway? We can't question *her* because she has conveniently disappeared from Nancy's employ. When did that happen? After George's death? Later?"

"Shortly before I came to stay at Rathmoor Park," Jane said sullenly. "But the present maid gave me Meredith's address in London, which means we can question her whenever you like." Her smile was cool. "You see? I'm perfectly willing to follow this wherever it takes us, as long as we base our conclusions on facts and not on your obvious bias against Nancy."

"I do *not* have a bias against Nancy," he gritted out. "But considering what's at stake, and this new information about the babe she bears—"

"*Possibly* bears. We're not even sure of that! Her new maid said that her mistress had shown signs of being with child, but they weren't so pronounced as to make it certain. And even around her, Nancy was cautious about claiming absolutely that she was pregnant."

"That doesn't mean she wasn't."

"No, of course not. But you'd think that if she had been sure, she would have written to her supposed lover to tell him. And according to her maid, Nancy never corresponded with any gentlemen."

Dom shook his head. "Just because her maid didn't see such letters doesn't mean they never existed. Perhaps that's why Nancy was so familiar with the schedule for the mail coach—because she preferred to post and receive her mail in person."

Jane lifted her gaze heavenward. "Has it occurred to you that perhaps her association with Samuel wasn't romantic? They've known each other for years. So perhaps she went off with him to London because . . . I don't know . . ."

"Because she was completely unaware of how it would appear for her to be seen traveling to London with a known rogue," Dom said coldly.

A sigh escaped her. "I know how this looks, but you still have nothing but the words of an innkeeper and an ostler. What if they confused the situation? Or they lied? Or—"

"Come now, Jane, you're not that credulous," he said softly. "It wouldn't be the first time a woman decided to pass her lover's child off as her husband's so she could inherit."

"That's not even logical! For one thing, if Nancy had . . . shared a lover's bed while also sharing George's, no one could ever know for certain whose child she bore. So why run off to London with her lover to have her baby, and draw attention to herself? She'd be better off staying at Rathmoor Park."

"Unless she knew she'd conceived the child too long after George's death to be able to pass it off as his."

The color drained from Jane's face. "*That* is a truly horrible assertion."

He strode up to her. "*Think,* Jane. If she disappears for the next six or eight months, an examination is impossible. She could simply show up with a baby she claimed as George's, and none could prove otherwise, no matter what their suspicions."

She snorted. "No doctor worth his salt would confuse a newborn for a three-month-old."

"Ah, but it needn't be so great a difference for her to be worried. The law says that the babe must be born within forty weeks of the husband's death to be considered his, which means she can't bear the child even one week later. So why should she risk its being declared illegitimate, when she can put the matter in doubt by giving birth in secret whenever she pleases, then coming out of hiding to declare that the child was born before the forty weeks were done?"

Jane's stony gaze pierced him. "You don't think *someone* would witness that birth? And testify to the truth of the matter?"

"Witnesses can be bought easily enough, my dear. Trust me on that."

"You really have become very cynical in these past few years," Jane said in a hollow voice, "if you're asserting that my cousin, a woman gently bred, is perpetrating a deception of such grand proportions as to make her a true villain! You may believe her capable of that, but I *know* she is not."

Dom stared her down. "A woman will do much to secure her future if she feels it's threatened. With things as they are now, Nancy inherits only her dower's portion—a third of the rents. Any illegitimate child of hers would get nothing. No monies, no land, no title. So if her child is born a bastard, he—"

"Or *she*," Jane put in. "You keep forgetting that none of this is by any means certain. Even Dom the Almighty cannot predict the sex of an unborn child."

"True," he conceded, trying not to bristle at the term *Dom the Almighty*. Did she really consider him such a pompous twit? "But after seeing what Father's negligence wrought, George took great care to make his own will ironclad. If he had no son and couldn't prevent me from inheriting the title and entailed estate, he dictated that anything not entailed be left to a daughter."

When Jane blinked, clearly unaware of the niceties

of George's will, he went on ruthlessly, "And if Nancy does happen to bear him a son?" He choked down his ire at the thought. "The boy will gain everything. That would be a temptation for any woman who wants the best for her child."

Though Jane blanched, she stood firm. "Nonetheless, Nancy wouldn't do anything immoral to obtain that."

Jane's persistence in the face of the facts was starting to chafe him raw. "No? Even *you*, as principled as you are, are willing to marry a man you don't love just to secure yourself a better future. So how much more would Nancy wish to do so, if she were—"

"Wait a minute." Jane narrowed her gaze on him. "Why the devil would you think I don't love Edwin?"

The question startled him . . . until he realized what he'd said.

He wasn't even sure why he'd said it. Perhaps because he wanted it to be true. Because he wanted to think that despite her engagement, he still had a chance with her. Because he was a fool—a reckless, besotted fool.

No, it was more than just wishful thinking; he was sure of it. She hadn't ever said anything about loving Blakeborough.

Then again, he hadn't asked. Perhaps instead of thrusting his head in the sand, he should do just that. Because this had suddenly become much bigger than a matter of Nancy's disappearance. The future of the viscountcy was at stake. And that meant the future of his life was at stake. In the midst of this turmoil, he needed one thing to be solid.

He needed to know where he stood with Jane.

"Dom, answer the question," Jane said tersely. "What reason have you for thinking I don't love Edwin?"

"*Do* you?" If she *did*, then Dom had already lost her. But if she didn't . . .

A scarlet blush stained her cheeks. "I'm marrying him, aren't I?"

In an instant, his world shifted. She hadn't said yes. She hadn't really even answered the question. He knew it, and she definitely knew it, judging from the way she averted her gaze.

So he had a chance with her after all. Perhaps not much of one, given that he could be about to lose the very things that would put him on a more equal footing with Blakeborough, but it was a greater chance than he'd had before.

"You don't have to love him to marry him." Deciding to take a risk, he stepped to within a breath of her. "I've been an investigator long enough to recognize the signs of love in a woman. You don't show any for your fiancé."

Her outraged gaze shot to him. "I beg your pardon?"

"You don't speak his name with that softness a woman reserves for her sweetheart, you don't refer to his opinions at every turn, and you don't seem to be itching to return to him." As she drew herself up for what would undoubtedly be a hot retort, he added swiftly, "And you didn't kiss me yesterday as if you were in love with Blakeborough."

Let her deny *that*, damn her.

A rigid mask descended over her features. "My, my,

what interesting observations," she said in a frosty tone. "I have to wonder exactly what sort of tawdry investigations you've been conducting all these years, to have learned what a woman 'reserves for her sweetheart' and how to read so much into a kiss."

She was baiting him again, but this time he was prepared. He'd spent half the night analyzing her words and smiles and kisses yesterday, and figuring out, without the distraction of her presence, what they meant.

Coupled with her reaction to his words about her engagement, they meant she cared more for him than she dared show.

"I didn't read anything into our kisses that wasn't there." His gaze locked with hers. "But I could use another test of my theory. Which would give *you* another chance to prove me wrong."

Given the sudden glitter in the dark bronze of her eyes, she knew he was baiting her, now. She hesitated, obviously torn between fleeing and rising to his challenge.

But this was not the Jane who'd run from him years ago when he'd driven her away. This Jane didn't run; she stood and fought.

Right now she seemed bent on fighting *him*, but that was all right. Let her get it out of her system. Then perhaps if he were careful and very, very lucky, they could move on together. If she didn't kill him first.

A taut smile crossed her face. "I don't have to prove anything to you."

"Certainly not. As long as you don't mind me drawing my own conclusions."

Her smile vanished. "Which are . . ."

He shrugged. "That you refuse to kiss me again because you don't trust yourself. Because you're afraid you haven't quite killed your feelings for me."

With her eyes sparking fires, she leaned up to whisper in his ear, "You have no idea how thoroughly I've killed my feelings for you."

That was definitely bravado in her voice.

"Well then, let's see how thorough that is, shall we?" And catching her by the chin, he tipped her head up for his kiss.

She froze. Snaking an arm about her waist, he pulled her up against him and proceeded to kiss her most ardently.

Curiously, though, she neither fought nor responded. She just let him kiss her, as if waiting for him to finish.

Damn her. He'd hoped that a surprise attack might give him the advantage, but clearly he'd put her too firmly on the defensive. It maddened him. He was *sure* her impassive acquiescence was an act. It was his own fault, too, for making the kiss into a challenge in the first place.

So be it. He would alter the challenge.

When he drew back to see the smug triumph in her face, he schooled his own expression to boredom. "It appears you really did kill your feelings for me. And now you've very nearly killed mine for you, too, because that had to be the most insipid kiss I've ever experienced. Though I suppose I should have expected that from a spinster of some years."

Her eyes narrowed on him. "Spinster?" Her voice rose. "*Of some years?* Oh, it's just like you to turn that back on me as if somehow it was *my* fault I've stayed unmarried. Next you'll be claiming that my 'insipid kiss' is why you found me so easy to toss aside."

She set her shoulders. "Well, Dom the Almighty, when I'm done with you, you will *never* dismiss me as a 'spinster of some years' again. But you will heartily wish that you could."

Then, clasping his head between her hands, she drew him back for a most un-insipid kiss.

Now *that* was more like it. Her lips were soft, her mouth luscious, and her lavender scent swirled about him so sweetly it made him dizzy with the delight of being this close to her again.

He fought the rampant urge to yank her up against him and kiss her with all the pent-up passion of their years apart. Better to let her control the kiss for as long as he could stand it.

He did, however, open his mouth. When she accepted the invitation to make their kiss more intimate by exploring inside with little darting thrusts of her silky tongue, he exulted.

When a moan sounded low in her throat and she threaded her fingers through his hair possessively, that was all he could take. He wrapped his arms about her waist and dragged her flush up against him.

She went still, and for half a second he feared he'd

acted too hastily. But then she melted against him and slipped her arms about his neck to anchor him to her, and his mind went blank.

There was only Jane in his arms again, Jane kissing him again . . . Jane, the only woman he'd ever truly desired, sharpening that desire to a keen edge that cut through the past and left him open and bleeding and yearning for nothing but her.

How had he ever let her go? He must have been mad. She was everything he remembered and more—lush and womanly and passionate, the grown-up version of his young sweetheart. He couldn't get enough of her.

He feasted on her mouth as his hands roamed her back, memorizing curves, finding the feminine shape that lay beneath her layers of clothes.

She tore her mouth from his. "You . . . you tricked me . . ."

"Did I?" He nuzzled her ear. "As I recall, *you* kissed *me.*"

"You practically dared me to."

"After you drove me mad with your coldness." He laved her ear with his tongue. "After you refused to answer my question."

"What question?" she breathed against his cheek.

"Do you love Blakeborough?"

"Ah. *That* question." She flattened her breasts against his chest, making him ache to touch them, fondle them.

She'd probably done it purposely, the sly minx. And most effectively, since now that the idea of touching her breasts had been planted in his head, he could scarcely think of anything else.

He fought clear of the fog of desire. "I want an answer, Jane," he choked out, then nipped her earlobe.

"You don't have the right to an answer." She nipped *his* earlobe.

"That's what you said yesterday about kissing, too, yet here we are again." He dragged openmouthed kisses down her jawline. "Kissing. A lot."

"I know, curse you. But . . . but we shouldn't."

He buried his face in her neck. "I'll stop whenever you ask."

She didn't ask, though she did groan most feelingly when he tongued the pulse that beat wildly in her throat. Inflamed, he tried to kiss lower. When her tucker got in the way, he ripped it from her bodice, desperate to see the soft upper swells of her bosom that had tortured his memory since the Keanes' ball three months ago.

"Dom! What the devil are you . . ."

He scattered kisses along the freckles dotting her nicely displayed décolletage.

She caught her breath. "Sweet Lord, Dom! Your family could come in any minute!"

"They know better." His sister for certain would give him enough rope to hang himself if it meant pairing him off with Jane.

"Still . . . You shouldn't . . . That's not . . ." Her protests trailed off as he took his time kissing every inch of her partially exposed breasts.

But soon it wasn't enough. Soon he wanted the forbidden. Driven by the fire burning in his blood, a decade-long, smoldering flame, he cupped the pillowy softness of one breast through her gown.

Her eyes went wide, her cheeks turned scarlet, and she covered his hand as if to pull it away. Before she could, he kneaded her breast with his palm, knowing it might be his only chance to do so. He had to touch her intimately. Know her more intimately.

To his amazement, she didn't stop him. She watched him wide-eyed, then whispered in a voice full of shock and awe, "Ohhh, Lord, *Dom* . . ."

What else could he do? Filling *both* his hands with her breasts, he took her mouth once more.

8

THANK HEAVEN JANE still had her arms looped about Dom's neck, or she would surely collapse onto the floor. Bad enough that his bold tongue driving inside her mouth over and over reduced her to pudding. But his hands were now doing things . . . Oh, *Lord,* such *wonderful* things!

He rubbed and fondled her breasts through her gown until her nipples felt hard and aching, until a strange stirring far below made her squirm and press her thighs together.

She should stop him, really she should. Even her tolerant fiancé would not approve of this. *She* shouldn't approve. At the very least, she shouldn't . . . like it quite so much. Though how she was to stop that, she wasn't sure.

Through a haze of pleasure and need, she felt Dom draw down the bodice of her gown and her corset to bare her breasts, draped only in her thin shift. What was wrong with her? Why wasn't she protesting this . . . this *outrage*? This amazing . . . intoxicating . . .

Hunger rose up in her . . . sharp, piercing, and so strong she ached. For him. For the only man who'd ever commanded her heart . . . and was now commanding her body.

Except that it wasn't the cold, arrogant Dom who'd always set her off, but the ardent suitor she'd first fallen in love with. She'd begun to think that *that* Dom had vanished. Clearly he had not.

His kiss grew harder, hotter. He thumbed her nipples through the linen, and sensations screamed through her, so foreign and delightful that her head spun. The room spun. Lots of things were spinning. Perhaps that was why she felt dizzy.

"Do it again," she whispered against his mouth, then cringed at the breathless wantonness of the request.

He paused, then said huskily, "How about if I do something even better?"

"B-better?" she squeaked.

Locking his gaze with hers, he drew down her shift, then lowered his head to suck her nipple.

Oh, Lord, *better*.

She slid her hands up into his hair, fully intending to pull him away. But her hands ignored her orders and clutched him tightly to her breast instead.

So she gave up. Because what he was doing to her breasts with teeth and lips and tongue was astonishing.

"You taste even better than I imagined," Dom whispered against her skin. "Sweet, delicious Jane."

"This is . . . mad . . ." Anything this wonderful *had* to be some form of insanity.

"Then I've been mad for twelve years." He tugged at her nipple with his teeth, and she gasped. "Because I imagined this often. Holding you . . . touching you." He laved her nipple with his tongue as if to soothe it. "I tried not to torture myself, but . . . it was impossible that I should *never* indulge in . . . the fantasy of you like this, in my arms again."

He'd thought of her all these years? And done nothing about it?

"You could have . . . had me whenever you wanted," she choked out, even as she thrilled to his words. "You just didn't . . . want me."

"Not true." His breathing labored, he dragged his mouth from her breast to kiss his way back up to her throat. "I couldn't *allow* myself to want you. There's a difference."

None that she could see. But just now, she could hardly think. One of Dom's hands worked its magic on her breast, his mouth seared kisses into her tender skin, and his other hand snaked around to cup her derriere and pull her flush against him.

Something hard pressed into her through her skirts. What the devil?

"Jane," he rasped against her lips. "My darling Jane . . . still mine . . ."

The possessive note in his voice drove out every other thought. She was losing the fight against him.

Sweet Lord, she couldn't. Mustn't, until she was sure

he wouldn't become Dom the Almighty again. Until she was sure he wouldn't trample her into dust, the way he had before when things hadn't been exactly how he wanted them. She couldn't go through that again.

She pushed him back, breaking his hold on her. "Not yours," she said firmly. Her breath still came in heavy gasps, and she fought to get it under control. To get herself under control. "Not anymore."

He stared at her a long moment, his eyes ablaze and his hands flexing at his sides as if regretting the loss of her already. "Will you never forgive me for what I did so long ago, Jane?"

The soft question caught her off guard. "Would you do it again if you had the chance?" She could hardly breathe, awaiting his answer.

With a low oath, he glanced away. Then his features hardened into those of the rigid and arrogant Dom he had become. "Yes. I did the only thing I could to keep you happy."

Her breath turned to ice in her throat. "That's the problem. You still really believe that."

His gaze swung to her again, but before he could say anything more, noises in the hall arrested them both.

"It's gone very quiet in there." It was the duke's voice, remarkably clear, sounding as if it came from right outside the door. "Perhaps we should knock first."

Oh no! As Jane frantically set her gown to rights, she heard Lisette say, "Don't you dare bother them, Max. I'm sure everything's fine. Let's come back later."

With panic growing in her belly, Jane glanced around for her tucker. Wordlessly, Dom plucked it from the back of a chair and handed it to her.

Without meeting his gaze, she pinned it into her bodice, hoping to hide the tiny holes where Dom had unwittingly ripped it free of its pins.

"Besides," drawled Tristan, "it's not as if Dom will seduce her or anything. That's not his vice."

Sweet Lord, were they *all* right outside the door?

"I'm not worried about that," Max answered. "Miss Vernon isn't the sort to *let* him seduce her."

As Jane tensed, Dom hissed under his breath, "Do the blasted idiots not realize we can hear them?"

"Apparently not."

Dom furtively adjusted his trousers, which seemed to be rather . . . oddly protruding just now.

Ohhh. Right. This was one time she wished Nancy hadn't been so forthcoming about what happened to a man's body when he was aroused. So *that*, not his pistol, had been the odd bulge digging into her.

Definitely not a pistol. Her cheeks positively flamed. Faith, how could she even face his family after this and not give away what she and Dom had been doing?

Mortified, she hurried to the looking glass to fix her hair. While she stuffed tendrils back into place and repinned drooping curls, Dom came up behind her to meet her gaze in the mirror. "Before we let them in, I want an answer to my question about Blakeborough."

Curse the stubborn man. How could she tell Dom she was so pathetic that she hadn't even managed to find another man to love in all the years they'd spent apart? That she'd been foolish enough to wait around for Dom all this time, when he'd happily gone on living his life without her? Her pride couldn't endure having him know that.

To her relief, Tristan said, "Well, whatever they're up to, we have to get moving." A knock sounded at the door. "Dom? Jane? Are you done talking?"

She met Dom's gaze with a certain defiance, and he arched one eyebrow in question.

So she took matters into her own hands and strode for the door. Caught off guard, Dom swore behind her and snatched up his greatcoat just as she opened the door and said, "Please come in. We're quite finished."

In more ways than one.

Their companions trooped in, casting her and Dom wary glances. Jane looked over to see Dom holding his greatcoat looped over his arm as if to shield the front of him. That brought the blushes back to her cheeks.

She caught Lisette furtively watching her, and she cursed herself for wearing her emotions on her sleeve. Better shift her attention elsewhere before Lisette guessed just how shameless she'd been.

"I assume you now know of Nancy's possible pregnancy?" she said baldly.

The others exchanged glances.

"Tristan filled us in, yes," Lisette said.

"As I explained to Dom, it is by no means a certain thing." Swiftly Jane related what she'd revealed to him about Nancy's past miscarriages and friendship with Samuel.

The minute she was done, Dom said, "Jane seems to think that Nancy would never behave so duplicitously as to try passing off Samuel's child as George's own."

"Then perhaps we should listen to her," the duke said.

"Max!" Lisette said. "Don't you realize what would happen to Dom if Nancy gives birth to a son who could lay claim to the estate and title?"

"Of course. But that's beside the point. And it doesn't change the fact that none of us are remotely familiar with George's wife. I'm not sure I've even met her." He nodded to Jane. "Whereas Miss Vernon has had an intimate acquaintance with her for years. If anyone knows the woman's character, it ought to be she."

Jane could have kissed him for that. "Thank you, Your Grace."

"Call me Max, please," he corrected her. "I learned a long time ago that this family doesn't stand on ceremony."

"Then do call me Jane," she answered. "It's beginning to look more and more like we'll be thrown into each other's pockets quite a bit in the next few days, given that I'll be traveling on with you and Lisette to London."

"Speaking of that," Tristan said, "Max and I came up with a plan while you two were having your discussion . . . or whatever it was." When his knowing tone provoked a foul glance from Dom, Tristan added hastily, "Max has an estate near Newark, about seven or eight hours' drive from here. It's a logical stopping point on the road to London, since you'll need to break the trip up into parts. Since we're getting a late start, we thought that you three could head on to Max's estate in Newark while I stay to do more nosing around in York."

"For what?" Dom asked.

"Information on Barlow. Other than what the innkeeper said about the post chaise to London Barlow hired for him and Nancy, we didn't learn anything about whether they've been spending time together. It would be good to know the exact nature of their . . . er . . . friendship."

"I think we can guess, can't we?" Lisette said stoutly. "Given all the gossip about Mr. Barlow, I mean."

Jane winced. It had probably been too much to expect that Lisette would be on *her* side and not Dom's, but still it hurt to see the duchess so ready to assume the worst about Nancy.

"I'm sure all the rumors about Mr. Barlow and women are true," Jane said. "But that speaks more to his character than to my cousin's. It certainly doesn't mean Nancy ran off to have the man's baby, for pity's sake." She glanced at the three siblings, who'd unconsciously moved together, ranging themselves against her. "Have any of you considered the possibility that she didn't go with him of her own accord?"

"No," Dom growled, "because it's absurd."

Jane pinned him with her gaze. "Why? Simply because you wish it to be? Was there any *evidence* that she went with him willingly? Did the innkeeper say anything about how she behaved? Did he even see her get into the coach *with* Samuel?"

"No," Tristan put in before Dom could growl something else at her. "But what would Barlow's purpose be in abducting her?"

"Marriage, of course," the duke answered. "As Nancy's husband, Barlow would have complete control over her widow's portion. And if Nancy is bearing George's child, then Barlow would be stepfather to the new viscount. He'd be able to mold the lad however he wished and run the estate however he pleased until the lad came of age. He could bleed it dry before the heir ever reached his majority."

"You see?" Jane said. "Even the duke understands that more could be at work here."

Dom met her gaze balefully. "First of all, we have no evidence that Barlow took her against her will, and we have plenty of evidence that he did not. We know she came here purposely to meet him."

"That's probably true," Jane conceded, "but I don't think she intended to run away with him, or why bother to tell the servants she'd be back that night? She could have just said she was going to Bath with her aunt. Then she could have packed up all her baggage and gone off, with nobody the wiser. Besides, as I already told you, she would never willingly leave her dogs behind."

"All good points, you have to admit," the duke said.

Jane flashed him a smile. "Thank you, Max." He was

obviously a very wise man, and Lisette was a very lucky woman.

Though judging from the scowl Lisette leveled on him, the woman didn't particularly agree with that assessment at the moment.

Dom crossed his arms over his chest. "But if Barlow kidnapped Nancy in an attempt to force her into a marriage, wouldn't he have carried her to Gretna Green? He'd want her married to him as quickly and easily as possible. Instead, they're going to London."

"None of it makes any sense, I'll admit," Jane said.

Tristan nodded. "And that's precisely why we need more information. So I'll stay in York however long it takes to find it, and then I'll catch up to you in Newark or even London to tell you what I've learned."

Dom eyed him warily. "Won't your wife have something to say about your traveling so far off?"

"I already knew this was probably not going to be swift or easy, so I prepared her for any eventuality. She'll understand." Tristan shoved his hands into his coat pockets. "You may need me once you reach London. I realize that Victor and Isa are there, but who knows what else we'll uncover as this investigation goes on? Your entire future could be at stake. So I'd rather err on the side of caution and pursue this to the end with you."

Dom got a strange look on his face, surprise and affection mingling. "Thanks," he said, his voice taut with emotion. "Though I do welcome the help, you don't have to do that. This isn't your fight, after all."

"It wasn't your fight when you stood up to George

on my behalf, either," Tristan said softly. "The least I can do after all you did for me is add my support to this endeavor."

The two brothers stared at each other a long moment, and Lisette looked a little misty-eyed.

Then Tristan cleared his throat. "Besides, ever since Zoe got pregnant, she's been craving those sour pickles sold only at Fortnum & Mason in London. So I'll bring her back jars of them, and she'll instantly forgive me for being gone so long."

"Not if she finds out that you think her forgiveness can be bought with jars of pickles," Lisette said dryly.

"You'd be surprised how much a jar of those pickles could buy me right now." Tristan grinned. "Or perhaps not, since you've already endured having a baby."

"Lisette craved Russian caviar," the duke said. "Slightly more difficult to come by than pickles."

"And slightly harder on the purse," Dom put in. "Good thing she's married to *you*."

"For your next pregnancy," Tristan told his sister, "you should crave pearls. So much more practical than caviar."

Lisette stuck her tongue out at him, and Max said, "Don't give her ideas," though he then smiled at her.

Jane got the feeling that the duke would buy his wife the moon if he could find a way to dislodge it from the night sky, and her throat tightened with envy. Dom hadn't even been willing to swallow his pride for *her*.

"Speaking of babies, actual and prospective," the duke went on, "I know Lisette is eager to get home to ours, and Dom is eager to find out for sure about Nancy's, so we'd better be off. We've already lost a great deal of time just trying to find out the circumstances of Nancy's disappearance."

"True," Dom said. "We'll be lucky if we catch up to the pair before they disappear into the crowds of London."

Tristan's expression hardened as he walked toward the door. "Don't worry. If Victor and I have to comb every slum in the city, we'll find them. You can be sure of that."

Jane believed him. The Duke's Men had quite the reputation for finding people, and they had more reason than usual to find Nancy.

Now if only she could be sure that Barlow wouldn't destroy Nancy's reputation or steal her future before they did.

9

HALF AN HOUR later, as they left York headed for Newark, Dom stretched his legs out in Max's spacious and comfortably appointed traveling carriage. Another carriage behind them carried the ladies' maids and the duke's valet. It was all very civilized and proper, the very epitome of how gentlemen like them should travel.

A pity that Dom wasn't feeling particularly civilized and proper just now, and he certainly wasn't feeling like a gentleman. How could he, when the woman he ached to possess sat directly across from him, ignoring him?

Jane looked so pensive and aloof and pretty in the violet walking dress he'd wanted to strip off her earlier, that just gazing at her made his chest hurt.

The years had been kinder to her than to him. Not a single line creased her features, and not a thread of silver appeared in her unfashionably red hair . . . her beautiful, unruly red hair that he still itched to unpin and take down, to tangle between his fingers as he tasted again those lush breasts of hers, with their pert russet nipples hardening while he . . .

He bit back an oath as his cock stirred. Jerking his gaze to the window, he fought for mastery over it. He had to stop thinking about her naked! Otherwise, he was going to be giving quite the show to his companions.

Clearly, after all these years, he had finally lost his mind. This infernal lust wasn't like him at all, and acting on it as he had earlier certainly wasn't. All right, perhaps he'd enjoyed a few intimate encounters with Tristan's actress friends in Paris some years back, but generally Tristan had always been the only one to do things like that.

Yet even now, Dom burned to touch Jane, caress Jane, *know* Jane. Even in the biblical sense. *Especially* in the biblical sense.

Meanwhile, she wanted nothing to do with him. Since their discussion in the inn, she hadn't said more than two words to him.

And before that, she'd flat-out refused to answer his question about her fiancé. What did that mean? That she didn't love the man? If her bloody fiancé was so bloody important to her, she'd certainly hidden it well while Dom was kissing and caressing her.

Unless she'd been using his lust against him, tormenting him for what she saw as his throwing her away years ago. Punishing him for refusing to apologize for doing what he'd had to in order to ensure her happiness.

That's the problem. You still really believe that.

Yes, damn her, he did! Though it was getting harder to do so, with the scent and taste of her filling his mind. That was probably what she intended, to show him what he'd lost. To make him regret it.

If that was her purpose, it was certainly working, blast it.

"There's one thing I've been wondering about, Jane," Max said from beside him. "Why on earth did your cousin choose to marry George in the first place? I met the man once, and he didn't strike me as the sort to make a woman's heart quicken, if you know what I mean."

Dom glanced furtively at Jane. Would she reveal the truth of what had prompted George's interest in Nancy? Would she tell his family what had actually happened that blasted night in the library?

If it was revenge she wanted, then that would certainly be a fitting one. Lisette would never let him hear the end of it.

"George could be very charming when he wished." Jane looked pointedly at Dom. "I believe they grew interested in each other one night at a ball when he behaved very gallantly in defending Nancy from some . . . untoward fellow. That made a great impression on her, and apparently she made an even greater impression on George."

Dom just stared at her. So it wasn't revenge Jane sought. Then again, perhaps she just felt that the truth of that "one night at a ball" would somehow not reflect well on either of them. She might be right.

"So, was Nancy's marriage to George a happy one?" Lisette asked. "Because I don't see how it could have been, if she's been engaging in an affair with the likes of Samuel Barlow."

"She has not been engaging in an affair with anyone!" Jane cried. When the others fell into an uncomfortable silence, Jane tipped up her chin. "She hasn't, or I swear I would have known it."

"Forgive me for saying so," Max remarked, an edge to his voice, "but women can be adept at hiding such secrets, even from their families."

Ah, yes, Max's mother had cuckolded his father, hadn't she? Dom had forgotten that. Max himself hadn't known it until Tristan uncovered it last year.

"Perhaps so," Jane said hotly, "but not Nancy. I can imagine her flirting with Samuel, perhaps, but sharing his bed while also married to George? Never."

"Because she *loved* him?" Dom said sarcastically.

"Because by then, she feared him." Jane leveled him with a dark look. "Surely you can understand that, knowing him as well as you did."

"Then she shouldn't have married him," Dom said.

And she shouldn't have maneuvered that encounter in the library so that George saw her supposedly being assaulted by me.

Dom couldn't say that in front of the rest of them. But when he got the chance to be alone with Jane again, he would be sure to point it out.

"She was foolish to wed him, I'll admit," Jane said. "She was swept up in the idea of becoming Lady Rathmoor. Sadly, my uncle's concerns over George's character could never convince her, because she thought him merely overcautious. Considering what had happened to—"

Halting abruptly, she jerked her gaze from Dom.

"To you?" Dom snapped, insulted that her uncle could have spoken of him and George in the same breath.

"Of course not," Jane mumbled, but color stained her cheeks, making her freckles stand out, and he wasn't sure he believed her.

"Then to whom?" he snapped.

Myriad emotions crossed Jane's face, so many he couldn't sort them out. She opened her mouth, closed it. Paused a moment.

Then she squared her shoulders, as if coming to a decision. "To his sister—my mother. Considering what happened when Mama drowned."

Lisette gaped at her. "Your mother *drowned*?"

"She fell into a swollen river," Dom answered. What did Kitty Vernon's drowning have to do with anything? "Jane's father jumped in to save her, but he was pulled under, too, and they both perished. It was very tragic."

"Oh, Lord," Lisette said. "You didn't witness it, did you?"

"No, I was with my nurse." Jane's gaze shifted to his. "But as it turned out, events weren't quite as I was led to believe when I was a child."

The haunted look in her eyes struck a chill to Dom's bones. "What do you mean?"

"Mama did not 'fall' into the river. She was pushed."

"By whom?" Dom asked, though he began to fear he knew.

"My father." Her voice held an edge. "He flew into a rage—not for the first time, I might add—over some misstep he fancied that Mama had made. Only after he realized what he'd done did he jump in to save her. But neither survived."

A shocked silence fell on the carriage.

Dom could hardly take it in. Her mother was killed by her father? "But the official story—"

"Uncle Horace convinced the constable that with both parties dead, there was no point in dragging the rest of the family through a scandal. The two servants who'd witnessed the attack agreed to keep quiet, and it was ruled an accidental drowning."

Jane tipped up her chin. "That's why Nancy would never, *ever* have cuckolded George. She knew just how dangerous an angry, unpredictable man can be when he's crossed. She wouldn't have risked having the same thing happen to her."

Dom's head reeled. Her father had been such a monster? And she'd lived with the man until she was eight. Good God. Had he ever hurt *Jane*?

"Why did you never tell me this?" Dom asked.

"I only learned of it after you and I parted ways. It's not as if my uncle and aunt were going to admit such a thing to a mere child. But once George began courting Nancy, my uncle grew concerned. He begged me to keep her from making the same mistake Mama had. That's when he told me the truth about his sister's death, about what Papa did to her."

First she'd been saddled with what she'd thought was Dom's betrayal. Then she'd learned the truth about her parents. And he hadn't been there to help, to ease her way.

A tendril of guilt crept around his heart. He tried futilely to ignore it.

"I wasn't entirely surprised to hear it," Jane went on coldly. "What little I did remember from my childhood was of Papa bullying Mama."

"And you?" Dom asked hoarsely. "Did he ever—"

"No." She released a shaky breath. "It was Mama he always . . . pushed around. I was shielded from most of their arguing by my nurse, but the few times I dined with them were very upsetting. He spoke so harshly to her, it made me cringe. Only years later did I come to understand that not all men treated their wives that way. Uncle Horace certainly didn't."

"But still . . . good heavens, Jane," Lisette said, grabbing her hand. "That sounds dreadful."

After a quick squeeze of Lisette's hand, Jane released it. "And in the end, telling Nancy the truth about it didn't stop her from marrying George. She craved the chance to be a viscountess, and she thought him gravely misunderstood."

She slanted a glance at Dom. "Uncle Horace could always see George for what he was. He knew about George burning the codicil, because I'd told him. He understood how heinous that was. But Nancy didn't see it. And to her, George and my papa were nothing alike, anyway."

"But she learned otherwise later?" Max asked, his eyes full of sympathy.

"I'm honestly not sure," Jane admitted. "I'll grant you that George was prone to fits of temper, but I don't think he ever struck Nancy. Certainly he never did in my presence, and she never complained of mistreatment. Mostly he just . . . berated her. I suppose that can be just as bad."

A troubled frown creased her forehead as she gazed out the window. "It seemed so to me, whenever Papa spoke cruelly to Mama. My uncle told me that Papa dictated every aspect of Mama's life—what she should eat, where she should go, to whom she could speak." Her voice turned brittle. "She never did anything without his criticizing it or wanting to control it."

"Oh, God," Dom said as something occurred to him. "That's why the terms of your father's will were so strict. The bloody arse wanted to control *your* future from beyond the grave."

She bobbed her head. "Papa intended to run my life as he'd run Mama's," she said bitterly. "Of course, I didn't realize that until later. I just thought Papa had been overly protective, and Uncle Horace was being equally so."

Steadying her shoulders, she lifted her gaze to Dom. "So you see, Nancy wouldn't have been foolish enough to take Samuel as a lover during her marriage. She might have ignored her father's warnings as a girl intent on marrying a lord, but not after she'd experienced life with George."

"On the other hand, that might have made her yearn for some happiness," Max pointed out. When Jane scowled at him, he added, "I'm just saying that a woman, when pressed to the wall, sometimes reacts perversely."

Jane bristled. "Perhaps, but no one has found any proof that she did."

Dom conceded that with a nod. "Neither have we found any proof that she did not. And there's still the possibility that she became intimately involved with Barlow *after* George died." His voice softened. "You can't ignore that, Jane."

"No, but I don't know when she would have done so. I came to Rathmoor Park only a short while after George's death." She flashed Dom a pleading glance. "And even if Nancy *did* have an affair afterward, it wasn't because she wanted to steal your inheritance for her child. She wouldn't do that."

When Dom snorted, Max flicked a look at him. "But I gather that Barlow might."

Jane sighed. "It's possible he would attempt it. Though he would never convince Nancy to go along with it."

"So you know Barlow well, then?" Max asked. "I mean, you must. You're engaged to his brother."

That made Jane bristle. "Neither Edwin nor I have seen Samuel in years," she said frostily.

Lisette patted Jane's knee. "Max isn't accusing *you* of anything criminal."

"I should hope not," Jane said. "I realize that Nancy is my cousin and Samuel is my fiancé's brother, but I assure you I had nothing to do with it."

The defensiveness in her voice cut through Dom's anger at this situation with Nancy. He hadn't meant to treat her as if she were somehow guilty of something. But between the way he'd tormented her about not telling him of the pregnancy and the way he'd taken advantage of her in the inn room, she probably didn't know what to think.

"No one blames you," Dom said. "You've done nothing wrong, and I, for one, would never think that you had."

An uncomfortable silence fell on the group that was all the more awkward because they knew they had a full day's journey ahead of them.

After a short while, Max flashed Jane a smile. "So, Jane, why don't you tell us how you met your fiancé? I've chatted with Blakeborough a time or two at my club. He seems a decent chap, if a little surly."

"Max!" Lisette protested, with a furtive glance at Dom. "That's hardly an appropriate subject under the circumstances."

"No, I'd like to hear it," Dom said, keeping his eyes trained on Jane's face. "Blakeborough and Jane were already friends when I first met her, so I never knew what brought them together."

And perhaps she would finally reveal the truth about what she felt for Blakeborough.

She avoided his gaze. "Actually, I can't recall exactly

when we met, because I would have been very young. We grew up together in Preston, before . . . I went to live with my aunt and uncle. His parents occasionally came to dinners at our house."

A faint smile touched her lips that made Dom's heart stop. "I'm told that Edwin once pushed me into a puddle to make me stop following him everywhere. I don't remember it, though. I was only four." Her eyes twinkled. "He *claims* not to remember it either, but given that he was seven, I find that highly suspicious."

"How old were you when your parents . . ." Lisette trailed off with a pained look.

"I was eight." Jane smoothed her skirts, a nervous habit he'd noticed early on in their courtship. "And I didn't see Edwin again until my come-out, when he asked me for advice regarding his little sister."

"I forgot that Blakeborough has a sister," Dom said. "Her name's Yvette, right?"

Jane nodded. "She's quite a bit younger than he and Samuel."

"And quite a handful, too, from what the gossips say," Max added.

"Oh, yes," Jane admitted ruefully. "There are days when Edwin despairs of ever finding her a husband."

Lisette chuckled. "That sounds familiar. Dom and Tristan had begun to despair of ever finding *me* a husband." She shot Max a coy glance. "So I found one for myself."

"And you managed to hold on to him until you got

him to the altar, which seems to be the most difficult part," Jane said with a quick glance at Dom.

"No," Dom said, "the most difficult part is being sure that he's the right man for you. Sometimes it takes a while to figure that out. Some women even know a man for years before they accept his proposal of marriage." He couldn't keep from smiling smugly at her. "I wonder why that is."

A sudden glint in her eyes told him he'd made his point. "Probably because when *some* women find their hearts trampled on by some *men,* it takes them years to recover enough to accept another man's proposal."

He cringed. It hadn't taken her years to recover, had it? That hadn't been his intention.

"But," she went on, "once they do, they realize they had a jewel under their noses all the time. For example, my Edwin can be surly if you don't know him, but beneath that cold and bitter exterior is a very accomplished and intelligent gentleman who can have quite a soft heart."

My Edwin. Damn her for that.

For the next hour, Jane proceeded to sing Blakeborough's praises. To hear her tell it, Blakeborough could win at whist in his sleep, do complicated mathematical equations in his head, and ride a mile-long racecourse in five seconds flat. He even gave generously—and anonymously—to several charities, a fact that she'd only discovered when a friend running one of those charities had revealed it.

But just as Dom was ready to hunt the man down and beat him to a bloody pulp just for being a paragon, it occurred to him that she still hadn't mentioned Blakeborough and "love" in the same breath.

Only then did he relax. Let her go on and on about Blakeborough's brilliance if it made her feel better. As long as she didn't mention loving the blasted fellow, Dom was content.

And he would tell her so as soon as he could get her alone again.

10

SEVERAL HOURS LATER, as the group sat down to dinner at the duke's estate in Newark, Jane was relieved to find the seating somewhat informal. The table was too massive for anything else, unless they all wanted to shout to each other during the meal.

Still, everyone had dressed formally, including Jane, who'd taken great care with her attire. Not because she was dining with Dom, oh no. It was because of the duke and duchess. She'd figured they would expect it. That was the only reason. Truly.

Unfortunately, although Jane's maid had assured her that she looked like a queen, she still felt like a queen's *mount* ridden to exhaustion. For the last two hours in the carriage, she'd slept, no longer able to keep her eyes open, and she was still groggy.

Stealing a glance at Dom, who sat across the table from her next to his sister, she stifled a groan. *He* looked like a king—self-assured and positively regal. It was the first time she'd seen him in evening dress since

Lady Zoe's ball, and she'd forgotten how very well he wore it.

He tended to be a sober dresser, leaning more toward practicality than fashion. As he had at the ball, he wore a plain tailcoat and trousers of black superfine, the requisite white shirt, and a simply tied white cravat. But tonight his waistcoat was a gorgeous figured green silk that made his eyes glow like jade in the candlelight. He looked like a viscount in his full glory, not a second son auditioning for the part.

Sweet Lord, she hoped he did become viscount. Nancy could bear a daughter—that would make her perfectly happy. But Dom deserved the title and the estate after everything he'd been through.

Even if he did persist in thinking ill of Nancy. Though perhaps he didn't think *quite* so ill of her now.

Jane had never revealed the truth about Mama's death to anyone. It was her family's most scandalous secret. But she'd had to make them see, make *Dom* see. She'd had to make them understand.

The profound shock of Uncle Horace's tale, the horror of such a dark family secret, had rocked Jane's vision of her past. Coming on top of what she'd initially seen as Dom's betrayal, it had sent her into reclusiveness for quite a while. In time it had faded into a dull memory, a disturbing part of her youth.

Until Dom had come back into her life and stirred it all up again.

As he was doing now, his eyes seeking hers as he sipped his wine. "You look beautiful this evening."

She fought the urge to preen. "Thank you." She could hardly compare to Lisette in her duchess finery, but she was glad she'd had her gown of ruby silk with her and her favorite garnet necklace. "You look very well yourself."

"Except for his hair," Lisette said. "Jane, do persuade him to let it grow. He keeps it so unfashionably short that I keep expecting him to whip out a powdered barrister's wig and plop it on his head."

"As soon as I can hire a valet who can cut hair to my liking, I'll be happy to let it grow out to its former wild and unmanageable length," Dom quipped. "In the meantime, this is easier."

Lisette eyed him warily. "Please tell me you don't cut it yourself."

"All right. I won't tell you."

"Dom!" his sister cried. "You don't really—"

"He's teasing you, dearling," Max drawled. "Can't you tell?"

Lisette caught Dom winking at Jane, and she rolled her eyes, then dipped her spoon into her bowl of turtle soup. "You're becoming as bad as Tristan, I swear."

"I doubt there's any chance of that." Dom cast Jane a sly look. "Tristan was 'born in a merry hour.'"

Jane didn't miss a beat. "No, sure, my lord, his mother cried, but then there was a star danced, and under that was he born."

"*Much Ado about Nothing*?" Max asked.

"Slightly paraphrased," Jane answered.

"Well, clearly Dom has been spending too much

time around Shaw." Lisette buttered her roll. "Though I don't know why *Jane* is quoting Shakespeare."

Because it had been their favorite play. It was still *her* favorite.

Jane shared a knowing smile with Dom, but when his gaze heated and drifted to her bosom, it reminded her exactly what they'd been doing earlier.

Feeling the color rise in her cheeks, she forced her gaze from his. "So," she said brightly, scrambling for a less dangerous topic, "who is Shaw?"

The duke laughed. "You haven't met Skrimshaw? He used to be Dom's butler . . . of sorts. 'Shaw' is his stage name; he spends most of his evenings performing in the theater."

"And his afternoons and his Saturdays and every other Wednesday," Dom grumbled.

"Good thing he's not your butler anymore," Lisette said lightly. "Now he's Victor's problem." Lisette looked at Jane. "Victor and his wife have taken over Manton's Investigations for Dom."

"Assuming I don't have to return to it before the year is out," Dom said coolly.

When Nancy's child is born.

They all thought it, which cast a decided pall over the company.

A few moments of silence passed while they ate, but Jane didn't mind. She was famished, having eaten very little in the past two days, so she was happy to concentrate on her soup.

Then Lisette cleared her throat. "Speaking of theatrical performers, did I tell you, Dom, that I ran into one of Maman's cousins in London two weeks ago?"

Dom laid his spoon down. "I thought they were all still in France. What was this particular cousin doing here?"

"You won't believe this." Lisette leaned forward, clearly delighted at the chance to share a choice bit of gossip. "She was brought to England by Sadler's Wells Theatre. She's a successful opera singer, of all things!"

"I'm not surprised. It runs in your family." Dom shifted his gaze to Jane. "Mrs. Bonnaud, Lisette's mother, was said to have captivated many an audience with her voice before our father whisked her away from Toulon."

Lisette sighed. "I miss Maman's singing."

"So do I," Dom said softly.

"Do you remember when she used to direct us in performances of little *opéras comiques*?"

Dom chuckled. "As if I could forget it. I was the one humming the accompaniment, remember?"

"That's right!" Lisette said. "I haven't thought about that in years. And you were such a good sport about it, too."

"I would have enjoyed it more if I'd known any French arias. But since all I could hum were the bits of Mozart I'd heard played at the manor house, we ended up with a very limited repertoire."

"Until later," Lisette said. "You did add *The Marriage of Figaro*. We were all grateful for that, especially Maman, who made much of it."

"Your 'maman' made much of any piece of music derived from something French," Dom said amiably. "And *The Marriage of Figaro* was taken from a French play."

"Maman was nothing if not proud of her national origins. Otherwise Tristan wouldn't have tried so hard to play that French bagpipe-type oddity she had brought to England with her."

"The *bousine*." Dom shook his head. "That horrible thing sounded like a mare in heat."

"More like a mare in the final throes of death," Lisette said. "Thank heaven Tristan tripped and dropped it off that cliff at Flamborough Head, or he would probably still be playing it."

Dom winced. "Actually, he didn't exactly . . . er . . . drop it. He got mad at me when I criticized his playing, and he threw the thing at me. He missed."

A look that was equal parts delight and horror came over Lisette's face. "You and Tristan *destroyed* Maman's favorite instrument? Why, she cried for days over that!"

"I know. We felt terrible. Well, I only felt terrible because it made your mother cry, not because of the loss of the damned thing." Dom leaned back as the servant replaced his bowl with an empty plate. "And I'm not even sure Tristan felt all *that* terrible. He seemed relieved that he no longer had to attempt to master it."

"He couldn't master it because he has a tin ear. Always did." Lisette smiled. "Maman used to say that you inherited more of her musical inclination than any of her natural children."

Jane had been watching them for some time in rapt

amazement. Lisette and Dom shared the sort of memories a real sister and brother would have, and not what Jane would have imagined of the illegitimate daughter of a man's mistress and the man's legitimate son.

Jane caught Max watching her. "You didn't know, did you?" he said softly. "It's all right to be surprised. It came as a shock to me, too."

Dom looked perplexed. "What did?"

"That you and Lisette grew up so much in each other's pockets," Max said.

Jane glanced nervously at Max. "I suppose I *should* have known. Lisette and Tristan were both at our engagement party, and Tristan and Dom attended a number of assemblies with their father. But I assumed that it was only because the old viscount encouraged them to be friendly for such formal occasions, and they acquiesced to please him."

Dom gave a bark of laughter. "We did it to please ourselves. We preferred each other's company to that of most of the people we met in supposedly 'good' society."

Jane tried hard not to show her shock. Such behavior wasn't common among her peers. Many men treated their illegitimate children well—tried to find suitable matches for them or gain them good positions of employment—but they rarely introduced them to their legitimate children. And for the two sets to be raised together? It was unheard of.

Lisette carved some roast beef. "What did you think made us all so chummy?"

"I don't know. Dom's championing of you, I suppose.

I just . . . I never put it together until now." She ventured a look at Dom, who watched her with a hooded expression. "Have the three of you known each other since birth?"

"Pretty much." Dom smiled at Lisette. "I first met Mrs. Bonnaud when I was five and Father took me to the cottage to see my new baby sister."

Lisette eyed him askance. "He didn't call me that, did he?"

"Not yet, no. I was too young." Dom let the footman serve him some beef. "That didn't keep me from being curious, though. Tristan was toddling about, and Father and Mrs. Bonnaud were clearly very friendly, so I asked where Mrs. Bonnaud's husband was. Father, evasive as usual, said he was helping her get on without one."

Lisette snorted. "Helping her? That's what he called it?"

"You know Father. Never wanted to state the truth outright. And being a nosy little fellow, I persisted in my interrogation. I asked him if Mr. Bonnaud had died, like my mother."

With a sidelong smile at Jane, Lisette said, "Leave it to Dom to pose the hard questions."

"For all the good it did me," Dom said. "He brushed off that particular detail. He never liked to *answer* the hard questions." His face seemed to ice over. "Of course, George was more than happy to answer them on his leave from school. That was when I first heard the words *whore* and *bastard*."

"I can only imagine what he told you." Lisette

looked over at Jane. "George was never as happy about the arrangement as the rest of us."

"So he wasn't part of those jolly family get-togethers where you performed operas?" Jane said.

"He could have been, when he was on holiday," Dom answered in a hard voice. "Father invited him. And when Father was off on one of his trips, Mrs. Bonnaud invited George over. *I* invited George over. He always said it was beneath him to associate with them. And once he got old enough to spend holidays with friends, he preferred that. So did we, quite frankly."

"I can understand why." Jane shook her head. "The way he used to talk about Tristan and Lisette made even my blood boil. But I dared not voice my opinions. I never wanted to make things harder for Nancy by rousing his anger."

"I don't know how you were even able to tolerate him," Lisette said incredulously.

Jane shrugged. "I didn't spend much time with him. He was fairly easy to avoid whenever I was in the country visiting Nancy; he was always hunting or going to some horse race. And in London, when I dined with them, he and Nancy just spent the meal relating whatever gossip they'd heard." She grimaced. "That was one thing they had in common. Both of them loved to gossip about the *ton*."

"I'll admit we did our share of gossiping, too," Lisette said, a bit shamefacedly. "When he was home, Papa would read us the papers and make fun of the people in them. Perhaps that's who George got it from."

"When he was home?" Jane echoed, eager for more stories of their odd upbringing that might shed light on Dom's character. "What happened to Dom when your father was gone?"

"Well, though I don't remember it myself," Lisette said, "Maman told me that Dom was left with an indifferent nurse back then. So when he was about six, Maman complained about that situation to Papa and won the right to have Dom visit us whenever he wished."

"Which was pretty much all the time." Dom swallowed some wine. "Rathmoor Park was large and rather scary for a boy alone with 'an indifferent nurse.'"

A lump stuck in Jane's throat. "It must have been lonely, too."

He nodded tersely. "Even after Father hired me a tutor, I preferred to spend my spare moments at the cottage."

"And we had such grand times, the four of us, even without Papa," Lisette said cheerily. "Our own footraces and readings and musicales. Dom, do you remember . . ."

For the remainder of the dinner, Jane listened in fascination as Dom and Lisette traversed the years of memories that had ended abruptly when Dom turned nineteen and their close-knit family was shattered. As they talked, Jane realigned and reconstructed her assumptions about Dom and the Bonnauds.

How she wished she'd known some of this years ago. It would have explained a few things, softened a few blows. Though it did leave her with questions for Dom. Unfortunately, this was neither the time nor the place to ask them.

As they finished dessert, Lisette said, "After the *bousine* incident, Papa gave Maman a harpsichord he found in their attic. But she could never master it."

"Because she never practiced," Dom said with a laugh. "And neither did you."

Lisette gave her characteristically Gallic shrug. "What would have been the point? I have two left thumbs when it comes to any sort of instrument." She slanted a glance at her husband. "But did you know that *Jane* plays? And quite well, too."

"Oh? When did you hear her play?" Max asked, eyeing Jane with surprise.

"At her engagement party to Dom, of course. He insisted upon it."

Dom regarded Jane with a warm gaze. "She played Mozart's Nineteenth Piano Sonata. Even though she prefers Beethoven. She did it for me."

The fact that he remembered what she played, coupled with the way he was looking at her, made Jane's breath catch in her throat. With some difficulty, she tore her gaze from his and lied, "I only did it because Beethoven's sonatas are all too long."

"Right," was all he said. With his extensive knowledge of Beethoven, he could challenge the lie easily. Thankfully, he didn't.

But she could feel his eyes on her, feel the very air crackle between them.

"Well, the Mozart was lovely," Lisette said. "I know! You should play it for us now!"

Jane blinked. The last thing she needed was to rouse her bittersweet memories of their engagement party. "I-I don't have the music."

"Oh, I'm sure we must have a copy somewhere in the music room," Lisette persisted. "Max's mother loved playing the pianoforte. Max, do you think—"

"Lisette," Dom broke in with that firm tone that brooked no argument, "can't you see that Jane is tired? She couldn't have had more than two or three hours of sleep last night, and her nap this afternoon couldn't have made up for that. We've already spent most of dinner boring her with tales of our childhood. Let her be."

Jane's gaze shot to him, and the compassion and understanding she saw in his face made her heart constrict. Just when she thought there was only one Dom—the stiff and controlling one who worried her with his similarity to Papa—he showed glimpses of that other side to remind her of the man she'd once loved.

Once. That was the important part. Though sometimes she had trouble remembering it.

"I really am exhausted," she said, flashing him a grateful smile. "We have a long journey ahead of us tomorrow, and I would very much like to retire."

"Oh, of course, my dear," Lisette said readily. "I wasn't thinking."

"We should all probably retire," Max said. "Lisette, why don't you and Jane go on up now that dinner's finished? Dom and I will have our glass of port and be along shortly."

"Excellent idea." Lisette rose and held out her hand. "Come, Jane, let me show you to your room. This house can be impossible to navigate when you're not familiar with it."

With a nod, Jane joined her. But as they climbed the stairs, the earlier conversation at dinner rose to haunt her.

She looked over at Lisette. "I know that Dom's mother died in childbirth. Was that before your mother became your father's mistress, or after? Dom never said." And she'd never asked.

Lisette tensed. "After. We recently learned that, much like Nancy, the previous Lady Rathmoor had some difficulties bearing children. The doctor had told her after George's birth that she mustn't get pregnant again."

"So your father turned to your mother."

Lisette nodded. They climbed a few more steps in silence.

Then Jane ventured another question. "You said that your mother 'won the right to have Dom visit us whenever he wished.' So she *wanted* him there, right? Even though he was son to the woman who'd first had your father's heart?"

"I'm not sure anyone ever had Papa's heart," Lisette said dryly. "In case you hadn't guessed, he was a rather selfish man."

"But he did let Dom spend time with all of you. So

he must have believed that your mother really cared about him."

"We *all* really cared about him," Lisette said fiercely. "He was big brother to Tristan and me, and he played the dutiful son to Maman. I missed Dom terribly during the years we were in France. He came to visit a couple of times on business, but other than that, we didn't see him."

That raised more of Jane's questions, but these were ones that only Dom could answer. And she wouldn't be able to sleep unless she asked them.

"Um, I think I left my handkerchief on the table," Jane said. "I'll just run down and fetch it. There's no need to wait for me—you go on to bed."

Lisette stopped to stare at her in bewilderment. "Your handkerchief will be perfectly fine where it is. A footman will find it and give it to you in the morning."

"No, I dare not leave it or I'll forget about it in the confusion of our departure." She was already turning to descend the stairs. "And it's my favorite."

Jane didn't stop to see if Lisette believed that nonsense. She just hastened down, trying to figure out how to get Dom alone.

Fortunately, just as she approached the dining room, she heard the duke say from inside, "Sorry to be a wet blanket, old chap, but I shall turn in, too. Lisette and I don't usually rise as early as we did this morning."

"So I've noticed." Then Dom added hastily, "Not that it matters, mind you. Everyone has his own habits."

"Yes, that's true." The duke's puzzled tone showed he

was unaware of what his wife had said yesterday about his "habits."

"Don't forget that we must leave as early tomorrow as possible."

"Of course."

"I'm hoping Tristan will have arrived by then, but if not, we'll press on without him."

"Certainly," Max said, rather stiffly now. He probably wasn't used to being ordered about by anyone, even his brother-in-law. "Well, good night, then."

Hearing footsteps approaching, Jane darted quickly into an alcove and waited with heart pounding as the duke emerged from the dining room. He strode, with a surprisingly quick step for a man who claimed to be tired, in the direction his wife had gone.

Only after he'd disappeared up the stairs did Jane relax. This was her chance.

✦ ✦ ✦

DOM SWALLOWED THE last of his port, glad that Max had retired. He was in no mood for company right now.

Had he really never told Jane what Lisette and Tristan and their mother had meant to him? He supposed not. Though he probably shouldn't have let Lisette go on and on about their early years at Rathmoor Park—Jane must have found the stories deadly dull. Still, they had to have been better than hearing Lisette speak of the engagement party.

He groaned. The look of panic on Jane's face when

Lisette had proposed having Jane play the Mozart sonata again had thrust a knife into his chest. He recognized that look. Jane had worn it when she'd found him and Nancy together.

Feeling the servants watching for him to leave so they could clear the dining room, he rose from the table and walked out into the hall. He and Jane still hadn't talked much about that night in the library beyond settling the fact that he'd arranged the encounter. Now he wondered if a tiny part of her still believed what she'd seen.

"Dom, may I speak to you a moment?"

He started, his blood quickening as he whirled around to find Jane standing in the hall. Good God, was she some sprite he conjured up whenever he thought of her?

Sadly, no, or she would have shown up in his bedchamber at least once a night in the past twelve years.

Voices sounded in the dining room as the servants stacked up dishes. They would soon emerge into the hall. Without a word, he drew Jane through the nearest open doorway, then shut the door to give them more privacy.

A low fire burned in the hearth, and one lamp was lit as if someone had expected to use this room. Belatedly he realized this was the music room Lisette had mentioned earlier.

Jane didn't seem to notice. She stood there anxiously, her gaze fixed on him.

"What is it you wish to discuss?" he prodded. Watching indecision play over her face, Dom braced himself for anything.

Then Jane steadied her shoulders. "You loved her very much, didn't you?"

His heart dropped into his stomach. "Who?"

"Mrs. Bonnaud."

Oh, thank God. For half a moment, he'd thought she was talking about Nancy. "Yes, I did. She was the closest thing I ever had to a mother."

Jane wouldn't meet his eyes, and her hands were a veritable flurry of smoothing and straightening her skirts. "At least that explains why you chose her and her children over me."

That flummoxed him. "I didn't choose them over you, Jane."

"Not directly," she said hastily. "But the result was the same. You chose to help them, and George punished you for it by refusing to give you any money or support. Which kept you and me from being able to marry. So, in a way, you did choose them. I mean, you probably didn't think of it that way at the time but—"

"No, I didn't." He had to make her understand. "And I didn't have any choice, either. George demanded that I hand Tristan over to him and his men to be hanged. What else was I to do?"

The color drained from Jane's face as her gaze shot to his. "Hanged! You never said anything about hanging."

He gaped at her a moment before the past came flooding back. "God, I'm an idiot. I forgot that I never told you about the horse theft."

"You certainly didn't." She crossed her arms over her chest. "You told me that after your father died and George burned the codicil, George added insult to injury by kicking the Bonnauds out of the cottage your father had given to them. You said you helped them leave England, which so infuriated George that he wouldn't give you a penny of the inheritance you ought to have received. There was no mention of any hanging."

"I . . . er . . . well . . ." Dom dragged one hand through his hair. "I suppose there's no point in keeping it secret now, with George dead." He released a heavy breath. "Tristan stole the horse Father bequeathed to him, then sold it to gain funds to support his mother and Lisette. He thought George wouldn't be able to prove the theft, but George found someone who'd seen Tristan do it. So George was bent on having Tristan hanged."

Her eyes got huge.

"George came to the cottage looking for Tristan. I happened to be there, but I refused to reveal where Tristan was hiding, so George essentially disinherited me. That's why the Bonnauds fled to France, and why I helped them. Because I saw no other way out."

"Of course not!" Jane said. "You couldn't let him hang your brother."

"Exactly."

A frown knit her brow. "Still, you could have told me. If I'd had any idea that your rift with George was over something so . . . so . . ."

"Illegal?" Dom said dryly. "I didn't dare tell anyone, even you. One word to the wrong person about my helping a fugitive would have meant an end to my new position as a runner. I couldn't risk it."

"But if I'd known, I would never have brought George into the library. I wouldn't have gone near him."

He blinked. "Don't be silly—that wasn't *your* fault. Barlow talked you into that at Nancy's instigation, so she'd have a titled knight errant who'd feel sorry enough for her to marry her."

Jane's eyes narrowed. "What do you mean? Nancy had nothing to do with George's presence."

A sudden unease rose in his belly that he instantly squelched. Nancy had to have been responsible somehow. Jane simply didn't understand. "I take it that Nancy told you it was all Barlow's idea."

"No." Jane looked thoroughly bewildered. "She never said a word about that. Because I was the one to decide that he should accompany me."

His unease grew to a churning in his stomach. "That can't be. Barlow had to have . . . manipulated you somehow. Why on earth would you have brought George in there when you knew about me and him?"

"I didn't know everything, did I?" she said irritably. "I thought I could mend the rift by getting you two to discuss things." Eyes alight, she planted her hands on her hips. "If I'd had any idea that George had tried to get your brother *killed*, I certainly wouldn't have pursued such a foolish plan."

Dom could hardly breathe. All this time he'd been sure that Nancy had somehow convinced Barlow to involve George, that she'd done it to further her own future as she helped him alter his. "So it was *your* idea to bring George in," he said inanely.

"Yes. *Entirely* my idea. I can't believe you ever thought otherwise." Jane shook her head at him as if he were a child. "She was risking her reputation to help you. Why would she do that in front of someone as dangerous and unpredictable as George?"

"She didn't know he was dangerous," Dom said hollowly.

He didn't need Jane's snort to tell him how idiotic that sounded. Because it finally hit him why he'd deliberately misconstrued the situation. It was easier to believe that Nancy had ended up with George through her own machinations than to admit his own part in bringing it about.

"Samuel tried to stop me," Jane went on, "but I didn't listen. I got rid of him and took George in there instead."

"Oh, God, Jane. I never thought . . . I always assumed . . ."

"That's what happens, Dom, when you play the puppet master. People aren't puppets. *People* make decisions on their own and behave as they will." Her voice was cold, accusing. "You can set a plan in motion, but as soon as it involves *people*, it will rarely commence exactly as you wish."

The taunt sank deep inside his soul. He remembered a far more disastrous case of a plan going awry. It hadn't been his plan, thank God, but he still hadn't been able to alter its deadly outcome.

Men had died. Women and *children* had died, and all because some fool had thought to control an unruly crowd with violence. All because Dom's hands had been tied. That was when Dom had learned the lesson that plans must be carefully laid whenever they involved *people*.

"It works far better," Jane went on, apparently still intent on berating him, "when you trust those people with the truth. When you give them all the facts."

Her tone put him on the defensive. "You mean, the way you did when you told me about Nancy's disappearance?"

Jane paled. "Well . . . that was different."

"How so?" He approached her with a scowl. "You left out the important fact that she might be pregnant. If I'd known, we would all have left for York as soon as Tristan could join us, and we wouldn't have wasted so much time."

Her throat moved convulsively. "You can't blame me for that. I was protecting Nancy."

"And all those years ago, I was protecting *you*," he said fiercely. He took another step toward her. "I know you resent how I manipulated you into jilting me, but my damned brother had just torn my family apart, and I wasn't sure what lay ahead of me. I couldn't bear to watch your love for me die in the slums of London."

"So you killed it instead?" she choked out.

His heart faltered. "*Did* I?"

Alarm spread over her face. Then she turned, as if to flee.

He grabbed her arm to tug her up close to him. She wouldn't look at him, which only inflamed him more. "I answered your questions," he rasped. "Now answer mine."

He could feel her tremble, see uncertainty flash over her face in profile. Utter silence reigned in the room. Even the servants had apparently finished in the dining room across the hall, for no sound penetrated their private little sanctuary.

"I can't," she whispered at last. "I don't know the answer."

11

JANE KNEW FROM Dom's flinch that he'd been hoping for a different response, but she couldn't help it—she spoke the truth.

When he acted like a gentleman, as he had at dinner, she remembered exactly why she'd fallen in love with him. But when he reminded her of how he'd made assumptions and, worse yet, used those assumptions to decide her future for her, she couldn't bear it. Because he was still doing it, still demanding his way and dictating terms and ignoring her concerns.

She understood the courtly gentleman. It was the autocratic devil she had trouble understanding.

And she might as well admit it. She twisted her head to look up at him. "I don't know *how* I feel about you anymore."

The pain that slashed over his features only confused her further. Was he genuinely hurt by the thought that he'd killed her love? Or was his pride merely bruised because he hadn't been able to step right back into her life as if the past meant nothing?

"At least tell me the truth about Blakeborough," he said hoarsely. "Do you love *him*?"

"Why does it matter?"

His eyes ate her up. "If you do, I'll keep my distance. I'll stay out of your life from now on."

"You've been doing that easily enough for the past twelve years," she snapped. "I don't see why my feelings for Edwin should change anything."

"Easily? It was never easy, I assure you." His expression was stony. "And you're avoiding the question. *Are you in love with Blakeborough?*"

How she wished she could lie about it. Dom would take himself off, and she wouldn't be tempted by him anymore. Unfortunately, he could always tell when she was lying. "And if I say I'm not?"

"Then I won't rest until you're mine again."

The determination in his voice rocked her. Unsettled her.

Thrilled her.

No! "I don't want that."

His fingers dug into her arm. "Because you love Blakeborough?"

"Because love is a lie designed to make a woman desire what is only a figure of smoke in the wind. Love is too dangerous."

He released a heavy breath. "So you *don't* love him."

His persistence sparked her temper, and she pushed free of him. "Oh, for pity's sake, if you must know, I don't." She faced him down. "Not that it matters one whit. I don't need love to have a good marriage, an amiable marriage. I don't even *want* love."

It hurt too much when her heart was trampled upon. Dom had done that once before. How could she be sure he wouldn't do it again?

Eyes gleaming in the firelight, he said in a low voice, "You used to want love."

"I was practically a child. I didn't know any better. But I do now."

"Do you? I wonder." He circled her like a wolf assessing its prey's weaknesses. "Very well, let's forget about love for the moment. What about passion?"

"What about it?" she asked unsteadily as he slipped behind her. Nervous, she edged nearer the impressively massive pianoforte that sat in the center of the room.

"What part does passion play in your plan for a safe and loveless marriage?"

She pivoted to face him, startled to find that he'd stepped to within a breath of her. "None at all."

He chuckled. "Does Blakeborough know that?"

"Not that it's any of your concern, but Edwin and I have an arrangement. He'll give me children; I'll help him make sure Yvette finds a good husband. We both agree that passion is . . . unimportant to our plans."

"Really?" He raised an eyebrow. "It certainly aids in the production of those children you're hoping for. To quote a certain lady, 'You can set a plan in motion, but as soon as it involves *people*, it will rarely commence exactly as you wish.' You may not want passion to be important, sweeting, but it always is."

"Not to us," she said, though with him standing so close her legs felt like rubber and her blood raced wildly through her veins. "Not to *me*."

With his gaze darkening, he lifted his hand to run his thumb over the pounding pulse at her throat. "Yes, I can tell how unimportant it is to you."

"That doesn't mean . . . anything."

"Doesn't it?" He backed her against the pianoforte. "So the way you trembled in my arms this morning means nothing."

It meant far too much. It meant her body was susceptible to him, even when her mind had the good sense to resist.

And curse him to the devil, he knew it. He slipped his hand about her waist to pull her against him. "It means nothing that every time we're together, we ignite."

"People do not . . . ignite," she said shakily, though her entire body was on fire. "What an absurd idea."

She held her breath and waited for his attempt to kiss her, determined to refuse it this time.

But he didn't kiss her. Instead he fondled her breast through her gown, catching her so by surprise that she gasped, then moaned as the feel of his hand caressing her made liquid heat swirl in her belly.

Devil take the man.

"I don't know," he rasped, "you certainly feel warm to *me*." He kissed her flaming cheek, then dragged his mouth down her jaw to her throat. "God knows *I'm* on fire. You've set me aflame."

She curled her fingers into his coat sleeves, meaning to pull him away. But he was tonguing her throat and kneading her breast, and her mind was all a muddle. It felt so . . . so *good*. Which meant it had to be wrong.

"Dom . . . we mustn't . . ."

"No?" His thumb stroked the edge of her bodice. "Why did you wear this provocative bit of scarlet silk to dinner, then, if not to entice me? You can't tell me you had no other gowns in your trunk."

She closed her eyes in a vain attempt to steel herself against his words. "Perhaps I simply wanted to torture you for not choosing me when you had the chance."

"Then it's working." His voice turned ragged, rough. "I spent the entire dinner desiring you, yearning to touch you like this."

"Good," she said, rather gratified that he saw her as such a siren.

"You like that, don't you? You enjoy tempting me into madness." His breath beat hot against her cheek as he thumbed her nipple.

It instantly hardened, the traitorous thing. He'd taken control yet again, turning her to putty just by touching her.

All right, then. While it might be beyond her power to stop desiring him entirely, she didn't have to let him control the attraction. In her years of dreaming of him—the admittedly chaste dreams of a virgin—*she* had been in control, making him burn and yearn, making him regret that he'd ever put her aside.

Perhaps it was time to fulfill those dreams.

She opened her eyes to find him watching her with a heavy-lidded gaze that promised all manner of sensual pleasures if she would just give herself over to him. She would make him keep that promise . . . but without giving up herself.

Edwin would undoubtedly disapprove of this dalliance, but just now she didn't care. Dom was about to learn that she wouldn't be ruled by him or any other man.

Looping her arms about his neck, she rose up on tiptoe to kiss his mouth. This time she was the one to instigate the duel of tongues and lips that sent her senses reeling. This time she was the one in control.

Until Dom pulled down her bodice and corset and shift to bare her breasts. Oh, sweet Lord in heaven. He was more wicked—and more wonderful at this—than even she could have imagined.

But she could be wicked, too. Remembering what Nancy had told her about men, she reached down between them to cup the hard length of him through his trousers.

He jerked back. "What are you doing?"

How wonderful to be the one to shock *him!* Though she noticed he didn't step away or pull her hand off him. And his flesh seemed to grow beneath her very fingers. "Don't you like it?" she said in what she hoped was a sultry-sounding voice.

"Good God, yes." He practically groaned the words. "But where the blazes did you learn to do it?"

"Nancy said men like to be touched . . . down there."

"Wonderful. Now the sinner is instructing the saint," he muttered before he took her mouth again, giving her no chance to protest that she wasn't as saintly as he assumed.

But clearly he'd guessed because he leaned into her hand, letting her fully explore the male appendage that Nancy had only described in furtive whispers.

To Jane's delight, the more she rubbed him through his trousers, the more his kiss changed, grew bolder, hotter, fiercer. How delicious! They had certainly never done anything like *this* in their youth. Perhaps if they had, he wouldn't have been so content to toss her aside.

It was definitely making her ignite. Or perhaps it was his hands roaming her body doing that. Whichever the case, an unfamiliar ache began between her legs that made her want to squirm. So she focused on caressing him with renewed vigor, hoping to regain control over this . . . insanity.

He grabbed her hand to still it.

She tore her mouth from his. "What? Am I doing it wrong?"

"If you do it any more right, I will embarrass myself." He fixed her with a dark stare. "Or perhaps that's what you want. Another way to torture me."

"I don't know what you mean. Am I doing it right or am I torturing you? Which is it?"

He searched her face, then, apparently satisfied with

what he saw there, smiled faintly. "Both." Taking her by surprise, he dropped onto the pianoforte bench and tugged her across his lap. "Here, I'll show you."

As he drew her skirts up to her knees, she froze. "I don't know if this is . . . such a good idea, Dom."

"Oh, trust me, it's a fine idea." He smoothed his hands up her stockings and past her garters until he came to her drawers. "Before you go running off to seal your 'arrangement' with Blakeborough, you should at least have a *taste* of passion. Just so you'll know how important it really is." Pressing his mouth to her ear, he added, "Men aren't the only ones who like to be touched there, sweeting."

That remark *really* made her want to squirm, but before she could ask about it, he kissed her mouth again and she gave herself up to the kiss. And then he was stroking her between her legs, right where she ached.

Her legs fell open, she wasn't even sure how. Then his clever fingers were inside her drawers and finding the delicate flesh beneath her curls and doing outrageous things to it that made her shimmy and wriggle on his lap.

"Feels good, doesn't it?" he rasped against her lips.

"Yes. Is it . . . too very wicked?"

He gave a strained laugh. "Not too very wicked." He delved inside her with one finger.

"Dom!" she squeaked, but he continued the caress, and her heart felt as if it might leap from her chest, it raced so hard. "*Dom* . . . That's . . . oh . . ."

"God, sweeting," he said as he slid his finger in and

out, driving her insane, "don't ever tell me again that passion means nothing to you. You're so warm and wet. Perfect. So beautifully perfect."

Seizing her mouth again, he stroked her with slow, sensuous movements that melted all her insides. Then he kissed his way down her chin to her neck and farther as he bent her back so he could reach her breast.

She made no attempt to halt him. She wanted his kiss there, as it had been this morning through her gown, wanted his tongue on her nipple. With a growl of pure satisfaction he took her breast in his mouth.

"Oh, sweet Lord," she whispered.

His fingers fondled her oh so cleverly below, and his mouth sucked her oh so cleverly above, and all she could do was clutch his neck and hang on for dear life as a rush of feeling swept up her body.

So *this* was passion, these intense sensations centered below her belly that made her feel boneless as satin and . . . and hot as . . .

Faith, she couldn't think what. Her knees were open and her bosom bare, and she just wanted more. *More.* More heat, more stroking, more . . .

A keening began low in her throat that matched the building intensity between her legs. His fingers inside her fell into a provocative, rushing rhythm that was like . . . like . . .

"That's it, my lovely Jane," Dom whispered against her breast. "Give yourself to the dance."

Ah, yes, like dancing. Only better. Because the music rising inside her came from her pounding heart and beating blood, from Dom's devilish playing upon her privates, from the crescendo . . . of her own . . . quickening . . . gasps . . .

Someone screamed. Her, apparently, for Dom uttered an oath seconds before he swallowed her cry with his kiss.

And just like that, she vaulted out of the dance into heaven. Her body shook and her hand gripped his neck hard enough to leave marks, and it was *marvelous*. Every inch of her felt alive, from bones to flesh to skin.

She wanted to shout, but Dom's mouth wouldn't leave hers. His tongue slid silkily in and out, slowing, softening, bringing her down from wherever it was she'd been.

After a while, his kiss gentled to a tender sweetness that made her ache in a different way.

In her heart. Her stupid, foolish heart.

Regretfully, she drew her lips from his, and he let her, though his gaze didn't leave her face. He drew up her bodice, pulled down her skirts, and lifted her until she was sitting straight up on his lap.

His *thing* felt like a rod of iron beneath her bottom, but he made no move to have her touch it again. Which was good because at the moment, she could only sit there, limp and panting.

He briefly kissed her forehead. "That, sweeting, is passion," he said in a throttled voice.

She nodded. It was all she could manage.

"And if you wish to leave this room an innocent, you'd best go without delay."

That startled her. But she was grateful for the warning. Because now that their encounter was done, and she was returning to reality, she realized how mad this was. If she still meant to marry Edwin . . .

No, she couldn't think about that. Not right now, when she had Dom's taste in her mouth and his scent engulfing her senses.

Blushing, she rose from his lap and straightened her clothes, sure that if she came across anyone in the halls, they would guess at once what she'd been doing. Thank heaven the servants had probably already retired to their quarters. She would die if any of them saw her and guessed she'd been playing the wanton.

"Dom . . ." she began, not sure what to say. *Thank you? That was lovely? When may we do it again?*

Not that. If they ever did *this* again, she wouldn't rest until he made her his. And she still wasn't sure she wanted that.

"It's all right, Jane," he said tightly, as if he could read the conflict inside her. "Get some sleep. We'll talk tomorrow."

She bobbed her head and fled. But an errant and disturbing thought hit her as she climbed the stairs.

If I, as a maiden, can so readily give in to Dom's charms, how much more readily will an experienced widow like Nancy give in to Samuel's?

12

Dom sat there in a state of acute arousal long after Jane left. He was out of control. He *hated* that. Most of the time he knew exactly what he wanted and how to get it in the most efficient manner. But when it came to Jane . . .

Damn the wench, but she destroyed his control whenever she entered a room. Seeing her at dinner in that crimson dress, with garnets sparkling at her throat, had made it impossible for him not to touch her when she'd shown up outside the dining room alone.

Though he didn't regret it. The feel of Jane coming apart in his hands was like nothing he'd ever known. Just remembering it had him fully aroused again. Blast.

Then he heard a noise in the hall. Was that Jane, come back to finish their encounter? But no, when a figure appeared in the doorway, it proved to be Tristan.

Good God. "How long have you been here?" Dom remained seated, hoping that the position would make it easier to keep his brother from noticing the arousal emblazoned on his trousers.

Tristan thrust his hands in his coat pockets. "Long enough to see Jane leave looking rather . . . disheveled." His voice had an edge to it. "Take care, Dom. She's toying with you."

I know. "What makes you say that?"

"For one thing, she seems none too fond of you. For another, she's engaged to someone else." Tristan came into the room. "Yet every time the two of you get the chance to be alone, we find you . . . well . . ."

"Talking? That's all we're doing, you know."

Tristan snorted. "Right. Because you're on such good terms."

Dom tensed. They could be. If he could manage to melt the glacier of a past that lay between them. "We get along well enough, under the circumstances."

"Yes, and what are those circumstances, exactly?" Tristan walked closer. "She's behaving rather like a woman scorned, which is odd when one considers that *she* jilted *you*. She did, didn't she?"

Dom avoided his brother's speculative gaze. "It's a bit more . . . complicated than that."

"I thought it might be." Tristan dropped into a chair before the fire. "But she really *is* engaged to Blakeborough, is she not?"

A sigh escaped Dom. "That's complicated, too." Especially now that Dom had learned she wasn't in love with the chap.

Love is too dangerous.

She certainly was right about that.

"Leave it to you to complicate a simple situation," Tristan said.

With his arousal effectively banished, Dom rose. "You and Zoe did the same," he said irritably.

Tristan shrugged. "Not really. I got her into my bed as soon as I could manage it, and all our complications vanished after that." He watched as Dom paced the room. "Though I wouldn't attempt that with Jane if I were you."

"I wouldn't dream of it."

Yet he *was* dreaming of it, of having her right where he wanted her, where he could tease and taste and touch every fragrant inch of her to his heart's content. Where he could have her beneath him, where he could be inside her. After all, if he compromised her, she'd *have* to marry him.

But if he did that, she would never forgive him. It would be hard enough to get her to forgive him as it was. She seemed to think he'd been dictatorial in his decision to force their parting. And though he knew he'd done the right thing, there was no point in adding more ice to the glacier by arguing the matter.

"Are you still in love with her?" Tristan asked.

Tristan always got right to the point, damn him.

"I don't know. If love is an obsession that grabs you by the throat and won't let go, then I very well may be."

"That sounds more like lust to me."

"Aren't they supposed to go hand in hand?" Dom snapped. He couldn't believe he was having this conversation with his brother.

"For men? Not always. But for gently bred women, almost certainly."

Dom hoped to God that was true. Because Jane had been pure liquid fire beneath his touch. And he fervently prayed that she would be so again. He would *not* let her marry Blakeborough without a fight.

But he didn't mean to tell Tristan that. The bloody devil had already guessed far too much about the situation between him and Jane as it was.

Dom halted to stare at his brother. "Did you learn anything more in York?"

"So, we're changing the subject now, are we?" At Dom's dour look, Tristan laughed. "Fine, have it your way." Leaning forward in the chair, Tristan rested his elbows on his knees. "I did actually learn a few things. Had you heard what Barlow does for income these days?"

"I assumed it was gambling or some such."

"Tangentially related. He arranges prizefights in York and the surrounding areas. He uses his connections among the *ton* to find backers who don't mind traveling up to York for a really good mill. He's not getting rich, by any means, but he makes enough to keep him in brandy and cravats."

"So he definitely might be interested in marrying Nancy."

"Actually, I found out more about that, too."

Dom's gut clenched. "They've been spending time together."

"Yes, but not the way you'd think. I spoke to everyone in his lodging house. No one had *ever* seen them together there."

"They could have gone to an inn."

"Perhaps, but I couldn't find any evidence of that. I did, however, speak to several shopkeepers who knew Nancy. They said that Barlow sometimes joined her and her maid while they shopped."

Tristan leaned back to put his feet on the hassock. "But although the shopkeepers described a definite flirtation, it didn't sound like anything more. Barlow flattered Nancy, she teased him, and that was that. He didn't even buy her gifts. It was all perfectly respectable."

"I wonder if George would have seen it that way," Dom muttered.

"I doubt it. But from what I heard, they did nothing truly wrong. Nancy had Meredith with her at all times, they were never seen without the maid, and at no point did anyone suspect a physical relationship."

"That doesn't mean there wasn't one."

"No." Tristan crossed his ankles. "And in fact, I have one rather large piece of information that could imply that there was."

"Oh?"

"It took me awhile, but I finally found an inn servant who'd actually witnessed them leaving for London together."

Dom lifted an eyebrow. "Don't tell me. Nancy went with him of her own accord."

"Not only that, but the servant overheard Barlow

telling her that the doctor they were to see in London was the best money could buy. That she needn't worry about that."

"The doctor who was meant to confirm her pregnancy?"

"I don't know. That's all the servant heard."

"Damn." Scrubbing a hand over his face, Dom paced to the fireplace. "If she's seeing a doctor, she probably really is pregnant. And Barlow did tell the innkeeper as much."

"Yes, but if she has a history of miscarrying, wouldn't a carriage trip to London increase her risk of losing the child? Why would she take such a chance?"

"Nancy may not have considered that possibility," Dom said. "She's not terribly bright."

"Or Barlow might have forced her hand somehow."

Dom frowned at him. "Don't tell me you're listening to Jane's wild theories now."

"I'm not listening to anyone's theories. I am trying to keep an open mind and listen to the facts, and the facts aren't making sense."

Blast. Was Jane right? Had Dom been so biased against Nancy heretofore that he hadn't thought rationally about this? "But we're still sure that they're headed to London?"

"I've seen nothing to indicate otherwise."

"Do you have any idea where he would take her in the city?"

Tristan shook his head. "We could probably track them to the inn where the rented post chaise ends up, but they're too far ahead of us now for us to catch up to them before they disembark. So finding the inn won't do us any good unless we happen to stumble upon the hackney that took them to their destination from there."

"Not much chance of that at a busy coaching inn," Dom said, "although I suppose it's worth the attempt." He thought a moment. "Or . . ."

"Or what?"

"Our route from here to London takes us right by Saffron Walden, does it not?"

Tristan shrugged. "I suppose."

"Ravenswood's estate is near there. And with Parliament not in session because of Whitsuntide, we might actually find him at home."

"*Viscount* Ravenswood? The undersecretary to the Home Office?"

Dom smiled grimly. "Also a spymaster with whom I've had substantial dealings."

"Oh, right. I forgot that you worked for him at one point."

"He's had his finger in every pie. He may know what caused the rift between Barlow and his family, which could help us figure out the man's purpose. And Ravenswood would also have kept an eye on Barlow because of the man's involvement with boxing and the *ton*. Prizefights are still illegal, no matter how many gentlemen attend them."

"But will he give us the information we need? Spymasters are notoriously closemouthed."

"He'll give it to me." Dom rubbed his scar, remembering that awful day in Manchester . . . and Ravenswood's part in sending him there. "He owes me."

"Then we might as well stop to speak with him. It's quite a drive from here to Saffron Walden, but it's on our way and with good weather and the longer days we ought to be able to reach it by evening tomorrow, as long as we leave early."

"I've already warned Max of that. Although we ought to start out tonight. The less time we waste on the road, the more chance we can find Barlow and Nancy once we reach London."

"I agree," Tristan said, "but it's dark as pitch out there. We're not getting much of a moon tonight. I don't think we should risk it, especially since one of us at least will have to drive the phaeton. Besides, the rest of our party has retired, and I've gone two days already with little to no sleep. As have you."

"You're right. And we both need to be fresh when we reach London, if we're to track down Barlow and Nancy."

"Exactly."

Dom stared into the fire. "I wish you didn't have to tell Jane any of what you've told me about him."

Tristan eyed him askance. "Why?"

Because Dom had her so close to being his again that he could practically taste it. Merely reminding her of his suspicions regarding Nancy might send Jane back behind her stalwart defenses.

"I hate upsetting her until we know more," Dom said.

"I can understand that. But she's going to ask me what I found out, and I have to tell her *something*."

"I know. Just try to keep to the bare facts, will you? No speculations."

"I'll do my best."

Dom snorted. He knew what that meant—that Jane wasn't the sort of female to be fobbed off with bare facts. So tomorrow's drive to Saffron Walden was going to be anything but easy. Unless . . .

He began to smile. Yes, that would definitely work.

+ + +

THE NEXT MORNING, Jane stood in the foyer of Max's country house in Newark, hardly able to believe her ears. "What do you mean, they're gone?"

Lisette seemed rather flustered as she directed the servants on where to place her trunk in the coach. "Apparently Tristan arrived late last night, after we'd retired. He reported to Dom, they went to bed for a few hours, and they rose early to head off in Dom's phaeton."

To avoid speaking with Jane, no doubt. Bad enough that she had tossed and turned half the night, but now to have *this* happen . . .

What if Tristan had learned something truly alarming? What if *that* was why they'd raced off? "Did they leave a note to explain?"

"No."

She was going to kill Dom. Or his brother. Or both. "So they left us behind to go investigate, without a word as to what Tristan had learned in York."

"Not quite. According to our butler, we're to meet them at some man's estate in Saffron Walden this evening. By the time we arrive, they will have gathered all their information, and then the five of us can go straight on to London. I gather that Dom wanted to lose no time, which is why he and Tristan chose to go on ahead."

That mollified her a little. At least they weren't trying to cut her out of the search completely. Still . . . "Did they mention whom they were going to see?"

Max came up beside her. "The Viscount Ravenswood."

"Oh! Isn't he quite high in the government?"

"You could say that." Max flashed her an indulgent smile. "He works directly for the Home Secretary. Rumor has it that they're grooming him to be prime minister."

Jane blinked. "But . . . But what could he possibly have to do with Nancy and Samuel?"

"Dom is undoubtedly relying on Ravenswood for information," Max said. "The Home Office is in charge of the Bow Street Runners, you know. So I'm sure Dom worked for the man at some point."

Of course! The Home Office—and Dom in particular—had been lauded for halting the members of the Cato Street Conspiracy, among other things. Obviously, there was a connection there. Still . . .

"What kind of information does he hope to glean?"

"We've no idea," Lisette said testily. "Before we

could even leave our beds, my two idiot brothers went galloping off like the tight-lipped fools that they are, leaving us to wonder and fret and—"

"I doubt they did it purposely, dearling." Max laid a gentle hand on her shoulder. "Perhaps they were following some lead where time was essential."

Lisette exchanged a glance with Jane. "What do *you* think? Did they do it on purpose?"

"Undoubtedly." Jane fought down anger. Dom could be so devious. "Either Tristan learned something damning about Nancy that neither wants me to know, or he's afraid to admit that he learned nothing."

Get some sleep. We'll talk tomorrow.

Yes, what about that? How was she supposed to talk to Dom when he ran off to escape her?

Oh no. Perhaps Dom had learned for certain that Nancy was pregnant. Perhaps he'd returned to his old ways of being cautious, in preparation for possibly losing the viscountcy. After all, the last time he'd lost his birthright, he'd manipulated Jane into jilting him.

She scowled. Fine. If that was causing his silence, then he could go to the devil. She'd put up with that once; she wouldn't put up with that again. Especially after last night. He'd roused her hunger for him with his incredible kisses and sly seductions and tender care for her virtue . . .

When her heart did silly little jumps at the thought of how he'd warned her to leave, she wanted to cry. Curse him for tempting her to feel. She did not *want* to feel. Not for him. Not after how he'd ignored her for twelve years.

Yet she couldn't seem to stop it.

And now, some time later, riding in a carriage with his sister only made it worse. Jane could feel Lisette's speculative glances like needles pricking her skin, and the only way to banish them was to talk.

Unfortunately, all she could talk about were the many scenarios she imagined Nancy and Barlow in, each more alarming than the last. Max laughed off her worries, but that didn't stop Jane from fretting, rethinking every word Nancy had ever told her.

Meanwhile, Lisette was strangely silent. But when they stopped to change horses and she and Lisette got out to use the necessary, Lisette took her aside the minute they'd left Max.

"Please allow me to apologize on my brothers' behalf, Jane. I know that the uncertainty is killing you. Tristan really should have stayed long enough to tell you what he'd learned."

"I don't blame *him*." She sniffed. "I'm sure Dom is the one who insisted that he keep quiet."

"Probably. I'm afraid that Dom can sometimes be—"

"Manipulative? Arrogant? Infuriating?"

Lisette clearly fought a smile. "I was going to say, 'oblivious,' but apparently you have a different view of things."

"He's not oblivious," she said stoutly. She only wished he was. He'd realized right away that she wasn't in love with Edwin. "He notices everything."

"Not when something stands in the way of a notion he's got into his head. Once in a while he follows a plan of action so slavishly that he not only misses the forest, but the hills and the sky and every other thing surrounding the trees. Particularly if the plan involves someone he cares about. Like you."

"Dom doesn't care about me anymore," she told Lisette, mostly to divert her from her matchmaking.

It didn't work. Lisette rolled her eyes. "Who's being oblivious *now*?"

Later, as they barreled toward Saffron Walden, Jane couldn't stop thinking about what Lisette had said. Dom really *could* be terribly bullheaded when he thought he was pursuing the right course of action. Like the way he'd been with her years ago. And his insistence that Nancy was plotting to take the viscountcy from him.

Not to mention his blaming Nancy for George's presence in the library that awful night. If he'd had any sense, he would have realized how little his assumption made sense. But he'd been too caught up in creating an image of Nancy as some sort of schemer so he didn't have to dwell on his own culpability.

What did that mean for her future? For *their* future?

The thought tantalized her—a future with Dom. He still wanted her, in his bed and in his life. And she still wanted him. Lord help her, but she did.

She just didn't *want* to want him, not when he made plans for her without consulting her. Today was a perfect example. He didn't want to discuss what was going on with her, so he ran off, leaving her to fret. She couldn't live like that.

But could she live with Edwin now that she knew what being in Dom's arms was like? Or was she deceiving herself when she said it didn't matter?

A pox on Dom for rousing all these feelings again. And a pox on Nancy, too, for forcing her into this situation in the first place. When Jane caught up to her cousin, she was going to shake her senseless.

◆ ◆ ◆

JANE, LISETTE, AND Max arrived at the Ravenswood estate very late in the evening. There was no sign of Dom and Tristan or even the viscount, but his wife, the exotic-looking Lady Ravenswood, was there to greet them. Jane had heard much about the viscountess but had never met her, so Max performed introductions, since he'd apparently known the couple for some time.

"We are so sorry to intrude," Lisette told the viscountess. "If you could just direct us to my brothers, we'll take ourselves out of your hair."

"Nonsense," Lady Ravenswood said. "My husband and the other gentlemen have gone to visit an associate of his, but since they were uncertain how long that would take, I suggested to his lordship that you and the rest of your party should dine here and stay the night."

"We wouldn't wish to put you out," Max said without a whit of sincerity.

"And we can't stay," Jane put in hastily. "The matter that takes us to London is of the utmost urgency."

Lady Ravenswood smiled kindly. "That may be so, but the gentlemen seemed to think that a good night's rest wouldn't hurt." She cast a furtive glance at Lisette. "Besides, I understand that the duchess has recently borne a child, and I know very well how taxing those first months afterward can be."

After glancing at Lisette, Jane winced to see how the woman was flagging and chided herself for being so inconsiderate as to drag everyone along with her at such a reckless pace. The duke and duchess had only come along to chaperone, not to be run ragged.

"Of course you're right," Jane told the viscountess. "Lisette really should rest."

"I'll show you upstairs," Lady Ravenswood said. "The gentlemen may not return for hours, and they insisted that you sup without them. But since it's already quite late, you may prefer to have trays in your rooms."

"That would be lovely, actually," Lisette said with such relief that Jane realized just how weary she was. "We appreciate your kindness."

A short while later, the viscountess had settled Max and Lisette into a guest suite and ordered supper trays for them.

But as she guided Jane down the hall, Jane said, "If you don't mind, I prefer to wait downstairs for the gentlemen's return."

A frown furrowed Lady Ravenswood's brow. "It might be some time yet. And I gathered from their discussion earlier that Lord Rathmoor and Mr. Bonnaud may very well leave for London as soon as they're done with supper here."

Again? Dom meant to leave her without a word *again*? Not if she had anything to say about it.

Jane forced a smile. "Unfortunately, since the matter the men are pursuing involves me and my cousin, I really must consult with his lordship and Mr. Bonnaud before they head for London. And I do not mean to let them leave without giving me a report."

That seemed to startle the woman. "Forgive me, but I was given to understand by my husband that you and Lord Rathmoor haven't been friendly since the two of you were engaged and you . . . well . . ."

"Jilted him?" One day Jane was going to subject Dom to a long list of all the ways in which his subterfuge had created problems for her. But at the moment, she needed Lady Ravenswood on her side. "That is only partly true. Tell me, madam, have you ever been the victim of unfair or misinformed gossip?"

Pain glimmered in the viscountess's dark eyes. "I'm the American half-Senecan wife of a viscount with high-placed friends. So yes, you might say I have."

Jane gentled her tone. "Then you'll understand how easy it is for society to misconstrue matters. Lord Rathmoor and I . . . have a rather complicated association, which he seems determined not to complicate further. I believe that is why he refuses to give me my report. And that's why I could use your help."

"In what?" the woman said warily.

"Nothing too awful, I assure you. As you will under-stand when I explain."

She would tell her ladyship however much was nec-essary to gain her aid. Because it began to appear that the only way to fight Dom's sly ways was to take some devious measures of her own.

13

THE SOUND OF voices in the hall woke Jane with a start. Sweet Lord, she hadn't meant to sleep. But it had been hard not to in the richly upholstered wing chair where she sat hidden from view in Lord Ravenswood's library.

Now fully awake, however, Jane tensed when the voices stopped outside the library door. Once Jane had persuaded Lady Ravenswood to help her, the viscountess had readily agreed to guide her husband to settle with the gentlemen in here, where trays of food had been set out. Though Jane hated spying on them, she saw no other choice. Dom stubbornly insisted on avoiding her, and Tristan would do whatever he commanded.

The door opened, and Jane sank down into the high-backed chair that faced away from it. Lady Ravenswood had assured her that she couldn't be seen from behind.

"Does the coachman think he can repair them?" said a voice that had to be Lord Ravenswood's, since she didn't recognize it.

"He's not sure. They're newly patented, so he doesn't know if he can figure out how they work."

The low thrum of Dom's voice sent her pulse into a dance. Devil take him! She'd just seen him last night; his mere voice shouldn't make her swoon, for pity's sake. It shouldn't make her remember the soft words he'd whispered as he'd caressed her and kissed her and swept her into madness . . .

What was wrong with her? She wasn't letting that man sweep her anywhere, not as long as *he* only wanted to sweep her out of his way.

Now if only she could be sure why.

She strained to listen. For a while, the gentlemen were too intent on eating to say much of interest. But once the clink of silver ended and the clink of glasses began, their tongues loosened.

Thank heaven for brandy. She could smell it all the way over here.

"Even if the carriage lamps are repaired," Lord Ravenswood said, "it's not safe for you to leave tonight. And a few hours won't make much difference to your investigation."

"I told him that," said Tristan, "but my fool of a brother is obsessed with avoiding Miss Vernon's questions, and he thinks he can only manage that by staying ahead of our party."

"Ah," the viscount said.

Jane dug her fingers into her palms. After their intimacies last night, she'd thought they might have some chance together, but he only shared his body with her. Everything else he kept secret.

You're the one hiding here in the corner, her conscience said.

Yes, because it was her only way around the tight-lipped devil.

"How will you find Barlow?" Lord Ravenswood asked. "I don't suppose you'll want to talk to Blakeborough."

"The earl isn't going to give up his brother until he knows all the facts," Tristan said.

"Good luck providing them," Dom said. "So far even *we* can't seem to discover all the facts."

"I'm sorry I couldn't help you more with that," Lord Ravenswood said.

Tristan snorted. "I still don't understand how your associate here could be entirely unaware of Barlow's address in London."

"Men like Barlow move through the shadows. Since even arranging prizefights is illegal, those who do it don't exactly advertise where they live."

Samuel was involved with prizefights? How odd. She'd wondered what he'd been doing all these years, but never suspected it would be something so shady. Did Edwin know? By unspoken agreement, they never discussed Samuel.

"I've kept track of Barlow in York," his lordship continued, "but to my knowledge he doesn't set up fights in London, so I have no idea where he stays when he's in town."

"You surprise me, Ravenswood," Dom said dryly. "I thought you had your thumb on every miscreant of note."

"I'm not as active in such matters as I once was. My subordinate has taken over most of that work. These days, my world is all politics."

"Well," Dom said, "you've been a great help with the information about why Barlow was disinherited. It reinforces my suspicions about him. Though I do wish you'd give us the name of the young heiress whose life he ruined."

Jane tensed. She'd always heard Samuel was a rogue, but to ruin a lady? That went beyond the pale.

"She is now happily wed to a respectable gentleman who doesn't care what happened between her and Barlow," Lord Ravenswood responded, "and I wouldn't damage her marriage for the world by stirring up that muck again."

"Neither would I," Dom said icily. "I'm always discreet."

"I realize that, but I promised her father I'd never reveal her identity to anyone, and that includes you," Lord Ravenswood countered. "She won't be able to tell you anything, anyway. It's not as if Barlow took her back to his lodgings before they set off for Gretna Green."

If Samuel had eloped with this girl, how had she ended up married to someone else? Besides, an attempted elopement might tarnish his reputation, but it would hardly get him disinherited.

"The more you tell me about him, however," Dom

said, "the more convinced I am that Barlow is engaged in a scheme to wrest my property from me."

"You're probably right," Lord Ravenswood answered. "But I'm not nearly as certain as you that your sister-in-law is actively aiding him in the deception."

"Dom is a bit biased against Nancy," Tristan put in. "With her being George's widow and all."

"That's absurd," Dom retorted. "I am merely considering the facts that *you* uncovered, dear brother. You can't dispute that Nancy was seen leaving York of her own accord with Barlow, headed for London."

"Come now," Ravenswood said, "you know as well as I do that brute strength isn't the only way a man can force a woman to his will."

"I realize that," Dom said testily. "But until I can be sure Nancy means me no harm, I have to assume the worst." Jane heard the ring of a glass against the tray. "I'm going to check the progress of your man's repairs. Coming, Tristan?"

"No," Tristan surprised her by saying. "I agree with Ravenswood. We might as well wait until tomorrow to travel. And if you're still set on avoiding Jane, we can just get up early as we did this morning."

Jane made a face. Little did they know—she was *not* going to let them get away with that again.

A weighted silence fell on the room that was only broken when Dom muttered a coarse oath. "Fine. I'll tell the coachman that he can head for bed and not worry about the carriage lamps. You should go to bed, too, Tristan."

"I want a word with him first," Lord Ravenswood said smoothly.

"If you mean to suck him into your shadowy world—" Dom began.

"I told you, I'm not much involved in that business anymore." Lord Ravenswood's voice tightened. "But if that was my intention, you wouldn't have a say in it."

"The blazes I wouldn't. I refuse to see my brother end up with a scar like mine. Or worse."

Jane sat up straight. Had Lord Ravenswood caused Dom's scar?

"Blame me as much as you wish, but you know that wasn't my doing," Ravenswood said softly. "Nor yours. Stop tormenting yourself over something that was always beyond both our controls."

Ravenswood was wasting his breath. Dom believed nothing was beyond his control.

She waited for Dom to say as much, fancying she could feel the tension in the room. A hundred questions flooded her, questions she meant to ask as soon as she could get Dom alone again.

"Good night to you both then," Dom said stiffly as if Ravenswood hadn't spoken a word. "I'll have one of the grooms bring in our bags now that we're staying."

Then she heard the door open and close, and her heart constricted. Dom had more secrets than she'd guessed.

As soon as the sound of Dom's footsteps receded, Lord Ravenswood said, "Do you think Rathmoor really will go on to bed? Or will he set off for London on his own?"

"My brother is a careful man," Tristan said. "It's not in his nature to be reckless."

Except when it came to her. Dom was so determined to avoid her that he might just take his life in his hands for it.

"What do you think, Miss Vernon?" Lord Ravenswood asked in a raised voice.

Miss Vernon? Her heart sank into her stomach. Lady Ravenswood must have revealed Jane's intention to spy on the men. But then why hadn't the viscount said something sooner? Was he bluffing?

"No point in hiding in that chair any longer," Lord Ravenswood added. "I know you're there."

Definitely not bluffing.

With a sigh, Jane rose to face the gentlemen, who instantly stood, too. Tristan gaped at her. Lord Ravenswood did not. As his keen gray eyes assessed her from beneath a pair of nondescript brown brows, his face showed no expression.

That troubled her. It reminded her too much of Dom.

"It's good to meet you at last," the viscount said with a courtly bow.

"I wish I could say the same." She gazed at him warily. "I assume that your wife told you what I was up to."

"No, she's not one to tattle, but she *is* rather bad at deception. So when she insisted that we take our supper in the library, I guessed that something was afoot." He nodded to the high-backed chair. "Especially when

I saw that the chair had been turned around. And since I doubted that the duke or duchess would have cause to eavesdrop, that left only you." When she winced, he added, "Not for nothing was I appointed to my position, Miss Vernon."

Having gotten over his initial shock, Tristan eyed her cautiously. "You heard everything."

She shrugged. "As you said, your brother is obsessed with keeping things from me. You left me no choice."

Tristan whirled on the viscount. "And you were aware she was listening in! Why didn't you say something sooner?"

"She has a right to the truth," his lordship said simply. "You know she does, or you wouldn't be calling your brother a fool for keeping it from her."

Tristan crossed his arms over his chest. "Dom didn't want to alarm her until he had all the facts."

"No," Jane countered, "he didn't want to argue with me over what he *considers* 'facts.' But that isn't his decision to make. I'm the one who involved him in the search. I never would have if I'd known he would push me out of it."

The viscount's gaze shifted to her. "Still, I daresay you had your own reasons for involving him, given why you jilted him."

As she gaped at the man, Tristan muttered, "Hell and thunder, even I don't know why she did that." He slanted a glance at Ravenswood. "Dom wasn't lying when he said you have your finger in every pie."

Lord Ravenswood's tight smile didn't reach his

eyes. "Hardly. But a man generally turns confessional under the influence of laudanum, and we had to give your brother a great deal the day he got that scar on his cheek. It wasn't the only wound he received. It's just the only one he can't hide."

Her heart chilled. "He has other wounds? Where? How did he get them?"

"You'll have to ask him. If he won't even tell his family, I imagine he has his reasons."

Yet Lord Ravenswood had roused their curiosity enough to ensure that they *would* ask. The man was almost as wily as Dom, though in this instance she was grateful for it. The thought of Dom injured so badly that he required "a great deal of laudanum" alarmed her more than she could say.

"But I'm happy to answer your questions concerning your cousin and Mr. Barlow," Lord Ravenswood went on. "If you still have any after eavesdropping on our discussion."

She ignored his sarcasm. Because one thing about what she'd overheard still worried her. "You mentioned that Samuel eloped with a young woman. So why did she end up married to someone else?"

"Because she changed her mind about the elopement on their way to Gretna Green. She told Barlow she couldn't go through with it and tried to get him to return her home. He refused, and when she attempted to get the coachman to stop, he—"

"Don't tell her that," Tristan said in a low voice. "There's no reason to alarm her."

"Miss Vernon strikes me as a sensible woman not given to hysterics, one who can handle the facts," the viscount said. "Besides, just because Barlow forced himself on an heiress he was scheming to marry doesn't mean he would force himself on a widow when there's no need for it."

Horror gripped her. "Samuel *raped* a woman?"

"Hell and thunder, Jane!" Tristan cried. "What do you know of rape?"

She glared at him. "I am not the china doll wrapped in cotton that you and your brother think me. Women hear of these things—from the streets, from the broadsheets, from accounts of crimes and trials. We know that men rape women."

With a lift of her chin, she stared down the viscount. "*That* is why I involved Dom in this, sir—because I'm not fool enough to go off searching alone. But I didn't realize that he would take over the investigation to such an extent that I'd be kept out of it."

"Still, you understand why Dom did that, don't you?" Tristan put in. "He didn't want you worrying that Nancy might be in danger."

"But she might." Jane's heart stuck in her throat as she looked toward Lord Ravenswood. "What happened to this other woman after Samuel . . . assaulted her?"

"He thought he'd cowed her into submission—but when they stopped to change horses, she got away from him and found someone to help her get back to her family."

"Was he charged with a crime?"

"No. Her father feared that a trial would ruin her, especially since Barlow continued to insist that *she'd* seduced *him*. A family friend who was enamored of the girl stepped in to marry her, and then challenged Barlow to a duel. But Barlow fled instead of meeting his accuser on the field. That's when Barlow's family disinherited him."

No wonder Edwin had never told her this. It must mortify him. "And nothing was done about Samuel's crime."

"Nothing *could* be done. All parties involved agreed to let it go because it was unlikely that a trial would serve the lady well."

"Or so the men told her, I assume," Jane said bitterly.

"And she agreed with them. After having her idyllic life ripped from her, she didn't also want her pain exposed and picked over by the crowds."

Jane supposed she could understand that, but wondered if she could have done the same, given her own vindictive streak.

"The husband of the injured girl was able to get Barlow dismissed from his post in the navy," Tristan said, "which is why he now arranges prizefights for a living. But that's where the matter ended."

"Until he found another woman to assault." Jane couldn't breathe for thinking of Nancy at Samuel's mercy.

"He won't hurt your cousin," Lord Ravenswood said firmly.

"You don't know that!"

"I do. He'd be a fool to harm her when she is carrying the child who can make his fortune."

"And if she isn't?" she asked.

"We're fairly certain that she must be," Tristan said. "A servant overheard Barlow telling her about a doctor they could see in London. And the servant said she looked very ill, which she would if she's suffering morning sickness."

"Or if she'd already lost the baby," Jane said.

Lord Ravenswood steadied a gentler gaze on her. "Then why would she go with him?"

"You said yourself that a man can force a woman to his will without brute strength."

"Yes. But they were friends, according to what Bonnaud here discovered from the shopkeepers in York. That argues for her not being forced. Were you aware of their regular meetings in York?"

"No." She hadn't known any of that.

That's why it was more important than ever that she talk to Dom. She had to find out what he was thinking, hear what he was planning. She had to elicit his promise that he wouldn't cut her out of things anymore.

She forced a smile for Lord Ravenswood's benefit. "Thank you for telling me this. It's more than Dom would do."

"You're welcome."

"Now, if you gentlemen will excuse me, it's very late and I'm very tired. I think I shall go up to bed."

"I'll take you up," Tristan said.

"No, that's all right," she said, fighting to sound casual. "I know where my room is. You stay and enjoy your brandy with Lord Ravenswood. Besides, I believe he still has something to discuss with you."

"I do, indeed," Lord Ravenswood said.

But the viscount's eyes followed her as she walked out of the room, and the whole time she traversed the hall to the staircase she worried that he or Tristan might come after her.

Fortunately, they did not. As she neared the bottom of the stairs, she wondered if Dom might already be in his bedchamber. Somehow she doubted it. She'd be very much surprised if he intended to stay here tonight, no matter what he'd told his brother.

As she came into the foyer, a footman rose to ask her, "Were you just with the gentlemen, miss?"

"Yes. They're still in the library." She hesitated a moment, then asked, "Has Lord Rathmoor come in yet? The gentlemen wanted to know."

"No, miss. I believe he's still in the stable."

"Thank you. I'll tell them."

With a smile that she hoped hid her consternation, she headed down the hall as if she were returning to the library, but she passed it up to go toward the back of the house.

She hurried through halls and rooms. Somewhere there must be a rear entrance that led to the stables, and she meant to find it. Because there was no way she would chance Dom's running off again without her.

* * *

DOM STOOD IN the harness room of Ravenswood's stable, trying his hand at repairing the carriage lamps for his phaeton. Since neither the coachman nor the groom had succeeded, Dom had sent them on to bed with the assurance that if he got the blasted things working again, he'd rouse the men to put the horses in their traces.

He still hoped to go on to London tonight since it was only a few hours away. Although Ravenswood was right that it was foolish to drive without lamps on such a dark night, if they could be fixed, Dom saw no reason to stay.

Especially now that he'd learned why Barlow was disinherited.

"I knew you would ride off again to avoid me."

At the sound of the familiar female voice, he spun around, then groaned to see Jane standing in the harness room entrance. She was still dressed for travel, which was odd, given the footman's claim that everyone had retired.

Leave it to Jane to defy expectation.

"I'm not avoiding you," he said. "You wanted me to investigate, so I am."

She came closer, and he tried not to notice how lovely she looked despite her frilly, flouncy gown. As far as he was concerned, it gilded the lily. He itched to haul her into his arms and strip away the furbelowed green gingham and flimsy undergarments until only pure, unadulterated woman was left, standing naked in all her heartbreaking beauty.

Judging from her accusing scowl, that wasn't going to happen.

"I wanted you to investigate on my behalf," she said, "not go running off to do it on your own."

He returned his attention to the carriage lamp. It was the only way to restrain his impulse to tear off her clothes. "I wouldn't exactly call it 'running off,'" he said curtly to hide his agitation. "If I can't get these working again, I'm not going anywhere."

Coming up behind him, she peered around his shoulder to watch what he was doing. She smelled of lavender and honey, a scent that had haunted his nights for years. Now it nearly brought him to his knees.

He trimmed the wick too short, then cursed under his breath.

"I didn't know that repairing carriage lamps was one of your particular talents," she said.

"Obviously it isn't," he snapped, "since I've had no more success at it than Ravenswood's coachman."

"Yet that hasn't stopped you from trying," she said in an arch tone. "God forbid you should trust a mere coachman to handle anything so important."

Refusing to be baited, he stared coolly at her. "Is there something you wanted, Jane?"

"You know what I want. To be told what's going on. To hear why you're ready to risk life and limb to go on to London tonight when even your friends are against it." Her gaze, dark with anxiety, struck him hard. "Are you *that* worried about Nancy's being alone with Samuel? Lord Ravenswood says she's not in any danger, but clearly you think otherwise. His tale about that lady Samuel assaulted must have upset you as much as it did me."

"It didn't upset me so much as—" What she'd said registered, and his heart jumped into his throat. "Ravenswood told you about all that? When?"

"I . . . I . . . well . . ." A fetching blush stained her cheeks. "I . . . um . . . sort of listened in on your conversation with him and Tristan in the library just now."

God save him. He ran through what they'd said in the library, trying to figure out if any of it had been damning. "I don't recall Ravenswood's mentioning Barlow *assaulting* the lady."

"No, his lordship told me that later. Apparently, he'd already figured out I was in there and was just waiting until you left to rout me from my hiding place."

"The bloody arse ought to have said something the moment he realized it," he said hotly.

"Why? So you could hem and haw about the truth? So you could keep me in the dark about whatever danger Nancy is in?"

Blast Ravenswood to blazes.

Dom laid the carriage lamp down on the table to face her. "I doubt she's in danger. Assaulting Nancy wouldn't suit Barlow's purpose, which is to have her child inherit Rathmoor Park. Even seducing her would be unwise; he won't want to draw attention to their association right now. In fact, he was probably the one to insist that Nancy tell the servants she was visiting Mrs. Patch. If you hadn't returned to the estate, no one would have known anything was amiss."

Her troubled gaze bore into him. "His lordship said much the same. But if you really thought that, you wouldn't be racing off to London." She rubbed her arms. "You wouldn't be trying to hide the truth from me."

"I saw no reason to alarm you."

That made her bristle. "I am *not* a coddled child. I can endure hearing about the ugly side of life!"

"Except when your cousin might be part of it."

She searched his face. "If the facts demonstrate that Nancy is helping Barlow in some scheme, you should *want* to reveal them, if only to convince me to accept your version of things. But clearly they don't, or you wouldn't keep hiding them from me."

"I wouldn't *have* to hide anything if you would trust my instincts as an investigator, damn it!" When she flinched, he tamped down his temper. He hadn't meant to say that, but she'd struck a nerve. "Every time I mention Nancy in less than glowing terms, it puts your back up. Then you refuse to listen to anything else I have to say."

"It's not your mention of Nancy that does that. It's you, with your secretive ways and your running off without me. It's *you*, making decisions that concern us both." Her voice grew choked. "This . . . ongoing argument between us is about more than just the investigation. You want me to trust you, but how can I when you hide your whole life from me?"

She was staring at his cheek now, and he had the perverse urge to shield it, like a child covering up the evidence of some misdeed. Suddenly, he remembered what he'd accused Ravenswood of in the library earlier. What she must have overheard.

He groaned.

"Like that scar of yours, for example," she went on, confirming his fears. "You want me to trust you implicitly? Fine. Then trust *me* for a change. Tell me how you got it."

"What, your chatty new friend Ravenswood didn't explain it to you the minute my back was turned?" he said snidely.

A strange sorrow lit her face. "No." She reached up to trace the line of puckered flesh, and his breath caught. "Though he did say this isn't your only one."

The pity in her eyes unsettled him. "Damn Ravenswood. He ought to keep his nose out of it."

"I wish he'd told me more. Because Lord knows you never will."

Perhaps that was why Ravenswood had forced the issue. He was taking a page from Lisette's and Tristan's matchmaking book.

God rot them all. For years, no one had given a damn that Dom remained a bachelor. But once Jane had dropped into his life again, his bloody family and friends had apparently decided that Dom needed *their* help to get her back. That he didn't have the sense—or, more likely, the stones—to manage it himself.

Well, he had both.

He caught her hand. "Why do you want to know about my scars? What does it matter, if you mean to marry Blakeborough anyway?"

Her eyes turned that warm coppery brown that never failed to stop his heart. "I haven't yet decided what to do about Edwin."

"Then let me advise you." Lifting her hand to his lips, he kissed it, then each finger one by one. "Don't marry him. Marry *me*."

To blazes with being cautious. It wasn't getting him anywhere.

"Marry you?" she said tartly. "So you can give me half of yourself? Hide your past from me? Continue to shelter me from anything you think might alarm me? That sounds no better than the arrangement I meant to make with Edwin."

Meant to make. He wanted to take comfort in that, but he couldn't since she still hadn't said yes. She apparently wanted him to bare his soul before she'd even consider it.

"Fine," he bit out. "You want to know how I got the scar on my cheek? It was a slice from a saber."

"Where? By whom? Under what circumstances?"

"I got it while I was working. That's all I can say."

She snatched her hand from his. "That's all you *will* say, you mean."

When she turned on her heel and headed for the door, the thought of her leaving him with his proposal unanswered made his heart falter. "Wait, damn you."

"There's no point." She paused in the doorway. "Not when you insist on remaining a stranger to me."

Was that what she thought he wanted? "Jane—"

She walked out into the stable proper, and his gut

clenched. He'd never told anyone but Ravenswood what had happened that day, and even Ravenswood had only received the barest of facts.

Because Dom couldn't speak of it. Some days he couldn't even think of it for fear that the weight of it would crush him.

But he couldn't let Jane walk away, either. He couldn't risk the possibility that she'd never come back. So perhaps he could tell her something. Just enough to pacify her.

"I got my scar at St. Peter's Field in Manchester, all right?" he called after her. Perhaps she wouldn't know what that meant. Perhaps she wouldn't ask to hear more.

But when she halted and turned to retrace her steps with a certain horror in her expression, he realized such a hope was futile.

"When?" she asked hoarsely.

Damn her for making him do this. "You know when. I can see it in your face."

"Oh, dear sweet Lord. So you were at the Peterloo Massacre."

14

JANE WISHED THE words unsaid the minute Dom flinched. She wished she didn't know of the Peterloo Massacre, wished she weren't so avid a reader of newspapers. But she did, and she was.

Ten years ago, a meeting of radical reformers at St. Peter's Fields had ended in horror for hundreds of poor working men and women, earning it the name that compared it to Waterloo. But though Waterloo had been far worse, it at least had been fought during wartime, with real armies.

A thought stopped her cold. Dom would have been on the side of the militia who'd thundered in and wreaked havoc, not on the side of the meeting goers. But if that were the case, how had he been wounded?

"Were you among the soldiers?" she whispered.

"Don't call them that." His words were sharp, tortured.

Them. Not *me.* "Why not?"

"Because anyone who would cut down an unarmed

man for nothing more than speaking his mind doesn't deserve the title of soldier. Soldiers protect the innocent; they don't willfully slash and slaughter them."

She watched him uneasily. "Some said the crowd brought the violence upon themselves."

"Anyone who says that is a fool," Dom clipped out. "Anyone who says that wasn't there."

"So why were *you* there?"

She had to know, though she was wary of his answer. Because his eyes had gone bleak, like those of men who'd looked into shadows and seen themselves.

"Don't make me talk about it, sweeting. You don't want to hear—"

"I want to hear anything that will help me understand you." *Why you didn't come after me. Why you keep me out even now.* "Every time you refuse to reveal your secrets, Dom, I assume that you find me unworthy to hear them."

"That isn't remotely the case," he ground out.

"Then tell me what happened. Lord Ravenswood said you torture yourself over it. I want to know why. I need to know why." And she suspected he needed to tell it.

"Fine. Since you're giving me no choice . . ." He leaned back against the table and crossed his arms over his chest. "I was there with the Spenceans who were pressing for parliamentary reform. But I knew we were in for trouble when over sixty thousand people gathered in that field to hear them speak."

"You were worried they might turn violent?"

"The radicals? No. I'd spent months with the Spenceans as one of Ravenswood's spies, and I knew they were determined not to cause trouble. It was precisely because they feared violence from the local magistrates that they required that their people come unarmed, in orderly groups."

He stiffened. "But the minute I saw the special constables forming two rows to force a passage from the edge of the field to where the speakers stood, I feared the worst."

When he began to breathe more heavily as if struggling to keep himself under control, she swallowed hard. She'd never seen Dom so agitated.

"I even considered identifying myself to Hulton, head of the magistrates. He didn't know the Spenceans the way I did, and I thought I might convince him to refrain from taking any violent action."

He scrubbed a hand over his face. "But Ravenswood had ordered me not to reveal my purpose. No matter what, I was to maintain my role so I could continue to spy on the radicals. I was to keep my connection with the Home Office a secret, even from the authorities."

Lord Ravenswood's words came to her then: *Blame me as much as you wish, but you know that wasn't my doing. Nor yours. Stop tormenting yourself over something that was always beyond both our controls.*

The massacre? No, surely not. Dom wouldn't blame himself for such a monumental disaster, would he?

"So I did my duty." Dom's voice turned bitter. "Unfortunately, none of Hulton's advisors had the good sense to recommend restraint. He grew so alarmed by the size of the crowd that he decided the speakers should be arrested. Then he listened to his damned Chief of Constables, who argued that the warrant couldn't be served without a show of force."

When Dom fell silent again, his hands now gripping the edges of the table on either side of him, she prodded, "That's when Hulton called in the militia."

"Yes, the bloody idiot." He stared blindly out the harness room door into the stable. "The hotheaded young cavalrymen arrived on the field drunk. They pushed their way through the constables' too narrow passageway, and their horses floundered in the sea of people. So the riders began slashing about them with their sabers to clear a path."

Sweet Lord. "Is that when the crowd began to fight back?"

A foul curse escaped him. "You can't call it fighting when one side has swords and guns, and the other has a few bricks and fists. But yes, when the crowd realized that the militia was there to arrest the speakers, they fought back."

"Which only provoked the militia further."

He nodded tersely. "The drunk cavalrymen panicked and started sabering and bludgeoning anyone within reach. Meanwhile, I'm told that Hulton saw the ruckus from afar and ordered the Hussars in. They unwittingly blocked the crowd from dispersing, which only made matters worse, and before we knew it, the situation deteriorated into rampant violence."

"And you were in the middle of it."

How awful it must have been for him to see the authorities attacking the people when he could do nothing to stop it. With her heart twisting in her chest, she moved close to lay her hand on his taut arm.

He didn't even seem to notice. "Eighteen died, most of them civilians," he said in a hollow voice. "Five hundred more were injured, a third of them wom—" He broke off with a grimace of pain and guilt so profound that it cut her to her heart.

"Women," she supplied as tears stung her eyes. "Yes, I heard that." That must have been horrible for him, given his natural instinct to protect. "Why were so many women there?"

"There weren't." His breath came in harsh gasps now. "It was ten men for every woman."

"Then why were women a third of the wounded?"

"Because the damned militia targeted them!" As she gaped at him, his voice chilled. "I saw it with my own eyes. And most of the women's wounds were later found to have been caused by weapons, not trampling, which wasn't the case for the men." He shot her a despairing glance. "What kind of monster deliberately attacks women at a peaceful gathering?"

She thought of Papa. "The kind who doesn't like the idea of a woman expressing her own mind, fighting for her own freedom."

His jaw was as tight as an archer's bow. "You attribute to them some semblance of thought. But those animals were beyond thought. One of the Hussars—

a legitimate soldier who'd seen battle and knew how to behave in it—tried to reason with the militia. He cried, 'For shame! Gentlemen: forbear, forbear! The people cannot get away!'"

The howling pain in Dom's eyes would have laid a lesser man low. "The arses either didn't hear or didn't care. I got the scar on my cheek when I kept a special constable—*one of our own men*—from being sabered. I got the rest of my wounds when I . . . I . . ."

His words grew halting, his breathing tortured. "I came between . . . a pregnant woman and . . . her attacker." The catch in his voice was heartbreaking. "I survived my injuries. She . . . did not." He began to tremble, like the ground before a quake.

Jane choked back tears. She had to be strong for him. Wrapping her arms about his waist, she held him to her. How could she soothe him, when he'd witnessed such horrors?

"I heard that the poor woman lingered for days before giving birth to her babe too early, and then . . ." He shot her a helpless glance. "She left behind children. Six . . . motherless *children*, for God's sake."

"Oh, Dom . . . oh, my dearest." She stretched up on tiptoe to press her cheek to his, wishing she could do more.

"One woman was sabered to death," he said in a harsh whisper against her cheek, "another beaten with a truncheon. Two of the special constables died on the field. And there was a child—"

He choked off the word, shaking too violently now to go on.

"Enough." She clasped him close in a futile attempt to calm him. "No more."

Jane had heard about the child's death because the press had made much of it. The boy's mother hadn't even been at the meeting. She'd been carrying her two-year-old across a road as a cavalryman raced to catch up to his companions. His horse struck her, and the child was thrown from his mother's arms. The boy died instantly, the first casualty of a truly horrific day.

Tears stung her eyes. She'd never guessed at the darkness he'd held inside him for so long. How could she, when he closeted his pain inside his heart, refusing to let anyone else see it?

The poor dear fool had put the blame for the entire massacre on his own head, and he thought they would do the same.

"That's why you haven't shared this with your family?" she said. "Why do you keep all of us out? Because you think we'd blame *you* for the massacre? Because you blame yourself for it?" She brushed a kiss to his hair. "Oh, my sweet darling, it wasn't your fault."

His hands gripped her arms. "You don't understand," he said in a ragged voice. "I should have identified myself, made Hulton listen to reason."

"How?" She pulled back to gaze into his eyes, so haunted by shadows. "He had a score of magistrates behind him, not to mention years of hatred between the radicals and the local militia. How were you to change all that?"

His voice turned fierce. "I should have broken ranks with Ravenswood. I should have behaved as my conscience dictated and tried to stop it at the source. I should have *made* them listen! Perhaps if I had—"

"And perhaps not." When he tried to pull away from her so he could lick his wounds alone, she wouldn't let him. Catching his head in her hands, she forced him to look at her. "You did your duty. That's all you could do."

"My duty was to keep people from dying," he hissed.

"Your duty was to survive! There were thousands of people on either side. Only God could have stopped that disaster, and contrary to what you think, you *aren't* God." When he winced at that, she whispered, "You are just a man, my darling. You did your best with the terrible circumstances you were handed. That is all any of us can ever do."

For a long moment, he just stared at her, naked torment on his face. Then he uttered a fractured moan and clutched her to him. Burying his face in her hair, he stood there with his chest heaving and his heart thundering against her ear. His grip was so tight she could hardly breathe, but she made no protest.

He needed her, and that meant everything. Because Dom never needed anyone. So as tears streamed down her cheeks, she held him tight and pressed damp kisses to his neck.

It took some time for his storm to pass, some time for him to stop shuddering in her arms. But after they stood there locked together awhile, his strong arms began to loosen their grip and his shaking to subside.

Encouraged by that, she stretched up to brush soothing kisses over his jaw, his cheek, his lips.

He jerked back, and as he searched her face, the dark shadows in his eyes receded a little. "Oh, God, Jane, why did I let you go?" he asked in an aching voice that resonated to her very soul. "I've been lost ever since."

The words melted the last corner of ice in her heart, and when he lowered his head to hers, she rose to him like a shoot stretching for the sun.

Moaning low in his throat, he devoured her mouth, his kiss pure hot passion, so all-consuming that within moments she had to pull free just to breathe. Then he shifted his kisses to her cheek and ear and jaw, branding everything as his.

"I need you," he said against her throat. "God help me for it, but I do. All these years without you have been hell." Kissing her neck, he fisted his hands in her sleeves. "I want to strip this gown from you. I want to lay you down in that straw over there and have my way with you."

The words made her exult. "Then do it," she murmured against his hair. "Now. Tonight. Have your way with me, and I'll have mine with you."

"That's what I'm afraid of," he said darkly, but he seized her mouth again with such ferocity that it took her aback . . . then fed some feral part of her that had never felt like this with anyone but him. She couldn't get her fill of his mouth . . . or his hands, which roamed her most familiarly.

Wanting to touch him, too, she reached for the buttons of his waistcoat.

He broke their kiss to stare at her, a sudden sobering awareness in his eyes. "We shouldn't do this here."

There was no question what "this" meant. There was also no question that he was having second thoughts, pulling away from her. She refused to let him. "Why not? The grooms and the coachman have all gone to bed. And you did say you meant to marry me."

"Yes, but you're a lady," he said fiercely. "You deserve better than to be tumbled in a stable."

That was the trouble with Dom. Some part of him still saw her as the poor maiden needing his protection, not as a full-grown woman who had the same needs as he had. Who wanted and *yearned* just the same as he did.

He'd sent her away last night to protect her innocence, and then had avoided her for the next day. She wasn't giving him the chance to do that again, not now that he'd allowed her a glimpse into his soul.

Dragging her hands free of his grip, she went to shut the door to the harness room. "Twelve years ago you decided what I deserved, and I ended up alone. So this time *I* will decide what I deserve." Ignoring a twinge of self-consciousness, she faced him and began to undo the front fastenings of her pelisse-robe. "And I deserve this. I deserve *you*."

His breathing grew labored as he stared at her hands with a searing intensity. "What are you doing, Jane?"

"What does it look like?" She slid out of her gown and let it fall to the floor, leaving her standing before him in only her petticoats, corset, and shift. "I'm seducing you."

Dom's eyes narrowed on her, and she panicked. Was she being too bold? Too shameless?

Too daft?

She *was* daft, to be standing half-dressed like this in a stable, when all it would take was a groom coming down from his room above to turn this into the most mortifying night of her life.

But she'd die before she let Dom see her squirm. With forced bravado, she planted her hands on her hips. "Well? Are you going to leave me here like this?"

Even as the words left her lips, she spotted the rather pronounced bulge in his trousers. That's all she had time to notice before he was striding up to grab her head in both hands and seize her mouth with his once more.

This time their kiss was a war of tongues and teeth, both striving for mastery. Their hands darted everywhere in a thrilling flurry of unfastening and untying, a rush to see who could get the other one naked first. His boots ended in one corner, her half boots in another. Their clothes soon pooled around them on the floor of the harness room.

He got her shift off, then stepped back before she could divest him of his drawers, and for one heartstopping moment she feared he was having more second thoughts.

"Dom?" she asked, her cheeks flaming as she stood naked before him. She'd never stood naked before anyone, even a maid.

But the way Dom was scouring her with his rough gaze felt like a caress. A very carnal caress, which loosed a bevy of butterflies in her belly.

"I've spent years dreaming of you like this, sweeting," he rasped. "Give me a moment to take it all in."

"If you wish," she whispered. And that would give her a moment to take *him* in.

Although, sweet Lord in heaven, it might require more than a moment. She'd seen men half-dressed in paintings and even less-dressed in sculptures. But those smooth-skinned bodies were insipid compared to Dom's hard contours and scarred male beauty.

How could she have guessed that such sheer virility lay beneath his subdued clothes? His deliciously muscular chest gleamed with sweat in the warm stable, and his powerful arms lay tense at his sides. Then there was his lean waist, which gave way to rangy hips sporting quite a bulge beneath his drawers.

Lord help her. She couldn't take her eyes from that impressive thickness. And the more she stared, the more it seemed to grow.

"This is what you do to me, Jane," he said in a voice raw with hunger. He grabbed her hand to press it against him there. "I've desired you from the day we first met."

As his flesh moved beneath the stockinette, she swallowed. "I don't recall ever seeing you like *this* back then— all . . . big and thrusting. I think I would have noticed."

He choked back a laugh. "It's the sort of thing a gentleman generally takes great pains to keep his lady from seeing. But tonight you're making it difficult for me to behave."

"Good! I don't want you to behave. I want you to be wicked." She fondled him shamelessly. "With me."

A harsh breath escaped him. "You have no idea what being wicked entails."

"Then perhaps you should show me."

His eyes glinted in the lantern light and he growled, "Perhaps I should."

Next thing she knew, he was sweeping the tools and carriage lanterns off the table near them. Then he lifted her onto it and parted her thighs with his hands.

"This, my sweet, is wicked," he warned just before he knelt to place his mouth on the secret part of her that lay in the juncture of her thighs.

Shock gripped her. It had been one thing to have him touch her furtively beneath her skirts last night, but this blatant, outrageous—

"Ohh, *Dom* . . ." She clasped the edge of the table to keep from dissolving into a puddle. "That is . . . that is . . ."

"Wicked?" he asked hoarsely, his eyes dark with sinful promise.

She nodded. Her cheeks surely shone as red as the tongue he now used to stroke her. *Down there.* In an intimate caress that sent heat licking up her belly to her breasts, which were already aching to feel that tongue on them.

This was wicked, all right. Luxuriously decadent. It made her feel like a shameless wanton. But she didn't care as long as she was being a shameless wanton with *him*.

Then he began caressing her with his mouth in earnest, with teeth and tongue and lips, and her mind went blank.

Some of what she'd felt last night echoed along her nerves, like the tinkling of bells that rose to an urgent ringing. But tonight his mouth was amplifying the sensations until it was more like a gong being struck, lightly at first, then harder, faster, louder. The vibrations shook her until she was shimmying beneath his mouth and clutching his head.

When the final ringing bong sounded through her, she had to stifle her cry of pleasure. It was so intense, so delicious . . . so wonderfully *wicked*. Who would have guessed that such an outrageous act would feel that *magnificent*?

Dom rose from his kneeling position, a keen hunger shining in his eyes. "Was that wicked enough for you, sweeting?" he drawled as he used his cravat to wipe his mouth.

With her heart thundering loudly in her ears and her breathing staggered, it took her a moment to answer. "Not quite," she managed, then tugged at the waistband of his drawers. "You still have these on."

That seemed to startle him. Then one corner of his lips quirked up. "I never guessed you were such a greedy little—"

"Wanton?" she asked before he could accuse her of being one.

But he just shot her a smoldering smile. "Siren."

"Oh." She liked that word much better. Feeling her oats, she gestured to his drawers. "So take them off."

With a laugh, he did so. "There, my lusty beauty. You have your wish."

"Yes . . . yes, I do." Now she could study him to her heart's content.

But the reality was rather sobering. His member, jutting from a nest of dark curls, couldn't possibly be hidden behind a tiny fig leaf like the ones on statues. "Oh my. It's even bigger and more . . . er . . . thrusting without the drawers."

"Are you rethinking your plan for seduction now?" he asked, with a decided tension in his voice.

"No." She cast him a game smile. "Just . . . reassessing the . . . er . . . fit."

"It's not as fearsome as it looks."

"Good," she said lightly, only half joking. She looped her arms about his neck. "Because I'm not as fearless as *I* look."

"You're a great deal more fearless than you realize," he murmured. "But this may cause you some pain."

She swallowed her apprehension. "I know. You can't protect me from everything."

"No. But I can try to make it worth your trouble."

And before she could respond to that, he was kissing her so sweetly and caressing her so deftly that within moments he had her squirming and yearning for more.

Only then did he attempt to breach her fortress by sliding into her. To her immense relief, there was only a piercing pop of discomfort before he was filling her flesh with his.

All ten feet of it. Or that's what it felt like, anyway.

She gripped his arms. Hard.

He didn't seem to notice, for he inched farther in, his breath beating hot against her hair. "God, Jane, you're exactly as I imagined. Only better."

"You're exactly . . . as *I* imagined," she said in a strained tone. "Only bigger."

That got his attention. He drew back to stare at her. "Are you all right?"

She forced a smile. "*Now* I'm rethinking the seduction."

He brushed a kiss to her forehead. "Let's see what I can do about that." He grabbed her beneath her thighs. "Hook your legs around mine if you can."

When she did, the pressure eased some, and she let out a breath.

"Better?" he rasped.

She nodded.

Covering her breast with his hand, he kneaded it gently as he pushed farther into her below. "It will feel even better if you can relax."

Relax? Might as well ask a tree to ignore the ax biting into it. "I'll try," she murmured.

She forced herself to concentrate on other things than his very thick *thing*—like how he was touching her, how he was fondling her . . . how amazing it felt to be joined so intimately to the man she'd been waiting nearly half her life for.

Then it got easier. She actually seemed to adjust to his size. And when he slid his hand down from her breast to stroke that special spot between her legs that sent her flying, it was most effective. She wasn't quite flying, exactly, but she was definitely leaping a bit.

A giggle escaped her at that thought, and he bit out, "Something strike you as funny, sweeting?"

"I never guessed that . . . this would feel . . . so odd."

"You'll get used to it."

The hint of a future for them melted her even more than his hand down there. And that's when he began to move, sliding out and then back in. Heavens. That *was* intriguing. Rather nice, actually. The more he did it, the better it felt.

Then he removed his hand so he could better grip her hips, and he plunged harder into her. Oh, now *that* was quite . . . oh my. Very, *very* nice.

His gaze burned into her as he drove deep. "Less odd now?" he managed.

"Definitely . . . less odd." She kissed the taut line of his jaw. "Quite . . . enjoyable, in fact."

He grunted and buried his face in her hair the way he was burying his . . . thing inside her, and it was deliciously sinful. Now she really *was* flying, up toward the sun.

As if he realized it, he dug his hands into her hips and thrust fiercely, repeatedly, and she met his rhythm with a pushing of her own that sent her soaring.

"Dom . . . oh, Dom . . . oh my . . ."

"Jane," he rasped as his strokes grew frenzied. "It's always . . . been you. Only you."

"Only you," she echoed.

She'd been fooling herself about Edwin. There had only ever been one man in her heart. And as he drove himself deep inside her, he sent her vaulting into the sun.

When he followed her into the bliss, she clutched him close to her chest and prayed that he would let her inside his heart as deeply as she'd let him into hers. That she wasn't making a mistake by taking up with him again.

Because it was too late to go back now. This time, he had her for better or worse.

15

DOM HAD NEVER felt so close to heaven as he did wrapped in Jane's lovely arms, with her thighs hooked about his hips and her head tucked against his shoulder. If lightning struck the stables at this moment, he would die content. But he didn't want to die, not now that he had Jane.

He did have her, didn't he? Surely she wouldn't have given herself to him if she intended to marry Blakeborough.

They were still entwined, though Dom's cock was softening. He kissed her hair, which had somehow remained pinned up throughout their lovemaking, except for a few stray tendrils that tickled his nose. He wanted to pull it all down, just to see how long it was. He wanted to get a look at her arse without her clothes on, which he hadn't had the chance to do.

He wanted to make love to her again, somewhere more private. Somewhere he could take his time with her.

"I never dreamed it would be as amazing as that," she whispered.

"I did."

"Really?" Her soft voice was a caress. Everything about her was as smooth and silky and sweet as whipped cream.

Well, except for her tart opinions. And her fierce determination to make him tell everything in his soul. Though he had to admit that after confessing his secret fears to her earlier, he felt freer, as if the boulder he'd been carrying for years had dropped from his back.

"I knew it would be perfect." He gave her a lingering kiss, then drew back to cup her pinkening cheek. "With you it could be nothing less."

Shyly avoiding his gaze, she finger-combed his short hair. "Nancy always said that sharing a man's bed was something to 'endure.' That marriage was more pleasant without it, but it was required for having children so she'd had to put up with it."

He skimmed a hand down her lightly freckled arm. "And what do *you* think, now that you've experienced it for yourself?"

"I think I could 'endure' it with great enthusiasm." Jane flashed him a mischievous smile. "But I'm not really sure. Should we try it again so I can make certain?"

Stifling a laugh, he tried to look stern. "We're lucky none of the grooms have stumbled over us already." He managed to sound even-toned, though the prospect of taking her again—here, now—was already making him hard. "Speaking of that, we'd better get dressed, before someone finds us here naked."

A sigh escaped her. "You do have a point. Though I don't know how you can be so sensible and industrious when all I feel is lazy and content."

"I'm not being sensible and industrious at all." Reluctantly he slipped from her arms to go hunt up his drawers. "I'm simply being selfish. The longer you stay naked, the more the chance that I will attempt to ravish you again."

"That sounds perfectly . . . awful," she said as she struck a seductive pose.

God save him.

He swept his gaze over her thrusting breasts, her slender belly with its delicate navel, and her auburn thatch of curls. The taste of her was still on his lips, the smell of her still in his nostrils. He wanted her again. And again and again . . .

Muttering a curse under his breath, he tossed her shift at her. "Put some clothes on before I combust."

She laughed, a delicate tinkling sound that tightened his cock. Fortunately for his self-restraint, she did as he bade and donned her shift. Only then was he able to breathe, to concentrate on putting on his trousers rather than on the erotic sight of her drawing her stockings up those luscious legs.

He turned and nearly stumbled over the carriage lamps. "These are a lost cause, now that I recklessly dashed them to the floor in my . . . er . . . enthusiasm, sweeting."

"Good," she said cheerily. "Now you *can't* run off to London without me tonight. Besides, I gathered from my eavesdropping that none of you even know where to go to look for Nancy and Samuel."

"I *have* decided on a starting point." He weighed the wisdom of revealing it, but she most assuredly had the right to know *that*. Besides, it would allow him to gauge her feelings. "I mean to speak to your fiancé as soon as I reach London. Surely he knows something about where his brother lives. Assuming that he'll tell us."

With a scowl, she tied her garters. "Of course he'll tell us. He'll certainly tell *me*. That is, if he knows. I'm not sure that he does."

Dom watched her shimmy into her stays, wondering if she would say any more about Blakeborough. She couldn't still be thinking of marrying the man, could she? It wasn't in her character to let one man bed her and wed another.

But she merely turned her back to him. "I'll need help lacing up."

He moved behind her to tighten her laces. The intimacy of it made a lump catch in his throat. "I suppose I'd better get used to this for when we marry."

A long pause ensued.

"Are we marrying?" she asked lightly.

"Of course." When she didn't say anything, he felt it like a punch in the gut. And as always, that made him dig in his heels. "We have to marry now, Jane. You know that. I took your innocence."

"You did not take my innocence," she said with a bit of an edge to her voice. "I gave it of my own free will."

Was she really arguing the matter? "That doesn't change anything. We still must marry."

She slid away from him to pick up her petticoat. "So I get no say in it?"

"You had your say when you let me bed you," he remarked, more coldly than he'd intended.

But damn it, he had understood from her giving herself to him that she meant to marry him. Otherwise, he would never have made love to her. And there was no way in blazes he would let her go off to wed the earl. Not now, not ever.

"You're not marrying Blakeborough," he added. "Not after this." He'd meant to phrase it more as a question, but fear of losing her to the bastard had twisted it into a command.

And she most definitely heard that, for she tensed and finished tying on her petticoat with rigid motions. Then she faced him with a challenging glance. "Edwin won't care that I'm not chaste."

Edwin? God, was she still considering marriage to that arse? "I doubt that. And if you think I'll let you test that theory, you're mad." Jealousy made him harden his voice. "You and I *must* marry, and that's an end to it."

"Is it?" With a storm building in her expression, she planted her hands on her hips. "Tell me, Dom, do you ever *ask* for anything? Or do you always just assume that everyone will fall in line when you give orders?"

That took him aback. Hadn't he asked? Perhaps he

hadn't. But then, he shouldn't have had to after what they'd just done.

In any case, he'd be damned if he let her flounce off after Blakeborough. "Jane, you must listen—"

"*Must!*" Her eyes blazed at him. "Stop issuing commands! That's what Papa always did to Mama: 'You must obey me, Kitty. You must keep quiet around the servants. You must not coddle Jane so much; she needs a strong hand.'"

A strong hand?

Too late he noticed the latent fear in her face. Too late he realized his mistake.

Yesterday when she'd told them about her father, she'd made it painfully clear how she felt about men who gave orders, but he'd been too focused on what her tale had to do with the hunt for Nancy to recognize how having a bullying father must have affected Jane.

This argument they were having wasn't about Blakeborough at all. It was about her father. And not just her father, but *Dom*—the way he'd made the choice for them both years ago, the way he was making the choice for them now.

Blast, what an idiot he was.

Jane showed her agreement with that assessment by glaring at him. "I'm not just going to fall in with your plans because you dictate them. I did that once; I'm never doing it again. If we marry, it will be because we *both* choose it, because you trust me enough to *ask* me. Not because you have *willed* its occurrence."

Good God, he'd gone badly awry. But surely she knew him better than to think—

"Dom, are you out here?" called a voice from somewhere beyond the stables.

Damn it all. It was Tristan.

Swiftly Dom donned his shirt. "Be quiet," he whispered to Jane, "and he'll go away."

Tristan's voice sounded again, even nearer now. "I swear to God, Dom, if you ride off to London in the dark and make a liar out of me before Ravenswood, I will kick you from here to France!"

"He won't go away," Jane whispered back, a hint of desperation in her voice. "He promised Ravenswood that you wouldn't head for London with broken carriage lamps, and now he'll want to make sure that you don't."

Which meant his arse of a brother wasn't going to stop looking for him. Any minute now, he'd be striding into the harness room.

Then Jane would *have* to marry Dom.

As soon as the thought entered Dom's head, it apparently occurred to her, too, for she paled and stepped near enough to whisper, "Please. Not like this."

He stared at her ashen face, and his stomach sank. He couldn't force her to wed him. After what had happened between them years ago, she would never forgive him for taking her choice away from her yet again.

Besides, he didn't want to force her into anything. The only way he could prove that he didn't intend to run roughshod over her for the rest of their lives was to walk away now. Even if it killed him.

Bloody hell. "I'll draw Tristan away from the stables," Dom said tersely as he shoved his stocking feet into his boots. "That will give you a chance to finish dressing and sneak back into the house."

Relief spreading over her face, she bobbed her head.

He buttoned up his shirt. "It will also give you a chance to decide what you want." Gathering up his coat, waistcoat, and cravat, he added in a low murmur, "But know this, Jane. I am *not*, nor ever intend to be, a man like your father. Somewhere inside of you, you must . . ." He winced. "You surely *do* know it."

He waited long enough to see uncertainty flicker in her eyes. Then he strode out of the harness room and closed the door behind him.

Hoping to have time to finish dressing before his brother found him, he halted. Then he spotted Tristan down the corridor searching the stalls, probably look-ing for Dom's team of horses.

Best to take the offensive. Perhaps that would dis-tract Tristan from Dom's state of undress. "Good God, man, what are you doing?" Dom called out.

Tristan spun around. "What do you think? I'm look-ing for you, you dunderhead." Then his gaze swept down Dom, and his eyes widened. "Why the hell are you half-dressed?"

So much for distracting him. "It's damned hot in here, in case you hadn't noticed."

Dom made a show of wiping sweat from his brow with his sleeve and hoped that his excuse would pass muster. After all, the only clothes he wasn't wearing were ones he would actually have taken off if overly warm.

But Tristan looked suspicious. "Even I have never seen you without a cravat."

"That's because you've never seen me toiling in a hot stables," Dom snapped, then swiftly changed the subject. "As you can probably guess, I couldn't fix the carriage lamps."

Tristan glanced behind Dom to the closed harness room door. "Do you want me to look at them?"

"No," Dom said curtly. "It's a lost cause. Besides, we'll be in London soon enough where I can get an expert to repair them." He drew on his waistcoat and coat, stuffed his cravat in his pocket, then headed for the stable entrance. "It's late. Might as well get some sleep."

Thankfully, Tristan acquiesced and followed him out the door.

As they walked, Dom buttoned his waistcoat, then pulled his cravat out of his pocket and tied it around his neck.

Big mistake. He could smell Jane on the strip of silk from when he'd wiped his mouth with it. The scent made him want to throw caution to the winds, march back into the stables, and carry her out over his shoulder and off to gain a marriage license without delay.

Which of course he *couldn't* do, if he wanted to win her.

Damn it to blazes, how could he have bungled things so badly that he still had to *win* her, even after bedding her? But he had. And now he had to leave her back there.

At least for the moment. He'd promised her, after all.

To keep from thinking about her stewing in her anger at him, he said, "So, what was it Ravenswood wanted to discuss with you privately, anyway? Or are you allowed to say?"

They walked a short distance in silence before Tristan answered. "Actually, he wanted to talk about you."

"Me?" Dom said, surprised. "What about me?"

"He's worried about you. About how you'll react if Nancy ends up bearing George's son, and you lose the estate and have to go back to running the agency again." Tristan slanted a glance at him. "He's not the only one."

"I'll be fine." To his shock, he realized it was true. He wouldn't be happy about it, of course, but he had learned how to cope. Compared to the first time, this was nothing. "I lost everything once and survived it well enough. I can do it again. Besides, I have a business concern that I can return to now, so it'll be easier."

"Not if this nonsense with Nancy means you lose Jane again, too."

He sucked in a harsh breath. "I am not losing Jane." The words were a vow, to himself and to her. He would do whatever it took to keep her this time.

They'd almost reached the house when Tristan spoke up again. "In the course of my discussion with Ravenswood, I tried to get him to tell me how you got your scar, but he wouldn't. He said I'd have to ask you."

Jane's words came suddenly into his head: *That's why*

you haven't shared this with your own family? That's why
you keep all of us out? Because you think it was your fault?
Oh, my sweet darling, none of it was your fault.

When Dom didn't answer right away, Tristan went
on, "I told Ravenswood you'd always brushed off the
question with some nonsense about a fight you got into.
But that isn't true, I assume."

Dom ventured a glance at his brother and winced
to see the hurt on his face. Jane had said, *Every time*
you refuse to reveal your secrets, Dom, I assume that you
find me unworthy to hear them. Apparently, that was how
he'd made *all* of them feel. As if he were somehow too
important to let them into his life.

Only God could have stopped that disaster, and contrary
to what you think, you aren't *God.*

When she'd said it, he hadn't understood why she
would accuse him of such a thing. Why she sometimes
called him "Dom the Almighty."

But he understood now. By shielding his guilt from
the world, he'd shut himself off from his family. From
her. He'd pushed away the very people he should have
embraced.

Having just watched Jane retreat into fear and shut
him out, he now knew precisely how painful it could
feel to be on the receiving end.

If he wanted to change all that, he would have to
start opening his heart, letting his family—and her—
see the things he was most ashamed of, most worried
about. He would have to trust them to understand, to
empathize, to love him in spite of everything.

The only other choice was to keep closing himself up until, as she'd said at that ball last year: *One day that church you're building around yourself shall become your crypt.* He didn't want that.

He took a steadying breath as he and Tristan walked up the steps to Ravenswood's manor house. "As it happens, I *did* receive my scar in a fight. But it was a fight against the militia at the Peterloo Massacre."

When Tristan shot him a startled look, Dom halted at the top of the steps to face him. "If you want to hear the story, I'll tell you all about it. Right now, if you wish."

Tristan searched his face, as if not quite sure he believed what he was hearing. "I'd like that very much." Then he broke into a grin. "But only if we do it over a glass of Ravenswood's brandy. That's the best damned brandy I've ever tasted."

"One of the privileges of being a spymaster is that you can get your hands on the good stuff," Dom said lightly, though his stomach churned at the thought of revealing his most humiliating secret, even to his brother.

Still, as they headed inside, Tristan clapped him on the shoulder, and that reassured him. Telling Tristan about Peterloo represented a beginning of sorts, toward a closer friendship than Dom had allowed himself to have with his brother in recent years.

Jane would be proud.

16

JANE HAD AN awful night. First, there was the nightmare that began with Papa calling Mama "ignorant" and "willful" while Jane hid behind her mother's skirts. It ended with Dom assuring Papa that he would take Jane in hand.

After Jane awoke gasping, she lay there shaking, unable to go back to sleep.

Did she really believe that Dom was like Papa? He was certainly arrogant, and he could drive her mad with the firmness of his pronouncements. It still rubbed her raw that he'd ordered her to marry him rather than asking her.

But he *had* bowed to her request not to let Tristan catch them together, even though he'd clearly realized that putting her in a compromising situation would inevitably lead to a marriage. That was something, wasn't it?

And she *had* seduced him, after all. She could see how he might interpret that as a tacit agreement to marry him. Especially since she'd meant it as such. Indeed, she'd been more than eager to become his wife, until he'd taken it for granted and started ordering her about like . . . like . . .

Dom the Almighty.

She blew out a breath. That was the trouble. She had no way of knowing which Dom she'd be marrying. The one who said he'd been lost ever since he'd let her go? The one who took such care with bedding her?

Or the one who dictated to her? Who wouldn't even have revealed his most recent discoveries about Nancy's situation if Jane hadn't eavesdropped to get them?

A sudden scratching at the door of her bedchamber startled her. Could that be her lady's maid so early? She sat up, surprised to see from the clock that it was already six A.M. They were to leave Saffron Walden at seven; Lady Ravenswood had told her so last night.

For the next hour, Jane thankfully didn't have to think about her and Dom at all. By the time she did her ablutions, dressed, packed up, and had a bit of toast with tea, it was time to head off for London. Indeed, she was the last person to appear on the steps of the manor house where everyone else was assembled, saying their goodbyes to the viscount and his wife.

"So, you're heading to the Earl of Blakeborough's in London, right?" Lord Ravenswood asked Tristan.

"Yes. Dom and Max and I agree that it's our best course of action."

The four men briefly discussed the quickest routes to London. Though she could feel Dom darting glances at her the whole time, she couldn't face him, couldn't even look at him. Not just now, when she was still in turmoil about what they'd done.

About what he'd said to her at the end. *It will also give you a chance to decide what you want.*

That was the trouble. She didn't know what she wanted. Well, she *did* know—she wanted to marry Dom the courteous gentleman. But not Dom the Almighty. She wanted the Dom who mourned for the six children who'd lost their mother needlessly, not the Dom who was sure Nancy was a whore because she'd married his bastard of a brother.

But what if both parts were him? What if she couldn't have one without the other? Why, he hadn't even said he loved her!

Then again, neither had she, so she could hardly fault him for that. Their past was still too raw, and they were both still afraid. Perhaps he'd been waiting for her to say it. She'd certainly been waiting for him. Because then she might really believe he meant to make a life with her again, and not go running off at the first sign of disaster.

Like, perhaps, if Nancy proved to be bearing George's son.

"Since it's such a beautiful morning," Dom said, "I was thinking that someone might prefer to ride in the phaeton with me. What do you think, Jane? Shall you join me?"

He was asking. Deliberately *asking,* not ordering. And she could feel his expectant gaze on her, indeed, feel *everyone's* expectant gazes on her. But her thoughts were too jangled right now, and an enforced ride with him would only jangle them more.

Especially since they'd be trapped together for half the day. She wouldn't be able to escape. Not that she necessarily wanted to escape. Did she?

Oh, Lord, she couldn't handle this at the moment. "Actually, I was looking forward to chatting with your sister in His Grace's coach. If you don't mind."

Only then did she meet his gaze. It showed nothing of his thoughts, which made everything worse. She'd begun to recognize that bland expression; he only wore it when he was protecting himself. And if he felt a need to protect himself, then she'd hurt him.

She swallowed hard. She hadn't wanted to hurt him. Perhaps she *should* ride with him. Clear the air. Perhaps she was being a coward.

"Whichever you prefer," he said curtly. Then he walked briskly down the steps to his waiting phaeton, leapt in, and set it going.

And the decision was made for her. Again.

No, she couldn't blame this one on him. This one was entirely hers. She'd sent him running away.

Everyone knew it, too, which was nowhere more apparent than in the carriage once they were all settled in and headed off. Lisette was unusually silent. The duke's wooden expression said that he wished he could be anywhere else but here. And Tristan was studying her with a cold gaze.

He did that for a mile or so before he spoke. "You're a cruel woman, Jane Vernon."

"Tristan!" Lisette chided. "Don't be rude."

"I'll be as rude as I please to her," he told his sister, with a jerk of his head toward Jane. "That man is mad for her, and she just keeps toying with him."

Guilt swamped Jane. And she'd thought that spending half a day trapped with *Dom* would be bad? She must have been dreaming.

"It's none of our concern," Lisette murmured.

"The hell it isn't." Tristan stared hard at Jane. "Is this about Nancy? About the fact that if she has a child, Dom will lose the title and the estate?"

"No, of course not!" How dared he!

"Tristan, please—" Lisette began.

"That's why you jilted him years ago, isn't it?" Tristan persisted. "Because he no longer had any money, and you'd lose your fortune if you married him?"

"I did not jilt him!" Jane shouted.

An unnatural silence fell in the carriage, and she cursed her quick tongue. But really, this was all Dom's fault for never telling his family the truth. She was tired of being made to look the villainess when she'd done nothing wrong.

"What do you mean?" Lisette asked.

Jane released an exasperated breath. "I mean, I *did* jilt him. But only because he tricked me into it." When that brought a smug smile to Tristan's face, she narrowed her eyes on him. "You knew."

"Not the details. I just knew something wasn't right. But since it was clear that neither you nor my idiot brother were going to say anything without being prodded into it, I . . . er . . . did a bit of prodding." He smirked at her. "You do tend to speak your mind when you get angry."

Jane scowled at him. "You're just like *him*, manipulative and arrogant and—"

"I beg to differ," Tristan said jovially. "He's just like *me*. I taught him everything he knows."

"Yes, indeed," Lisette said with a snort. "You taught him to be as much an idiot as you." She glanced from Tristan to Jane. "So, is one of you going to tell me what is going on? About the jilting, I mean?"

Tristan cocked an eyebrow at Jane. "Well?"

She sighed. The cat was out of the bag now. Might as well reveal the rest.

So she related the whole tale, from Dom's plotting with Nancy at the ball to George's involvement to how she'd finally discovered the truth.

When she finished, Tristan let out a low whistle. "Hell and thunder. My big brother has a better talent for deception than I realized."

"Not as good as you'd think," Jane muttered. "If I hadn't been so wounded and angry at the time, I would have noticed how . . . manufactured the whole thing felt."

Lisette patted her hand. "You were young. We were all more volatile then." Her voice hardened. "And he hit you just where it hurt, the curst devil. No wonder you want to strangle him half the time. I would have strung him up by his toes if he'd done such a thing to *me*!"

To Jane's surprise, the duke kept silent, though he appeared to be musing on something.

Tristan did *not*, however, keep quiet. "Now see here, sis, Dom thought he was doing right by her. You know what life was like for him then—running here and there for Ravenswood and Pinter, living in garrets, learning investigations from the bottom up. It wasn't the sort of existence for a lady."

Jane sniffed. "Lisette lived it. She helped you in Paris, didn't she?"

"Not until I was much older," Lisette admitted. "And not until Tristan had established himself with the French secret police and Eugène Vidocq. By the time I was working for Vidocq myself, Tristan and I had a very nice apartment adjoining his town house, and I was already twenty-three. You were, what, seventeen when you and Dom got engaged?"

"And you weren't bred for such a life," Tristan put in. "Whereas Lisette had been scraping by with me and Mother for years."

Jane crossed her arms over her chest. "All right, so my circumstances were a bit different. But I had been managing the household for my aunt for some time by then." Although Dom hadn't apparently known that.

"That's still a far cry from garrets in Spitalfields," Tristan said.

"I would have shared any garret with him if he would only have asked!" Jane cried. "But from the beginning, he urged me to jilt him. I *told* him I wouldn't, yet he refused to listen!"

"In other words, you left *him* no choice," the duke

said, the first time he'd spoken since they entered the carriage.

It caught Jane off guard. "What do you mean?"

Max shrugged. "You just said he wanted you to end it. Well, he knew *he* couldn't end it without damaging your reputation. So he must have thought he had no choice but to manipulate you into acting to preserve your future. He did it for you."

"He did it for himself!" Jane cried. "So he wouldn't have to be saddled with a . . . a gently born wife who might drag him down in difficult times."

As the stark words echoed in the carriage, she realized that was exactly what hurt so much about their parting. That Dom hadn't had the faith in her to believe her love would survive even a garret.

Lisette reached over to squeeze Jane's hand, but it was the duke's reaction that Jane most noticed. His eyes shone so kindly upon her. "That's why you never went after him later. Why you never sought him out once you knew the truth. Because you were afraid that it was always about you and your 'flaws.' Not him."

Tears clogged Jane's throat. "I waited for *years*. I was sure he would come to his senses and seek me out. But he never did."

"Not because of anything to do with you," Lisette said.

"You can't know that," Jane choked out. "Once he established the agency, he could have approached me again. But he didn't want me."

"I doubt that," Lisette said reassuringly. "He never

married anyone else, did he?" She sighed. "What you don't understand is that Dom, of all of us, was the one most hurt by Papa's . . . lack of affection. Papa showed Tristan a great deal of attention and I was his only daughter, his little girl. But Dom—"

"Was the one whose birth killed your father's wife." Jane remembered that bit of their family history.

Lisette nodded. "If what George said before he died is true, then their mother bore Dom at great risk to herself, because she was jealous over our mother. So Papa must have looked at Dom as . . . well . . . a living representation of how he'd failed his wife."

Tristan snorted. "Father didn't feel deeply enough for that. He just saw Dom as the second son, like every other man of his ilk." He glanced at the duke. "No offense, Max."

"None taken," the duke said. "But I think Lisette is mostly right. Your father doted on his bastards; that's not typical. And for all that he and George didn't get along, he certainly had him well educated and gave him plenty of responsibility."

"Whereas he just stuck Dom off at school and ignored him." Lisette glanced at Jane. "I know it's no excuse for his behavior, but Dom has always blamed himself for too many things—his mother's death being only the first. If he'd married you, he would have blamed himself for every moment of unhappiness the two of you suffered as a result of his being disinherited and your losing your fortune. Perhaps he couldn't face that."

Jane thought of Dom last night, brought low by the conviction that he'd caused a massacre, of all things, by not acting upon his conscience. Might he have been the same if in marrying her, he thought he'd made her life a misery?

"All the same, it should have been my choice, too." Jane glanced at Max. "And he did have other choices. He could have consulted me on a plan whereby we would wait five years until he established himself, and then we would reconsider marriage. I might have agreed to *that*. But he didn't even try."

Max's gaze held a trace of pity. "Perhaps he didn't want you to wait. If he thought you'd be better off without him, then perhaps he believed you would come to think so, too, if he took himself out of your life."

"Yes," Jane snapped, "he thought me so shallow and foolish that I would fall out of love with him the minute things got hard. How flattering."

"Or perhaps he just thought *himself* incapable of holding on to the love of a woman as fine as you," Tristan ventured. "God knows I had my own doubts about holding on to the love of a good woman, after growing up with our feckless father."

What had Dom said about why he hadn't come for her? *The point is, you would have been a fool to choose me over one of them. And I was astute enough to realize it.*

When he'd told her all the reasons he'd been convinced that she would never accept him, she'd focused on his inability to believe her strong enough, determined enough, to share his trials.

But there were two ways to see it. Perhaps *he* hadn't thought himself worthy enough to keep her love.

She didn't want that to sway her emotions, but it did.

"I know it sounds as if we're making excuses for him," Lisette said, "and clearly he did act with great presumption toward you, but at the time he obviously thought he was doing the right thing."

"He still does," Jane said dryly. "He has expressed no remorse for what he did. He says he would do it again if he had the chance."

All right, so last night he *had* murmured those special words that had prompted her to seduce him: *Oh, God, Jane, why did I let you go? I've been lost ever since.* But that was regret. Not remorse. Not exactly.

"That does sound like Dom," Lisette said with a shake of her head. "Never admit you're wrong, even when you are. Never let anyone too close. He doesn't like to bare his heart to anyone for fear they will destroy it."

"But I think he's changing," Tristan said. "Last night he told me how he got his scar."

"He did!" Lisette cried. "Oh, Tristan, you have to tell us what he said. I'm sure Jane wants to know as much as any of us."

Jane bit back the impulse to admit that she already knew. After all, when she'd last seen Tristan, she'd said she didn't, and she certainly didn't want Tristan figuring out that she must have met up privately with Dom in the interim. It wouldn't take much for him to figure out the real reason Dom was half-dressed in the stables.

Still, it warmed her that after Dom had revealed his secret to her, he'd done the same with his brother. If he could change that much after so many years, it gave her hope for their future together. And right now, she could use a little hope.

17

IT WAS WELL past noon as they approached Blakeborough's town house in the most fashionable part of
Mayfair. Dom hadn't had the chance to speak to Jane
alone since they'd rushed to London so quickly, but his
one glimpse of her, looking fresh and pretty and bright
in her sun-colored pelisse-dress, had made him want to
howl his frustration. Especially when she'd refused to
ride with him.

Damn it, this had gone on long enough. He would
take her aside and make things right between them the
minute they finished consulting with her fiancé about
Barlow.

Fiancé. The very word scraped him raw. Dom had
met Blakeborough half a dozen times back when he'd
been courting Jane, but their paths hadn't crossed since
then. As Dom recalled, the earl had been too handsome
for his own good.

Through the years, however, rumors had begun to
circulate about the man's disposition—that he was a

curmudgeon of sorts, cynical about women and about marriage in general. Which is why Dom had initially been surprised to hear that Jane was engaged to the arse.

Still was engaged to the arse.

Dom scowled. He'd spent the entire trip imagining what he would do when confronted with the man.

The idea of challenging Blakeborough to a duel over Jane was tempting, but not remotely practical. For one thing, it would hurt Jane's reputation. For another, it might result in Dom losing her anyway. Because if afterward Dom had to flee to avoid prosecution, she might not agree to leave England with him. Besides, it would be awfully hard to drag Rathmoor Park out of arrears from afar.

Dom had even considered telling Blakeborough that his fiancée was no longer chaste. But that would send her into an apoplectic fit, and rightly so. A gentleman didn't impugn a woman's reputation to gain what he wanted. Even if what he wanted was the woman as his wife.

No, he would just have to hope that Jane did the right thing and broke with the fellow. In the meantime, Dom would pray he could speak to the man with civility . . . or at least without wanting to call him out.

A few moments later they converged on Blakeborough's doorstep, startling the poor footman who responded to their knock. He clearly recognized his master's fiancée, but having a duke, duchess, and viscount unfamiliar to him show up en masse seemed to unsettle him.

While they waited to be announced, Dom tried not to remember the last time he'd been in this house—the night Jane had jilted him. He shot her a furtive glance. Clearly she remembered, too, for she wouldn't look at him, and her gaze kept darting past the massive staircase and down to where the library was situated.

Or perhaps she was just looking at the large Botticelli hanging in the hall. Or the thousand-year-old marble bust of Homer sitting atop a costly mahogany table with ivory inlays. Or even the umbrella-stand of gilded bronze.

Blast the man and his blasted Botticelli and bust and bronze umbrella-stand. No wonder he wanted Jane. He had everything else. Now all he needed to make his life complete was a beautiful and accomplished lady to manage all his pretty things and adorn his arm at parties.

That annoying thought was still ringing in his head when Blakeborough himself strode into the foyer, accompanied by a surprise guest, walking more slowly and stiffly. Jane's uncle. Damn it all to blazes.

"Uncle Horace!" Jane cried, clearly taken as off guard as Dom.

They'd intended to wait until they had more news before informing Sadler about his missing daughter. No chance of that now.

Since Tristan and Lisette knew Blakeborough and Sadler from Dom and Jane's betrothal party years ago and Max knew Blakeborough from his club, there was little need for introductions. Instead, they all stood uncomfortably by as Sadler hugged Jane fiercely.

"My dear girl!" Sadler held her at arm's length, as if to look her over. "What has happened?"

She turned wary. "What do you mean?"

"After I got your letter, Nancy's housekeeper wrote to say that Nancy was supposedly off in Bath with Mrs. Patch and that you and Lord Rathmoor and his family had gone to look for her. I didn't know what to make of that. *Supposedly off in Bath?* What does that mean?"

When Jane looked at a loss for words, Dom jumped in. "We're happy to explain all, sir, but if I may ask, why are you here?"

Sadler shrugged. "I got the housekeeper's letter this morning, so I drove here to consult with Blakeborough, hoping he might know more. That Jane might have bent the rules of propriety to write to her fiancé."

Blakeborough was watching Jane closely. "As I told your uncle, however, you never bend the rules of propriety."

The blush that stained her cheeks made Dom want to leap between her and the earl to defend her honor. But since the man hadn't actually impugned it, that would alert the man to the fact that her honor *needed* defending.

Still, it was clear Blakeborough had noticed her blush, for his gaze flicked suspiciously between her and Dom. "Of course, I was glad to hear that Jane was among friends. I shouldn't have liked to think of her riding the roads alone."

Dom forced a smile. "Despite everything that happened between me and my brother, I do still consider Nancy my responsibility. So Jane came to me the moment she realized her cousin was missing."

"Missing!" The color drained from Sadler's face. "Are you sure?"

"I'm afraid so." Dom glanced at the servants who were avidly listening. "We're happy to give you more details, but we've come a long way and—"

"Of course, forgive me," Blakeborough said hastily, exchanging a glance with Dom that said he understood the need for privacy. "You'll want to be more comfortable for this discussion."

He ordered that refreshments be brought to the drawing room, then led them there down a different hall from the one leading past the library. Thank God. Even passing by it might send Jane right over the edge, especially with her fiancé right in front of her, reminding her that she could have a more amiable husband than Dom if she wished.

Dom silently groaned. How was he to go on if she chose to stay with Blakeborough?

As soon as they entered the drawing room, Jane followed her uncle to the settee. Dom noticed that Sadler had to hold on to her to sit down. Well into his sixties now, he apparently had bad knees. Dom sighed. He hated telling the aging fellow bad news about his only child, but that couldn't be helped.

Meanwhile, Blakeborough placed himself behind them like a guard. The investigator in Dom went to work analyzing the man's attire—expensive but not ostentatious, studied but not affected—and Blakeborough's wary stance, closed manner, and stiff expression. Was that just his usual response to strangers or a sign that he was bracing for trouble about his brother? Which could mean he was well aware of Barlow's scheme.

But the *man* in Dom noticed none of that. It just wanted to march over and punch bloody Blakeborough in his perfect, unscarred face for being too rich, too eligible, and too thoroughly engaged to Jane. The *man* in him wanted to throttle the earl for standing guard over Jane when she should be *Dom's* responsibility, *Dom's* to protect. *Dom's* to marry.

The man in him had to shut up, unfortunately. Or this investigation wouldn't progress very far.

As soon as Max and Lisette were seated in two wing chairs and Dom and Tristan stood next to them, Sadler turned to Jane. "Now, what's this about Nancy being missing?"

Jane grabbed his hand. "I hate to tell you, Uncle, but she's gone off somewhere with Edwin's brother."

Despite hearing Sadler's gasp, Dom kept his gaze fixed on Blakeborough to assess the man's reaction. There was shock, alarm, dismay. But no guilt. The man was either a brilliant actor . . . or entirely unaware of his brother's scheme.

A pity. Dom would very much have enjoyed arresting him. For anything.

But Blakeborough seemed utterly undone, for he now gripped the top of the settee behind Jane. "*Samuel* has something to do with this?" he asked hoarsely.

Briefly, Dom and Tristan laid out all they had discovered, refraining from posing their speculations about what was afoot. Dom first wanted to see what the earl and Sadler would make of the bare facts.

"So, Blakeborough, as you might imagine," Dom finished, "we need to speak to your brother. And Nancy, too, of course. It's most important. We were hoping you might know where he stays when he's in London."

"I wish I could tell you, but I have no idea." Blakeborough raked his fingers through his black hair. "I gather that you already have his address in York."

"Well, this all seems entirely outrageous," Sadler put in, though his wan cheeks showed he had some notion of the ramifications. "My girl would never run off with that scoundrel. She knows better."

"Does she?" Blakeborough said cynically, to Dom's surprise. "Until she ended up with Rathmoor's brother, you feared she might actually marry Samuel."

"But that was long before he got cut off by your esteemed father," Sadler said. "Once that happened, Nancy agreed with me when I stated that the fellow was a rascal and not to be trusted." He winced. "If you'll pardon me for saying so, Lord Blakeborough."

Blakeborough's hard laugh cut through the room. "No need to beg pardon from *me,* sir. I know what my brother is capable of."

Jane twisted to look up at him. "And what is that, Edwin? I mean, he . . . he wouldn't hurt Nancy, would he?"

The earl glanced at Dom, as if appealing to him for help in dealing with Jane's delicate feelings.

"She already knows what got Barlow disinherited, I'm afraid," Dom said. "I consulted with Lord Ravenswood on the matter, and she overheard our discussion."

"Dear God," Blakeborough muttered.

"What?" Sadler asked. "What is it?"

"Well, Edwin?" Jane asked anxiously. "Would he *hurt* her?"

Blakeborough squeezed Jane's shoulder, then left his hand resting there. That seemed remarkably intimate for a man who supposedly had only a platonic-sounding "arrangement" with her.

Dom tamped down his urge to go knock the earl's hand from here into the next county.

"It depends on how you define 'hurt,'" Blakeborough mused aloud. "I don't think he'd . . . do what he did before with that other poor girl."

"What other poor girl?" Sadler cried.

"It's all right, Mr. Sadler," Dom cut in. "Tristan and I agree with the earl's assessment. We think Barlow is enamored of your daughter and wouldn't harm her."

He probably shouldn't mention his suspicions about what *Nancy* was capable of. Her father might not handle that well at all.

With an uneasy glance at Sadler, Blakeborough said, "But I wouldn't put it past Samuel to . . . er . . . lay on the charm so he could persuade Nancy to marry him."

At Blakeborough's tactful wording, Sadler stiffened. "'Lay on the charm.' You mean, 'seduce her,' don't you?" When the other men exchanged glances, Sadler pushed himself to a stand. "Don't talk to me as if I'm some sentimental old fool. I know what men do to women, especially vulnerable ones like my girl."

"Uncle," Jane said gently as she, too, rose. "By every account, Samuel and Nancy have had only a friendship, nothing more."

Sadler arched one gray brow. "It won't remain that for long if she's in Barlow's power."

"Look here, my brother is a selfish arse," Blakeborough broke in. "But I don't think he'd force Nancy into anything. Even his mistress said—" He halted when every eye swung to him.

"Barlow has a mistress?" Dom asked. "Here in London?"

"I believe she's still here, yes. When she came to see me a couple of weeks ago, she gave me an address somewhere in Cheapside."

Cheapside? Something niggled in the back of Dom's brain, but he couldn't put his finger on why Cheapside seemed significant.

"Why did she come to see you?" Tristan asked.

Blakeborough got a disgusted look on his face. "Well, initially she told me that my brother had gotten her with child when she was working in Yorkshire. So she'd moved to London to stay with her family while she had the babe, but she hadn't heard from him since her arrival. She asked for my help in pressing him to answer her."

"How long ago did she move here?" Dom asked sharply.

"I don't know. Three months? Four? I told her I

would do what I could to convince Samuel to own his flesh and blood, but I also warned her that he has an unreliable character and probably wouldn't pay me much heed."

Blakeborough's voice hardened. "In the end it didn't matter. A few days ago, she sent a note here saying that she'd been mistaken about being pregnant. I suppose she'd merely been hoping to wheedle some money out of him. Or me."

"That's about the time when Barlow would have reached London," Tristan said. "The mistress might have found him, and he might have asked her not to involve herself with his family."

Dom only shook his head. He'd finally remembered where he'd seen the word *Cheapside* recently. "More likely Barlow had a far more sinister motive." He glanced at Tristan. "Don't you find it a convenient bit of happenstance that this woman came here from Yorkshire to stay with her family a few months ago? And that she suddenly lost her baby right before we arrived?"

Tristan's eyes widened, and he let out an oath. "As you're so fond of saying, 'happenstance often happens by design.'"

Jane had gone pale. "Oh, Lord, Cheapside." She looked up at the earl. "Did the woman leave her name?"

"Of course. I have the note somewhere." Blakeborough rounded the settee, headed for a writing table. "It was Merry or something."

"Meredith," Jane said hollowly. Her gaze met Dom's. "She's part of it."

So Jane had put it together, too, the clever girl. "Which means Nancy is part of it."

"Not necessarily," Jane said.

"What are you two talking about?" Sadler stared at Jane. "Wait, isn't Nancy's *maid* named Meredith?"

"Her former maid," Dom said. "Who accompanied Samuel and Nancy every time they shopped together in York."

"I guess the man was seducing the maid and the mistress both," Tristan said. "Looks like you were right to be concerned, Dom. Barlow really is trying to make sure that Nancy's child inherits—even if it's not actually *her* child."

Dom nodded. "That's why Meredith renounced the pregnancy. She didn't want anyone tracing the babe back to her. That wouldn't have helped their scheme."

"*Whose* scheme?" Blakeborough asked. "The maid's and my brother's?"

"Your brother's and Nancy's." Ignoring Sadler's shocked gasp, Dom added, "When Meredith became pregnant, she left to come here, probably hoping that Barlow would follow eventually. Back in York, Nancy began to fear she might lose or had already lost her own baby, so she and Barlow cooked up a scheme to appropriate Meredith's child. That's when they headed here."

"Now wait just one moment," Sadler cried. "Are you suggesting that my daughter is helping that scoundrel pass off his mistress's child as George's *heir*? So the child can inherit what is rightfully yours?"

Placing her hand on the man's arm, Jane shot Dom an accusing look. "Yes, Uncle, that's precisely what he's suggesting. Dom insists on seeing Nancy as some sort of scheming villainess, no matter how much I argue with him over the matter."

"Jane," Dom said softly, "my theory makes the most sense."

"Only because you've got it fixed in your head that it does!" She left her uncle's side to approach Dom. "Do you really think that Nancy would put up with having Samuel's babe by another woman foisted on her?"

"When a great deal of property and a title are at stake? Yes, I'm afraid I do."

"But the scheme only really works if the child is a boy!" Jane said. "And only if Nancy wrests the babe from poor Meredith to raise as her own."

"She would probably just *hire* 'poor Meredith' to take care of the infant."

"Oh, for pity's sake," Jane said. "Nancy may be dim-witted sometimes, but she's not so stupid as to hire back the one woman who might tempt her husband to cheat under her very nose."

"Perhaps she doesn't know that Meredith's child is also Samuel's."

Even before Jane gave an inelegant snort, he had to admit that it sounded unlikely. As she said, Nancy was not *that* stupid. Still . . . "If this isn't some scheme to steal my title and estate, then why did Meredith suddenly claim she was no longer pregnant?"

"Perhaps because it's Samuel's and *Meredith's* scheme?" Jane snapped.

"I wouldn't put it past my brother to concoct such a thing," Blakeborough put in.

Annoyed by the earl's interference, Dom narrowed his gaze on the man. "If Meredith was in on it from the beginning, why would she have asked you for money? Because she hadn't heard from your brother. Because he and Nancy were sure at that point that Nancy had a babe in *her* belly. It's only after they decided otherwise that they shifted tactics."

Jane planted her hands on her hips. "So your theory is that Nancy plans to marry Samuel, pass off as her own the child he fathered on her maid, and then raise it, assuming it's a boy, to be heir to the title. That doesn't gain *Nancy* much, does it? It's not her son, and she's not Samuel's only lover. He and his mistress and the son get everything; she gets only the privilege of knowing she's married to a seducer."

Dom ignored the fact that some of what she said made sense. "She gains an exalted rank as mother to the new viscount. She gains a husband she's always coveted. And she might not even care if Samuel was having an affair with her maid—you said yourself that Nancy wasn't fond of the intimate side of marriage."

The moment Jane paled, he realized what he'd said. Something highly inappropriate. Something that revealed just how frank he and Jane had been in their conversations. God only knew what Blakeborough would make of that.

Bloody hell. Whatever it was, it wouldn't help Dom's situation with Jane any. Not that any of this would. Damn Nancy for coming between them yet again.

Jane's gaze turned stormy as she poked him in the chest. "You've got it all figured out, don't you? But as usual, you ignore all the ways that your theory *doesn't* fit."

He stared her down. "Such as what?"

Again she poked him in the chest. "Why did Samuel mention coming to London to see a doctor if they were sure that Nancy had lost the baby?" Another poke. "Why did she leave York in such strange circumstances that she roused our suspicions?" Poke. "Why did she not even pack bags for the journey?"

When she started to poke him once more, he grabbed her hand. "Perhaps she and Barlow worked up the scheme once she got to York."

Jane snatched her hand free. "And she didn't try to return to Rathmoor Park to allay the servants' suspicions or pack or even take her dogs?"

"Nancy didn't take her dogs?" Sadler echoed. "That's not right, not right at all. That girl carries those deuced dogs everywhere. Many is the trip I've taken with her when I've had to endure the mutts in my lap." Sadler approached to stand beside Jane. "I tell you, the only way she'd leave them behind is if Barlow abducted her and forced her to do his bidding. That's what has happened. I know it!"

With a smug lift of her eyebrow, Jane crossed her arms over her chest and dared Dom to refute that.

He couldn't. Because until he could investigate more, he simply couldn't be sure of the truth, damn it.

"Think what you like," he said. "But whether she's complicit or no, we have to stop them before Samuel takes Nancy somewhere we'll never track him. He's still got five months to wait out the birth. If he succeeds in hiding her until then and they reappear married, with a babe in arms that they claim is George's, we'll have a hard time proving them wrong."

Jane swallowed. "That's true. And even if Nancy isn't complicit now, by then she's likely to be. A man can work any woman round to his way of thinking if he has her to himself for five months, I daresay."

A chill ran down his spine. He fought to ignore it. Nancy was in on this. She had to be. "So I must go to Cheapside. Our best lead right now is Meredith. At least we have *her* address."

"Do you want me to go with you?" Tristan asked.

"Actually, you and I should head for Manton's Investigations to fetch Victor. Then the two of you can hunt Samuel down while I go after Meredith." Dom glanced at Blakeborough. "I don't suppose you know a few of your brother's favorite haunts that my men can investigate."

"I do," Blakeborough said, "but they're places Samuel used to frequent when he lived here years ago. I don't know if he would return to them now."

"People are creatures of habit," Dom said. "And he has no idea that we're close on his heels. No doubt he assumes that Nancy's spurious letter about going on a trip to Bath has fooled everyone. That should buy us a little time to search without spooking them."

Blakeborough nodded. Going over to the writing desk, he drew out some paper and grimly began to jot down information.

"Blakeborough," Dom said, "if I find your brother—"

"Do whatever needs to be done." The earl shot him a hooded glance. "I long ago realized that Samuel could not be trusted. If he has committed a crime, prosecute him to the fullest extent of the law. I wash my hands of him."

Dom nodded. This smacked a bit of how George had felt about Tristan. Except that by all accounts, Blakeborough had tried to help his brother, tried to save his brother from himself until his brother had raped the young woman Ravenswood mentioned. Grudgingly, Dom admitted that the earl was showing himself to be a rather decent man. More decent than his brother, in any case.

"I want to go with you, Dom," Jane said.

Her uncle put his arm about her shoulders. "Let the men do their work, my dear. You should stay here with your fiancé."

The reminder of her still-standing betrothal made Dom want to smash something. But her uncle was right—she would only get in the way if she joined them. And there *was* the problem of her riding off unchaperoned with two gentlemen.

"Listen to your uncle," Dom said. "It's best if you

remain here with your . . . friends." He couldn't bring himself to use the word *fiancé*.

Her eyes sparked fire. "So you mean to just go rushing off with your mind set? You'll almost certainly put Nancy in danger if you continue assuming she's part of the scheme."

"You must trust me, Jane." When the word *must* made her flinch, he cursed his quick tongue and deliberately softened his tone. "I know it's hard for you to believe sometimes, but I do know what I'm doing. No matter what my opinions, I'll let the facts stand for themselves. I promise I won't harm her or allow anyone else to harm her, sweeting."

Only after a stunned silence fell on the room did he realize what he'd called Jane. She did, too, for her eyes went wide and a blush stained her cheeks again.

Blakeborough's eyes glittered like sleet on slate as he strode over to Dom and thrust the piece of paper at him. "Here's the list of Samuel's haunts. You'd best go if you mean to catch them."

They stared each other down, silently acknowledging their status as rivals for Jane's hand. How Dom wished he could set everyone straight, tell them that he and Jane were going to be married, and to blazes with Sadler and Blakeborough and anyone who stood in their way.

But he'd tried to force the issue once and that had only muddied the waters. It was time to let Jane make up her own mind.

So he forced himself to be cordial and thank the earl, forced himself to seize the sheet of paper, then walk out. But just before he and Tristan left the room, Dom saw Blakeborough take Jane by the arm and urge her to sit beside him on the settee.

Damn it all to blazes—Dom hated having to leave her just now, in the very house where he'd first torn them apart, with things so unsettled between them.

But even if Barlow succeeded in ripping away everything Dom owned and Dom had to return to grubbing around in the muck to catch criminals, he meant to get Jane back. No matter what claim the earl tried to place on her, Dom meant to convince her to be his once more.

And once he did, he would move heaven and earth to hold on to her.

18

AFTER DOM AND Tristan left, the servants brought in the refreshments. Right now Jane had no more desire to drink tea than she had to watch Dom ride off without her, but it would give her time to come up with a plan for joining him. Because if he thought she would just sit here and wait while he corralled Samuel without a care for Nancy's guilt or innocence, he was mad.

She was *not* waiting on Dominick Manton anymore. She was certainly not waiting to see if he ruined her cousin's life by blundering in, full of unfair assumptions, and provoking Samuel to do something awful to Nancy.

Unfortunately, she was still trying to figure out how to go after Dom when the duke exchanged a glance with his wife, then rose. "I suppose we should probably be going on."

When everyone else rose, too, and Max held out his hand for Lisette, panic swelled in Jane's chest. Once they left, she would have no way of getting to wherever

Dom was. Uncle Horace certainly wasn't going to take her, and she began to doubt that Edwin would, either.

"If you don't mind," she burst out, "I shall go with you." She fumbled for some excuse that made sense. Ah, yes. "My bags are still in the carriage with your servants, the one that went on to your town house. So I'll just ride home with you to fetch them, if that's all right."

She held her breath. They'd actually separated out her bags only this morning, but perhaps the duke and duchess wouldn't recall that.

No such luck. Max frowned. "Wait a minute. I thought that we—"

"No, my dear," Lisette put in as she grabbed his hand, "don't you remember? Since we weren't expecting Jane's uncle to be here, we sent all her bags on to our town house."

Judging from the momentary confusion in Max's face, he thought Jane and Lisette had both gone temporarily mad. But then his face cleared. "Right. Of course." His voice turned a bit sarcastic. "It completely slipped my mind." He smiled at Jane. "But we're always happy to take you wherever you need to go."

"Oh, yes," Lisette added. "Delighted to help."

Edwin placed a proprietary hand on her back. It was the second time since she'd arrived that he'd touched her in such a fashion, and it perplexed her. He'd never behaved like a true fiancé to her.

When she cast him a quizzical look, he said smoothly, "The duke and duchess can just send your bags to your uncle's once they reach home, Jane. That way you won't have to inconvenience them."

She stared hard at him. And now he was trying to control her? Sweet Lord, what had gotten into him? Was it because of Dom? Were *all* men like dogs, snarling at each other the moment a woman they'd marked as their own came into the room?

But Edwin had never really marked her as his own. Not the way Dom had, anyway. So what was he up to?

Meanwhile, Uncle Horace mumbled, with a mouth full of tea cake, "Yes, yes, his lordship is right. Just let the duke and his wife take care of it at their leisure."

"It's no inconvenience at all," Lisette said brightly, her eyes meeting Jane's. She wasn't a fool. She could obviously guess what Jane wanted.

"And there are things in my bags that I need right away," Jane persisted. "Personal items."

Nothing was more certain to send a man fleeing than mention of a woman's "personal items." The phrase covered a number of feminine ills, all of which men would rather eat nails than discuss.

"If you must go, then go," Edwin said in his usual surly tone, to her immense relief. Then he added, "But I do wish to speak to you alone before you leave."

She stifled a groan. No doubt he wanted to ask about her "friendship" with Dom. She'd hoped to put off any discussion of ending the engagement until later, but obviously that was unwise. And unfair to Edwin. He deserved to know where he stood with her.

"If you don't mind waiting for me a short while longer," she told Lisette and Max crisply, "I do need to have a word with Edwin first."

Max nodded. "No problem at all. We'll be in the carriage."

"I'll just go see to having my own equipage brought round, Jane," Uncle Horace said. "That way you and I can follow the duke and duchess to their abode and fetch your bags together."

Jane wanted to scream. There were times when propriety—and overprotective men—were an annoyance beyond endurance.

But before she could think of a way to discourage Uncle Horace, Lisette said in that imperious duchess voice she'd learned to affect, "No need to trouble yourself, sir. I wish to introduce my little boy to Jane and show her some designs I have for a party I'll be throwing next week. We'd bore you to tears, I'm sure."

Lisette smiled. "But I promise we'll take good care of her. Besides, her maid is at our house already, so she can return with Jane when Jane and I are done. We'll be happy to send them back together in our carriage."

"Oh!" Uncle Horace exclaimed. "Well then, that's very kind of you, Your Grace. Very kind indeed."

At his about-face, Jane fought a smile. A duke's carriage dropping off his niece? That would be quite a coup in their neighborhood. It would raise his credit with the neighbors. The news might even get round to his business and improve his connections.

Thank heaven for matchmaking duchesses.

"I won't be too long, Uncle," Jane said, to prod him out the door.

"Right," he said, taking the hint. "Best be getting home then." He allowed Lisette to take his arm and help him out of the drawing room, with Max trailing behind them.

Once she and Edwin were alone, she shifted away from his curiously possessive hand. This would be hard. What could she say? How could she break it to him gently?

Then Edwin glanced at her with the accusing gray eyes that made her feel like a schoolgirl being taken to task by her papa, and she squirmed guiltily.

"I take it that you are not really heading to the duke and duchess's town house from here," he said coolly.

Sweet Lord, but he was astute. "No."

"And I suppose that means that you and Rathmoor have renewed your . . . er . . . friendship."

Blunt, too. Not that she was surprised. Edwin had always been blunt. But he'd never taken that hard tone with *her*, and it rankled a bit.

"Yes." She tipped up her chin. "I'm afraid we have."

Edwin strolled over to the fireplace and stood with his back to her, rigid as the pokers next to him. "You and I had a deal."

A long sigh escaped her. "I realize that. And I feel bad about reneging on it. I was looking forward to helping Yvette in society. She deserves a good marriage." She squared her shoulders. "But I think I deserve one, too. With a man who wants me to be more than just a companion to his sister."

He muttered something under his breath. "I did intend our marriage to be a real one, you know."

That was a shock. Edwin had always been cynical about the institution.

"Surely you're not serious." She wished he would look at her again so she could better guess what he was thinking. "Don't tell me you're going to give me some nonsense about how you've fallen in love with me."

"No." As if realizing how sharply he'd answered, he shot her a rueful glance. "I suppose I could eventually come to love you. I'd at least make the attempt."

Poor man. "There's no *attempting* with love. You either love someone or you don't. Trust me on that."

He searched her face. "Are you in love with Rathmoor, then?"

"Yes."

The answer came without her even thinking about it. Because she was. She probably always had been. She'd told Dom that he'd killed her love for him, but the truth was, it was unkillable. Though she'd thought to root him out of her heart, he'd merely lain dormant in the wintry ground, waiting until spring when he could grow over her heart like the pernicious honeysuckle in Uncle's arbor.

She should have told Dom last night how she felt, but she'd been too afraid that loving him might mean forgiving him for what he'd done. And she hadn't been quite ready for that. She wasn't sure she was now, either. All she knew was she loved him.

Whether she could live with him was another matter entirely.

"Does he mean to marry you?" Edwin asked.

"He proposed marriage, yes. I haven't answered him. I wanted to speak to you first." That was a bit of a prevarication, but not too awful of one, was it?

Edwin faced her, looking mulish. "He doesn't deserve you."

"And you do?" she teased.

He scowled at her. "That's beside the point. You deserve a man who will stand by you through thick and thin, and Rathmoor's record in that regard leaves much to be desired."

"I agree. Which is why I haven't yet said I would marry him. I want to be sure before I do."

"Ah." Edwin cocked his head to one side. "So there's still a chance for me?"

Oh, dear. "I'm afraid not. If Dom has taught me anything, it's that given the choice between a marriage of convenience and no marriage at all, I would choose the latter."

"But what you're really angling for is a marriage for love." When she cast him a sad smile, Edwin rolled his eyes. "You and Yvette are both cloyingly romantic."

"Which is probably why neither of us has managed to gain a husband."

"True." He crossed his arms over his chest. "Well, if you change your mind about that arse Rathmoor, look me up. I may not love you, whatever that ridiculous word even means, but I do respect and admire you. And

I'd still be willing to make a go of it if that's what you want."

She pretended to swoon. "You really do know how to sweep a girl off her feet, Edwin."

"Watch it, minx," he said with one eyebrow raised. "Or I might actually *try* to steal you from Rathmoor."

"I doubt that." She softened her tone. "But thank you for pretending that you would make the attempt."

He gave a self-deprecating chuckle. "You'd think I would have learned a trick or two from my brother by now, about how to tell a woman what she wants to hear. But alas, I am not of his poetic bent."

"Nor are you a liar," she said gently. "That's a mark in your favor. In fact, you have a great many marks in your favor. Any woman would be lucky to have you."

His easy manner vanished, replaced by the mask of cool reserve he usually wore. "If you're starting to blather nonsense, you'd better go, before I lose all respect for your intelligence."

With a strained laugh, she turned for the door.

"Oh, and Jane?" he called out.

"Yes?"

Edwin placed his hand casually on one of the fire pokers. "Tell Rathmoor that if he breaks your heart, I will find him and skewer him with one of these."

She started to make some teasing remark but the cold glint in his eye made her think better of it. "I will. And thank you for understanding, Edwin."

"I don't understand a damned thing," he drawled. "You're tossing aside a wealthy earl to run after some fellow you jilted twelve years ago. That makes no sense. And it means I am now once more in need of a wife who can tolerate my bad-tempered growls long enough to get my sister a husband."

She hoped he found someone better, someone he could love. But there was no point in saying it. He would just mock her. "I do hope we can continue to be friends."

He snorted. "I doubt Rathmoor will allow that."

"He doesn't have a say in it," she said, then turned on her heel and left.

When she reached the duke's coach, she was relieved to find that Uncle Horace had already headed home and only Max and Lisette were waiting for her.

"Where to?" Max asked as she climbed in. "I assume that you had some destination in mind when you cooked up that nonsense about needing your bags."

"I want to join Dom." She stared him down, daring him to gainsay her. She'd take a hackney if she had to. "He's probably still at Manton's Investigations, so let's start there."

Though a smile tugged at the duke's lips, he merely gave the order to the coachman. As soon as they set off, however, he said, "You do realize that Dom is going to throttle me for helping you."

"I don't see why," she said lightly. "You *are* head of the Duke's Men, aren't you? Surely you can go wherever you please and involve yourself as much as you like."

As Lisette burst into laughter, Max shook his head. "My brother-in-law doesn't exactly *like* having his agency called 'the Duke's Men.' I'd keep that appellation under your hat, if I were you."

"Oh, that sounds so much like Dom," Jane muttered, "not to appreciate a fellow who showed faith in him and was willing to use him to find his own cousin, not to mention invest in his business concern."

Lisette laughed even harder now, which only made Max wince.

"What?" Jane asked. "What is it?"

A flush spread over Max's face. "Let's just say that my part in . . . er . . . 'the Duke's Men' has been greatly exaggerated by the papers. Rather tangential, really."

"In other words," Lisette teased, "he pretty much did nothing. He didn't even come up with the name, and he certainly didn't hire Dom to find Victor. Tristan stumbled across Victor himself, and then . . ."

Lisette spun out the story of how she had met Max and how Dom had become involved. How Max had made a grand gesture for the press to protect Tristan from George.

"Oh, Lord," Jane breathed. "That's why you were all at George's house that day." The day she'd first seen Dom after nearly eleven years apart.

"Exactly. I mean, Max does what he can to recommend the agency, and certainly Dom benefits from the excellent press he received as a result of Tristan's finding Victor. But beyond that, Max has nothing to do with it. He has *tried* to invest in it, but Dom gets all hot under the collar every time he suggests it."

"What a shock," Jane said sarcastically.

She thought of Dom the Almighty, having his hard work and keen investigative sense attributed to some duke who'd simply taken up with his sister, and began to laugh. Then Lisette joined her, and eventually, Max.

They laughed until tears rolled down Jane's cheeks and Lisette was holding her sides.

"Poor Dom," Jane gasped, when she'd finally gained control of herself. "No matter how carefully he plans, someone always comes along to muck things up. We must all be quite a trial to him."

"Oh, indeed, we are," Lisette said, sobering. "But honestly, he takes himself far too seriously, so it's good for him." She smiled at Jane. "*You're* good for him. He needs a woman who stands firm when he tries to dictate how the world must be, a woman who will teach him that it's all right if plans go awry. He needs to learn that he can pick up the pieces and still be happy, as long as he does it with the right person."

"I only hope he agrees with you," Jane said. "I really do."

Because if she could be that woman for Dom—if he could *let* her be that woman for him—then they might have a chance, after all.

19

Dom sat hunched atop the box of a dilapidated coach just a block away from where Meredith's family lived. He'd purchased the former hackney carriage a few months ago to use for investigations, and it had proved invaluable. A stranger lounging in a doorway might be seen as suspicious, but a hackney hoping for a fare? No one looked twice.

It enabled him and Tristan and Victor to be invisible. If they were all three required, one could sit on the seat as the driver, and the others could pretend to be fares, waiting for a friend in some nearby lodgings.

Today, however, it was just him, cursing the London drizzle that seeped through the box coat with shoulder capes that he wore as part of his disguise. He swigged from the brandy flask tucked inside his coat, seeking a bit of liquid comfort. After all, he was going to be here for some time.

No one had answered the door at Meredith's family home. Fortunately, a neighbor had told him that she and her family worked at some coaching inn, returning home at seven o'clock every night. Not so fortunately, the man didn't know which one or even what part of town it was in.

Dom had no choice but to wait for her to return. He drew out his pocket watch. Five o'clock. Two more hours to keep watch. Damn.

The wails of a baby wafted down to him from farther up the street, and he looked up to see a young woman coming toward him, with the crying infant slung on her hip and two squabbling children walking beside her.

"Stop your jawin', the both of you!" she cried at the girl who looked to be about eight and the lad who couldn't be more than five. "You've set Billy off again, you have. If you keep it up, you won't get no cake after supper, and that's a promise."

As he watched them approach—the children still jostling each other and the mother trying to settle the baby—a fantasy leapt into his head.

He saw Jane playing the old pianoforte at Rathmoor Park. A little boy much like that one sat beside her on the bench, poking at the keys with his chubby fingers and adding dissonance to his mother's performance. His sister, a little girl much like that one, leaned over her mother's shoulder to watch how Jane fingered the keys.

Meanwhile, Dom stood nearby, jiggling a crying babe of his own, trying to console it, swinging it up into the air until it hiccupped, then laughed.

He saw the scene as clearly as a painting—the babe

and young boy still in skirts, the girl with brown curls tumbling down her back, their mother glancing back at him with a gleam in her eye and a teasing smile on her lips that hinted . . .

"Hey, what're you looking at, guv'nor? Ain't you ever seen a crying babe?"

He started. God, he'd been staring. What was wrong with him? He was supposed to blend in, not make a spectacle of himself. He never let his mind wander like that while he was on a case.

Then again, he never had Jane to preoccupy him. To make him want things. To make him hope. That was the worst part—the hope she dangled before him.

With a sigh, he slouched down and tugged his broad brim over his face. Another ten minutes passed. He wondered if he could slip into the coach and nap until Meredith returned. But given how little rest he'd had the past few days, he was liable to sleep well beyond the allotted time.

The clatter of hooves approaching made him glance up at the street ahead. Bloody hell. Was that Max's coach? What was *he* doing here?

It pulled up beside the hackney, and Dom jerked his gaze forward for the benefit of anyone who might be watching. When he heard a window being lowered, he hissed, "You can't be here, blast it. Go away. If Meredith should return early and see you—"

"You don't even know what she looks like!" a familiar feminine voice protested. "But I do."

For one foolish moment, his heart leapt. Until he

remembered where he was. And what he was supposed to be doing.

With a scowl, he looked at Jane, who sat at the coach window staring out at him. "I don't *need* to know what she looks like. She and her family will enter that house over there at approximately seven, at which time I will knock on the door and ask to speak to her. So go home. You'll just make everything worse."

He glanced beyond her to Max. "Take her back to her uncle's. If our quarry spots a ducal coach hanging about in the neighborhood before we spot her, it might spook her."

Jane's lips thinned into a line. "Fine. Then Max and Lisette can go, and I'll wait with you. I'll pretend to be your fare. Or your wife. Or whatever suits you. But I'm not leaving."

He was still assembling reasons she shouldn't stay, when the door to Max's coach opened and Jane stepped nimbly out, then quickly slipped into his hackney. Before Dom could even protest, Max's carriage was pulling away.

Damn, damn, damn. She shouldn't be here. It wasn't wise. So why was part of him ridiculously glad to see her?

Chiding himself for letting his obsession for Jane overrule his investigative good sense, Dom made a furtive survey of the street. But no one seemed to be around to have noticed the short encounter between the two carriages.

A long breath escaped him. It wasn't as if he couldn't

leave the box; he *had* just been thinking that he ought to go inside and sleep. The curtains could be closed. Meredith wouldn't return for a couple of hours.

So he could talk to Jane and find out what had happened between her and Blakeborough after he left. He could finally get an answer to his marriage proposal.

Proposal? Jane would probably call it a marriage *command*.

He groaned. Perhaps it wouldn't be a bad idea to talk to her while he waited. He could always pack her off in another hackney before it was time for Meredith to return home. Yes, that would be best.

Climbing inside the hackney, he doffed his hat and shrugged out of his box coat. But all of his perfectly logical reasons for being there went right out of his head the moment he saw her looking so luscious and lovely in her sunny gown.

Because he desired only one thing. Jane. In his arms. Now.

She must have seen the feral need flare in his face, for her eyes went wide. That was the only reaction she had time for, however, before he dragged her into his embrace so he could take her mouth in a hard, urgent kiss.

God, he wanted her. He would never stop wanting her. Fisting his hands in her puffy sleeves to hold her still, he plundered her mouth the way he ached to plunder her body.

Suddenly she shoved him back. "What are you doing? That's not why—"

He clasped her head in his hands, dislodging her bonnet, which tumbled to the floor. Then he kissed her again, demanding her to kiss him back, to *need* him back. It took her a moment, but then she moaned low in her throat and melted against him.

And he exulted. She was soft, so wonderfully soft, his Jane. So wonderfully giving. Surely she wouldn't be responding to him this way if she had cemented her engagement to Blakeborough.

But then, he'd thought that last night.

He jerked back, gratified to see from her flushed cheeks, reddened lips, and bright eyes that she was now as eager and aroused as he. Indeed, she was already looping her arms about his neck to draw him close once more.

Stopping just short of her mouth, he rasped, "Are you still engaged to Blakeborough?"

Her gorgeous eyes narrowed. "My engagement didn't stop you last night."

"It would now."

A coy smile broke over her lips, and she tightened her grip on his neck. "Then I suppose it's a good thing I am not."

With a growl of triumph, he kissed her once more. She was here. She was his. Nothing else mattered.

Still kissing her, he jerked both sets of curtains closed. Then he tugged her onto his lap and began to tear at the fastenings of her pelisse-dress. He wanted to touch her, taste her . . . be inside her. He could think of naught else.

"I take it that you mean to seduce me," she murmured between kisses.

"Yes." Seduce her and marry her. And then seduce her again, as often as he could.

"Well then, carry on."

So he did. He unfastened her clothes just enough to bare her breasts, then seized one in his mouth. God, she was perfect. His perfect jewel.

She buried her hands in his hair to pull her into him, sighing and moaning as if she would die if he didn't make love to her. Which was exactly how *he* felt.

Working his hand up beneath her skirts and into the slit in her drawers, he found her so wet and hot that he nearly came right there. He slipped a finger inside her silky sweetness, and she gasped, then began to tug at his trouser buttons.

"You're all I want, Jane." As he stroked her, he used his other hand to brush hers away so he could unfasten his own trouser buttons. "The only woman I ever cared about."

"You're the only man *I* ever cared about." She undulated against his fingers, begging for him with her body. "Why do you think . . . I waited for you so long?"

"Not long enough, apparently," he muttered, "or you wouldn't have gotten yourself engaged to Blakeborough." He tugged at her nipple with his teeth, then relished her cry of pleasure.

"I only . . . did it because I was . . . tired of waiting." She arched against his mouth. "Because you clearly weren't . . . coming back for me."

"I was sure you hated me." At last he got his trousers open. "You acted like you hated me still."

"I did." Her breath was unsteady. "But only because . . . you tore us apart."

He shifted her to sit astride him. "And now?"

Flashing him a provocative smile he would never have dreamed she had in her repertoire, she unbuttoned his drawers. "Do I look like I hate you?"

His cock, so hard he thought it might erupt right there and embarrass him, sprang free. "You look like . . . like . . ."

He paused to take in her lovely face with its flushed cheeks, sparkling eyes, and lush lips. Then he swept his gaze down to her breasts with their brazen tips, displayed so enticingly above the boned corset and her undone shift. He then dropped his eyes to the smooth thighs emerging from beneath her bunched-up skirts.

Shoving the fabric higher, he exposed her dewy thatch of curls, and a shudder of anticipation shook him. "You look like an angel."

She uttered a breathy laugh. "A wanton, more like." Taking his cock in her hand, she stroked it so wonderfully that he groaned. "Would an angel do this?"

His cock was a rod of iron. "Jane . . ." He covered her hand to stay it, but she ignored his attempt.

"I love it when you can't control yourself," she whispered. "I love having you at my mercy. You have no idea . . . how much I enjoy seeing Dom the Almighty brought low."

He barely registered her words. What she was doing

felt so good. So bloody damned good. If she stroked him much more . . .

"I want to be inside you." He gripped her wrist. "Please, Jane . . ."

Her sensuous smile faltered. "You've never said 'please' to me before. Not in your whole life."

"Really?" Had he only ever issued orders? If so, no wonder she'd refused him last night.

Perhaps it was time to show her she didn't have to seduce him to gain control. That he could give up his control freely . . . to *her*, at least. "Then let me say it now. Please, Jane, make love to me. If you don't mind."

She stared at him. "I . . . I don't know what you mean."

He nodded to his cock, which looked downright ecstatic over the idea. "Get up on your knees and fit me inside you." Realizing he'd just issued yet another order, he added, "Please. If you want."

Jane got that sultry look on her face again. Like the little seductress she was rapidly showing herself to be, she rose up and then came down on him.

By degrees. Very slow degrees.

He had trouble breathing. "Am I hurting you?"

Her smile broadened as she shimmied down another inch. "Not really."

Stifling a curse, he clutched her arms. "You just . . . enjoy torturing me."

"Absolutely," she said and moved his hands to cover her breasts.

He was more than happy to oblige her unspoken

request, happy to thumb her nipples and watch as her lovely mouth fell open and a moan of pure pleasure escaped her.

His cock swelled, and he thrust up involuntarily. "Please . . ." he said hoarsely. "Please, Jane . . ."

With a choked laugh, she sheathed herself on him. Then her eyes went wide. "Oh, that feels *amazing*."

"It would feel more amazing if you . . . would move," he rasped, though the mere sensation of being buried inside her was making him insane. When she arched an eyebrow, he added, "Please."

"I could get to like this," she said teasingly. "The begging."

But even as he groaned, she began to move, like the sensual creature that she was. His sweetheart undulated atop him, her head thrown back and her eyes sliding closed, and for the first time in his life, he was happy to give himself up to someone else's control. To relish her pleasure, which was also *his* pleasure.

Somehow he'd stumbled into paradise, ruled by his own personal angel. His own personal siren.

"You like having me . . . in your power, do you?" he said.

"Yes, oh, yes." Her eyes brightened as she rode him, harder, faster. "Say it again."

"What?" He could hardly think for watching her take him. For being inside her so deeply he fancied he could feel her heart, her very soul.

"Please." Her face was flushed, rapt. "Say . . . 'please' again."

"Please."

Why had he never thought to say it before? This was all he'd ever wanted—to have the enthralling, intoxicating Jane in his arms, in his life. Forever.

A "please" from time to time was little enough to give for that. "Please, my wanton angel." He clutched her close, his rhythm quickening. "Please . . . be mine. Please . . . marry me."

His release approached like a carriage thundering toward the heavens. Toward paradise. And as the blood roared in his ears, he plunged his cock deeply and emptied himself inside her, crying, "Please . . . Jane . . . love me!"

"I do." With a hoarse cry of her own, she strained against him and found her own release, milking his cock with the force of it. "I do, my darling . . . I do."

20

JANE FELT LIMP and sated and thoroughly wicked
as she snuggled against Dom. They were still joined
below, though he'd begun to soften inside her. Still, how
naughty it was to be here like this, how deliciously carnal to have made love while they were both half-dressed.
Why, Dom still even wore his cravat! She didn't know
why that excited her, though it did.

But not as much as Dom saying "please" over and
over. Letting her take control of their lovemaking.
Even *encouraging* her to do it.

And not nearly as much as Dom asking her to marry
him.

Well, he didn't really *ask*, exactly. He demanded it yet
again. But he'd said "please," and that made all the difference. Especially since he'd then asked her to love him.

Silly man. As if she had any choice in the matter.

"I do love you, you know," she whispered. "I can't help
myself. I fell in love with you practically from the moment we met, and I never stopped."

"I love you, too, sweeting," he murmured into her shoulder. "Always have, always will."

Her heart thundered in her chest. She'd waited so long to hear those words again, she could scarcely believe them.

She pulled back to search his face. "Truly?"

"Truly." With infinite tenderness, he brushed her fringe of curls from her eyes. "I tried so hard to forget you after we parted. But I couldn't. Not for one day."

That earned him a long kiss . . . that, and the prospect of him as hers. Her very own *husband*. Oh, yes. She could let herself think it now. They could marry at once, or at least as soon as this business with Nancy was over.

Nancy! Oh, Lord, she'd forgotten all about her cousin.

Sliding off him, she frantically sought to put her clothing to rights. "You don't think that Meredith returned while we were . . . you know . . ."

"No." A faint amusement lightened his tone as he tucked himself back into his drawers and buttoned them. "The man I spoke to said she and her family return at seven every night." He pulled out his pocket watch. "It's only six now."

"Thank heaven." She tugged her skirts and petticoats into place and patted her hair. "I do wish that hackney coaches came with mirrors."

Dom's eyes gleamed at her. "Be glad I didn't take your hair down completely, while I was mauling you with all the self-control of some half-grown lad."

She shot him a teasing glance. "I didn't mind. You

maul very well. And making love in a carriage, with the world passing by unsuspecting, was rather . . . well . . . thrilling."

"I can do without that kind of thrill, frankly. If anyone had discovered us . . ." He shuddered. "Next time we make love, it will be in a bed, and I will treat you with the tenderness you deserve." He watched her smooth her stockings and retie her loosened garters. "How did you find me, anyway?"

"We went to your office, and your butler told us you had left to come here." She laughed, remembering it. "Max said, 'What, already?' and Mr. Shaw said, rather loftily, that you could 'wait for no man's leisure' and 'tend on no man's business.' I gather that the man is as fond of *Much Ado about Nothing* as we are."

"Oh, he likes them all," Dom said dryly. "Too many years spent as a bit player in the theater, I'm afraid. He keeps hoping that if he memorizes every play in existence, he will advance to a lead role." He fastened his trousers. "But how did you even get away from your uncle and Blakeborough? They just let you ride off after me with Max and Lisette?"

"Well, Blakeborough had no choice since I had just jilted him." She sighed. "Oh, Lord. I have once again jilted a fiancé, haven't I? I'm forever going to be known as the woman who jilted two men." She made a face. "I should have calling cards made—'Jane the Jilt,' to go along with 'Dom the Almighty.'"

"I will never carry a card with the appellation 'Dom the Almighty,' so just put that right out of your head," he said irritably. "In any case, since you're marrying me, I'm no longer jilted." He paused a moment to shoot her a wary glance. "You *are* marrying me, aren't you?"

That was even closer to asking. "Say 'please,'" she teased.

Though he eyed her askance, he pulled her close for a long, lingering kiss, then said, "Please, Jane, will you marry me?"

She beamed at him. "I do believe I will."

He sobered. "Even if Nancy actually does turn out to be bearing George's son, and he inherits everything?"

"Of course. You're head of the Duke's Men. I would be a fool to pass up such a match." When he scowled at her, she burst into laughter. "Max and Lisette told me all about how your agency got the name. I must say I found it vastly amusing."

"You would," he grumbled. "And you still haven't said why your uncle let you go off with them." After she related her elaborate deception, he shook his head. "All this subterfuge in order to talk to me could have been prevented if you'd just ridden with me earlier today, when I asked."

"Really?" She smoothed his disordered hair, which was sticking up at all angles. "You wouldn't have spent the entire trip detailing reasons why I 'must' marry you?"

He flinched. "I'm sorry, Jane. Apparently, when I find myself with my back to the wall, I bark orders."

"I know." She straightened his cravat. "And in case you hadn't noticed, I don't do well with men who bark orders or make plans for me. It makes me want to shove them off a cliff."

"Or refuse to marry them?"

"That, too."

"Then I can see it's a habit I shall have to break, if I am to keep you happy." He glanced away. "Sometimes, it's just . . . I don't know . . . easier to bark orders than to ask. Safer. No one has a chance to say no."

It hit her then. That was precisely why he felt more comfortable ordering people about, setting up plans, being in charge. Because when he wasn't in control, there was a chance he'd be left out in the cold. Left in a house with oblivious servants and a brother who despised him for taking his mother away by the simple fact of being born.

Left alone. Her poor, dear love.

Jane kept her eyes trained on his cravat. "But if you don't ever give people a chance to say no, you can never know if they will rise to the occasion or not."

He tipped up her chin until she was staring into his eyes. "I wronged you terribly by not trusting you to rise to the occasion, didn't I? If I'd married you and carried you off to the garret, I daresay you would have stayed by my side. Loved me. Cherished me."

Tears stung her eyes. "I like to think I would have. I certainly would have tried. It would have been worth it to be with you."

"Leaving you was the biggest mistake I ever made," he said earnestly. "I once told you I would do it again, given the chance. But I was lying, to myself as well as you. I could never do it again. Certainly not now that I know what it's like to have you for my own. You have no idea how much I've missed you all these years."

It was all she could do not to burst into tears right then and there. But that would only alarm him. So she choked them down enough to say, "No more than I missed you, I expect."

With a groan, he kissed her, long and hot. It was a sweet promise of things to come, a portent of their future together.

When he was done, she wiped away tears. "To be fair, if we *had* married then, who knows what would have become of us? I doubt I would have liked your running about the country as a spy, leaving me alone for weeks at a time. And I daresay you would have had trouble concentrating on your work for worrying about me."

His grateful smile showed that he appreciated her attempt to mitigate his betrayal.

She swallowed. "Of course, later you could have . . . well . . . come after me. Once you established your business. While I was still un-betrothed. Why didn't you?"

"I don't suppose you would accept rampant idiocy as a reason?"

"I would . . . *if* I really thought it were the reason." When he stiffened, she added archly, "You aren't generally an idiot. Daft and a tad overbearing, yes, but not an idiot."

A sigh escaped him. He leaned past her to pull the

curtain open just enough so he could keep an eye on the street.

When it looked as if he might not answer, she added, "Tristan thinks you didn't come after me because you were afraid that I *couldn't* love you."

He cast her a startled glance. "You told Tristan the truth about us?"

She winced. "And Lisette and Max. Sorry. Tristan sort of . . . forced it out of me."

"Well, that explains why Max and Lisette were willing to bring you here in the midst of such a crucial investigation. They've been pressing me for a long time to give you another chance. Because they thought *you* betrayed *me*."

Grabbing her hands, he gazed down at them with a haunted look. "And I suppose there's some truth to my brother's words. But I also didn't come after you because that would have been a tacit admission that I'd made a mistake. That in so doing, I'd ruined our lives. I was afraid if I admitted I'd been wrong, then it had all been for nothing. I'd sacrificed my happiness—*your* happiness—for nothing."

"Oh, Dom," she whispered and squeezed his hands.

"A part of me also thought if I didn't approach you at all, there was still a chance we could be together again. But if I asked and you said no—or worse yet, said that you no longer cared about me—it would be over for good. As long as I didn't ask, there was always hope. And hope is what kept me going."

A muscle flexed in his jaw. "Until you got engaged. That quashed my hope. It was what I'd told myself I wanted for you. Because it proved that I'd been right to put you aside."

He lifted his gaze to hers. "Unfortunately, being right was cold comfort when it meant I'd lost you for good. By the time you came to me that day at Rathmoor Park, I was in a very dark state. I was resigning myself to a lifetime of loneliness, of wanting you and not having you."

"You would have let me marry Edwin?" she said incredulously. "Even though you still loved me?"

"You were still going to marry *him*, weren't you?" he countered. "Knowing that you still loved *me*."

"True." She attempted a smile. "I would have done it just to bedevil you."

"No doubt," he said dryly.

"But it would have been a mistake, and I'd have been miserable."

He pressed a kiss to their joined hands. "Then I suppose we should really thank Nancy for her shenanigans. Or else we'd still be separate and miserable."

The mention of Nancy made her start. "What time is it?"

"It's early yet," he said, but released her hands to pull the curtain aside once more. Then he froze. "Damn."

"What?"

He nodded out the window. "Is that Meredith?"

She followed his gaze and caught her breath. "Yes. And she's with Samuel."

"Hard to tell if she's pregnant when she's wearing that loose gown. And I don't see her family. She must have left them at the coaching inn where they work so she could come away with Barlow."

Her heart sank. "There's someone else I don't see— my cousin, devil take it. Where's Nancy?"

The couple stood right in front of Meredith's home, engrossed in what appeared to be a heated conversation.

Dom opened the window, but the pair were too far away to be heard. When Meredith turned as if to go inside, Dom reached for the door handle.

Jane stayed his hand. "You can't go out there!"

"Why not? I have to catch Barlow before he runs off."

"But we still don't know where Nancy is."

Dom stared at her. "Once we have Barlow and Meredith, one of them will surely give us her location. For all we know, Victor and Tristan may already have learned where he's staying. I told them to come here if they couldn't find out anything. I've been here since three and they haven't shown up yet."

Panic tightened her throat at the thought that he might depend on such uncertainties rather than go after Nancy. "But if they don't learn where he's been staying, and Samuel refuses to reveal it, then what?"

He shrugged. "She'll probably come to her father's herself, since she'll have nowhere else to go."

"If she *can*," Jane said, desperate to convince him. "Doesn't the fact that she's not with either of them alarm you? It certainly does me."

His jaw tautened. "I suppose you have a point." He searched her face. "But are you willing to risk the possibility that I—that *we*—could lose the estate? Because if you're wrong about Nancy, and if Barlow somehow escapes my grasp, then we might still lose everything. The two of them would just find another babe to take the place of Meredith's."

She considered that. But she *wasn't* wrong about Nancy. She knew it in her heart. "You accused me last night of not trusting your instincts as an investigator," she said, choosing her words carefully. "But that's not true. I do trust them. So, if you're absolutely certain that Nancy is willingly participating in a scheme to defraud, then I will bow to whatever plan you implement."

He eyed her skeptically.

"I mean that." She cupped his cheek. "But if you have even a wisp of a doubt that she's involved, then I beg you to trust *my* instincts regarding her character. Because they're telling me she would never set out to steal your rightful inheritance."

With a coarse oath, he shifted to look out the window. Then his gaze sharpened. "Barlow is leaving now that Meredith has gone inside. So exactly what do you want me to do?"

She caught her breath. He was asking her. Considering her opinion. *Trusting* her. "I-I want you to follow him. He's bound to lead you to Nancy eventually."

"And if he doesn't?"

A shudder wracked her. "Lord, I don't even want to think about that." She donned her bonnet and tied the ribbons. "But you can't really follow him forever, so I suppose you'd have to capture him."

"All right." He shrugged into his coat, clapped his hat on his head, and opened the carriage door on the side Samuel couldn't see. "What about Meredith? What if *she's* the one hiding Nancy?"

When he climbed out, Jane followed him. "Don't worry about Meredith. I'll take care of *her*." Jane wasn't about to let the maid escape scot-free.

Dom edged to the front of the carriage to look past the horses. He scowled. "Barlow hailed a hackney. I must go. But I don't like leaving you here alone."

"I'll be fine," she said, shoving him toward the box. "Go, go! He's getting away! Meredith and I will be waiting right here for you once you've found Nancy."

He hesitated a moment more. Then with a muttered curse, he climbed up onto the box and rode off.

She watched him go, her heart in her throat. What if he *did* lose sight of Samuel? What if . . .

No, she was *not* going to think about all the things that could go wrong. She was going to hedge their bets by getting the truth out of Meredith. Surely it would help to know the maid's side of things. Meredith might even possess crucial information.

Hoping that she didn't look too much like a woman who'd just been thoroughly bedded, she straightened her bonnet and walked briskly across the street to the house that Meredith had entered.

Noting the window nearby, she ducked her head to hide her countenance behind her bonnet as she knocked. It wouldn't do for the maid to recognize her and refuse to answer the door.

But Meredith must not have even looked out, for the door swung forcefully open, and she exclaimed, "Samuel, I swear that if you don't—" She blinked at Jane. "M-Miss Vernon! What are you doing here?"

"Looking for Nancy," Jane said bluntly, and pushed past the woman into the house. "You don't have her here, do you?"

The color drained from her already wan cheeks. "I . . . I don't have her anywhere. She's not at Rathmoor Park?"

Jane stared accusingly at her. "You know perfectly well that she's not. So you might as well stop lying right now. I already saw you with Samuel."

"Good Lord." Meredith looked positively ghostly as she grabbed for a side table near the door.

"Are you all right?" Jane asked. The woman was *not* playing the deceptive villainess very well.

"I . . . I . . ." Whirling on her heel, Meredith ran into the nearest room.

Jane followed just in time to watch the maid cast up her accounts in a chamber pot. "Oh, dear." Glancing around, Jane spotted a pitcher of water and hurried to dampen her handkerchief, then brought it over to Meredith.

Gratefully, the woman took it to wipe her mouth and forehead.

"Here," Jane said as she led Meredith over to a sofa, "you must sit down."

Some investigator *she* was, helping the woman who was supposed to be the enemy. Still, she couldn't help it. She could never bear to see a woman ill, especially one bearing a child.

But she had to know the truth. So, as soon as she and Meredith were seated, she said, "I assume that you and Samuel were arguing about your child. *His* child."

"You know?" Meredith squeaked, her hand going to her belly. Then she paused. "Oh. Right. I forgot that Lord Blakeborough is your fiancé." She scowled. "I should never have gone to him. But I didn't think he'd reveal my secret to *you*, of all people, especially after I told him I was mistaken about a babe growing in my belly."

"Except that you weren't mistaken, were you?" Jane prodded.

Meredith stared down at the handkerchief. "No. After Samuel showed up, I figured everything would be all right, so I lied to his lordship. I didn't want the truth to get back to you or my mistress. She thought I was helping my ill papa; she'd never take me back if she thought I was bearing a bastard. *Especially* Samuel's bastard."

Jane's throat tightened. "Because she was having an affair with Samuel."

Meredith eyed her incredulously. "No, indeed! It was naught but a flirtation until his lordship's death. Then she started talking about how she could marry Samuel, how he wanted to marry her. And I was in a pickle. I thought she was deluded about his intentions, but I could hardly tell her I was bearing his babe. I would have been turned off for good! So I asked for leave to come home to help my ailing papa."

The young woman rubbed her arms. "I really thought Samuel would marry *me*. He was always saying how he loved me. But after I sent that note to his lordship, Samuel admitted he was planning to marry her ladyship. That he and my lady wanted to take in my babe, since she'd lost her own. Only they . . . wanted to make it look like she'd borne it herself, he said. That it was her late husband's. So the babe could inherit, you see."

A vise tightened about Jane's chest. She'd been wrong about Nancy. Oh, Lord, how could that be?

"But that didn't sound right to me." Meredith glared into the distance. "I'm not as much the fool as Samuel takes me for, you know. I understood how wicked that was, and I knew my lady would never do such a thing."

The vise loosened a fraction, and Jane began to breathe again.

"So, I told him I wished to speak to her ladyship myself about it. He put me off for a few days, telling me nonsense about how she wasn't feeling up to it after losing the baby and such. This morning when he came to the inn where I work, I flat out told him I wouldn't do it unless I could talk to her. I gave him no choice but to agree."

Meredith met Jane's gaze. "So, this afternoon, he brought me over to the house where she's staying. It was *awful*, miss. A rough-looking bruiser friend of Samuel's was standing outside when we got there. He and Samuel went inside with me and stood about the whole time I spoke with her ladyship."

Jane swallowed, her heart clamoring in her chest. "What did she say to you?"

"Not much. She was cold and looked at me so suspicious-like . . . There's no telling what he'd told her about *me*, about my part in everything. We hardly spoke two words, because he kept breaking in and correcting her on things. She wouldn't say a word about my baby, though he kept prompting her to."

Meredith frowned. "The whole thing was odd, I tell you. So I started asking her if she was all right and how she was feeling and such, and that's when Samuel hustled me out of there and brought me home."

Sweet Lord. It sounded to her as if Samuel was keeping Nancy against her will. If that were the case, and Dom was walking into a situation against at least Samuel and one of Samuel's prizefighters, possibly others . . . "You know where this house is, right?"

"Yes, but . . . well . . ." She twisted the handkerchief in her hands. "When I told Samuel I wanted no part of his scheme, he threatened me if I didn't keep quiet. Said he would blacken my name so I could never get a position again, that he would ruin me."

"That's what you were arguing about," Jane said.

"I was just trying to think what to do when you knocked." Meredith seized Jane's hand. "Oh, miss, my papa really is ailing. I didn't make that up. He shouldn't even be working at the coaching inn, and Mama doesn't make enough to take care of us and a babe, too. I have to have a position! I can't lose it. It would have been hard enough to rely on whatever Samuel gave me, but if he won't marry me and won't help pay for the babe and I can't work . . ."

"You leave Samuel to me," Jane said fiercely. Edwin would help. He had to. Assuming that Meredith was speaking the truth, of course, about all of this. "But you *have* to tell me where he's hiding Nancy."

Somehow she had to get to Dom, to warn him. Oh, sweet Lord, she dearly hoped she hadn't sent him into danger!

A knock came at the door, startling them both. Meredith leapt up. "What if that's Samuel? What if he's come back, and he finds you here? Lord help us!"

Jane stepped to the window to look out, then sagged in relief. "Oh, thank heaven, it's Tristan." Without waiting for Meredith, she hurried to open the door.

"Jane!" Tristan cried. "What the hell are you doing here?"

"Dom's Jane?" the man with him asked.

She didn't recognize him, but he had to be Max's cousin Victor. He and Max had similar faces, not to mention similar coloring. There was a definite family resemblance.

"I presume you are Mr. Cale." She thrust out her hand. "I'm Jane Vernon, Dom's *fiancée*," she said, delighted that she could say it at last.

Mr. Cale shook her hand as Tristan muttered, "It's about damned time you two made it official." Then he gazed beyond her to where Meredith stood. "Where is Dom, anyway? We didn't see the hackney out front."

"He took it to follow Samuel, who was just here. He's trying to find out where Samuel is keeping Nancy." She fought, unsuccessfully, to tamp down the panic rising in her chest once more. "But he might be riding into danger, and I don't know where he's gone." She turned to stare at Meredith. "Please, you have to tell us. I can't take the chance that Samuel will hurt the man I mean to marry."

"L-Lord Rathmoor? Y-You're going to marry his late lordship's younger brother?"

Jane nodded. "And then I'll be mistress of Rathmoor Park, and I swear by everything that's holy, I will make sure—*we* will make sure that you're taken care of. You and your babe and your family." She seized Meredith's hands. "But you have to tell me *where Samuel is keeping Nancy.*"

Meredith glanced from her to Tristan and Victor, then released a long sigh. "All right. I'll tell you."

21

BY THE TIME the carriage carrying Barlow halted in front of a tumbledown town house across the Thames in Battersea, the light was fading. Dom pulled over a few doors back, then got down and pretended to check one of the horses' feet for a stone so he could keep an eye on his quarry.

Fortunately, Barlow didn't seem to be expecting anyone to follow him, for he didn't even glance around. He paid the hackney driver, who pulled off. Then he spoke to a beefy fellow lounging on the steps before using a key to go inside.

Those two things alone would have roused Dom's alarm, but coupled with Jane's concerns, he had to admit all wasn't quite right. The man with the look of a prizefighter about him appeared to have been standing guard. Given Barlow's present profession as an organizer of fights, might there be others inside?

The bruiser rose and headed up the street toward

Dom, whistling. The man was a good head taller than Dom, but that would make no difference if Dom took him by surprise. Laying his hand on the knife in his coat pocket, Dom waited until the man walked past him before following behind him . . . at least as far as the nearest alley.

Then before the big lug even knew what was happening, Dom lunged forward to catch him by the neck in a hold. Jabbing the tip of his blade into the brute's back, Dom dragged him into the alley.

A moment of struggle ensued until Dom hissed, "I'll bury this knife in your ribs, you bloody fool, if you don't stop fighting."

The man stilled. "If it's money ye're after—"

"It's not." Dom tightened his forearm across the man's throat, just enough to limit his breathing. "Who's in the house with Barlow?"

There was a long pause. "Don't know what ye're talking about," the man wheezed.

"Then we'll stand here until you figure it out." Dom stuck the bruiser with his blade just enough to make him bleed. "While we wait, I can do some carving."

"Now see here," the man warned him, "if you cut me, my friends will hunt you down and smash your face to bits. You don't know who ye're dealing with."

"Neither do you. Ever hear of the Duke's Men?" God, how he hated that term, but it was better known than Manton's Investigations. "I'm one of them."

"Ye're lying."

"Not a bit. I've got friends of my own. With guns.

And plenty of reason to shoot them. My name's Manton. Perhaps you've heard of me."

The man froze. "*Dominick* Manton? The runner what captured those rebels in Cato Street?"

"The very one." He dug his forearm into the fellow's windpipe. "Now, let's try this again. Who else is in the house with Barlow?"

The bruiser swallowed against his arm. "There's a lady in there by the name of Nancy. Barlow says he's planning on marrying her. That's all I know."

"Why did he have you standing guard?"

"To keep the lady from leaving when he ain't around."

Dom gritted his teeth. Jane had been right. And this had now become far more complicated. "So the lady doesn't actually *want* to marry Barlow, I take it."

"He won't say. But he keeps her locked in her room."

"Which room?"

When the man hesitated, Dom jabbed him again.

The bruiser hissed a curse through clenched teeth. "The one at the back, top floor."

"Is there anyone else in there? Aside from Barlow and the woman?"

The man hesitated. "Don't know."

That second's delay told Dom the bruiser was probably lying. Damn. Dom could spend all day trying to get the truth out of this idiot.

And now Dom could hear sounds of a carriage coming up the road. That could be another of Barlow's friends—or more than one. Dom didn't fancy being cornered by a pack of prizefighters.

So he tightened his hold on the bruiser until his breathing stopped and the man went limp.

As Dom lowered him to the ground, shadows darkened the end of the alley nearest the street. But before he could even reach for the pistol in his other pocket, a familiar voice drawled, "Told you he'd be in the alley. Dom always prefers seclusion for his interrogations."

Dom released a breath. Thank God Jane had sent Victor and Tristan here. Wait, how had she known where to tell them to find him?

Jane herself pushed past Tristan and Victor and ran to him. "I'm so glad you're all right!" Catching sight of the bruiser on the ground, she halted. "I-Is he dead?"

"Just unconscious." Dom glanced at Victor. "A trick your wife told me about after that mess with your brother-in-law last year. I finally found a wrestler to teach it to me, but I've never before used it on a case."

"Effective," Tristan said, nudging the prone man with his foot. "You'll have to teach us, too."

Victor knelt by the fighter. "Guess we'd better tie him up before he comes to, eh?"

"Yes," Dom said. "He won't stay out long."

The other two went to work, using rope Victor carried in the agency's traveling coach. Dom was glad he'd brought the massive thing. They might need it.

Meanwhile, Jane was busy opening Dom's coat and checking him over. "You *are* all right, aren't you? He didn't hurt you?"

Dom laughed. "I used to do this for a living, sweeting.

I'm fine." Then he sobered. "But you were right about Nancy. Barlow's keeping her locked up."

"I know. Meredith told me. That's how we knew where to find you." When he arched an eyebrow at her, she added, "It's a long story and I'll tell you later. Right now you have to get Nancy out of there."

"Agreed."

Victor brought his rig up alongside the alley, and he and Tristan tossed the trussed and gagged bruiser inside. Then they returned to the alley.

"So, what's the plan?" Tristan asked.

"You take Jane back to her uncle's," Dom said. "Victor and I will handle getting Nancy out."

Jane glared at him. "I'm not leaving."

"You most certainly are," Dom said firmly.

"But Dom, you need Tristan's help. Samuel has become a thorough villain. You don't know what you're walking into." She crossed her arms over her chest. "No point in losing a man by sending one off with me."

"She's got a point," Victor said.

Damn. She did. "Fine." Dom fixed Jane with a dour look. "But you have to *swear* you'll just sit in my hackney and stay quiet while we rescue your cousin. Understood?"

"Absolutely," she said with a sniff. "I don't want to get in the way."

When Dom snorted, Tristan and Victor both laughed.

"He's got it bad, doesn't he?" Victor said to Tristan.

"You have no idea, old chap," Tristan answered cheerily.

"Come on, you two dunderheads, night is falling and we don't want to finish this in the dark," Dom grumbled. "Let's see what we can find out before we go blundering in." He pointed to the other end of the alley. "That leads to the mews. We might be able to see the back of the house from there, where Barlow is keeping Nancy. If I can trust what that bruiser told me."

The three men started for the back opening to the alley. Then Dom paused to look back at Jane. "Well?"

"I'm going, I'm going! Be careful." She blew him a kiss, then disappeared into the street.

Damn it all. She'd better be true to her word. While he didn't think Barlow was as dangerous as she feared, the arse's prizefighter friends might be.

Fortunately, the house was easy to survey from the mews. With daylight waning, Dom, Victor, and Tristan were able to keep to the shadows and look the situation over. There were only two floors, which made everything easier. Less area to cover, and more chance at finding Nancy quickly. Not to mention, less chance that the house was filled with prizefighters.

"Judging from the number of windows, only two rooms are in the back on the top floor," Dom said. "That narrows down Nancy's location. Assuming that I can believe that bruiser's information."

"Do you think Barlow's got a man behind that back door?" Victor asked.

"He might," Dom said. "It would make sense; Nancy could skip out the back as easily as the front. But from what the bruiser said, any guard is there to keep Nancy in, not keep others out. I doubt that Barlow expects anyone to know where to find him."

"You might be right," Victor said. "No one was saying a word at Barlow's old haunts. We would never have tracked him down if you hadn't followed him."

"Or if Jane hadn't convinced Meredith to tell us where the house is," Tristan said. "Your fiancée is quite a woman."

"I know." And she never ceased to amaze him. Dom turned to Victor. "You haven't met Barlow, right?"

"I don't think so."

"Good. Then you can be the one to knock on the front door. Since he doesn't know you, he may actually answer. If he doesn't, you'll have to break in, but that shouldn't be a problem. The houses around here are cheaply made. Either way, while you're subduing Samuel, Tristan and I can break down the back door. I'll deal with whomever's in there while Tristan finds Nancy and gets her out."

"Hey, why am *I* stuck with Nancy?" Tristan asked.

"Because you're better with women than I am."

"Tristan's better with women than both of us put together," Victor said dryly. "And Max."

Tristan rolled his eyes. "Fine. I suppose that's a workable plan, since I can't imagine that Barlow has more than one extra fellow in there. It's not as if he's dealing with the likes of my bold wife. Zoe might attempt an escape out a window, but I doubt Nancy would."

"True," Dom said. "But for all we know, this house is where his prizefighter friends spend their leisure time. We'd better be prepared for anything."

Because Jane was right: they had no idea what they were walking into.

◆ ◆ ◆

JANE SAT WITH her face glued to the window of the hackney. Thankfully, the carriage was situated close enough to the house that she could just see the entrance up ahead. But it was getting darker now. Soon, she wouldn't be able to see much of anything, unless the lamps were lit inside.

Suddenly Victor emerged from the alley, making her start. What the devil was he doing?

He strolled up the steps of the house to knock on the door. Sweet Lord! Her pulse went into a stampede, especially when, moments later, Victor vanished inside.

Faith, she couldn't see anything else from here! The dratted house windows were curtained, too, which was vastly annoying. She lowered the carriage window, hoping to hear what was going on, but not a sound came from the house. Was that good or bad? Were they inside? How long did it *take* to corral a villain, anyway?

Oh, if only she dared get out, but Dom had been very firm about that. And though she might ignore some of his orders, she suspected that in this case, it was best to heed it.

Then a shot sounded from the house, and her heart jumped into her throat. Seconds later, a man darted from the house. He was running right toward her, so she got a good look at him.

Samuel. Sweet Lord. Somehow he'd gotten past

Victor. And he had a pistol in his hand. The blackguard had probably shot Victor, or worse, Dom! And he was getting away!

Not on her watch, he wasn't.

She didn't stop to think. As he came abreast of the carriage, she swung the door of the carriage open, directly into his path.

It knocked him right off his feet. As he lay there, stunned, she leapt out and marched over to him. A red haze filled her vision at the thought of everything he'd done, and she dug the heel of her half boot into the wrist of the hand holding the gun. As Samuel let out a howl, she wrenched the pistol from his hand. Then she backed up and aimed it at him, praying she could pull the trigger if she had to.

Not that she was likely to hit anything if she did; she'd never shot a firearm in her life. But he was *not* escaping, drat it.

Samuel stumbled to his feet, then blanched. "Jane!"

"Yes, it's Jane, you . . . you . . . vile . . . horrible . . . *arse!*"

"Give me the gun, Jane," he said hoarsely, fixing his gaze on it. "You don't want to be playing with that."

With her blood beating a fearful tattoo through her veins, she steadied the pistol in the general direction of his heart. Though she could think of better places to shoot him, frankly. "I'm not playing. And you're not going anywhere."

Samuel lunged at her, and the pistol went off.

Which was odd, because she couldn't remember

pulling the trigger. But she must have, because smoke came out of the end of the pistol and he cried out and dropped to the ground at her feet, grabbing his thigh.

As Samuel rolled there, clutching at his leg and howling, Victor skidded to a halt beside him.

"Good shot, Jane!" The grin he flashed her reminded her instantly of Max. "I saw you hit him with the carriage door, too. Excellent work. We'll have to make you an honorary Duke's Man."

"Over my dead body," Dom growled as he ran up beside her. He tried to divest her of the pistol, but she had a death grip on it. "Let go of it, love," he said, his tone gentler. "You got him. You're safe now."

Releasing the gun to him, she began to shake. "I-I wasn't worried about m-me; I w-was worried about *you*. I heard that shot and saw him with the pistol and I . . . I just knew . . . h-he'd killed . . ."

Dom pulled her into his arms. "We're all fine, I swear. The prizefighter who answered the door lunged at Victor with a blade when he realized what was up, and Victor shot him. The man's inside. He'll live." He pressed a kiss into her hair. "Samuel was with Nancy when Tristan and I broke in the back, and he tried to use her to escape. Held that pistol to her head, then pushed her at us right before he ran out the door."

She stared up at him. "So . . . So Nancy is—"

"Jane!" cried a voice from near the house, and she looked up to see her cousin following Tristan, who was shoving a bound fighter ahead of him down the steps.

"Oh, heavens, Nancy!" Jane cried. "You're all right!"

Tears started in her eyes as she ran past Samuel toward her cousin. They met in a tight embrace, both of them crying and laughing and babbling all at the same time.

Jane held Nancy at arm's length to look her over and be sure she was okay. Her cousin was pale and dirty, with dark circles under her eyes, but she didn't look seriously harmed. "He didn't . . . Samuel didn't . . . force you to . . ."

"No," Nancy said. "No, not that." Her voice hardened as she gazed past Jane to where Samuel still writhed on the ground. "What happened to him?"

Dom came up behind them. "Jane shot him."

"She missed his privates by only a couple of inches," Victor said in an admiring voice.

"A pity she didn't hit them." Nancy darted past Jane to stare down at Samuel with her hands planted on her hips. Then, to Jane's shock, she kicked him in the ribs. "That's for lying to me." She kicked him in the knee. "And that's for kidnapping me."

"Nancy, darling—" he choked out.

"Don't you 'darling' me, you worm!" She ground her heel into his wounded leg. "You held a pistol to my head, you disgusting, reprehensible—"

"Enough," Victor said, pulling Nancy away from Samuel. "I think he's got the point."

"You bitch!" Samuel cried after her. "I could have made you a rich woman! We could have had the whole thing, you frigid little—"

Jane kicked him herself. As a choked howl escaped

him, she glared down at him. "Now, you listen to me, Samuel Barlow. Next time you come near my family, I'll make sure I *hit* your privates! And furthermore—"

"Perhaps you should take the ladies home," Victor told Dom, "while we bring the three scoundrels to the magistrate's and have them held until charges can be brought. I begin to think they'll be safer with me and Tristan than with the ladies."

Dom chuckled. "I believe you're right." He slipped an arm about Jane's waist to pull her away from Samuel. "Come on, sweeting, time to go."

The last thing Jane saw of Samuel before Dom helped her and Nancy into the hackney was Tristan and Victor hauling him into a massive carriage. Dom climbed up onto the box and pulled away from the house.

And that's when Nancy fainted.

22

TWO HOURS LATER, Dom sat with Jane and her uncle in the Sadler house drawing room as they waited for Max's personal physician, Dr. Worth, to come down from Nancy's bedchamber. The man was taking an awfully long time, which concerned Dom immensely.

He took Jane's hand and squeezed it, alarmed by her pallor. Ever since Nancy had fainted in the carriage, Jane had been out of her mind with worry, although Nancy had come to shortly afterward and insisted that she was all right.

But Jane wouldn't rest until her cousin was examined by a competent physician. So Dom had sent for Worth, knowing that he was the best. Fortunately, Sadler had acquiesced to his choice.

"I do hope she's all right," Jane said for the fifth time. "She's been through a great deal."

"Yes," was all Dom could manage.

They weren't even sure *what* she'd endured. According to Jane, Nancy had claimed Samuel hadn't assaulted her, but that was all they knew. The time spent since rescuing her had been taken up with concern for her physical well-being.

Dom swallowed his guilt. He should have listened to Jane from the beginning, should have moved more swiftly. But he'd been so convinced that he was right. As an investigator, he should have known better. He needed to work on trying not to let his biases get the better of him, even though he wasn't going to be returning to that business.

Though he still wasn't absolutely certain about that. Despite what Meredith had told Jane, he couldn't be sure Nancy had lost the babe until he heard it from her own lips. Yes, she'd been through a great deal, but fainting was also something a pregnant woman might do if she'd been hauled from here to beyond with no care for her well-being.

"She'll be all right," Sadler said, as if to convince himself, though his face looked like ashes. "My girl's stronger than she looks." He flashed Jane a wan smile. "Besides, she has to be. She's got a wedding to help you plan, eh?"

"Yes," Jane said, with a shy smile at Dom. "And she'll be my bridesmaid, of course."

At least waiting for the doctor had given Dom the chance to ask her uncle formally for Jane's hand. To his surprise, the man had been eager to accept Dom into the family. Either he'd figured out that she would never marry Blakeborough, or he was still so stunned by the turn of events concerning his daughter that he would acquiesce to anything.

Regardless, Jane would be his. Which was all Dom had ever wanted.

Dr. Worth appeared in the doorway, and they jumped to their feet.

"How is she?" Sadler asked. "How's my girl?"

Dr. Worth smiled. "She's fine. A little rattled is all. But in time, she'll be her usual self."

"And the baby?" Jane asked.

The doctor's smile faded. "She lost it, I'm afraid."

Sadler sat down abruptly, his eyes haunted. "My poor girl."

Dom slipped his arm about Jane's waist. "I'm sorry," he murmured. He meant it, too. "I'm so sorry, sweeting."

She gazed up at him with a forced smile. "It's for the best," she said, though tears shone in her eyes. "And not a great surprise."

With a nod, Dom glanced at Dr. Worth. "Can you tell *when* she lost it?"

He had to know if Samuel had brought on the death of Nancy's child. It could alter the charges against him considerably.

Since Dr. Worth had done quite a bit of work for Manton's Investigations, he apparently guessed why Dom was asking. "Given what she told me about her previous history and the bleeding she had a week ago, I'm fairly certain the babe was already gone by the time she set out on this trip."

"I see," Dom said tersely. "Thank you for the information."

"I do believe the child was her husband's," Dr. Worth added. "There's no way of being sure, of course, but given what she told me about when she stopped having her menses, she was probably four months along when she lost the child. So it was almost certainly conceived when he was alive."

Jane choked back a little sob. "Like the others."

"Yes."

It hit Dom suddenly that if Nancy had borne three children, he would have had nieces and nephews long before now. And George would have had an heir. It was only because of Nancy's difficulties that Dom was even getting a chance to be viscount—to run Rathmoor Park—at all. A sobering thought.

Sadler was staring at the doctor. "Will she . . . that is . . . can my Nancy ever . . ."

"I don't know. But there's always a chance. There's nothing obviously wrong to prevent her from bearing children." Dr. Worth smiled kindly. "Some women simply cannot. That's merely a fact of life."

"So I may never have grandchildren," Sadler said. "I mean, assuming my girl even marries again."

Marries again? Good God. Dom had completely forgotten that Barlow had been aiming to be Nancy's husband. "Can we see her?" Dom asked the doctor. "I have some questions for her, and it's better to get the answers while they're still fresh in her memory."

"Yes, you can see her," Dr. Worth said. "Just don't overtax her. She'll be weak for a while from the combination of having lost the baby and then having been dragged across the country shortly thereafter. I'll wait down here in case you have any more questions for me."

"Thank you, Doctor," Jane said. "It's most appreciated."

Dom headed for the door with Jane at his side. When Sadler remained seated, Dom paused. "Sir, are you coming?"

Sadler shook his head. "I don't think so. I-I just can't bear to hear what she . . . what he . . ." He trailed off with a moan.

"I understand." Dom tucked Jane's hand in the crook of his elbow and headed for the stairs.

It was probably better that Sadler not be there. Fathers always saw their daughters as children, and the thought of something terrible happening to their little girls filled them with such guilt over not protecting them and such anger at the perpetrators of the crime that they could hardly be rational.

But rationality was what was needed if a prosecution against Samuel were to be attempted. Assuming that it even could be attempted.

As soon as they entered Nancy's room, Dom couldn't help noticing how blatantly girlish it was, with painted cupids on the ceiling, fashion dolls displayed in one corner, and pink frilly things everywhere.

It was more the bedchamber of an immature chit than the sly deceiver he'd thought her, and once more, he wondered how he could have been so wrong about her.

Nancy smiled wanly as Jane approached the bed. "You see? I *said* I was all right."

"Yes, dearest, you did." Jane sat down beside Nancy and took her hand. "But the doctor says you need to rest and get better. So I'm here to make sure that you do."

Nancy dropped her gaze to the counterpane. "I suppose he told you that I lost the baby."

Jane nodded, but said nothing. Dom resisted the urge to speak. Better to let Jane handle this for the moment.

"I was already almost sure that I had," Nancy went on. "That's why I hurried off to York to see a doctor."

"Wait—you went to York to visit a doctor?" Jane asked. "Not to see Samuel?" When Nancy blanched, Jane added, "We know about your shopping trips to York. That you always visited Samuel."

"Not *visited*," Nancy said defensively. "Not exactly. We just shopped together." She sighed. "Oh, Jane, what a fool I was, fancying myself in love with him. All the time he was flirting with me and professing his great affection, he was bedding my maid. And I didn't even know it!"

Jane patted her hand. "We talked to Meredith. She fancied herself in love with him, too. So you were both duped."

A hurt look crossed her face. "Yes, but Meredith knew how I felt about him. She never revealed that *she* was in love with him."

When Nancy fell silent, Dom held his breath, wondering if the woman would go on.

Jane clearly wasn't waiting for that. "When did Samuel start talking about marriage?" she asked bluntly.

Nancy plaited the counterpane with her fingers. "After George died. He wrote to me about it. I mean, I didn't go see him or anything—I couldn't, without someone wondering about it. A grieving widow doesn't merrily go off on shopping trips. It wouldn't look right."

Nancy slanted a nervous glance at Dom. "And then Dom moved onto the estate, and you came, and I thought I was pregnant and . . . well . . . I didn't know what to do. I was just so flattered that he asked. I took it to mean that he really was in love with me, since my dower portion is hardly enough to tempt a man."

"No," Jane said dryly, "but the prospect of being stepfather to a baby viscount certainly was."

"He didn't know about that!" Nancy paused. "Well, I thought he didn't, anyway. I never told him I might be carrying George's child." She scowled. "Of course, that traitor Meredith did. Probably while she was letting him have his way with her. She just spilled out all my secrets to him."

"Which only shows how thoroughly he'd deluded her, too," Jane said softly.

Dom snorted. "In what way?" He couldn't believe she was defending Meredith. Jane had already told him that Samuel had threatened the maid, but still . . .

Jane flashed him a sad look. "She probably thought that telling him Nancy was bearing another man's son would dampen his attraction to Nancy. Samuel has an amazing ability to disguise his mercenary streak. He presents himself as a hopeless romantic."

Ravenswood had said something similar, so perhaps Jane was right.

"I thought he was in love with me," Nancy said petulantly. "I truly did."

Jane let out an exasperated breath. "You knew he'd been disinherited. Didn't that give you *some* pause?"

"Yes, but . . . well . . . he told me it was all that girl's fault. That she'd led him on and spun a tale to deceive his father and—" She grimaced. "I suppose that was all lies."

"To say the least," Dom muttered. More and more, he began to see why Jane had defended the woman. Because she realized just how dim-witted her cousin could be about men.

"You said you went to York to see a doctor about the baby," Jane prodded. "Why not just use the doctor you've always used?"

He had to admit that Jane was rather good at the interrogation part. Perhaps the "honorary Duke's Man" thing wasn't so far-fetched after all.

Nancy thrust out her chin. "He would have gone straight to Dom with the news. I wanted . . . someone unrelated to the family."

Jane's eyes narrowed on her. "But why not ask *me* to take you before I left? I can see why you didn't want to involve Dom, given the sticky nature of the situation, but I wouldn't have told him, and I could probably have found you a doctor."

"Yes, but . . . well . . ."

"You also wanted to see Samuel," Dom said cynically.

"And you could hardly do that with Jane around to disapprove."

Nancy shrugged feebly. "I figured I would already be in York to see a doctor, anyway. And Samuel *had* asked me to marry him. What would be the harm in it?"

Jane glanced at Dom and rolled her eyes heavenward. It made him wonder how often she'd had to deal with such nonsense from her cousin in the past.

"But when he met me at the inn," Nancy went on, "he started working on me about running away to get married. He said we'd go right to Gretna Green. I-I told him I couldn't, that I had to speak to Papa first at least. That I had to be sure I hadn't lost the baby . . ."

She dropped her gaze to the counterpane again. "He got all strange then. He started asking me all these questions about the baby and why I thought I'd lost it. After I told him, he stopped talking about running off to Scotland and started saying how he knew an excellent doctor in London. That we would go there straightaway, and then go to Papa."

"Because he'd realized you'd probably lost the baby, given your past miscarriages," Dom said in a hard voice. "So, before he jumped into marriage with you, he had to get you to London and make sure he had a plan in place to provide you with a child."

When Nancy paled and Jane glared at him, Dom realized he'd been a bit too blunt.

"You must think me quite the fool," Nancy mumbled.

Dom sighed. "No. As Jane says, Samuel is a master of deception."

Nancy glanced at Jane. "But you would never have been so foolish, would you?"

"I believed that silly charade you and Dom cooked up." She smiled ruefully. "People in love don't always think straight."

Nancy shook her head. "I think I knew in my heart. It felt so wrong, writing that note about going off with Mrs. Patch to Bath. I knew it was foolish to travel to London if I might still have a baby growing in me." She started to cry. "I just so . . . wanted Samuel's attentions to be real. George never really loved me; he only married me because he thought it was a way to get back at Dom."

"You *knew* that?" Dom said, startled.

"He told me in one of his rages. And Samuel was always . . ."

"Enamored of you, I know," Jane said, cradling her cousin's hand in hers. Her voice hardened. "Some men are blackguards."

The words gave Dom pause. She was thinking of her late father.

Then Jane looked up at him, and her angry expression melted and she gave him a soft smile full of love. "It takes a great deal of time and effort to separate the good ones from the bad ones. But the good ones are out there, if you know where to look."

Dom's heart swelled. She considered him one of the good ones. Her past really was finally in the past.

"Well," Nancy said in a small voice, "I don't think I want to look anymore. I'm done with men."

Something in Nancy's tone made alarm flash in Jane's face. "You said Samuel didn't . . . force you. That was the truth, wasn't it?"

Gulping down tears, Nancy nodded. "But once we reached London, and he got me into that house, I could no longer pretend he was in love with me. It was clear we weren't going to see Papa. We weren't going to see any doctors."

She screwed up her face as if fighting the urge to cry, and even Dom felt sorry for her.

"Then he explained his whole . . . nasty plan about how my child, or rather, *Meredith's* child could still inherit, and I realized he was quite mad, and I told him so. That's when he got mean and nasty, and locked me up in that room and brought Meredith to . . . to torment me . . ."

She broke into sobs, and Jane held her, soothing her with soft words and sympathy as only Jane could.

A lump lodged in his throat. He was reminded of how Jane had behaved with *him* when he'd told her about Peterloo.

And it finally, really sank in what he'd lost by not having Jane all these years. Because she always knew exactly what to do and say when someone's heart was breaking. She knew how to heal the scars that ran beneath the surface.

If she'd been there with him after Peterloo, would he have spent so many years in pain? Somehow he didn't think so. He had truly been mad to let her go.

Thank God he had come to his senses at last.

Nancy's sobs finally subsided to a few sniffles. Jane was still holding her when Nancy murmured, "What will happen to Samuel?"

It took Dom a second to realize Nancy was speaking to *him*. "He'll be charged with kidnapping, since he carried you away 'by force or fraud' and kept you against your will. He'll also be charged with certain offenses relating to his attempt to steal my title. You'll get your justice," he promised her. "I can swear to that."

And he would get his. There would be no impostor to worry about. George was truly laid to rest.

Dom's past was finally in the past, too.

As he choked down the emotion welling up in his throat, Jane rose to look at him. "Is that all you need to know?"

He nodded. "I'll go see the magistrate so we can discuss what's to be done. I know you want to stay here and comfort your cousin." Then he headed for the door.

He'd just reached the hall when Jane ran out after him. "Dom, wait."

He smiled at her. "What is it, sweeting?"

"Thank you."

"For what?"

She came up to press a kiss to his cheek. "For letting me question her. For not turning all investigator-like and bellowing questions at her. I know she'll have to face plenty of that at the trial."

"I'll keep her out of it if I can, but if the choice is sending him to prison or covering up the scandal—"

"You should send him to prison," she said fiercely. "No question about that."

He chuckled. "You are far more bloodthirsty than I ever would have guessed."

"And more hardy, I hope?"

"Definitely."

Her eyes sparkled at him. "Does this mean you'll make me an honorary Duke's Man, after all?"

"Certainly not," he said in a falsely stern voice. When she lifted an eyebrow at him, he swept his gaze down her and grinned. "There is nothing remotely manly about you, sweeting. So you'll have to be an honorary Duke's *Lady*."

She beamed at him. "I'm going to remind you of that when I ask you to teach me how to shoot."

His grin faltered. "Teach you to what?" he said as she headed back into Nancy's room. "Have you gone mad?"

Her laughter wafted back to him as she closed the door, and he realized with relief that she was joking.

Or was she?

Good God. As a wife, Jane was clearly going to be a joy and a trial, a blessing and a curse. Once they married, she was going to throw all his plans into disarray, and all his careful control right out the window.

He smiled. He couldn't wait to begin.

EPILOGUE

London
September 8, 1831

THE DUKE OF Lyons's drawing room was full to overflowing as Jane came downstairs from nursing her darling Ambrose. Jane had never seen the town house so crowded. Of course, it was rare for them to have all the Duke's Men—and their families—in one place. Usually the Rathmoor Park contingent spent time with the Winborough contingent, while the Cale contingent socialized in London.

But they had all needed to be here for William IV's coronation. Dom, as the Viscount Rathmoor. Zoe, as the designated heir to the Earl of Olivier. Max, as one of the highest dukes in the land, of course. And even Victor, as *cousin* to one of the highest dukes in the land, though he hadn't marched in the procession of peers. He and Isa had taken seats in the special section reserved for those with invitations to the ceremony.

Fortunately, His Majesty, a more practical and frugal king than his late brother, had eschewed the expense of a grand banquet afterward in favor of having a dinner with intimate friends, so Max and Lisette had hit upon the plan of having their own family dinner on coronation night.

Now, as Jane scanned the room for her husband, she was reminded of that evening at Winborough when Dom had warned her to expect chaos. This was chaos times three. Victor and Tristan were in a corner, probably discussing the latest in investigative techniques. Isa sat beside Tristan's father-in-law on the settee, examining his broken pocket watch with a jeweler's magnifying glass.

The children had been allowed to join everyone for a few moments before dinner, so Lisette was trying to explain to three-year-old Eugene why he couldn't drag his one-year-old sister, Claudine, around the room by her feet, even if it did make her giggle. Meanwhile, Victor and Isa's twelve-year-old, Amalie, was dancing with her second cousin Max to a jig being played on the pianoforte by Zoe, as the pages were turned by—

Dom. Jane grinned. Of course. She should have known he'd be at the pianoforte. She reached it just as Zoe finished the piece.

"There you are," Dom said. "How was Ambrose?"

"Starving, as always. I swear he wants to nurse every two hours."

Zoe grinned. "It's because he's a boy." She pulled out some sheet music and began hunting through it for another selection. "Lisette says that Eugene nearly drove her mad. Even the wet nurse she used when she and Max came up to Winborough complained that she'd never seen a babe so lusty. But Claudine didn't give Lisette a bit of trouble. My little Drina was never a problem, either."

"Just as I always suspected," Jane said. "Men are insatiable from birth."

Dom's eyes twinkled at her. "In some things, anyway."

Her stomach flipped over. Dr. Worth had only yesterday told her that they could resume marital relations, but in all the chaos of the coronation preparations she hadn't had a chance to tell Dom.

"Oh, look, a waltz!" Zoe said, pulling out a piece of music. "And I do so like the Dettingen Waltz."

Dom rose. "Shall we dance, sweeting?"

"Absolutely," she said brightly and took his hand.

The music began, and they attempted to waltz, no small feat in the crowded drawing room. The tune seeped into her brain, sparking a memory. "Do you know that I danced to this with Samuel right before I jilted you at Edwin's?"

Dom blanched. "Good God, I had no idea. I wasn't exactly listening to the music that night. Do you want me to have Zoe play something else?"

"Certainly not." She smiled at him. "All that is past."

It was true. She knew Dom top to bottom and inside and out. She trusted him. She *loved* him, and not with the girlish adoration of apparent perfection that she'd felt in her youth, but with the messy kind of love that could accept a man, flaws and all.

Because his flaws were nothing compared to his fine character. He was good and honorable, with a generous heart and a lively intelligence. He was an excellent manager of his estate and a wonderful father to their son. Compared to all of that, the past was a distant memory.

Dom pulled her closer to press a kiss into her hair. She couldn't wait until later, when she would spring Dr. Worth's news on him.

"Speaking of Samuel," she said, "Nancy was relieved to hear that he received a sentence of transportation. She was afraid that Edwin would use his influence to get Samuel's sentence commuted, and she couldn't bear the idea that she might one day stumble across Samuel in the street. With Edwin supporting Meredith and her babe, Nancy wasn't sure *what* to expect from him, even though I told her he'd washed his hands of Samuel years ago."

"Blakeborough has never struck me as the kind of man to overlook criminal behavior, even in his brother."

"True. He has a strong moral sense, even if he does hide it beneath an equally strong aversion to people."

He drew back to stare at her. "Forgive me, sweeting, but I cannot imagine you married to him. His melancholy would give you fits within a month."

"Right," she teased, "because I'm much better off married to a man who follows plans so slavishly that he stays awake half the night for fear of oversleeping and missing the coronation."

He arched an eyebrow. "I couldn't sleep for watching you nurse Ambrose. It's been some time since I . . . well . . . saw your charms unveiled in any other capacity. I have to take my pleasures where I may."

"Aw, my poor dear," she said in mock concern. Deciding to put him out of his misery, she added, "I ought to say that's what you get for being so unfashionable as to share a bedchamber with your wife, but as it happens, Dr. Worth—"

The music abruptly ended, and the sound of a gong being struck broke into everyone's conversations. They fell silent as Max went to stand at the entrance to the room with Victor and Isabella at his side.

"Attention, everyone!" Max clapped his cousin on the back. "I am proud and pleased to introduce to you the new owner of Manton's Investigations."

Cheers and applause ensued.

When it died down, Tristan called out, "So the legal machinations are finally done? Dom has actually let go of the thing at last?"

"I signed the papers yesterday," Dom told his brother. He gazed fondly at Jane. "I decided I'd lost enough of my life to finding other people's families. Now I'd rather spend time with my own."

"I'll bet that didn't stop you from writing a contract of epic proportions." Lisette grinned at her husband. "How many stipulations did Dom make before he agreed to complete the sale?"

"Only one, actually," Max said.

Everyone's jaw dropped, including Jane's. She gaped

at her husband. "Only one? You didn't dictate how Victor is to run the thing and when and where and—"

"As you once said so eloquently, my love, 'you can set a plan in motion, but as soon as it involves *people*, it will rarely commence exactly as you wish.' There didn't seem much point in setting forth a plan that wouldn't be followed." Dom smirked at her. "I do heed your trenchant observations, you know. Sometimes I even act on them."

She was still staring at him incredulously when he shifted his gaze to Victor. "Besides, Victor is a good man. I trust him to uphold the reputation of Manton's Investigations."

Jane glanced at Victor. "You're not going to change the name to '*Cale* Investigations'?"

Victor snorted. "I'd have to be mad. Who wants to start from scratch to build a company's reputation? It's known for excellence as Manton's, and it will always be known as Manton's, as long as I have anything to say about it."

"So what was the one stipulation that Dom required?" Tristan asked.

Dom scowled. "That it never, in any official capacity, whether in interviews or correspondence or consultation, be referred to as 'the Duke's Men.'"

As everyone burst into laughter, Jane stretched up to kiss his cheek. "Now, *that* sounds more like you, my darling."

A few hours later, Jane came out of her boudoir to find her husband in his dressing gown, stretched out across the bed reading the newspaper and idly petting their spaniel Little Archer, a pup from Mrs. Patch's brood.

Seizing the moment, Little Archer leapt off the bed and into her dressing room, where he could chew up slippers to his heart's content. Dom, however, didn't even look up as she entered.

"They're calling this the most elegant coronation in history." He snorted. "I noticed there's no mention of its being the most interminable."

"Dom," she purred as she closed the dog into the dressing room for the moment.

"All that pomp and circumstance is so tedious." Still reading, he turned the page of the newspaper. "Ravenswood told me that King William is determined to make sure that parliamentary reform is enacted."

She walked languidly forward. "*Dom.*"

He snapped the paper to straighten it. "It's about bloody time. I should think—"

"Dom!" she practically shouted.

"Hmm?" He glanced up, then frowned. "Why are you wearing your coronation robe?"

"I was cold," she said with a teasing smile. She let the robe fall open. "Since I have nothing on underneath."

Dom stared, then gulped. Unsurprisingly, his staff jerked instantly to attention. "If you're trying to torture me," he said hoarsely, "you're doing a good job of it."

She sashayed toward the bed, letting the velvet and ermine robe swing about her. "No torture intended." She put one knee on the bed. "Dr. Worth said I may resume relations with my husband whenever I am ready."

He blinked, then rose to his knees and seized her about the waist. "May I assume that you're ready?" he rasped as he brushed a kiss to her cheek.

"You have no idea." She met his mouth with hers.

They kissed a long moment, a hot, heavenly kiss that reminded her of how very talented her husband was at this aspect of marriage. She untied his dressing gown and shoved it off his shoulders. He had just finished tearing off his drawers when she shoved him down onto the bed.

His eyes lit up as she hovered over him. "Ah, so it's to be like that, is it, my wicked little seductress?"

"Oh, yes." She grinned at him. "I do so enjoy having a viscount fall before me."

She started to remove her robe, but he stayed her with his hand. "Don't." He raked her with a heated glance. "Next session of parliament, I'll endure the boredom of the endless speeches by imagining you seducing me in all your pomp and circumstance."

"My pomp is nothing to yours, my love," she murmured as she caught his rampant flesh in her hand. "*Yours* is quite . . . er . . . pompous."

"That's what happens if the viscount falls." He thrust against her hand. "His pomp always rises."

And as she laughed, they created a pomp and circumstance all their own.

Want even more sizzling romance
from *New York Times* bestselling
author Sabrina Jeffries?
Don't miss the first book in her
sexy new Sinful Suitors series,

The Art of Sinning

Coming in Summer 2015 from Pocket Books!

LADY YVETTE BARLOW stood at the edge of the duke's ballroom, watching the dance with a hollow ache of envy in her stomach. She loved to dance. And the chances of her being asked were slim to none. She towered over half the men in the ballroom. Not to mention that the whole world had recently learned of her brother Samuel's perfidy. Even her eldest brother, Edwin, the Earl of Blakeborough, couldn't avoid being tarred by that brush.

As if she'd conjured him up, Edwin's voice sounded behind her. "Yvette, there's someone I'd like you to meet."

Good Lord. He'd been trying to cheer her up ever since they'd arrived, and he was very bad at it. Heaven only knew whom he thought might serve the purpose.

Pasting a smile to her lips, she faced him and his companion. Then her heart dropped into her stomach.

Standing beside Edwin was the most attractive man she'd ever seen—a golden-haired Adonis with eyes as deep a blue as the estate's prize delphiniums. Indeed, the man stared at her with an intensity that quite sucked the air from her lungs.

He was tall, too. Heavenly day. A decided improvement over the gentlemen Edwin usually foisted on her.

"May I introduce my new friend, Mr. Jeremy Keane?" Edwin said.

The man bowed. "I'm delighted to make your acquaintance, Lady Yvette."

His deep voice resonated through her like a piece of particularly delicious music. Even his accent was compelling. American perhaps? Oh, she did like Americans. They were so refreshingly forthright. And they used such interesting slang, too. Perhaps she could expand her collection of street cant to include American terms.

She dipped her head. "The pleasure is mine, Mr. Keane." But even as she said it, she put together the accent and the name. Oh dear, he was *that* Mr. Keane.

As if to confirm her realization, the man raked her in a blatantly admiring glance. A *rogue's* glance.

She groaned. Not again. Could she never meet a gentleman who was *not* a scoundrel?

Edwin went on. "Keane is an artist from—"

"I know all about Mr. Keane." When Edwin scowled, she caught herself. "From the exhibit of his works, of course."

Mr. Keane's warm gaze poured over her like honey. "I don't recall ever seeing *you* at my exhibit. And trust me, I would have remembered."

A shiver danced down her spine before she could steel herself against reacting. Very nicely done. She'd have to be on her toes with this one. "We attended it in the morning. I daresay you were still lying foxed in some gaming hell or nunnery."

"Good God, here we go," Edwin muttered under his breath, recognizing the cant for brothel.

"I am rarely foxed and never in a nunnery," Mr. Keane retorted, "for fear it might tempt the 'nuns' to bite me."

"I should love to know what you consider 'rarely,'" Yvette said. "That you even know that 'bite' means 'cheat' in street cant shows how you must spend your days."

"And how you must spend yours," he said with a gleam in his eye. "After all, you know the cant, too."

She stifled a laugh. Mustn't encourage the fellow. Still, she was impressed. Rogues always fancied themselves wits but seldom did she meet one who really was.

"Mr. Keane has kindly agreed to paint your portrait, Yvette," Edwin cut in. "Assuming that your tart words haven't changed his mind."

The scoundrel had the audacity to wink at her. "Actually, I like a little tart with my sweet."

"More than a little, I would say, having seen your paintings," she shot back.

Suddenly he was all seriousness. "And what did you think?"

The question caught her off guard. "Are you fishing for compliments, sir?"

"No. Just truthful opinions."

"That's what everyone always says, though they never mean it."

"Are you calling me a liar, Lady Yvette?" he said in that deadly tone men use when their honor is questioned.

"Of course not," she said hastily. A man's honor was nothing to be trifled with. "I was just speaking generally." When he continued to look at her expectantly, she struggled to put her uncertain feelings about his work into words. "As for your work, I would say that your idea of 'tart' borders on the 'acidic.'"

"It does indeed," he drawled. "I prefer to call it 'real life.'"

"Then it's no surprise you've taken up with Edwin. He considers real life to be acidic, too."

"Oh, no, don't drag *me* into this," Edwin put in.

Mr. Keane's gaze searched her face. "And you, Lady Yvette? Do *you* consider real life acidic?"

My, my. Quite the persistent fellow, wasn't he? "It can be, I suppose. If one wants to dwell on that part. I'd rather dwell on the happier aspects."

A sudden disappointment swept his handsome features. "So you would prefer a painting of bucolic cows in a field."

"I suppose. Or market scenes. Or children."

The mention of children sparked something bleak in the depths of his eyes. "Art should challenge the viewers, not soothe them."

"I'll try to remember that when confronted at my breakfast table by a picture of vultures devouring a dead deer. That *is* one of yours, isn't it?"

Mr. Keane blinked, then burst into laughter. "Blakeborough, you forgot to tell me that your sister is a wit."

"Trust me," Edwin said wearily, "if I'd thought it would get you to agree to our transaction sooner, I would have mentioned it."

"Transaction?" She stared at her brother. "What transaction?"

Edwin turned wary. "I told you. Mr. Keane is going to paint your portrait. I thought that a well-done piece of art showing what a lovely woman you are . . . might . . . well . . ."

"Oh, Lord." So *that* was his reasoning. A pox on Edwin. And a pox on Mr. Keane, too, for agreeing to her brother's idiocy. Clearly, the artist had been coerced into doing so. Mr. Keane was well-known for *not* doing formal portraits. Ever.

She fought to maintain her composure, to act nonchalant, though inside she was bleeding. Did Edwin really think her so unsightly that she needed a famous artist to make her look appealing?

"Forgive my brother, sir," she told Mr. Keane with a bland smile. "He's set on gaining me a husband, no matter what the cost. But I happen to have read the interview where you said you'd rather cut off your hands than paint another portrait, and I'd hate to be the cause of such a loss to the world."

Mr. Keane gazed steadily at her. "I sometimes exaggerate when speaking with the press, madam. But this particular portrait is one I am more than willing to paint, I assure you."

"Eager for the challenge, are you?" Tears clogged her throat that she swallowed ruthlessly. "Eager to try your hand at painting me attractive enough to convince some hapless fellow in search of a wife to ignore the evidence of his eyes?"

Belatedly, her brother seemed to realize how she'd taken his words. "Yvette, that's not what I was saying."

She ignored him. "Or perhaps it's the money that entices you. How much did my brother offer in order to gain your compliance in such an onerous task? It must have been a great deal."

"I didn't offer him money, Yvette," Edwin protested. "You misunderstand what I—"

"I *want* to paint you," Mr. Keane snapped even as he glared Edwin into silence.

With betrayal stinging her, she gathered the remnants of her dignity about her. "Thank you, but I am not yet so . . . so desperate as to require your services."

She turned to leave, but Mr. Keane caught her by the arm. When she scowled at him, he released her . . . only to offer her his hand. "May I have this dance, Lady Yvette?"

That took her by surprise. Only then did she notice the strains of a waltz being struck. She had half a mind to stalk off in a huff. But that would be childish.

Besides, other people had begun to notice their exchange, and she could *not* endure the idea of people gossiping about her making a scene at the wedding breakfast of her friend . . . who happened to have jilted her brother.

"Lady Yvette?" Mr. Keane prompted in a steely voice.

She cast him the coolest smile she could muster. "Yes, of course, Mr. Keane. I would be delighted."

Then she took his hand and let him sweep her into a waltz.

As soon as they were moving, he said, "You have every right to be angry with your brother."

"My feelings toward my brother right now are none of your concern."

"I was telling the truth about wanting to paint you."

She snorted. "I don't know how much money Edwin promised—"

"But not for a portrait." He bent close enough to whisper in her ear, "Though he doesn't know that."

That caught her so off guard that when Mr. Keane pulled back to fix her with a serious gaze, she couldn't at first summon a single answer.

"I see I finally have your attention," he said.

"Oh, you always had my attention," she said testily. "Just not the sort of fawning attention you probably prefer."

A faint smile crossed his lips. "Tell me, Lady Yvette, do you have something against artists in general? Or is it just I who rub you the wrong way?"

"I don't trust charming rogues, sir. My other elder brother was one of your kind, so I know all your tricks."

He arched one eyebrow. "I seriously doubt that."

When he then twirled her in a turn, she realized with a start that they'd been waltzing effortlessly all this time. That almost never happened with her. Few men knew how to deal with an ungainly Amazon like her on the dance floor. But clearly he was one of them.

That softened her toward him a little. A very little. "So what exactly *do* you want to paint me for, anyway?"

"An entirely different work," he said. "And agreeing to your brother's request seemed the only way to get close enough to you so I could arrange that."

She eyed him skeptically.

"Ask Blakeborough if you don't believe me. Before I knew who he was, who *you* were, I wanted you to sit for me. I decided it the moment I saw you enter the room. I asked your brother who you were, he asked why I wanted to know, and I told him."

His gaze locked with hers, as sincere a one as she'd ever seen. But then, Samuel had always looked very sincere, too, when he spun some tale. "Why on earth would you want to paint *me*?"

"No clue. I never know why particular models intrigue me; just that they do. And I always follow my instincts."

Yvette blinked. He *could* have claimed it had something to do with her looks. The fact that he hadn't lent more credence to his assertion. "That's the most ridiculous thing I've ever heard." Yet a tiny part of her found it enormously flattering.

"It *is* ridiculous, isn't it? But true, I swear. No matter what gossip you've heard about me, I'm always honest, no matter the cost."

"Fine. Then tell me this: Exactly what are the terms of your 'transaction' with my brother?"

He flinched. "Your brother is an ass."

"Not really. Just rather oblivious to other people's feelings sometimes." She cast him a hard stare. "Answer the question."

With a long-suffering sigh, he tightened his grip on her hand. "I am to paint your portrait. In exchange, he is to drum up some gentlemen who might be interested in courting my sister."

She gaped at him. "What a pair of nodcocks you are! Has it occurred to either of you that your sisters are perfectly capable of finding husbands on their own if they so choose? That perhaps we— Wait a minute, I thought your sister lived in America."

"She's on her way here. She means to drag me home to help her with the family mills." He cracked a smile. "I mean to fob some other fellow off on her who can go in my stead."

His look of boyish mischief seduced her. Briefly. Until she put herself in his sister's shoes. "First you abandon her to go flitting about Europe. And now that she has tired of waiting for your return, you think to get rid of her by marrying her off." She shook her head. "Your poor sister."

"Trust me, there is nothing 'poor' about my sister. Amanda can take care of herself." His smile smoldered. "As, it appears, can you. Which is probably what made me want you for my painting in the first place."

She fought not to be intrigued. "What is this painting about, anyway?"

"It's allegorical, about the sacrifice of Art to Commerce."

That took her by surprise. "Something like Delacroix's paintings?"

"You're familiar with Delacroix?"

His voice held such astonishment that it scraped her nerves. "I do read books, you know. And attend exhibits and operas with my brother . . . when I can drag him to town."

"Operas, eh? Better you than me," he teased. "I can't imagine anything more tedious than an evening of such screeching."

"My point is that I'm not some ninnyhammer society chit who only keeps abreast of fashions."

"I didn't think you were." He bent close enough to say in a husky tone, "Unlike your brother, I am fully aware of your attractions."

The words melted over her skin like butter. And when he then tugged her slightly closer in the turn, she let him.

Not because of his devastating attractiveness, no. Or his deft ability to dance. Or the glint of awareness in his startling blue eyes. None of that had any effect on her. Certainly not.

Fighting to keep her mind off the breathlessness that suddenly assailed her, she said, "So, which character would I play in this allegorical painting of yours?"

One corner of his mouth tipped up. "Does that mean you agree to sit for it?"

"Perhaps. It depends on your answers to certain questions."

The music was ending. Oh dear, and just when the conversation was getting interesting. Unfortunately, it would be highly improper of him to ask her for another.

But apparently he'd thought of that, for he waltzed her toward a pair of doors that opened to reveal a set of steps descending into the sunlit garden. And almost as soon as the notes died, he offered her his arm.

Cursing the curiosity that prompted her to take it, she let him lead her outside, but she was relieved to see that they weren't the only people strolling about. At least she needn't worry about rousing further gossip.

Besides, she was ready to be out of the stuffy ballroom. Here in the chilly autumn air, she could breathe at last.

"Now, then, madam," he said. "Ask me whatever you wish."

"Who am I to play in your painting? What am I to wear? Will sitting for your picture ruin me for life? Is that why Edwin would only agree to a respectable portrait?"

"That's quite a lot of questions," he said dryly. "Let's start with the last. Your brother and I didn't get as far as my describing the concept of my work. The minute I said I wished for you to model for me, he flat out refused to let you be part of any painting that wasn't dull as dirt, even though I told him you wouldn't be recognized."

"Won't I?" She felt a stab of disappointment at the thought that he didn't really want to paint *her*, as she was. And why did she care, anyway? "So I'm to be wearing a mask or a cloak or something?"

"No, indeed. But you will be in some kind of Greek costume quite different from your normal attire. I can even change your hair color if you wish. And you'll only be in profile, anyway. I doubt anyone will realize it is you."

She gave a harsh laugh. "Right. Because no one will notice that the woman in your painting happens to have my ungainly proportions."

"Ungainly!" He shook his head. "More like queenly. Majestic, even."

The compliment came so unexpectedly that it startled her. She was used to being teased for her height, not praised. She had to turn her head so he wouldn't see how very much the words pleased her.

"But your proportions are unlikely to signify, anyway," he went on. "You'll be lying down."

That arrested her. How had she managed to forget he was a rogue? "Why would I be lying down?"

He gazed at her as if she were witless. "'Art' sacrificed to 'Commerce'? Were you even listening? Damn, woman, I can hardly depict a sacrifice without laying you across an altar."

Stunned by his matter-of-fact tone, as if it were perfectly obvious to anyone with sense, she mumbled, "Oh, right, of course. I don't know what I was thinking."

Actually she did know. She thought him quite mad. When he spoke of his art, there was no trace of the rakehell in him. Was it by design? Was he *trying* to rattle her?

Because he was certainly succeeding at that.

"Will you do it?" he asked. "Assuming we can find a way to manage it?"

"Managing it isn't a problem," she said, thinking aloud. "Artists doing portraits generally reside with the family during the process. So if you come to our estate for the portrait, we can arrange some way to meet for the painting you wish to do for yourself." She slanted a glance at him. "If you're willing to leave London for a bit, that is."

"Oh, I don't know." He stopped beside a marble fountain to smile teasingly at her. "It would take me away from all those gaming hells and nunneries. However will I survive?"

"I'm sure you can find a sympathetic tavern maid or two in nearby Cheshunt to tide you over," she said dryly.

"So, no nunneries in your neck of the woods?"

"Trust me, if there had been, my other brother would have uncovered them long ago."

When he looked at her oddly, a blush rose in her cheeks. She didn't know why she'd said that. She couldn't seem to forget the request Samuel had made of her just before he'd been sent off to serve his sentence of transportation.

"I'll be fine, I promise," he said silkily. "Though you still haven't given me your permission to paint you. For *either* work."

And suddenly it hit her—the solution to her problem with Samuel. "I haven't, have I?" She stared him down. "Tell me something, Mr. Keane. Are you as willing to make a bargain with me for your painting as you were to make a bargain with Edwin for my portrait?"

His eyes turned wary. "It depends. What sort of bargain are we talking about?"

Avoiding his gaze, she twirled the water in the fountain with one finger. "I will sit for you—clothed, of course—as much as you like. You may draw as many pictures of me as you please."

"And in exchange?" he prodded.

"You will find some way to get me inside a nunnery in Covent Garden."

Get email updates on

SABRINA JEFFRIES,

exclusive offers,

and other great book recommendations

from Simon & Schuster.

_____

Visit **newsletters.simonandschuster.com**

or

scan below to sign up:

Can't get enough of the Duke's Men?

Read the first three books in the series!

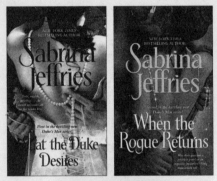

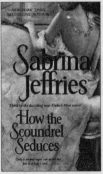